An Impartial Witness

An Impartial Witness

Charles Todd

An Imprint of HarperCollinsPublishers

HarperCollins books may be purchased for educational, business, or sales promotional use. For information please write: Special Markets Department, HarperCollins Publishers, 10 East 53rd Street, New York, NY 10022.

FIRST HARPERLUXE EDITION

HarperLuxe™ is a trademark of HarperCollins Publishers

Library of Congress Cataloging-in-Publication Data is available upon request.

ISBN: 978-0-06-200214-3

10 11 12 13 14 ID/RRD 10 9 8 7 6 5 4 3 2 1

In remembrance . . .

Samantha
June 1995 to September 2007

and

Crystal
November 1995 to March 2008

who gave so much to those who loved them

An Impartial Witness

Chapter One

Early Summer, 1917

As my train pulled into London, I looked out at the early summer rain and was glad to see the dreary day had followed me from Hampshire. It suited my mood.

I had only thirty-six hours here. And I intended to spend them in bed, catching up on lost sleep. The journey from France with the latest convoy of wounded had been trying. Six of us had brought home seventeen gas cases and one severe burn victim, a pilot. They required constant care, and two were at a critical stage where their lungs filled with fluid and sent them into paroxysms of coughing that left them too weak to struggle for the next breath. My hands ached from pounding them on the back, forcing them to spit up the fluid and draw in the air they so desperately needed. The burn victim, swathed in bandages that had to be changed almost every hour, was frightful to see, his skin still raw and weeping, his eyes his only recognizable feature. I knew and he knew that in spite of all his doctors could do, it would never be enough. The face he'd once had was gone, and in its place would be something that frightened children and made women flinch. I'd been warned to keep a suicide watch, but he had a framed photograph of his wife pinned to his tunic, and it was what kept him alive, not our care.

It had been a relief to turn our patients over to the efficient clinic staff, who swept them into fresh beds and took over their care in our place. The other nurses were already on their way back to Portsmouth while I, as sister in charge, signed the papers noting eighteen patients delivered still living, none delivered dead, and went to find a cup of tea in the kitchen before the next train left for London. The kitchen was busy and so I stood looking out the windows of the staff sitting room as I drank my tea. The green lawns of the country-house-turned-clinic led the eye to the rolling Hampshire landscape beyond, misty with the rain. So different from the black, battle-scarred French countryside I'd just left. Here it was peaceful, and disturbed by nothing louder than birdsong or the lowing of cattle. It had been hard to tear myself away when the driver arrived to convey me to the railway station.

Now as the train came to a smooth stop and the man sitting opposite me opened our compartment door, I smelled London, that acrid mixture of wet clothing, coal smoke, and damp that I had come to know so well. My fellow passenger smiled as he handed down my valise, and I thanked him before setting out across the crowded platform.

As I threaded my way through throngs of families seeing their loved ones off to God knew where, I caught snatches of hurried, last-minute conversations.

"You will be careful, won't you?"

"Mother will expect you to write every day—"

"I love you, my boy. You're in my heart always."

"Did you remember to pack your books?"

"I'm so proud of you, son. So proud—"

A pair of Highland officers stepped aside to allow me to pass, and I found myself facing a couple who were oblivious to my approach and blocking my way to the exit.

She was standing with her head bent and slightly turned toward her companion, her hat brim shielding her face. But even at a distance of several yards, I could tell that she was crying, her shoulders shaking with the force of her sobs. The man, an officer in a Wiltshire regiment, seemed not to know how to console her. He stood with his hands at his sides, clenching and un-clenching them, an expression of long-suffering on his face. I thought he must be returning to the Front and had lived through this scene before. She clutched an umbrella under her right arm while her left was hold-ing to his as if it were a lifeline.

Her distress stopped me in my tracks for a moment. Watching them, I wondered at his reluctance to touch her and at the same time I was struck by the air of desperation about her. I'd seen this same desperation in men who had lost limbs or were blinded, a refusal to accept a bitter truth that was destroying them emotionally.

But there was nothing I could do. Rescuing kittens and dogs was one thing, marching up to complete strang-ers and asking what was wrong was something else.

Still, I felt a surge of pity, and my training was to comfort, not ignore, as her companion was doing.

I was about to walk around them when a whistle blew and she lifted her head to cast an anguished glance at the train, as if afraid it was on the point of departing.

I had the shock of my life.

I'd seen her before. There was no doubt about it.

Hers was the face in the photograph that the pilot, Lieutenant Evanson, had kept by his side like a talisman during his treatment in France and in all the long journey home. His wife, he'd said. There was no doubt about that either.

I couldn't be mistaken. I'd seen that photograph too many times as I worked with him, I'd seen it that very morning, in fact, when I'd changed his bandages one last time. She was looking up at the officer now, her eyes pleading with him. I couldn't be sure who was leaving whom. But just then the engine's wheels began to move and the officer—I couldn't see his rank, he was wearing a trench coat against the rain—bent swiftly to say something to her, kissed her briefly, and then hurried toward the train.

She lifted a hand as if to stop him then let it drop. He swung himself into the nearest compartment, shut the door, and didn't look back. She stood there, forlornly watching him until he was out of sight.

It had all happened rather quickly, and I had no idea who this man might be, but I had the distinct impression that she never expected to see him again. Women sometimes had dreams or premonitions about loved ones, more a reflection of their own fears than true foreboding. They usually hid these well as they sent their men off to fight. But perhaps hers had been particularly vivid and she couldn't help herself. It would explain his restraint and her desolation.

Before I could move on, she turned and literally dashed toward the exit. I tried to follow, but I lost her in the crush. By the time I reached the street, she was in a sea of black umbrellas as people made their way toward the line of cabs waiting there.

I gave up my search after several minutes, and found a cab of my own to take me to the flat. I wasn't sure what I'd have done if I'd caught up with Mrs. Evanson, but I'd have felt better knowing she'd taken a cab rather than tried to walk off her low spirits in this chill rain.

Mrs. Hennessey opened her door as I came into the hall, smiling up at me in welcome. From her own ground-floor flat she watched us come and go, took in our mail when we weren't there, brought us soup when we were ill, and generally kept an eye on us without in any way intruding.

"Bess, my dear! And just look how wet you are."

She embraced me with warmth, then added, "You've just missed Elayne. She left this morning. Mary is in London, but staying with her brother's family, and there's been no word from Diana since she went back last week. Is there anything you need? I must say, you do look tired. How long will you be here?"

I laughed. "Thirty-six hours. Thirty-five now. And yes, I'm tired. And I'm glad to have the flat to myself. I want only to sleep."

"And you must do just that. I'll see that you have a nice tea. You look thin to me, Bess Crawford, and what would your mother say to that?"

"We sometimes miss meals," I admitted. "You won't tell Mama, will you?"

For some time I'd had a sneaking suspicion that my mother and Mrs. Hennessey had entered into a conspiracy to keep me safe. Choosing nursing as my contribution to the war effort hadn't been met with the greatest enthusiasm at home. The Colonel Sahib, my father, had no sons to follow in his footsteps, and while I believed he was secretly quite proud of me, he was also well aware that war had an ugly face, and nursing sisters saw the worst of what war cost.

Mrs. Hennessey said, "Which reminds me, Sergeant-Major Brandon stopped here last week. He took Diana to dinner before she left."

I felt a flicker of jealousy. Simon usually came to dine with me when he was in London. He'd served with my father in all our postings around the Empire, and now lived near us in Somerset when he wasn't doing whatever hush-hush work he and my father never talked about. No longer in active service, their experience was still invaluable, and the War Office sent for them often, sometimes for weeks at a time. My mother and I had tried to guess what they were doing, but I had a feeling we were well off the mark.

Simon had always been a part of my life. He'd picked me up at six when I fell off my first pony, he'd taught me tactics when I was tired of being a girl and bored with petticoats, he'd interceded with the Colonel Sahib when I was in disgrace. He'd listened to my secrets and comforted me when I was in the throes of first love and couldn't tell Mama, and he'd stood on the dock when my packet had sailed for England that last time and promised me I'd return to India some day, when the time was right. Half confessor, half godfather, half friend, half elder brother—Simon had no business taking my flatmates to dinner. Besides, Diana was in love with someone else.

Mrs. Hennessey finally let me go, and I went up the stairs. I was just plumping my pillow when she came in with a cup of tea. I think I was asleep before I'd finished half of it.

Twenty-four hours later, I was back in France. The next two weeks were a blur, broken bodies and long hours. Then one afternoon Sister James came in with a box that had just arrived from her family. Martha was two years my senior, plump, levelheaded, and a very experienced nursing sister. I'd learned a great deal from her, and we had become close friends as well as colleagues.

We had just finished an extra shift, and were tired and on edge from the German shelling that had gone on for hours. Although we were out of range, here behind the lines, the ground shook with the pounding until our heads were aching and our nerves frayed. It was usually a sign of an attack to come, and an ambulance had been sent back to the depot for fresh supplies to see us through. Harry, the driver, had also found time to walk across the camp to ask if there was any mail for our sector. Arriving at the hospital, he'd looked up Sister James and presented her with her package before unloading his cargo.

"I think Harry is half in love with you," I said as she let me feel the weight of the box. Hefty enough for sharing. I smiled, looking forward to seeing what was inside. It was a much needed distraction. "You seem to receive your post before anyone else."

Sister James laughed, then winced as another miniature earthquake shook the beds we were sitting on. Our only lamp had fallen over earlier in the day when the shelling began, but blessedly was still intact. A jar of tea hadn't fared as well. There was a crack down one side. And my mirror had come off the wall, fortunately landing on my spare pair of boots before tumbling to the floor.

The beds danced again, and Sister James said, "If this doesn't stop, we'll get no rest this night."

"Never mind the guns," I said, handing her my scissors to cut the string. "Open the box. There may be something perishable in it that we ought to eat at once."

"Chocolate," she said, "if it hasn't melted in this heat."

She managed to get the box open, and the first thing we saw was a small jug of honey from the hives on the James's home farm, swathed in a scarf her little sister had knitted, never mind that it was summer. Under that was a tin of fruit and another of milk for our tea. I wondered how her family could bear to part with such treasures, knowing as I did how scarce these were at home.

Around the whole was a folded newspaper, and Sister James gently pulled it out with a cry of delight. Just then the beds shook once more, and we both reached for the jug of honey, bumping heads as we caught it right on the brink of going over.

"Blast them!" she said, and then began to unfold the pages. It was a London newspaper, and in it was the engagement announcement of her middle sister. She read it hungrily, having missed the excitement of the proposal. Sitting back, she said, "Oh, how I wish I could be there for the wedding!"

We munched on stale biscuits that we'd found tucked in the scarf, and speculated on the chances of the marriage taking place in early autumn as planned.

I coughed as the next shell landed, catching me with a mouthful of biscuit crumbs. "If I were her," I said, clearing my throat, "I'd want to be married as soon as may be. Still, a Christmas wedding would be nice."

"If Henry can manage leave . . ."

We fell silent. Henry had proposed on his last leave. There might not be another.

Sister James said, "Well. We can hope." She took the engagement notice out of the newspaper and folded it carefully, stowing it in her trunk. I picked up the rest of the pages to search for the obituaries.

Instead I found myself staring at a pen-and-ink drawing of a woman's face. Beneath it was the caption: Police Ask for Witnesses—Evanson Murder Still Unsolved.

Startled—for I recognized the face—I read on.

The murder of Mrs. Marjorie Evanson, wife of Lieutenant Meriwether Evanson, presently in hospital in Hampshire, remains a mystery. Police are asking any witnesses who may have seen her to step forward. Mrs. Evanson left her residence shortly after noon on 15 May and was never seen alive again. Tracing her movements that fateful day has proved difficult, and Scotland Yard has now turned to the public for assistance in learning where she might have gone and whom she may have seen . . .

I put the newspaper down. Sister James, shoving her trunk back under her bed, said, "What is it? You look as if someone has walked over your grave."

It was just an expression, one I'd heard many times, but I said without thinking, "Not mine—but someone I may have seen. Look, read this."

Sister James took the newspaper from me and scanned the column. "I don't know her. Do you?"

"Her husband was among that group of wounded I escorted to Hampshire. The badly burned pilot. Remember? He kept his wife's photograph by him— and that's his wife. I can't bear to think how he must have felt when he was told."

"But, Bess, murdered? That's awful."

"Yes, but what's more important is that I saw her late that very afternoon. She was at the railway station, seeing off an officer in a Wiltshire regiment. She was crying. Terribly upset. I'm afraid I stood there staring. I was so surprised to recognize her." I winced as the next shell landed. They seemed to be coming closer together now.

"Who was the man with her?"

"I've no idea." I shook my head, trying to come to terms with the fact that she'd been murdered that very same day. "That poor man—her husband—was counting the hours until he saw her again. It was what kept him fighting to live. I wonder who had to break the news to him. I can't imagine having to do it."

"Bess, if you saw her that day, you must tell the Yard."

"But I don't know who she was with, or where she went after she left the station. Only that she was there for a few minutes, seeing someone off, and that's not terribly useful. It's been a week since this request came out in the newspaper—surely someone else has come forward. A waiter in a restaurant, a cabbie, a friend who ran into her somewhere." But what if they were saying the same thing: someone else will do it.

"If he's at the Front, this Wiltshire officer hasn't spoken to the police," she pointed out. "And just now, what Lieutenant Evanson probably wants more than anything else is for the police to find her killer."

"Does it say there how she died? I didn't read the rest of the article."

She went back to the newspaper, scanning down the column of close print. "Here it is. She was stabbed and then thrown in the river. They say that she was still alive when she went into the water, but was most likely unconscious."

"How awful." I tried to bring up the image of the woman I'd seen in London, her face streaked with tears. Yes, it was the same person. I'd have no problem swearing to that. And the man? Could I remember him as clearly? Dark hair, blue eyes, a rather weak chin . . .

More to the point, would I know him again?

"What if this officer hasn't seen the newspapers? Or been told yet that she's dead? If the police find him, it's possible he could tell them where she was going after she left the station. There's no way of knowing where that might lead," Martha James persisted.

"Yes," I said slowly. "You're right. I really should report what I saw, and let the Yard decide whether it's helpful information or not."

"They don't mention what time she died or when her body was found. More's the pity," she added, finishing the article. "You may have been the last person to see her alive, except for her killer. Now there's an unsettling thought. If he was looking for a likely victim, he might have followed you home instead. You were a woman alone too."

"You have a ghoulish imagination," I told her. "I'll write the letter now."

My voice suddenly seemed overloud.

We looked at each other. Silence had fallen, the earth was still. I felt almost dizzy with relief, my ears still ringing, my nerves still jangled, my teeth on edge.

"Oh, dear," Sister James said. "I have a feeling they'll be sending for us soon."

"Very likely. It shouldn't take long to put down what I saw. Could you make us a cup of tea meanwhile?"

But it proved unexpectedly difficult to compose that letter. I kept seeing Lieutenant Evanson's eyes peering through his heavy bandages, tenaciously holding on to hope even as time was running out for hope, trusting to his wife's love for him to help him survive and unaware that she would be dead before morning. And so I weighed each word, to make certain that I reported events accurately, uncolored by my own imagination.

After three tries, I was finally satisfied. I was just on the point of sealing the envelope when we could hear the first of the ambulances rumbling toward the wards, bringing in new casualties. I hastily finished my tea, put on a fresh uniform, and by the time Sister James and I were ready, there was a knock on the door and an orderly's voice summoning us to duty.

Chapter Two

I expected that the police would thank me for my information. And that would be the end of it. I wrote to Mrs. Hennessey, asking her to save the London papers, in the event there was any more news.

What I was not prepared for was a summons through channels to speak to someone at the Yard, an Inspector Herbert. I was given leave to travel to London for that purpose and two days later I was sitting in a grim little office at Scotland Yard, having been escorted there by a constable with a limp and lines of pain in his face.

After several minutes, a harried, balding man stepped into the room, introduced himself, asked me how my journey from France had been, and then lifted a sheet of paper from his desk and frowned at it. I recognized it.

"The Evanson case. We've had precious little help from the public, sad to say. I was on the point of giving up hope when your letter came." He lifted his gaze to my face, the frown deepening.

"You write that you recognized Mrs. Evanson from a photograph that her husband kept by his side. How long before encountering Mrs. Evanson at the railway station had you seen this photograph?"

"A matter of hours? That morning I'd transported her husband and other patients to a clinic in Hampshire and turned them over to the staff there. It was a little past five o'clock when my train pulled into London—I wasn't required to return to France for another day."

"Tell me again exactly what you saw."

"As I left the train and was walking toward the exit, Mrs. Evanson was literally in my path, and it was obvious that she had broken down. Her shoulders were shaking with her sobs. Of course, at that point I couldn't see her face because she was turned toward the officer standing beside her. Just then she looked up, and I realized I knew who she was."

"You also state in your letter that you recognized the cap badge but couldn't see the man's rank because of the trench coat he was wearing. But he was an officer in a Wiltshire regiment. Can you be quite certain about such details?"

"My father was in the Army for most of his adult life," I replied. "I know how to judge what rank a man holds and what regiment he serves with."

"And you are satisfied that he did take the train just as it was pulling away? He didn't pretend to board and then return to the platform?"

"I saw him take his seat. He didn't look back toward Mrs. Evanson. That distressed her, and she watched the train until it was out of sight. I don't know how he could have managed leaving without being seen. She turned then and left in a rush. I couldn't tell which way she went after that. It was raining, I had to hand in my ticket, and I was carrying my valise."

He nodded. "To be sure. And she was in great distress, you said."

"Yes. That's what drew my attention to her in the first place."

"What made her distress different from that of other women seeing off friends or loved ones?"

I frowned. "I thought at the time that perhaps she'd had a premonition or a dream that he wouldn't be coming back. She wasn't putting on a brave front, you see, as so many women do. She appeared to be giving in to her feelings."

"As you observed the two of them together—Mrs. Evanson and the officer—could you form an opinion of the relationship between them?"

"She clung to him. He hardly looked at her or touched her."

Inspector Herbert raised his eyebrows. "He didn't comfort her? Was he perhaps embarrassed by her behavior?"

"I—that's one possible interpretation. But he stayed there with her, he didn't walk away until the train began to move." It occurred to me then that by standing with her until the last minute, he'd kept her from following him to his carriage.

After a moment's thought, Inspector Herbert went on. "I am about to confide to you information that we haven't made public, Miss Crawford. And I hope you'll not repeat it. But I think it's necessary if we're to understand the facts you've placed before us. The coroner has informed us that Mrs. Evanson was nearly three months' pregnant. I must assume, from my exchange of letters with his commanding officer, that her husband, Lieutenant Evanson, couldn't have been the father of this child. By any chance, are you able to verify his medical history?"

I tried not to show my shock. "I know from his medical records that Lieutenant Evanson has been in hospital in France for two months. Before that, his aircraft had been shot down over German lines and it was at least two weeks before he made his way back to British lines. He wasn't hurt in that crash, at least not seriously, although he was sent to hospital for observation because of a blow to the head. There was no concussion, and he was released to his unit. But a few weeks later he wasn't so lucky—his aircraft caught fire and he was fortunate to survive at all. It must be four months or more since he was in England. At the very least."

I had heard one of the doctors say that Lieutenant Evanson had been returned to duty too soon, before the psychological effects of his first crash had worn off. But they were desperate for experienced pilots and he'd been eager to rejoin his flight.

"As we'd thought. The Army has supplied the particulars, but not in such detail. To the next question. You only saw Mrs. Evanson and the officer together for a brief moment. Do you think that this man might be the father of her child?"

I knew what he was asking: if not, did she have other lovers? I didn't want to believe that of her. But then I really knew nothing about her.

I pictured her again in my mind's eye. If I'd been touched by her anguish, why hadn't he? How had he managed to remain indifferent? Could that mean she'd only just told him her news? There at the station, where they were surrounded by strangers? She might have lost her nerve earlier, or been afraid that he wouldn't allow her to come to see him off.

I remembered a detail that I hadn't put in my letter. When he bent to kiss her on the cheek, she hadn't responded. She hadn't put her hand up to his face or turned to kiss him. It was as if he hadn't quite known how to walk away from her. And she had been numb, the perfunctory kiss a gesture on his part that she barely felt. That could mean he'd just made it clear that for him the affair was over. What if her distress was her bitter realization that he would do nothing to help her now, even if he knew about the child?

I took a deep breath. "It would be easy to read into what I saw all sorts of explanations that very likely weren't there. At a guess, there was more estrangement between them than passion. That's why I felt at the time that she never expected to see him again."

Inspector Herbert nodded. "I've drawn much the same conclusion. Still, there's always the possibility that he left the train at the next stop because he knew where to find her. I must keep an open mind there."

"If he was rejoining his regiment, he might not have had the option of waiting for a later train."

"Then we must find the man, if only to clarify that point. To be honest, we're no closer to discovering our murderer now than we were when our plea for information was published in the newspapers." Which

I interpreted to mean that he was in some way disappointed in my evidence.

"If you'd told me she was a suicide, I would have found that believable, given her state of mind. Or even if he'd been found dead instead of Mrs. Evanson. Not to suggest that she could have killed anyone. It's just that her death seems so—inexplicable."

Inspector Herbert smiled. "You have been very helpful, Miss Crawford. Thank you for coming forward."

I was being dismissed.

I rose to take my leave.

But at the door, I turned, my training reminding me. "Do you know—had she seen a doctor, to confirm her suspicion that she was pregnant?" She must have guessed by the third month.

"We've had no luck there either. I sent my men out with photographs of Mrs. Evanson, in the event she had used a false name. They spoke to doctors and their staffs all across London, and to midwives as well as—er—less savory practitioners in the poorer neighborhoods of the city. So far it would appear that she hasn't been to anyone. We had hoped that the father was decent enough to accompany her and someone remembered him."

Scotland Yard had been thorough.

"Surely her family must have some idea who her friends were. There must have been someone she'd seen more of than was proper."

"Neither her sister nor her sister-in-law had any inkling that there was someone. And the friends we've spoken to tell us the same thing," Inspector Herbert replied. "On the other hand, it's more than likely that when she was with this man, she'd avoid places where she might be recognized. Otherwise there could have been gossip, which might even reach her husband's ears in time." He paused. "You're a woman. Where would you look for help if you were in Mrs. Evanson's shoes?"

"I can't imagine that I'd turn to the man's family. I'm sure they were kept in the dark as well. I'm not sure about friends either. I'd be afraid they would stand in judgment of me. I expect I'd go somewhere I wasn't known, and pose as a war widow. People might be more kind in such circumstances. I'd be frightened about doing anything until I'd told my lover. And perhaps even after I'd told him."

"Frightened of him?" Inspector Herbert asked sharply.

"Frightened for myself and what was to come. I couldn't count on him, could I? He might be married. And even if he were not, I couldn't be sure he'd stand by me and marry me when—if—my husband divorced me. I'd have to face everything alone—my family, my husband, my friends. There's nowhere else to turn, then. And there's the child to think about. I wish now I'd caught up with her outside the station. But that's hindsight, of course. She wouldn't have confided in her husband's nurse, would she?"

"Quite. At least, thanks to you, we've discovered she was with someone later that day. That leaves only five or six more hours to account for. It had been ten, in the beginning. And in ten hours, she might have gone anywhere and still returned to London in time to be murdered. A needle in the proverbial haystack."

I remembered Sister James's comment. "I don't like to suggest—but there are men who prey on women, and if she had nowhere to turn, literally, if she sat crying on a bench along the Thames, or walked in Green Park—"

"We've had no problems of that sort—thank God— these past twelve months. But yes, we've taken that into account. Far-fetched, perhaps, but we haven't shut our eyes to the possibility. And her husband's family is pushing for an early conclusion. We have none to offer at present."

I thanked him and left. The patient constable led me down the stairs and out to the street. He asked as

I stepped out onto the pavement, "Shall I find a cab for you, Miss?"

"I'd like to walk a bit first. Thank you, Constable."

He smiled. "Safe journey home, Miss."

Little did he know that I'd be in France in another four and twenty hours.

I'd come nearly as far as Buckingham Palace, going over what I'd learned from Inspector Herbert. This meeting at Scotland Yard had been distressing. Both because of what I'd seen at the railway station and because I'd had Lieutenant Evanson in my care long enough to be concerned for him and his welfare. Yes, Marjorie Evanson had transgressed in the eyes of society. Sadly, such affairs were more common in the disruption of war. I'd heard patients worry about their wives when letters were slow in arriving, long silences that were never fully explained. They would ask me if I thought there was someone else, and always I'd tried to be reassuring, for fear of a relapse. And I'd had patients confess to me that they'd been unfaithful to wives or sweethearts, afraid to die with that on their conscience.

"Sister, I have to tell someone . . ."

But I couldn't judge Marjorie Evanson. I knew nothing about her, about what or who had tempted her, how she had come to do what she did. Whether it had anything to do with her death was something Scotland Yard must discover.

I found myself looking at the watch pinned at my shoulder. There was time—just—to find a telephone and put in a call to my parents, to say hello. And then I could take the early train to Portsmouth and stop at Laurel House on my way there.

I could see for myself how Lieutenant Evanson was faring, and it would help me put all this behind me. There was probably very little I could do for him, but perhaps a familiar face would cheer him, and we needn't mention his wife at all.

I felt a little better as I turned to hail a cab.

This was a lovely summer's day to be traveling, the roadsides and meadows rampant with wildflowers, villages quiet under the afternoon sun. A herd of sheep, recently shorn, ambled down a lane on their way back to pasture as we waited half an hour at a crossing to give a troop train priority. Lambs frolicked about the ewes, and robins were nesting in the hedgerow beyond. Birds had all but vanished in France, even the carrion crows.

I was looking forward to seeing Lieutenant Evanson, but I was beginning to wonder what I was to say to him. I needn't explain precisely why I was in England.

He would take it for granted that I'd brought other patients back. And I wouldn't speak of his wife unless he brought up her death. Least said, soonest mended, my mother had often warned me. There was no need to mention my encounter with Marjorie at the railway station either. And if there were other visitors, my stay could be brief. I'd know, after five minutes in his company, how he was coping.

At Marlyn Station, I found a man who could carry me on to my destination. And he promised to wait, because I dared not miss the next train south to Portsmouth. I'd have to stay the night, and my orders didn't leave me that option.

I had had other things on my mind the last time I was here, and it had been raining. Today as we came through the gates and up the drive, I could see that Laurel House was a handsome brick edifice in the Georgian style, with white stone trim and two broad half-moon steps leading up to the main doors. They stood open to the warm day, and I walked in, stopping at the small table that served as Reception.

I didn't recognize the middle-aged woman sitting there.

"Nursing Sister Crawford to see Lieutenant Evanson. He was my patient on his journey back to England, and I've stopped in to see him."

She gave me a strange look. I suddenly felt like an interloper, with no business here.

"Lieutenant Evanson?" I repeated.

"Perhaps you ought to speak to Matron, first," the woman said finally.

"Yes, that's fine," I answered. We walked down a passage between the graceful staircase and the doors to rooms that had once been fashionably decorated for social calls and parties and family evenings at home. Now they were bare wards for those who couldn't mount the stairs.

Matron had established herself in what had been a small morning room, and I remembered the pale lavender walls and a white coffered ceiling. Filing boxes still occupied all the free space, and the breeze from the open windows stirred papers on the desk. Matron looked as harried as she had on my last visit.

"Miss Crawford. How nice to see you again. Do sit down. May I offer you tea?"

"Thank you, no. I must make the next train to Portsmouth. I've come to speak to Lieutenant Evanson."

I realized suddenly that something was wrong. She had turned her head to look out the window as I was speaking, her gaze on the small gazebo in the garden. Then she turned back to me with an expression I instantly recognized.

"I'm so sorry to be the one to tell you—we lost Lieutenant Evanson six days ago."

I started to speak, but she held up her hand.

"He'd been very depressed since the death of his wife. Despondent might be the better word. We did all we could. And then on Tuesday night, we found him in his bed, dead. Somehow he'd managed to purloin a scalpel, we don't know exactly where or how. And he'd cut his own throat. It was the only death he could manage with his bandaged hands. Even so, it couldn't have been easy. But he was determined, you see."

I knew my face must be mirroring the expression on hers. Horror. Loss. Grief. And there was something more in her eyes, a sense of guilt, as if somehow she should have prevented his death. I sat there, stunned, and after a moment, she nodded, as if she understood what I was feeling.

I managed to say the proper things even as my mind struggled to accept what had happened. It was inevitable, given how much he loved his wife. What else was there to live for, without her, without a face or hands that resembled human features and fingers? And yet it was sad beyond words.

Why hadn't Inspector Herbert told me? But then he couldn't have known I was coming here. Still—

A brief silence fell. Then I asked the difficult question. "Who told him that his wife was dead?"

"His sister came down. It had to be done, of course. We couldn't have kept it from him. He'd been asking for her, you see. But we thought—he seemed to take the news as well as could be expected. He just stared at the wall and said nothing. He was very quiet for the next week, although he asked on two occasions if the police had made any progress in their search for her killer. Afterward, we realized he was simply biding his time. We kept an eye on him, well aware of how much—how important she was to his recovery. As soon as he'd arrived at Laurel House, he'd asked one of the staff to write to his wife, to tell her that he was back in England and how much he looked forward to seeing her. When she didn't come, he wrote to his sister asking if Mrs. Evanson were ill. His sister had hoped to spare him the news until he was stronger, but that was not to be. Mrs. Melton had no choice but to tell her brother the truth."

Even as he was dictating his first letter, it was too late. According to the police, Marjorie Evanson had left her house early to set out on the journey that would take her to the railway station and then to her death.

"He did inquire of the doctor if it would be possible for him to attend the funeral service. I needn't tell you it was out of the question. We asked our chaplain, Mr. Davies, to sit with him that day, and offer what comfort he could. I spoke to Mr. Davies that evening as he was leaving, and he felt that Lieutenant Evanson seemed reconciled to his loss. I wasn't convinced, however, and kept an eye on the lieutenant anyway."

So much for Mr. Davies's powers of observation. Still, he was undoubtedly the village priest, and had very little experience in suicide watches. There was something else to be considered. Lieutenant Evanson was trained as a pilot, taught to bury everything that might distract him from the intense concentration required to handle his aircraft and face a very aggressive enemy. He could well have concealed his intentions by drawing on that same training.

Remembering, I said, "What became of the photograph he carried with him?"

"The one of his wife? That was odd, you know. We had suggested that it be buried with him. It had meant so much to him. But his sister wouldn't hear of that. She left it on his bed when she came to collect his few belongings. That seemed so—so cruel to me, somehow."

I interpreted his sister's decision to mean that she had learned about the pregnancy, even if she hadn't told her brother or anyone else here at Laurel House.

Matron opened her desk drawer and took out an envelope. She passed it to me. "I kept it. I really couldn't bring myself to throw it away."

I took the envelope, but didn't open it. I could feel the edges of the thin silver frame through the brown paper. "I understand. I'd have felt the same. I nursed him for days. This was his anchor. Perhaps someone in Mrs. Evanson's family might care to have it later. What a pity."

"Yes, in spite of his burns, he was doing quite well. And he was a lovely man. You must have seen that too. Never complaining, never thinking of himself. No trouble . . ."

She took a deep breath, a middle-aged woman who had seen so much suffering, and yet still felt the tragedy of this one man's death. Her hair was turning gray, and there were dark circles under her brown eyes. I thought she had lost weight since I'd seen her last.

"Well. You have made this journey for nothing. But I can tell you that the other patients you brought us have done better than expected. Still, when the winter rains begin—" She shook her head. I knew what she was dreading, the stress of days of dampness on damaged lungs.

"Thank you so much for seeing me, Matron. It must have been difficult."

"Yes, well. Sometimes talking about things helps. And you knew Lieutenant Evanson too."

She rose to walk with me to the door. "You are looking tired," she commented. "How long have you been in France?"

"Since late January. Before that I was on *Britannic* when she went down."

"Ah, yes, I recall. And you're going back to France now?"

"I'm told to report to a small hospital just outside St. Jacques." Which sounded more grand than it was. St. Jacques had all but ceased to exist, muddy ruins in the midst of fields that no longer grew anything, even weeds. "A forward dressing station," I added. "Though it calls itself a hospital."

She nodded. "Two of my nursing sisters have spent some time in France. They are very good at improvising."

We had reached the main door. I smiled. "We often have no choice."

"This is your driver?" she asked, looking out at the motorcar by the door. "I wish you a safe journey, my dear. If you—should you find that Mrs. Evanson's family would like to have that photograph, do let me know. It will set my mind at ease. I believe the obituary listed Little Sefton as their address. Sadly, that's not all that far from here, but it might as well be on the moon. They never came to visit, you see."

And then I was on my way to the train, my leave nearly up, and France waiting for me across the Channel.

At the railing of the ship, staring out at the water as we passed out of The Solent and into the Channel, I found myself thinking that whoever had murdered Mrs. Evanson had killed her husband as well, just as surely as if he'd held that scalpel to the lieutenant's throat. Two victims—three if one counted the unborn child.

I found it hard to put Marjorie Evanson out of my mind. Perhaps because I'd first seen her through her husband's eyes as he held on to life amid great pain so that he could come home to her. Not to her as a murder victim or disgraced wife but as his anchor.

I had kept the photograph with me. Of course there was no time to find the direction of Mrs. Evanson's family and post it to them, but remembering her sister-in-law's emotional response as well as Matron's comment that they had never visited, I felt I ought to ask their wishes before sending it to them.

And in the weeks ahead I often caught myself looking for a face I was certain I would recognize, every time I saw an officer wearing the uniform of the Wiltshire regiment.

It had become a habit.

Chapter Three

I was hardly back in France—a matter of a fortnight— before we were given leave. It was unexpected, but the little dressing station in St. Jacques was too exposed and was being moved to another village. A fresh contingent of nursing sisters was assigned to take over there.

First, however, we were to escort a hundred wounded back to England. It was never easy, and on this occasion, even though our convoy moved at night, we were strafed by a German aircraft, racing down our lines with guns blazing and then swinging around behind the lines to find other targets of opportunity. Ambulances were clearly marked, so there was no excuse for the attack. The wonder was, only three people were wounded and no one died. I couldn't help but think the pilot had intended to frighten us rather than kill us. If that were true, he'd succeeded beyond his wildest dreams.

The weather had changed by the time we reached the coast, and on our crossing there was a storm that turned the rough Channel into bedlam. We were all seasick, patients, nurses, orderlies, and doctors, and probably half the crew if they were honest about it. I'd sailed from India to England and never met a storm like this.

My stomach agreed with me as I ran to the railing for the third time.

Then it was back below, cleaning sheets as best I could, washing faces, swabbing the decks. By the time we reached Dover, I could have kissed the quay from the sheer joy of having dry land under my feet once more.

Dover Castle was a familiar sight looming above us, half hidden in the clouds, its walls dark with rain. A friend was on duty there, but I didn't catch a glimpse of him. We were pressing on, for the sake of the worst cases, and pulled into London late in the afternoon. A watery sun greeted us, the worst of the storm well behind us.

I was relieved of my duties there, and after seeing the train on its way again, I took the omnibus to the corner of our street and walked down to the flat I shared with friends.

None of them was at home, but there were signs that Mary might be on leave again as well, and I left her a note before taking a leisurely bath and falling into bed. It was Thursday evening, and I'd have enjoyed dining out if I hadn't been so tired.

Mary came in later, bringing me a cup of tea and a plate of cheeses and biscuits that she'd just received from home. She was small, British fair, with rosy cheeks and dimples. The soldiers adored her, wrote poems to her blue eyes and curls, and flirted outrageously with her, but her heart was in the Navy, the first officer on a cruiser.

"You can't sleep away your leave," she said cheerfully. "How long do you have?"

"Ten days," I said, stretching and yawning. "I thought I might go home for the last half of it."

"Your parents will be delighted." She paused, then said, "I've heard stories. Was it a bad crossing?"

"Very bad. I thought I would never be able to swallow food again. Now I'm ravenous. Tell your father how grateful I am that he is in the cheese business. I haven't had a Stilton this good since the war began."

"And these are the leftover bits. Think what it would be like to have half a wheel to ourselves."

Laughing, we caught up on news, chatting among the biscuit crumbs, and then Mary said something that nearly caused me to choke on my tea.

"I've an invitation to spend the weekend with friends. A house party in the country. Would you like to come?"

"It would make a nice change. Do I know them?"

"I don't believe you do. It's the Melton family. But I think you convoyed Serena's brother home from France. Lieutenant Evanson. He killed himself not long ago, had you heard? Serena's husband will be coming home after a fortnight somewhere he can't talk about; it's his birthday, and she wants to do something nice to celebrate—here!" She reached out to pound me on the back as I turned red from coughing.

I cleared my throat and said politely, "Surely this is a family occasion—she wouldn't care to have strangers hanging about."

"The truth is, nearly everyone they know is somewhere else—in France, at sea, in the Middle East. She told me I could bring one of my flatmates with me, if I cared to. She wants it to be a gay weekend, no sadness to mar it."

I thought of the envelope with Marjorie Evanson's photograph still sealed in it. I'd carried it through France and now it lay in the top drawer of the small chest under my window, where I'd put it when I unpacked. It was Mrs. Melton who had decided that it shouldn't be buried with her brother. I thought I'd guessed why, but both Matron and I had felt it was—wrong. I really shouldn't go to this house party.

On the other hand, I hadn't had any news about the search for the killer. Perhaps I could satisfy my curiosity without causing any trouble.

"Yes, all right. If she'll have me. But it might be best if we don't say anything about my having nursed her brother. It could bring up—painful memories."

"If you don't mind, then I won't."

Which is how I found myself on a crowded train to Oxfordshire, with malice aforethought.

The house where the Meltons lived was within walking distance of the station. We arranged to have our valises brought there by trap and set out on foot. It was a lovely day, and the dusty scents of summer wafted from the front gardens of the small village of Diddlestoke, and then from the pastures and fields that surrounded us as we reached the outskirts. Another quarter mile, and we could see the gates of our destination.

Melton Hall was a charming old brick house with a central block, spacious wings to either side, and a small park through which the drive meandered on its way to the handsome Pedimented front door. Two small children ran out to greet us, the girl taking my hand and the little boy clinging to Mary's.

"Niece and nephew," she said over their heads, and I nodded. "On Jack Melton's side. Serena told me they'd be leaving before dinner."

We were greeted in the marble foyer by Serena Melton herself, and I was most interested in my first impression of her. Tall, dark, and rather elegant, she embraced the shorter, fairer Mary, then held out her hand to me. "Elizabeth! I may call you Elizabeth, may I not? We are so pleased you could come."

I hadn't met Lieutenant Evanson before he was burned, and so I couldn't judge the likeness between brother and sister.

And then she was leading the way up the stairs to our room, which overlooked the east gardens. Over her shoulder, she was telling us about her plans for the grand celebration and then, while we washed away the dust of travel, she was asking me about my family, expressing interest in the exotic places where my father had served, and then wanting to know about my work in France.

"I hear it's frightful to be the first to deal with the severest wounds. My brother was badly burned. I was never so shocked as I was when I saw him the first time. They were changing his bandages, and his skin was raw and weeping. It was all I could do to keep myself from showing what I was feeling, that he could have been a complete stranger."

"I hope he's continuing to heal," I said, though Mary cast me a sharp glance.

"Alas, he didn't survive," Serena Melton answered, her eyes filling, and I made appropriate noises of sympathy. I could see how much she cared for her brother. In her shoes I might have felt the same about Marjorie Evanson. After all, it was Marjorie's betrayal of her husband that had led to his suicide. Sometimes in cases of sudden death, people needed someone to blame. Or blamed God.

Taking a deep breath, Serena added, "I was never so grateful than when they found that Jack was good at numbers, and assigned him to break codes instead of carrying a rifle. He was furious, but as I told him, one martyr to the cause in a family is enough. If he can protect a convoy or warn of an attack, he saves hundreds of lives. Surely that's more useful than slogging through France in the hope of killing a few Germans. I don't know why men think that they aren't doing their part if they aren't up to their knees in mud and frightfully cold and hungry and tired."

We followed Serena down the stairs. She and Mary were having a conversation about a mutual friend serving in the Navy, and exchanging news about him. Then we were in the kitchen, where she was supervising the main course for dinner. Serena said proudly, "I got my hands on a roast. Don't ask how! It nearly cost me my virtue and my firstborn. But it's Jack's favorite."

From the oven came the most tantalizing aromas—beef, I was sure of it. After a quick look at her prize, and a few instructions for the cook, a Mrs. Dunner, Serena whisked us out to the north terrace where her husband was sitting with several other guests. There she made the introductions.

Captain Truscott, Lieutenant Gilbert, and Major Dunlop were Army of course, while Jack wore his naval uniform with panache. I thought perhaps that he was making up, a little, for not having war stories to tell, for he worked in the Admiralty in Signals. He looked particularly handsome, regular features, his hair only lightly touched with gray, and his eyes without that haunted look one so often sees among men who've served at the Front. Still, there were lines in his face, and I had the feeling that he knew more about the war than most, and carried different burdens because of it.

I realized very quickly that everything happening outside this household had been set aside for the weekend. Talk ranged from past shooting parties in Scotland to the Thames regatta. Any topic would do that didn't remind us of war and death and destruction. We laughed at stories that weren't really funny, made no mention of absent friends, and pretended to be happy and lighthearted. Other guests arrived in the next hour, but none of them was a certain officer in a Wiltshire regiment. Not that I'd expected him to be here, he was no doubt still in France. But Marjorie Evanson must have met him somewhere, in just such a social setting. It was entirely possible that someone would mention him. *Remember Fred? Serving with the Wiltshires? We had a letter from him last week . . .*

Of course he could be a complete stranger. Someone Marjorie met in London and never introduced to anyone she knew. That was surely the safest way to conduct an affair. But people don't fall in love with safety in mind. Sometimes risk must be half the excitement of a secret affair.

Neither Mary nor I wore our uniforms to dinner. Nurses at a dinner table tend to cast a pall over conversation. Men in uniform on the other hand tend to look dashing, whether they are or not.

The roast was indeed heavenly. There was even horseradish sauce, and Yorkshire pudding. For an hour the war faded into the background and it was 1914 again, when food was plentiful and parties like this frequent and fun.

That evening we played croquet on the lawn in the long summer twilight, a ruthless game with no holds barred. The next morning, Saturday, we played tennis and were silly over the litter of pups that one of the English setters had produced in the stable-cum-garage instead of the box carefully prepared in the house for her accouchement.

As we admired the little family, under cover of the ohs and ahs someone behind me commented quietly, "That was Evanson's bitch, you know. He'd arranged to breed her to FitzGerald's dog, the one the King admired. He'd hoped to give HM the pick of the litter."

"Pity about all that," the other voice said. "His wife. I mean to say, *murder.*"

But before I could turn and see the speakers, we were being handed pups and I couldn't be sure who had been just behind me.

The warm, furry little bodies, wriggling and squirming in our arms, licking our faces, kept us occupied for another half an hour, and then it was time for our luncheon.

We trooped out of the stables in good spirits, and I listened for the same voices as people laughed and congratulated Serena on the litter. Still, the two men had been nearly whispering, so it was harder to identify them with a normal voice.

Serena said nothing about the mother of the pups being her brother's dog.

Not an hour later, I overheard her speaking to Jack as I passed the study.

She was saying, "I don't believe any of them could have been Marjorie's lover. It was sheer foolishness to think we could find out this way."

Her husband answered quietly, "You were desperate. It was the best I could do on short notice. So many of the people we know are in France, or God knows where. The man may even be dead, as far as that goes."

"By his own hand, I hope," she retorted viciously. "After all he's done to us."

Jack said nothing.

"It's not your family," she went on into the silence, answering it as if her husband had spoken aloud. "I'm the one who has to live with the whispers and the shame. I can read pity in my friends' eyes. That is, when they can't avoid me. And wherever I go I can feel the stares behind my back. 'Did you know? Her sister-in-law was murdered, and then her brother killed himself.' As if I've done something wrong. No one asks how I'm coping, for fear I might embarrass them by telling them and expecting a little comfort in return. What if they knew the rest of it? I'd never dare show my face in public again." Her voice broke, but not with tears. "I should have had that damned bitch put down!"

"I understand," her husband answered her. "But you're tormenting yourself as well, you know. As for the poor dog, find her another home if you feel that way. Don't blame her."

"I'm not blaming her. I see her looking up at the door sometimes, as if she's waiting for Merry to come through it any minute. She loved him. Probably more than Marjorie did, if you ask me. And how do you tell a dumb brute that her master is dead?"

"I think she knows Meriwether is dead. I think she also hopes it isn't true."

"This is the third time we've had one of these parties. I don't know if I can face another one, Jack. But I can't think of a better way to question someone about Marjorie's friends than inviting them here under false pretenses. And the women come out of curiosity, hoping I'll drop some crumb of gossip that they can take home with them. The men come because they like you, but I watch their faces when I mention Marjorie, to see if she meant more to them than she should have. Surely whoever that man is, he still feels something. He's bound to give himself away. A shift in the way he looks at me, a tightness in the mouth. I want to know who it is. I won't have any peace until I do and can put the blame where it belongs."

"You may be right, my dear, but the truth is, I don't hold out much hope."

I walked on down the carpeted passage for fear one of them might come out and find me there, eavesdropping.

But I carried with me food for thought.

For one thing, Inspector Herbert hadn't told Serena about the man at the railway station. And probably wouldn't until he knew whether or not it was pertinent to his investigation.

For another, it appeared I wasn't the only one searching for Marjorie Evanson's lover. Even here. And I had the very strong feeling that if Serena found the man before I did, she would take savage pleasure in exposing him to the world.

Before she killed him . . .

The thought occurred to me out of the blue. I didn't know whether she was capable of such a thing or not, but her brother's death had affected her deeply, and sometimes people who turned to anger as they grieved acted rashly, in the heat of the moment, wanting to hurt the person who had hurt them.

Still, now I knew the purpose of this wartime birthday party and why it hadn't mattered if Mary had brought a friend. Serena Melton saw me as a smoke screen, added to make up the party's numbers and conceal her true purpose in inviting certain guests. Well, I needn't feel quite so guilty now about coming here under false pretenses, out of curiosity.

Last evening during croquet and again during the tennis match this morning, I'd seen Serena casually drawing aside first one guest and then another. She and Captain Truscott had had a long conversation, and soon after that, Lieutenant Gilbert. I'd thought she was making them feel at home, just as she'd chatted to me about my father and my duties.

And that reminded me of the naval commander she and Mary had discussed. Had Marjorie known him as well? I'd tried, politely, not to listen at the time. Now I made an effort to bring the exchange back. I didn't want to mention it to Mary.

"When was his last leave, do you remember?" she'd asked. *"Was he in London then?"* And when Mary told her he'd taken the train directly to Scotland, to see his parents, she'd replied, *"No wonder Marjorie had missed seeing him. I must say, Jack was wondering about him too."*

Serena must not have been very close to her sister-in-law or she wouldn't be fishing among Marjorie's friends for answers.

And that brought to mind another question.

Was there jealousy between Marjorie and Serena? Had Meriwether Evanson's marriage caused a rift with his sister?

Chapter Four

I'd taken refuge in the Meltons' dining room from a storm that had suddenly blown up, sending us all dashing for the house. As I stood there looking out at the rain sweeping across the lawns, I heard someone come in the door behind me, and turned.

It was Lieutenant Bellis, one of the late arrivals last night. He'd missed the tennis match, pleading fatigue, and I hadn't seen much of him at lunch. He was drenched, his hair plastered to his skull, and he said lightly, "Is there nowhere in this house that a man can find a drink?"

I laughed. "I suspect Jack keeps what's left of his precious stock under lock and key."

"I'm beginning to think you're right. Known him long, have you?"

"Actually, not very." I took a chance. "I met his brother-in-law once, I think."

"Meriwether? A good man. He didn't deserve what happened to him." He'd found a table napkin in one of the drawers of the sideboard and was busy toweling his head. Pausing, he looked at me from between the folds. "I thought I remembered you. A nursing sister, aren't you? From *Britannic*, I think. I was in Mesopotamia."

I fished quickly for a face in a hospital bed, then smiled as I remembered. "George Bellis! The leg's healed, I see." I didn't add that the thin, sun-baked man with a broken leg and cracked ribs, a fractured skull and the bites of myriad insects looked nothing like the tall, muscular officer standing before me now. His brother was a captain in one of the county regiments. I tried to recall which. Wiltshire?

"Indeed it has," he said as we shook hands like lost friends. "I was sent to France after I recovered. Were you still with *Britannic* when she sank? I'd wondered."

"I was," I told him, "and escaped with a broken arm."

"Harrowing experience, I should think."

"I still dream of it sometimes."

He nodded, folded the napkin, and put it aside. "Not surprising. My dreams aren't what they once were."

He made a gesture intended to lighten his next words. "My favorite is finding myself flying through a hail of bullets, diving headfirst into the nearest trench, only to find it crowded with the most despicable collection of Turkish soldiers you can imagine. Bazaar thieves, guttersnipes, and murderers all. Better than any rooster for a fast wake up."

But the lines around his mouth as he spoke told me that it had really happened, only to be repeated over and over again in his dreams.

I smiled, as I was expected to do, and then said, "Who wins?"

"I never find out. Since I'm still here, I expect it was me."

We laughed together, then I quickly changed the subject. "Wasn't there a girl? I seem to remember writing a letter for you. You could have written your own, but you were malingering."

"So I was. A few minutes with the pretty ward sister, and I was envied by every man present. Yes, there was—is—a girl. She's in Norfolk, helping her family grow whatever it is they grow in Norfolk. Worse luck, she couldn't meet me in London. It was harvesttime for something."

I could hear the disappointment in his voice. "Why didn't you go to her?"

He grimaced. "Apparently marrows or parsnips or whatever they are rank higher than a mere lieutenant." And then he brightened. "But I'm taking the train from here to London, meeting my brother, and we're driving on to Gloucestershire."

"How nice!" I was trying to think how to bring Meriwether Evanson back into the conversation when George did it himself.

"When did you know Merry? After his first crash or his second?"

"The second."

"Ah. The burns." He stared out the window, watching the rain. "I've always had a horror of fire. I can't imagine finding myself aflame. How bad were they?"

"Head. Hands and feet. Part of his torso. Infection is the greatest danger."

"Bloody hell," he said, shuddering as he considered that. Then he realized he'd sworn aloud and was busy apologizing.

"Did you know his wife?" I asked.

He smiled. "If you knew Merry, you knew Marjorie. She's all he ever talked about. I'm surprised he didn't name that bitch in the stables for her." And once more he realized he'd put foot in mouth. "Sorry—I didn't mean it the way it came out."

"I'd seen her photograph. She seemed to be such a lovely woman. In every sense."

"Yes, well, she most certainly was pretty." He smiled, remembering. "But it hadn't turned her head. Do you know what I mean? She was a thoroughly nice person. That's what makes it so hard to believe she was murdered. I mean to say," he went on, frowning now, "one doesn't think of murder touching *nice* people."

Before I could stop myself, I spoke in defense of Marjorie Evanson. "I don't think murderers care if one is nice or not."

"Oddly enough, Serena asked me yesterday if I thought Marjorie had fallen in with the wrong sort of people. I couldn't imagine what she was getting at. Marjorie wasn't like that." He took a deep breath. "Is there something worrying her?"

"I expect she's also having trouble understanding murder," I said. "Grasping at straws—the wrong sort of people, money, debts, secrets—anything to explain what happened."

"I doubt if it was money or debts. Marjorie was comfortably off in her own right, but not rich. As I remember, she and her sister shared the inheritance from their father."

Someone—Inspector Herbert?—had mentioned a sister.

"As for secrets," he went on, "Marjorie was hopeless there. Merry told me she couldn't wait for an anniversary or a birthday, and was forever asking if he wanted to know straightaway what she was giving him."

And yet she had kept a very different secret from her husband and everyone else.

Lieutenant Bellis began to pace restlessly. "How did we get on such a morbid subject? The weather is wretched enough."

Taking the hint, I said, "It does seem a little lighter in the west."

"Your imagination," he replied, grinning, coming to stand by me at the windows. "It's still as black as the bottom of a witch's kettle out there. This could go on for hours."

But it didn't. A tiny square of blue grew to the size of a counterpane, and then spread quickly, offering us the spectacle of a rainbow as the sun finally burst through.

The grass was too wet for sport, and so we collected in the study for our tea.

Jack was looking tired, as if he rather regretted inviting so many guests for the weekend. Watching him, I thought perhaps he was feeling the strain of his duties. It must be a burden to know the truth about what was happening in France or the North Atlantic and say nothing. I'd noticed several times that when he was asked for his views on the course of the war or the prospect for the Americans to come in, he evaded a direct answer, giving instead the public view we could read for ourselves in any newspaper.

My own father had told me privately that if the Americans didn't commit themselves soon, we would run short of men. I'd asked him if the Germans were in the same state, and he'd answered gravely, "We'd better start praying they are." It was a worrying possibility that we could lose the war. That so many might have died in vain.

The men drifted off to the billiard room, and the women settled down to read or knit. We were all expected to do our share with our needles, and most of us were thoroughly tired of the drab khaki wool intended for stockings, scarves, gloves, hoods, and even waistcoats to keep men warm in the trenches.

Serena came to join us after seeing to matters in the kitchen, and I noticed the shadows on her face as she sat by one of the lamps, rolling yarn into a ball.

Cynthia Newley said, "Serena, is there any news regarding Marjorie? Has the Yard learned anything more?"

"Apparently not," she answered coldly. "At least we haven't been told."

"It seems so—odd. You would think Marjorie's death would receive top priority."

"Indeed."

I glimpsed Serena's eyes as she looked up briefly at her friend. There was angry denial there. It was a pity the police had had to tell her about the unborn child. It had only added to her distress. Any indiscretion on Marjorie's part should have died quietly with her. But this was murder, and there were no secrets in cases of murder.

And then Serena was saying, as if unable to stop herself, "I don't know what's wrong with me. I can't seem to concentrate on anything. You knew Marjorie, Cynthia. So did you, Patricia. Those last months in London—what did she do? Where did she go? I wasn't in London often, I seldom saw her. When the police asked me if she had met any new friends, I had no idea. Or if she was worried about something. I was so out of touch, I couldn't give them an answer."

Patricia, a quiet woman with dark hair, said, "These past few months—well, since late winter for that matter—I saw her hardly at all. A few memorial services, and once at a morning church service. I asked Helen Calder if Marjorie was all right. Helen replied that she was probably worried sick about Meriwether. Let's face it, pilots don't have very long lives, do they?"

Juliana said, "Well, I can vouch for the fact that she didn't spend much time with her usual friends. I invited her to several parties, and she declined."

"Which could mean," Cynthia commented dryly, "she must have made new friends."

"Still, you must have seen her somewhere. Dining out, volunteering somewhere, the theater." Serena looked around the room, inviting comment.

Cynthia, sitting by the window, peered over her glasses. "Well. Since you ask. There must have been a man."

Serena bristled. "That's disgusting!"

"Is it?" She ran her fingers through her fair hair. "Look, we're not the innocent lambs we were in 1914, are we? If Marjorie stopped seeing her friends and family, there's probably a good reason. She had new friends—or she had something to hide. And what would she have to hide, if it wasn't a man?" Cynthia added bitterly, "She's not the first, Serena, and nor will she be the last. You're fortunate, you know where Jack is, even if he's not at home. He isn't off in France or God knows where, being shot at, and his letters coming in bunches or not at all, and you're left wondering if he's dead or wounded or missing. You can't stand in judgment of Marjorie, you haven't lived with her fears."

Serena said, "She never said anything to me about any fears."

"No, I'm sorry. But you're Meriwether's sister, you had your own worries there. I expect she didn't want to add to them."

Mary said, trying to pour oil on troubled waters, "There's been nothing more in the newspapers. Have the police made any progress at all?"

Serena gave her a cold, hard look. "The inquest was adjourned at the request of the police, citing the ongoing inquiry into her murder by person or persons unknown."

Mary answered mildly, "I was in France, Serena. I didn't know."

Nor did I.

Cynthia held her ground. "There's no use asking us about Marjorie. Talk to her sister. It's possible she knew more about what was going on. Marjorie may have confided in her."

"I doubt it," Patricia interjected. "My impression was that they didn't get on."

Serena turned to Cynthia. "You seem to feel there was something to hide. No one else does. It must mean that you know something you aren't willing to tell me."

"If you're asking if I know who murdered her, I don't. She avoided all of us these past few months.

Even you, if you think about it. One doesn't advertise adultery, Serena, but the signs are there. If you haven't noticed them, I'm sure the police have. If the man she was seeing killed her, then she threatened him somehow. But I hardly think, knowing Marjorie, that she would do such a thing. So who else could it be? That's a matter for the police. But you won't get anywhere unless you look the truth in the face."

Patricia winced. We were all feeling decidedly uncomfortable. One didn't discuss such things openly, and yet Cynthia had.

Juliana was bent over her ball of yarn, rewinding it after dropping it, avoiding looking at any of us.

I shot a quick glance at Serena's face. I don't think she'd bargained for someone as strong willed as Cynthia.

And then Serena surprised me. She said, "I don't want to believe there was someone else. After all, Marjorie was married to my brother. But I'm grateful for your honesty. I'll speak to the police. I wasn't supposed to mention it, but they're of the opinion now that someone noticed the rather fine lozenge brooch she was wearing when she was killed. It's missing, of course. Along with her purse. These new friends she possibly made—the police ought to be aware of them. Surely it won't hurt to look into who they are." She glanced at the clock on the mantelpiece and set aside her knitting.

"I think the gentlemen have had long enough to bore themselves to death. Let's rout them out and have our tea brought in."

She turned away to ring for tea, but her shoulders were stiff, and I thought she wouldn't soon forgive Cynthia for being outspoken and voicing what Serena already knew to be true.

As for a missing brooch, Inspector Herbert hadn't asked if she was wearing it at the railway station.

Serena had just lied to distract Cynthia and the rest of us from any thought of a lover.

She went in search of her husband and his guests.

A silence filled the room after she'd gone. I realized the sun now coming through the window was warm on my feet. I shifted a little in my chair.

Everyone looked at me as if I were about to speak.

Finally Mary said, "I didn't know where to look when she was talking about Marjorie."

Patricia said, her voice irritable, "We'd be liars if we didn't admit that we've been curious about what happened."

"Well, she certainly put paid to any more gossip, didn't she? I think we all must have had in the back of our minds that Marjorie must have done something to lead to her death. Making her as guilty as whoever killed her," Cynthia said. "The police should have made it clear about the missing brooch. It would have quelled a good deal of speculation and talk."

I put my knitting into its bag and said, "I'm cross-eyed from counting stitches. At least the sun has come out. It will be good to walk a little after tea."

The others turned to me as if I'd changed the subject on purpose. Which I had.

Chapter Five

Lying awake in my bed that night long after Mary was asleep, I considered Serena's lie about the brooch.

It had been a foolish thing to do. She was bound to be found out when Marjorie's murderer was caught and tried. I couldn't help but wonder what other lies she might have told people who came too close to the mark, as Cynthia had done.

And Cynthia Newley had brought up a very interesting point. That if Marjorie was meeting a man in places where neither of them was known, she was outside that safe circle of acquaintances and familiar surroundings that made it possible for women to move about London on their own. If her murderer had come from those shadows, the chances of finding him would be very slim indeed.

On the other hand, if the killer wasn't a stranger, Serena was running a risk openly digging for information. Just as one of her guests might unwittingly know this person, one of them might just as unwittingly tell him how close Serena was coming to uncovering the truth.

None of her efforts would bring her brother back to her, even if she could personally hand Marjorie's killer over to the police.

I was surprised that Jack Melton hadn't reined in her attempts to question his guests. But perhaps he saw this as a harmless way to deflect her grief and anger. And he could always say, later, "You must remember how recent it was, and how upset she's been, especially since the police have got nowhere."

I drifted into sleep and dreamed not of murderers but of India. It's strange how smells and sounds come back so vividly in a dream. The dust, ancient and full of an exotic mix of scents from dung to rare spices. The muffled sounds of car wheels in the distance, harness bells jingling, and the creak of wood as the oxen put their shoulders into pulling. The feel of the dry wind on one's face, just before the monsoon rains come. Voices in a bazaar, a dozen different dialects, all talking at once. I was back in a familiar and happy past, safe in a world I knew so well, my father walking through the compound gate, Simon Brandon at his heels.

Sunday morning it rained again. Not just the occasional shower, but a hard steady rain that had no intention of going away.

Most of us went with Serena to attend morning services at St. Ambrose Church in Diddlestoke, and listened to a homily on faith in times of trouble. The rector, aptly named Mr. Parsons, was eloquent. Most of the congregation were wearing black, although the Government had tried to persuade people to eschew mourning, to keep up the spirits of those at home as well as the returning wounded. My blue uniform coat stood out among them.

On the walk home, I asked if anyone knew someone in the Wiltshires, adding casually, "I haven't heard from friends in a while. Are they facing serious opposition? Should I be worrying?"

There was a general shaking of heads. Lieutenant Bellis added, "I shouldn't, if I were you. Your letters probably haven't caught up with you yet."

I had to leave it there.

Jack and Serena had gone ahead, to see that breakfast was ready for us, and afterward we played bridge. It was fun at first, but then the friendly bickering grew more strident as the better players argued over each hand. I lost interest and wandered away.

Captain Truscott was a tall, thin man suffering from nerves. His hands shook as he dealt the cards, almost like a palsy. No one had said anything as he twice dropped cards, or his fork fought to find his mouth at meals. But his mind was sharp and his sense of humor intact.

He too was soon banished from the tables, and he came in to join me in the music room. He'd asked me earlier to call him Freddy.

"May I join you?" he asked politely.

"Of course. This is a sanctuary for hopeless bridge players."

He laughed. "Do you play?" He gestured toward the piano.

"Not as well as I should like." Pianos are delicate creatures and dislike being shipped around the world, much less being carted from cantonment to cantonment on the backs of camels or in swaying oxcarts, absorbing dust and monsoons in equal measure. Lessons were possible only when my mother could find an instrument in fair enough tune to make learning the rudiments of playing even possible. She has perfect pitch, and I realized much later what agony of spirit she must have endured, even trying to pass on a little of her skill to her only daughter.

Captain Truscott walked across the room, sat down at the piano, adjusted his chair a little, and began to play.

Freddy, I discovered, was amazingly gifted, his hands steady and sure on the keys. I came to join him, turning pages in the music he'd found. It was a pleasure to listen to him.

He smiled up at me, but I could see his mind was elsewhere, as if the music reached deep inside.

As he moved on to another piece, this one from memory, he said, "Marjorie Evanson liked to listen to my playing. Her husband was Serena's brother. A pilot. They don't have much of a record for longevity. Marjorie formed a sort of club for women who were the wives or widows of fliers. They met once a week in her London house to give each other support and comfort."

Something else I didn't know about this woman.

"Who has taken over the group now?"

He shrugged. "I hope someone has. But she was the driving force. It may have collapsed without her."

Moving effortlessly to another piece, this one an Irish ballad, the keys rippling softly under light fingers, he fell silent.

Then to my astonishment he said, "There was another man. I don't think Serena knows. But I saw them together some months before Marjorie's death. Two? Three? I'm not sure. At any rate, they were in a small restaurant on the outskirts of Rochester. Not a place

I'd expect to find her, but I knew her at once. I'd had a flat, you see, and had to wait for it to be repaired. So I'd come to The Black Horse to have something to eat while I waited. There was a girl with me—she was engaged to someone else and worried about gossip. I was taking her back to London for her fiancé, it was completely aboveboard, but you know how people talk."

I could easily see how that might happen. With trains so crowded and having to wait for troop-train priority, everyone asked for lifts from someone going their way.

"Did Marjorie see you?"

"Oh, yes, I'm sure she did. She was facing the door as I stepped into the room. She looked away at once, and I backed out, telling Nancy I didn't care for the restaurant after all. I couldn't see the man she was with. His back was to me, the lights were dim, and there must have been something wrong with the chimney, because there was a smoke haze hanging about. I knew it wasn't Meriwether, but that's about it. The man was dark, and looked to be about my height. Before Marjorie saw me, they had their heads together in a way that seemed rather—intimate, if you know what I mean."

I did. And his description matched that of the man I'd seen. "Could you tell if he was in uniform? Anything to indicate rank or regiment?"

He shook his head. "I was too busy beating a hasty retreat. He could have been—"

And at that critical moment, the door opened and Cynthia came in with Lieutenant Gilbert.

"We heard the music," she said. "It's war in there—" She gestured over her shoulder. I could just hear Patricia arguing with Jack Melton about a hand. "We've escaped."

That was the end of a private conversation, but just before lunch, when we had no more than a minute alone, Freddy said, "I can trust you to keep that confidence? I wouldn't want to hurt Serena."

"Of course."

And that was that. I walked over to where Jack was showing off his gun collection. The cabinet was mahogany and lined with a pale velvet. Two prizes were there on display. I'd noticed them before. Jack was just pointing to the early American Colt revolver.

"My uncle went out to the American West to raise cattle. He had a weak chest and he hoped either for a cure or to die of it more quickly out there. To everyone's amazement, he survived, made a fortune, came back to England, and lived to be seventy-seven."

Everyone laughed, as they were meant to, and Jack's hand moved onto a pair of dueling pistols. Halfway there I saw his fingers pause for an instant where the lining was indented but nothing lay in that spot. It was an infinitesimal pause, but I saw the flicker of expression on his face and then he went on smoothly, "These belonged to my great-grandfather. Handsome, aren't they? He bought them not to kill anyone but because he believed a gentleman ought to own a pair. They were never fired in anger, but I have it on good authority that when he tried them here at the Hall, they pulled slightly to the right, and he missed his target, hit his coachman's pet goat instead, and there was a terrible uproar. The goat survived, but the tip of one horn was shorter than the other for the rest of its life, and my great-grandfather was required by the magistrate to pay compensation. Only no one could decide on the value of a goat. In the end my great-grandfather paid the coachman five pounds, a princely sum in that day, and was ordered to swear he would never dismiss the coachman or eat the goat."

I moved past them as his audience laughed again, and went to find Mary. Our train left for London an hour after lunch, and we were nearly ready.

She was rather quiet on the first leg of our journey. Busy with my own thoughts, I was content to let the silence between us lengthen.

After a time she said, "You know, it just goes to show that to eat well, one should live on a farm."

That was not as far-fetched a conversational gambit as it might sound. She was seeing a naval officer whose father was a gentleman farmer, like Jack, and she had been dithering over whether to marry him should he propose or find someone more likely to enjoy the social whirl in London.

I murmured something noncommittal, and she went back to her own reverie.

I myself had been thinking about Serena Melton.

I'd had no brothers—or sisters for that matter—to help me judge how one might feel in Serena's shoes, having lost Meriwether. Would I have been forgiving or vindictive? The closest I could come to imagining her emotional state was to consider something happening to Simon Brandon. He wasn't related, but I'd known him all my life and loved him dearly. If someone caused his death, I'd be furiously angry and determined to see that person punished.

Soldiers are mortal, we had all been touched by that loss. But Serena's brother hadn't given his life for King and Country. He'd died under tragic circumstances, just after the doctors had felt it safe enough to send him home. He'd had a good chance of surviving his wounds. First hope, then despair.

I myself had grieved in my own way for Meriwether Evanson. And so had Matron, for that matter.

I took a deep breath, more like a sigh, and Mary said, "Was it a boring weekend? I'm sorry for dragging you there."

"I was very glad I went," I told her truthfully. But I was looking forward to spending the rest of my leave with my family. I'd had my fill of spying.

I had been back in France nearly ten days when the letter came from Inspector Herbert at Scotland Yard.

It was brief, and it contained a photograph. I turned it over, to find myself staring into a dead man's face. I could see clearly the bullet wound in his temple.

I turned to the letter.

This is Lieutenant Fordham. He died of a single gunshot wound to the head. Forgive me for sending this to you without some warning, but I'm told you're in France and there's no other way. Fordham's death appears to be a suicide. I use that word, appears, *because there is a modicum of doubt. He was an officer in the Wiltshire Fusiliers. Are you still certain that the man with Marjorie Evanson the evening of her death was in this regiment? Could this be the man?*

I looked again at the photograph. But I already knew the answer. This was not the man at the railway station.

I felt a chill. Suicide among soldiers was more prevalent than the Army admitted. It wasn't good for morale to give exact numbers, they said. Why had Lieutenant Fordham chosen to kill himself? What demons drove him? And why—other than his regiment—had Inspector Herbert thought this might be the man I'd seen with Marjorie Evanson?

Was there something in his suicide note that pointed in that direction?

And what did Inspector Herbert mean by "appears to be a suicide"?

His brief message told me so little that my curiosity was aroused. I found myself thinking that he'd have done better to satisfy it.

I reached for pen and paper to answer him before the next post bag left.

Poor man. To answer your questions: I am not mistaken in the matter of the Wiltshires. And this is not the person I saw at the railway station.

But even as I finished putting those words down on paper in black ink, stark on the page, I glanced again at the photograph. Lieutenant Fordham was a handsome man even in death, and if he were charming into the bargain, he might easily turn a lonely woman's head.

He was the sort Serena Melton should have invited to a weekend party, not a Lieutenant Bellis, who considered himself a friend of Meriwether Evanson's, or Captain Truscott with his shaking hands. They were loyal to the dead, and not likely to confide anything they might know to a grieving sister.

I added another line to my message.

What weapon did Lieutenant Fordham use to kill himself? Service revolver? Other?

It was the price Inspector Herbert must pay for not being more straightforward. For something had just struck a chord of memory.

Thinking about Serena and her house party had brought to mind a vivid image of Jack Melton's hand pausing over an empty depression in the lining of his gun cabinet.

To suspect Serena Melton of killing a man she thought was her sister-in-law's lover was ridiculous. And yet—and yet I had seen for myself how deep her grief and anger ran. If she'd found someone she believed was the guilty man, and there was no way of proving it, what would she do?

For one thing, she wouldn't have a weapon handy, in the event she needed to use it. That was a very different thing from being so angry one could lash out with the first thing that came to hand. Besides, Lieutenant Fordham was a soldier, with a soldier's reflexes. He wasn't likely to let someone walk up to him, revolver in hand, and fire at him.

I was letting my imagination run away with me. But as much as I didn't want to believe it, there was most certainly the possibility that Marjorie had had more than one lover. And Lieutenant Fordham could have had his own guilty conscience.

And so I didn't tear up the reply to Inspector Herbert and start again. I left the query in my letter.

But Scotland Yard never answered. Not even to thank me for helping them with their inquiries.

Chapter Six

Finally I wrote to Simon Brandon.

He had been my father's batman, his friend even though he was less than half my father's age, and eventually his RMS, his regimental sergeant-major, a position of some responsibility as well as prestige. If anyone could find the answer to my question without involving the police or causing a stir, it was Simon. His contacts were myriad, and they had long memories of service together.

I knew my father well enough to be sure he'd find the answer to my question, and then want to know why I had asked it. The Colonel Sahib, as we called him behind his back, was accustomed to commanding troops in battle. Raising a daughter would—he'd thought—be as simple as taking a seasoned company on maneuvers. He could do it blindfolded. Hands behind his back.

By the time I was walking, he was in full retreat from that position. "She'll be running the British Army before she's ten!" he'd warned my mother. It wasn't long before all the servants and half the men in his command were enlisted in a conspiracy to keep me safe. Not to mention our Indian staff and all their relatives.

The Army has a code of its own. I had been well taught not to air its dirty linens in public, and in India my father would have made short work of finding out who had been involved with Lieutenant Evanson's wife, and seeing to it that he was disciplined. Or learning how Captain Fordham had shot himself. It would have gone no further, been dealt with quietly and appropriately. We weren't in India now, but the same circumspection was still there, inbred in us.

A letter came back faster than I'd expected. It occurred to me that Simon had somehow arranged to have it sent with dispatches. The post where I was presently stationed was notoriously slow. And sent with dispatches, the letter wouldn't pass through the hands of the military censors.

I opened it quickly, eager to see what he had discovered.

Bess. It's been hushed up. I can't discover why.
What's this about? Do you know this man?

Before I could answer Simon, we were moved again, this time to the tiny village of La Fleurette, so destroyed by war and armies that I could find nothing to show me what it might have looked like, once upon a time.

There was a pitted street, half buried in piles of rubble, only the west wall of the little church still forlornly standing, and miraculously, a stone barn that had somehow escaped damage. It was whole, even its roof intact.

"Praise God," Sister Benning said, looking up at it. "Now to see if we can do anything about the inside."

The lane into the barn's forecourt was no more than a muddy and rutted track. The barnyard was already jammed with lorries and ambulances jostling for room, and we had orderlies clearing up the interior as fast as they could, so that we had a space in which to work.

The walking wounded were already sitting on benches, shoulders drooping, bloody bandaging around heads, torsos, or limbs. Sometimes all three. Stretchers with the worst cases were being set across frames made from mangers, and a surgeon was already at work, calling for us to hurry and bring him what he needed. The first of the dead had been taken away, out of sight in what had been the milking shed.

It was chaos, and we were accustomed to it, having packed in such a fashion that we could find anything we wanted immediately.

Ambulances were coming in now in twos and threes, and I was meeting them, trying to sort the wounded into those who could wait, those who needed immediate attention, and sometimes, offering up a brief prayer as I came across a soldier who had died on the way to us.

We worked almost thirty-six hours without respite on one broken body after another. Someone had managed to brew tea, and we drank gallons of it without milk or sugar, to stay awake. I took my turn at the tables where Dr. Buckley was operating, my eyes on his hands and the wound. Ellen Benning, on the other side, was constantly mopping his brow, and as I looked up, I realized he was flushed, perspiration rolling down his face, and I wondered if he were ill. At a break while the patients were being shifted, I led him outside and asked, "Sir, what's wrong?"

He looked at me, his eyes so tired that they seemed sunk in his head, lined and puffy with lack of sleep.

"I'm well," he told me irritably. "Don't hover."

I said nothing more, letting him go back to work without protest.

And then as suddenly as the flood had begun, it started to taper off.

I saw Dr. Buckley huddled with one of the ambulance drivers, their faces grim.

We had reached a point where we could actually catch our collective breath when Dr. Buckley began to load the wounded, ambulatory and stretcher cases, into whatever vehicles we had, sending them back down the line. The empty vehicles were returning for their next load when I quietly asked what was happening.

"The Germans are about to break through along the Front. We're moving out as quickly as possible. The Army is trying to hold them, but I don't think there's much of a chance now. Best to be prepared."

It was the story of this war—a few yards gained at horrendous cost, then lost again with even more casualties from trying to hold on against all odds. A retreat today, an advance tomorrow, and then retreat again before the next advance, like a bloody tug of war.

I nodded, and went about helping him, smiling and offering comfort where I could, assuring the soldiers we'd just patched up that this was too exposed a location and they'd be better off in one of the trench hospitals down the line.

One of the Scots officers agreed. "This wasn't supposed to happen. We'd won the ground, HQ told us we could hold on to it. But their intelligence was wrong."

We were down to the last half dozen walking wounded, who were being handed into ambulances, and the staff was packing one with what was left of our stock of supplies. A lorry was filled with the dead.

I looked around in the pale morning light, feeling rather exposed here in this shattered place. I'd been too busy to notice before this. Still, I was tired enough to sink to the ground and sleep where I was.

Dr. Buckley had come out of the barn to supervise the last of the stretcher cases, those he had waited as long as possible before moving. I was just about to go and help when I heard a faint new sound in the distance.

Almost in the same instant, I recognized what I was hearing above the rumble of the German guns down the line. It was an aircraft, and it was coming closer.

Searching the sky for it, I felt my heart rate rise. I don't know why, but something, some instinct born of working so near war at its worst, warned me. Why was an aircraft heading this way? The British aerodromes were west of here. Was it in trouble? And then I saw it, coming low and fast. The shape was distinctive—the two wings and the different body of an Albatross. I had only a second to wonder how a German pilot could have flown this far behind our lines, and then remembered that our lines were collapsing. I was already running, pointing, shouting to everyone to take cover, one eye still to the sky.

The orderlies, patients, and nurses clustered around the great doors of the barn probably couldn't see what I did, but my alarm was all too apparent. They glanced up, then heard the aircraft's motor, and dashed for the security of the barn.

The German flier, perhaps on a simple reconnaissance mission to see how the wavering front was holding, had seen us as well, and he veered in our direction, one of the Spandau machine guns already stuttering angrily, ripping up the earth and tracing a line across the bonnet of one of the ambulances. It burst into flames as the orderly who had taken cover behind it flung himself to one side. I could see the bullets coming my way and dove behind one of the horse troughs, and then he was gone, only to swoop past and swing around to bear down on the barn itself.

I saw one of the wounded with a rifle in his hand, and he stood there, in full view, carefully taking his aim, firing and then waiting for death to come. But the pilot hadn't seen him and fired at the barn instead. I could see Dr. Buckley standing there, his mouth opened wide in a wordless shout, his fists raised above his head, cursing the pilot.

I realized he was trying to distract the German at the stick, and just as the pilot veered, a tiny plume of white smoke showed beneath the aircraft, turning black quickly and growing larger by the second, until it was a column trailing the aircraft like the shadow of death. I knew what was coming—I'd seen Lieutenant Evanson's burns and those of other fliers.

Dr. Buckley and the barn were forgotten as the pilot pulled up sharply and turned away in a frantic dash for his own lines.

By some marvel of aim, that soldier must have hit the German.

I was already at the barn, climbing into one of the other ambulances, ramming the burning one to one side, where it could do no harm to the barn's wooden doors. Just at that moment, the German Albatross exploded into flames, spiraling toward the earth. A cheer went up, and then Sister Benning was pointing, saying something to me that I couldn't hear over the explosive sound of the crash.

I closed my eyes for a second against the sound, then turned in the direction she'd indicated, and there was Dr. Buckley on the ground in a heap. All I could think of was that he'd been hit.

I ran to him as Sister Davis asked, "Isn't anyone going to see if that pilot survived?" No one stopped to tell her that he'd burned alive in that conflagration.

Bending over Dr. Buckley, I searched for blood, a wound, then felt for his pulse. It was slow, labored. An orderly was there, and I told him to put Dr. Buckley into one of the ambulances. "We ought to be going," I added. "If that Albatross got through our lines, the rest of the German army may be on its heels."

Sister Williams caught my own alarm and called, "Hurry!"

We got Dr. Buckley into the nearest ambulance. There was no room, with one ambulance destroyed, for six of us, and Sister Benning said, "Well, it's shank's mare, then."

The lorry with the dead was already pulling out, and the ambulances followed. We began to march in its wake, and I thought that all we needed now was for one of us to twist an ankle in the ruts and pits of the road. I was concerned as well for the wounded, bounced and shaken in spite of the care their drivers took to spare them the worst of the ride.

Sister Davis was saying, "They're getting ahead of us. What if the Germans are closer than we know?"

"Keep walking," Sister Williams answered her sternly. "And pay attention to where you're putting your feet. There's no one to carry you if you stumble or fall."

I looked over my shoulder. The black plume that marked where the German flier had gone down was dwindling, as the fire had consumed the wooden body of the Albatross and there was less and less fuel to feed on. I tried to put it out of my mind and did as Sister Williams had asked—silently concentrating on each step.

My main worry was that another pilot from the same squadron, seeing the telltale black smoke, might come to investigate. We could still be spotted.

We'd marched nearly three miles through desolation and the French summer sun, thirsty and wishing for nothing more than an hour's rest. Sister Benning had already asked if we needed to find some shade for five minutes of respite from the heat, but we all knew it would be the height of foolishness.

And then a lorry came barreling toward us, crashing about like an erratic monster, and it slowed in a shower of dust and loose stones.

"Get in," the sergeant at the wheel shouted to us, standing on no ceremony. "We lost this round, and the Hun will be at La Fleurette in twenty minutes."

We didn't need a second invitation. We scrambled into the back of the lorry and held on tight as the driver swung it in a wide circle to make his turn. Then we were heading back the way he'd come, gripping whatever we could find to keep ourselves from being thrown about. I could feel the bruises accumulating. But we were safe, and that was all that mattered.

The driver slowed after what seemed to be hours of torture, and he called back to us, "We should be in the clear. Sorry about the rough ride."

I asked if there was news of Dr. Buckley, but the driver shook his head. "No idea, Sister. But not to worry. We'll be back in La Fleurette soon enough. Word is the Huns can't hold what they've gained today."

And then he turned back to the wheel, and Sister Benning said, "Well. I know what it feels like to be on the rack, now," as we gathered speed again.

But I wasn't fated to return to La Fleurette, although later I was told that we'd regained the lost ground, just as the sergeant had predicted, and a dozen yards beyond it. But at the cost of how many lives, how many wounded who would never be whole again?

Dr. Buckley was being sent back to England. He resisted going at first, and then relented finally, asking if I could escort him—"She doesn't fuss," he had told the worried doctors who had examined him. At the same time I was informed that I was to be given leave, although I knew very well that in the rotation, I had weeks to go.

I never knew—although I had my suspicions—if my leave had to do with Dr. Buckley, or if Inspector Herbert had had some say in it. That was rather far-fetched, but stranger things, I'd learned in dealing with the Army, could happen. It was entirely possible that Simon Brandon had pulled some strings. Between them, he and my father knew everyone from General Haig to the lowliest subaltern down the line of command.

It was Simon who met my train as it came into London, and I'd sent no telegram.

Chapter Seven

Simon greeted me, took my satchel away from me, and walked with me to the motorcar that was waiting outside the station.

My father's motorcar, in fact.

Simon smiled. "It's home for you, Miss Crawford. Orders from the Colonel-in-Chief."

That was my mother. None of us disobeyed her when she issued a command.

I had delivered Dr. Buckley to a doctor waiting for him in the hospital in Portsmouth. Once he'd been settled and the papers I'd been carrying about his condition were handed over to Matron, who took charge of them and Dr. Buckley with quiet efficiency, I had been free to leave.

I was just as glad to be going home again. Standing at the rail of the ship bringing us into Portsmouth,

I'd watched the smooth waters of The Solent and the irregular shape of the Isle of Wight rise out of the darkness like some fantastical place in dreams—quiet and peaceful. At the back of my mind, unbidden, were the sounds of that Spandau machine gun firing round after round. And then an officer of the Wiltshire Fusiliers came to stand beside me, looking out toward the busy harbor.

"I miss the lights," he said without turning. "I could pick out the villages by their lights as we came into port."

They had been turned off to make the enemy blind. Portsmouth, across The Solent, was a major port and a tempting target for submarines.

I looked up at him, but it wasn't the face I'd hoped to see.

And that encounter had brought Marjorie Evanson back to mind. I still had her photograph.

Turning to Simon as we drove toward Somerset, I said, "What did you learn about Lieutenant Fordham's death?"

"It's still under wraps. A police matter. How did you come to hear about his death? Your letter was brief."

"I was worried about the censors. Scotland Yard wanted to know if he was the man I'd seen with Marjorie Evanson at the railway station, the day she died."

"And was he?"

"No. I can't even be sure he knew Mrs. Evanson. He was just in the same regiment as the officer the Yard is looking for. To help with their inquiries, as they say. Scotland Yard might even have asked me just on the off chance it would connect the two cases. Apparently they haven't made much progress in finding her murderer."

"That explains the fact that so little has come to light about Fordham's death. The Yard kept it out of the newspapers. Did you know that? But then Fordham was from a prominent family. I suspect they'd rather believe he was murdered than that he killed himself. He was a serving officer, recovering from wounds. Suicide smacks of not being able to face going back into the line."

"Was there an inquest?"

"It was adjourned at the request of the police."

"I did ask Inspector Herbert for the particulars, when I answered his letter. But he never replied. Where does the Fordham family live, do you know?"

"In Wiltshire. Leave it to the police, Bess."

"I know. They have more resources, and all that." I gave the matter some thought, then asked, "Was Lieutenant Fordham married?"

"I don't know. Bess——"

He turned to look at me, taking his eyes off the road for a moment. And that was when I realized that he was not telling me everything. I know Simon Brandon as well as he knows me.

"There's something else. What is it, Simon?" He was concentrating on passing a small dogcart driven by a heavyset man asleep on the seat, the pony trotting purposefully toward its destination as if it had done this a thousand times before. I waited until we were safely past pony and cart. "You might as well tell me."

"There's nothing to tell."

I smiled. "Must I spend my entire leave making your life miserable, wheedling and pleading and issuing ultimatums?" His profile was like stone. "I'll even cry."

He laughed then. "I haven't seen you cry in years."

I let it go. We drove in silence for some time.

Finally, Simon said, "All right. A fortnight before he died, Lieutenant Fordham was invited to a weekend party at Melton Hall."

I stared at him. "Melton Hall? But—" I stopped, then asked, "And did he accept?"

"He refused the invitation."

There could have been any number of reasons for refusing. But what had Serena Melton made of that?

"How on earth did you discover that?"

"Quite by chance. I was asking someone about Fordham, but she hadn't seen him for weeks. And then she added that, in fact, she'd just missed him. Apparently she'd attended a party where she'd been looking forward to seeing him—she had heard he was to be a fellow guest. But he never came. When she asked her hostess if he was all right, she was told that Fordham had pleaded another engagement. When she learned afterward that he'd died, she had wondered if his wounds were worse than she knew."

"I was a guest there one weekend. Simon, he must have known Marjorie—that's the only reason he'd have been asked to the party."

"That's why I didn't want to tell you. I knew you'd jump to conclusions."

I let it drop. But the rest of the way home to Somerset my mind was busy.

Inspector Herbert had asked me if the face in the photograph was the man I'd seen in the railway station with Marjorie Evanson. And I'd replied that he wasn't.

Granted, a good deal ot time had passed since that night. But Inspector Herbert must have believed that I could still recognize him. Otherwise, why send the photograph?

If there was some evidence I didn't know about, why hadn't he said so? Something that pointed to

Lieutenant Fordham, something to show that the man at the station had had nothing to do with Marjorie's death later that night. Yet he'd asked if they were one and the same.

Surely he wouldn't simply close the case now, whatever evidence he had uncovered, and never identify Marjorie Evanson's lover? Yes, Lieutenant Fordham had taken his own life, there could be no trial, the matter could be hushed up and the family's good name protected. But what about justice for Marjorie and her good name?

The silence, keeping the facts of the lieutenant's death out of the press, adjourning the inquest—it all made a certain sense whether I was comfortable with it or not.

After all, it was her murderer Scotland Yard wanted. It didn't matter about her private life if that private life had nothing to do with her death. Even if it had been responsible for her husband's suicide, the police could wash their hands of the case.

That seemed so unfair to Marjorie, so unfair to her husband, and to the families that grieved for them.

"You've been quiet. Are you all right?" Simon was asking as we came down the street and could see the house gates just ahead.

"A little tired, that's all."

Thinking that I must be remembering what I'd left behind in France, he said, "If you need to talk to someone . . ." He left the rest unfinished.

I thanked him, and then I was being welcomed with open arms. There was no fatted calf, there not being one handy for this occasion or any other, but I was safe and at home.

It wasn't until after dinner that I found a moment to put through a call to Scotland Yard. I only wanted to be reassured, told that I was wrong about Lieutenant Fordham.

A constable at the other end identified himself and asked how he could help me. I asked for Inspector Herbert.

"Your name, please?"

I gave it.

"I'm sorry, Miss Crawford. Inspector Herbert isn't in at present."

"When do you expect him to return?" I asked.

"I can't say, Miss."

"Tonight? Tomorrow?"

"I can't say, Miss."

I waited for him to ask if there was a message. But there was only silence.

I thanked him and put up the receiver.

Then I went to find my mother.

For someone who had spent most of her married life following my father around the world, she seemed to know half of England.

My father always explained that without any difficulty. "In the first place," he'd told me soon after we'd returned to Britain, "she needs to know anyone of importance, with an eye to providing you with a suitable husband."

Shocked, I'd blurted, "I'll find my own husband, thank you!"

"I'm sure you'll try," he'd replied doubtfully. "In the second place, if you've never noticed it for yourself, your mother has a winning way. People flock to her, wanting to be her friend. I've never understood it, to tell you the truth. But I've found that fact helpful more times than I've chosen to tell her."

Laughing, I'd answered, "Come to think of it, you're right."

"And lastly, who will people think of the instant they suspect trouble is stalking them? Complete strangers, mind you, but they'll turn up on our doorstep seeking an audience with your mother for her advice."

I could clearly remember asking my mother when I was a child in India why there were always people at our door, natives and Europeans alike. She'd answered, "I never know, my dear. I think the wind blows my name to them."

And for days, I'd watched and listened, hoping to hear her name in the wind for myself.

At the moment, knowing half of England was going to come in handy.

My father had gone out to walk—a habit left over from his days in the Army—and my mother was reading in the small sitting room she used most often.

She looked up. "There you are. I thought there was something on your mind. I sensed it at dinner." Drawing up another chair, she said, "Is it France?"

"Not France. Do you think, Mother, you could arrange an introduction to someone who lives in or near Little Sefton, in Hampshire?"

"And what, pray, is in Little Sefton that takes you away just as you've walked in the door?" my suspicious mother wanted to know.

"It's where Marjorie Evanson grew up."

She repeated the name, then said, "Isn't she the woman who was found murdered in London not so very long ago?" She picked up her knitting.

"In fact, yes. I knew her husband. He died of a broken heart after she was found dead. He had a long recovery ahead of him. Severe burns. I expect he had nothing to live for after that. He was devoted to her."

"One of your wounded? I see. Meddling again, are you?"

I tried a smile, to see if it would help. "Not so much meddling as trying to understand why the police haven't made more progress. Or if they have, why they've kept it quiet. Most of us live in London peacefully. We aren't murdered in our beds or on the streets, and tossed into the river."

"I should hope not," my mother said, not losing a stitch. "Your father has gone to great lengths to enlist Mrs. Hennessey in his campaign to see you safe."

I had to laugh. Still, I answered her, "I can take care of myself."

The words were no sooner out of my mouth than I had a flash of memory, of the German pilot firing his machine gun and the bullets tearing up the earth toward me.

"I'm quite sure Marjorie Evanson felt exactly the same," she reminded me.

"Yes," I began, ready to argue the point, then thought better of it. "The truth is, I have a photograph of her." I went on to explain how I had come into possession of it. "I'm not sure—given the circumstances—that Marjorie Evanson's family will want it any more than Serena Melton did. I thought perhaps I should find out before I sent it."

"And quite right," my mother nodded. "Tell me more about this man you saw at the station. Why do you think he's never come forward?"

"I have no way of knowing whether he has or not. I rather think not. But something happened recently that made me believe the police are looking in the wrong direction."

"Perhaps he has a good reason for not contacting the police. That's to say, if he knows they're looking for him. Either he's married, or he's in a position that would make an affair with a married woman bad for his reputation."

Depend on my mother to reach the heart of the matter.

"It doesn't speak well for him, I agree."

"Are the police quite sure he had nothing to do with Mrs. Evanson's death?" She turned the heel of the stocking she was knitting. Then she looked up at me.

"They felt it was possible, but not likely. I don't see how he could have managed it. Once they find him, they'll know whether he met his ship on time or not."

"Has it occurred to you, my dear, that if you're the only person who can identify this man, it might put you in some danger? Especially if he killed Mrs. Evanson. And even if he didn't."

"I don't think it's very likely that he even knows I exist."

"I wouldn't be too sure about that. If you saw *him*, how can you be so certain he didn't see you standing there staring at the two of them?"

"He didn't look my way. He was staring straight ahead."

"But you were looking at Mrs. Evanson."

A point well taken.

I said, "All the more reason to rid myself of this photograph as soon as may be. And put the Evansons out of my mind."

But I wasn't sure I could do that. And so I added, to ease some of the worry I could read in my mother's eyes, "He could be dead, of course. For all we know."

"Don't make excuses for him. And Scotland Yard can find him without your help."

"The thing is, they have no name, no photograph, only my description." I sighed. "It's been long enough now. I have a feeling Mrs. Evanson's murder will never be solved. And I find that abominable. He was my patient—her husband—and that makes it personal."

"Yes, you always did have an extraordinary sense of fair play. For better or for worse. Well, perhaps it would be wisest if I helped you, and made certain you don't come to grief."

She sat there, staring into space, thinking. I said nothing, almost afraid that if I spoke, she might change her mind.

Finally she said, "Do you remember Dorothea Mitchell?"

"She was a school chum of yours."

"We've kept in touch all these years, and I've met her in London a time or two for lunch. I'll have a word with her."

I was reminded of what my father had said in his second point about my mother, that she won and kept friends easily.

And so it was that Dorothea Mitchell—now Dorothea Worth—was engaged to find someone in her own vast acquaintance who could provide an introduction into Little Sefton for me. It didn't take her very long.

Mrs. Worth knew someone in Gloucester who had a friend in St. Albans whose younger sister happened to live in Little Sefton, Hampshire.

It was that simple.

Armed with a letter from my mother, I drove myself to Little Sefton—a good four-hour journey—and presented myself at the door of one Alicia Dalton.

I'd expected someone of my mother's age, but the woman who answered my knock was only about ten years older than I was. She was fair, with blue eyes, and her smile was warm.

"Miss Crawford? How nice to meet you. Do come in."

The house was stone, with lovely windows and colorful flower beds that ran down the short drive to the gates. Inside it was cool, with high ceilings and paneling in the hall, stairs running up to one side and a passage to other rooms on the left.

"I've been looking forward to your visit ever since my sister wrote to me. She didn't tell me why you were so interested in Little Sefton, but I was delighted to have your company even if only for a short while. My husband just went back to France, and I've been fighting tears and melancholy for two days."

"I'm interested in Marjorie Evanson," I told her truthfully. "I knew her husband—he was one of my patients after his last crash—and her death has been on my mind as well as his. I thought perhaps it would help if I came here and tried to put the past to rest."

That wasn't the whole truth. But it would do as a start.

"I knew Marjorie, of course. Not well—she was a rather private person, even as a child. But do come in, you'll want to settle yourself in your room, and then we can sit in the garden and talk." As she led the way upstairs, she said over her shoulder, "You're in luck, actually. We're having a garden party to raise money for children whose fathers have been killed. I'll take you around and introduce you to people."

She chattered all the way to my room, which was down the passage to the left, and when she opened the door, I smiled.

The room was large and airy, with windows looking out across the gardens toward the church that stood on a slight rise to the north, the rooftops of cottages clustered around it. The coverlet on the bed was a soft yellow, with flowers embroidered in a circle in the center, and the window curtains were cream with pale green ties.

"How lovely!" I said.

"I'm glad you like it. It's Gareth's sister's room. She's in London awaiting the birth of her first child. It's a nervous time, and she wanted to be near her doctors. I'll leave you to freshen up. Come down the stairs, go to the second door on your left, and I'll have tea waiting."

I thanked her, changed out of my traveling clothes and into a dress that was more comfortable in the afternoon heat, then went down to find Alicia.

She was in a small room with delicate French furnishings, a very feminine room with walls painted a soft rose and trimmed in cream.

We were soon on first-name terms, and I discovered that she was a fund of information about Marjorie.

"She has a sister, you know. Victoria. Marjorie was always in her shadow, a quiet girl who never fussed about anything, tried hard to please, and was never in trouble of any kind."

"Marjorie is younger than Victoria?"

"Oh, no, Victoria was several years younger, but you'd never guess it, really. She was domineering from childhood, always wanting her own way, always making certain that no one forgot her. I thought her quite bossy, and said as much to Marjorie one day when we were twelve. She gave me her quiet little smile, and said, 'Yes, it's simpler to give in than to fight. There's peace at home when Victoria is happy.' I told her that was arrant foolishness, that Victoria needed to learn her manners and her place. But her father doted on her, you see—Victoria, I mean—and he thought her behavior was a mark of strong character. In truth, she was quite spoiled."

"And Marjorie always let her have her way?"

"At least while she was living at home. But when Marjorie went away to school, and then to live with her aunt in London, on her next visit here she surprised us all by telling Victoria she was a bully. Publicly."

I laughed. "And what did Victoria have to say about that?"

"She left in a huff, vowing never to darken the door of any house where Marjorie might be invited. But it must have given her pause, because Marjorie and she were on better terms for a time."

"Does this aunt still live in London?"

"She died just after Marjorie and Meriwether were married. There's a distant cousin, Helen Calder, but no other family that I know of."

I found myself wondering how Serena Melton, Lieutenant Evanson's sister, and Victoria, Marjorie's sister, had got on. Like oil and water, very likely. They were both strong-willed women.

"Did the family approve of Marjorie's marriage to Meriwether Evanson?"

Alicia refilled my cup as she answered.

"It was a very good match. I think Mr. Garrison was pleased. Victoria wasn't. All the same, she was soon enjoying being the only child in the bosom of her family, and until her father's death, she showed no interest in leaving home. The Garrison house was left to her."

"Did you know Lieutenant Evanson well?"

"I stayed with Marjorie and Meriwether in London for two weeks in the autumn of 1915. I'd seen Gareth off to the France and I needed cheering up."

"How did they get on?"

"It was a love match, you know. They were quite happy. I think Marjorie had hoped that she might have a child before very long, but it never happened. Probably for the best, with both parents dead now."

It was a very practical point of view. But I thought perhaps Alicia was convincing herself that it was just as well she had no children yet.

If Victoria and Marjorie hadn't got on, I'd probably come here on a wild-goose chase. Still, sudden death could change attitudes, smooth over rifts.

As if she'd read my thoughts, Alicia said, "I couldn't believe it when I heard that Marjorie was murdered. I've never known anyone who was murdered. It was rather frightening. I couldn't help but wonder how it had happened. I mean, no one walks up to you and says, 'Hallo, I've just decided to kill you.' It's hard to comprehend." She shivered.

I said, "I expect there must have been a reason. Love. Hate. Fear. Greed. Passion. Some strong emotion that got out of hand."

"They did say that her purse was missing. It doesn't bear thinking of—killed for a few pounds. And then Meriwether dying so soon afterward. I saw Serena Melton at her brother's funeral, and she was in such distress. I heard her say to the rector, 'It's not fair, you know, for me to lose Merry on her account.' Meaning Marjorie. I thought it was a terrible thing to say. But they were close, Serena and her brother. I remember Marjorie telling me once that their parents had died at a very young age, and the two of them had depended on each other for support. Their guardian was not particularly good at dealing with distraught children, and left them to their own devices. A roof over their heads, clothes on their backs, food on their table and he felt his duty was more than satisfactorily done."

It explained Serena's feelings for her brother. Serena and Meriwether had been thrown together in a time of grief, when there was quite simply no one else to comfort them. It was a powerful tie.

I also understood why Marjorie might not have turned to her own sister, in her distress. Then where had she gone?

"What about Marjorie's mother? How did she feel about her daughters?"

"She's dead." Alicia's answer was short.

Marjorie had been utterly alone. No wonder she had been crying as if her heart were broken.

If anyone had a reason for suicide, she did. And yet she'd been murdered.

The garden party the next day was held at the rectory, and according to Alicia, it was a pale shadow of former days, when food was plentiful and two-thirds of the male population wasn't away fighting a war.

The food was makeshift, the women were in black rather than the usual array of summer dresses bought or made for the occasion, with matching hats to protect one's complexion. And except for the rector, the men were in uniform.

Little Sefton was small enough for everyone to know everyone, and I was one of the handful of outsiders in their midst. Alicia and I walked across the green lawn to the booths set out on the grass, their poles decorated with loops of flowers and bows of ribbons and bright fabrics. People nodded to us as we passed, and children ran about playing, chased by excited dogs.

Alicia was saying, "Let me present you to Rector Stevens. He's a lovely man. Do you play chess, by any chance? He quite fancies himself as the best player in Hampshire."

Not wanting to spend my afternoon in a chess match, I hemmed and hummed a bit, and Alicia said, "Well, never mind. One of the wounded is sure to oblige him."

I had seen far too many of those, walking with canes, arms in slings, or even being wheeled in invalid chairs.

She began to point out people to me. "That woman in puce. She was housemaid to Marjorie's mother. She puts up the best pickle relish in the county. Over there, the one with red hair—she was a friend of Marjorie's mother—" The list went on, and then Alicia stopped.

"What is it?" I asked.

"Victoria is here. I'd never have guessed it. I owe the rector's wife a dozen brown eggs."

"You had a wager on whether or not she was coming?"

"Oh, yes. I was nearly certain that with everyone discussing poor Marjorie's death, she wouldn't wish to be here."

I looked at Marjorie's sister. She was about my height, with fair hair and hazel eyes. But her mouth, unlike Marjorie's more generous one, was thin lipped, and I found myself thinking that I shouldn't like to cross her.

A family resemblance was there all the same, especially around the eyes, but I wouldn't have picked Victoria out on my own as Marjorie's sister.

Victoria turned away as we came nearer, and the rector was engaged with an older man who was speaking earnestly to him.

Alicia said, "That's Mr. Hart. A gentleman farmer. He owns the largest farm in Little Sefton. He's kind enough to send his workmen around to help with things like repairing chimneys or patching roofs or heavy lifting. It's a blessing, with Gareth in France." She turned away, to allow the two men a little privacy. "And that handsome devil sitting in the white elephant booth—the one with his arm in bandages—has been breaking hearts since he arrived a few weeks ago. He's staying with the Harts. Their nephew."

I could see the man she spoke of. An officer in the Wiltshire regiment, tall, very fair, a deep voice and a laugh that began in his chest and a smile that was devastatingly sweet. But with a roving eye as well. I watched him try his charm on a girl of perhaps fourteen, who blushed to the roots of her hair, then he switched his attention to her mother, but she must have been used to it. I heard her say, "Oh, behave yourself, Michael. One would think you were the Prince of Wales, the way you carry on."

He laughed and leaned across the booth's counter to kiss her cheek. "Dear Mrs. Lucas, if I ever marry anyone, it will be you."

She nodded. "Yes, and what shall I tell Henry when we elope?"

Henry must have been her husband, because Michael dropped his voice to a conspiratorial level and asked, "Must we tell him?" He looked around. "Come to think of it, I haven't seen him today. His back, again?"

"Sadly, yes. He's gone to see a doctor in Salisbury."

She moved on and he turned our way. "Ah, a new blossom in our garden," he exclaimed, seeing me. "And who is this, pray?" he asked Alicia.

Alicia took me across to the booth, presenting me. "Bess Crawford, this is Michael Hart. He's not to be trusted."

He bowed over my hand and welcomed me to the fete.

Close to, I could see the lines of strain around his mouth and the shadows in those wonderfully blue eyes.

"How is your shoulder?" I asked.

"Never better." But it was a lie. "I'll be returning to the Front by September, they tell me."

"How many surgeries have you had?"

"Enough for a lifetime," he replied tersely, and then laughed to cover his lapse.

Alicia left me there while she spoke to an elderly woman leaning heavily on a cane.

Michael Hart said, "Do you need a white elephant?" He was pointing to one—literally—made of porcelain. It was quite charming, and so I bought it, and he wrapped it carefully before handing it to me. I paid him and was about to turn away when he caught my hand in his good one, and said in a low voice, "No, don't go."

Out of the corner of my eye, I could see Victoria bearing down on us, and I stayed for the opportunity to meet her. But when she realized that I had no intention of leaving, even after my purchase was completed, she veered away.

"Do you know her?" I asked, interested to hear what he had to say.

"I knew her sister," he said in that same terse manner.

Marjorie.

He was beckoning to a woman just coming up the grassy avenue. "Mrs. Hampton, would you mind the booth for a bit?"

She came over to him and said at once, "Do go and sit down, Michael. You must be in terrible pain. I thought someone was to assist you?"

"No one came," he told her. "I'll be back in half an hour."

"Take as long as you like." She noticed the little box stuffed with coins and said, "I see you've done quite well. I told the rector's wife you were the perfect one to sell our little treasures."

Once more I began to turn away, but Michael took my arm and said, "Stay with me."

Chapter Eight

I did as he asked. The debonair officer had vanished, and there was perspiration on Lieutenant Hart's face, a tightness to his mouth. I'd seen this happen with wounded men. Off parade, so to speak, they let down their guard and admitted that they were in pain.

We walked together along a short path that led to the side door of the rectory. He reached for it out of habit, but I was there first and held it for him. Inside it was cool and dim, and I realized we were in a small plant room, where secateurs and trowels, baskets and pots lined the shelves on either side. Below were vases of all kinds. A dry sink where plants could be repotted or divided held a vase of wilting blossoms. Here flower arrangements were made up or cuttings were prepared for setting out.

My escort led the way through the second door and into a wider passage, then up a short flight of steps to a book-lined room that was clearly the rector's study.

"No one will think to look for us here." He sank into a leather armchair to one side of the desk, and closed his eyes.

I took the one opposite him. After a moment, he opened his eyes and said, "You're a good sport, Sister Crawford. Thank you."

I smiled. "Not at all. Is there anything I can bring you? Water? A pillow?"

"I'm all right."

Which I translated as, Don't fuss.

After a time, as the pain eased, he said, "I didn't know Victoria would be here today. I shouldn't be telling you this, but I owe you some explanation. Victoria's sister was killed some weeks ago. Victoria appears to think I know something about that. She hounds me every time she sees me. I couldn't deal with it today."

"And do you know something?"

He'd closed his eyes again. "I don't make a habit of killing women."

Which wasn't precisely an answer to my question.

"You'll hear about it soon enough if you stay in Little Sefton for very long," he went on after a moment, as if he'd made up his mind. "Marjorie Evanson was murdered in London. She was a friend of mine. Her sister is not."

"I didn't know Mrs. Evanson, but I was in charge of the wounded when her husband, Lieutenant Evanson, was brought home with burns."

Those marvelous eyes opened and seemed to spear me. "Were you indeed? A small world. I liked Merry, you know. The first time I met him, I knew he'd be right for Marjorie."

"Alicia told me you were a nephew of the Harts."

"I often stayed with my aunt and uncle on school holidays. My father was in the Army and my parents were half a world away most of the time. That's how I came to know Marjorie. She lived close by. A sweet girl. I liked her immensely. I wasn't in love with her," he added hastily, "but I liked her. We played together as children and sometimes she'd confide in me, and I in her. I think our two families are related somehow— a distant this or that. So we called each other cousin, Marjorie and I. She had no brother, and I had no sister. It was a good relationship."

I believed him. There was the ring of truth in his voice now.

"I read something about her death. Did the police ever discover who had killed her?"

"I don't know that they've made any progress at all. Although I'd had my suspicions that something was wrong."

"Had you?"

"About five or six months ago—you won't say anything to Alicia about this, will you?" I promised and he went on. "About five or six months ago, late winter anyway, her letters changed. They were shorter and not as full of news. Distracted. Unlike her. I put it down to worry about Merry—his squadron had been posted to France. And then the letters were fewer, as if she'd written out of duty when she remembered she owed me one."

"Did you see her after that?"

He sat up as a clock somewhere in the house struck the hour. "I must return to the booth. I don't know what possessed me to agree to man it."

I considered him. Friend or not, cousin or not, Michael Hart was very attractive. But he wasn't the man I'd seen with Marjorie Evanson in London.

I was tempted to ask him if he knew Lieutenant Fordham, but they were in the same regiment, and Simon had told me that the lieutenant's death had been kept out of the newspapers. Instead I asked, "There might have been another man. Had you thought of that?"

His eyes sharpened, and an ugly twist reshaped his mouth. "What do you mean? What have you heard?"

I shrugged. "You suggested there was a change in her. There's usually a reason for it. Perhaps there was something she didn't want to tell you or was afraid you'd read between the lines in her letters."

He got up and swung around the room, as if he were trying to find a way out of it, like an animal pacing his cage at a zoo. "That's nonsense. Besides, it doesn't explain her murder, does it?"

When I said nothing, he went on as much to himself as to me. "I can't drive, and I'm forbidden to take the train. I need to go to London. To talk to her friends. There was a women's group she belonged to, they met every week. I asked my uncle to drive me there, but he has his hands full with the farm just now—everyone is shorthanded, I know that's true, but still—" He took a deep breath. "It's been weeks already."

"What does Victoria have to say? Surely Marjorie confided in her."

"She wouldn't tell me even if she knew the name of Marjorie's killer. She was an insufferable little beast, always prying, always tattling. Neither of us could abide her. Marjorie tried to make peace with her, but confide in her? Never." He considered me. "Have a motorcar here, do you?"

"Yes, I—"

"Excellent. You can drive me to London, if you please. I'll start with the servants. They'll talk to me. I helped her choose most of them when she opened the house."

It was tempting. But I said, "My family lives in Somerset. I'll be going back there, not to London."

"How long have you known Alicia?" he asked shrewdly. "You don't strike me as old friends. I've known Alicia for years, and I've never seen you in Little Sefton before. You said you knew Meriwether. Did his sister send you here? I wouldn't put it past her."

"I told you the truth. I brought Lieutenant Evanson back to England, to Laurel House. He had a photograph of his wife, and it was pinned to his tunic where I could see it every day. He wouldn't let it out of his sight. I couldn't help but see it."

I didn't tell him that it was even now in my valise at Alicia's house. But I found myself adding, "I was told by Matron that Lieutenant Evanson's family didn't want it buried with him."

Under his breath he swore with some feeling. "Serena's doing, very likely. I think she felt as elder sister she ought to have a say in the woman Evanson married. She'd introduced him to several friends of hers, but nothing came of that."

I could hear people talking in the passage. "We should go out to the garden. They'll be looking for you."

"I've lost interest in the blasted white elephant booth."

"It is for a good cause," I reminded him.

"I'd rather give them the money and be done with it."

"That's charity."

Suddenly he chuckled, that same deep rumble that began in his chest before erupting into deep laughter.

"You're an extraordinary woman, Sister Crawford. I think Marjorie would have approved of you." Cradling his shoulder, he added with resignation, "Come along then. But think about it, won't you? Driving to London, I mean."

We walked together out of the rector's study, down the passage, and back to the fete.

As we stepped out into the gardens, Alicia raised her eyebrows at the sight of us together, and on the other side of the palm reader's booth, Victoria was staring.

I could almost read their minds as they wondered how I had so successfully cornered the Prince of Wales.

Behind me, Michael Hart said just loud enough for me to hear him, "Is this where you slap my face and walk away?"

Unable to stop myself, I smiled broadly.

But Michael had already slipped away and left me standing there alone.

The rector stepped into the breach and introduced himself, welcoming me to Little Sefton and asking where I was from. "Somerset," I told him, and then we played the social game of do you know . . .

We did indeed have a connection in common. It seems that the chaplain of my father's old regiment—now long since retired to grow roses and tomatoes in Derbyshire—had been a friend of the rector's father, and with those bona fides, I was accepted into the bosom of Little Sefton.

The afternoon turned out to be lovely in every sense. I found I was enjoying myself as the rector and Alicia between them presented me to everyone. I took my turn in the white elephant booth, and even sold tickets for the little raffle. Michael was least in sight, and I heard someone, a woman, say, "He's probably gone to have a lie down. He told me that Sister Crawford had advised him to rest and take a little something for his pain."

My back was to the speakers, and so I couldn't see who answered that remark.

"I wonder if she knows that he's altogether too fond of that little something for the pain." Another woman's voice.

Just as I turned to see who it was, I found myself almost face-to-face with Victoria.

I had wondered if—when—she might speak to me. She had no way of knowing who I was, but seeing me with Michael had for some reason ruffled her feathers.

As if to prove it, her first words were, "Have you known Michael very long?"

"Approximately two hours," I answered with a smile, refusing to be drawn.

"Alicia told me she hadn't realized you were acquainted with him, or she wouldn't have invited you to Little Sefton. She doesn't care to be used in this way."

Alicia had said nothing of the sort. She knew why I was here.

"How odd," I replied. "It was she who introduced us. She did mention that he was considered the exclusive property of someone—Victoria, I believe she was?"

Her face went beet red.

"I'm Victoria Garrison. And that man is of no interest to me."

"I'm Elizabeth Crawford," I went on. "Are you by any chance related to Marjorie Evanson?"

"It's clear to me that you've been reading the London papers. Who told you that Garrison was her maiden name? Alicia, of course. Our little scandal attracts all manner of curiosity seekers."

"As a matter of fact," I answered her serenely, "I was Lieutenant Evanson's nurse while he was in hospital in France."

That stopped her cold. But she recovered quickly. "Did Serena Melton send you here to annoy me?"

Intrigued by the fact that both she and Michael Hart had leapt to that conclusion, I hesitated a second too long.

She turned away, then swung around again to face me. "Well, you can tell her for me that while a murder in the family is not something to cry from the rooftops, a suicide is even worse." And she walked off, her shoulders stiff with anger.

I stood there thinking it was sad that two families had been torn apart by one act of violence, rather than being brought together in common grief.

Behind me, Mrs. Hart said quietly, "Poor girl. She's taken her sister's death hard. They were never close. Perhaps she has come to regret that now."

I hadn't heard her come up behind me. I'd have liked to disagree with her, but said, "I'm sorry."

"Victoria takes after her father. He was a hard man to like. Marjorie was more like her mother, which is probably why Mr. Garrison was fonder of Victoria." She shifted the course of the conversation. "Alicia tells me you've come just for the weekend. Have you known each other long?"

"She's the friend of a friend who thought we might enjoy each other's company," I answered. "And we have, I must say."

"She's missed Gareth terribly. Of course there are no children. That's been a sorrow for both of them. One might say early days, but for the war. One can only pray that Gareth returns safely. I fear for Michael. You're a nursing sister. Will that shoulder heal cleanly? I don't know what they've said to Michael. He puts up a good front, and we try not to ask too many questions. I do know he secretly dreads the possibility that he might lose his arm. I've heard him cry out at night, dreaming they're taking it."

"It's too soon to judge these things," I said, the only hope I could offer, not knowing the details of the case. "I'm surprised he's out of hospital. But that's a good sign, you know. When was he wounded?"

"It was no more than a fortnight, if that, after dear Marjorie was killed. When the news came, I said to my husband that I wondered if Michael had got careless, worrying over her death. They kept him in hospital as long as they could, but he's not one to be penned up. He brooded too much. We were happy to have him back and safe."

I remembered him pacing the rector's study.

"He's no trouble at all," she went on. "He can do everything for himself except dress. But he won't take his morphine when he needs it. He says fighting the pain is good for the constitution." She smiled sadly.

She moved on to speak to a friend, and I went to find Alicia. The garden party was coming to a close, and she was helping to pack away the remnants of food from the stalls, preparing to take them around to those who weren't able to attend. I volunteered to help, and she and I crisscrossed Little Sefton, answering questions at each door about who was at the affair and who was not, and of course having to explain who I was and why I was here in Little Sefton.

Along the way, Alicia pointed out the Garrison house. It was stone, and unlike its neighbors, was set well back from the road, with lovely roses climbing almost to the windows of the first storey, and a low wall around the front garden, which was ablaze with blooms of every kind, the hollyhocks just coming into their own.

Tired and ready to put our feet up—"with a little sherry," Alicia suggested—we returned to her house. But when we got there, she discovered a letter from Gareth had arrived in the post, and she quickly excused herself to run up the stairs and read it in private.

There was a knock at the door before she'd come down again, and I went to answer it.

Michael Hart stood on the doorstep.

"I've just been to see Dr. Higgins," he informed me lightly. "He says I'm fit enough for London if I don't drive, carouse, or chase unsuitable women."

"How dull for you," I responded. "But I'm not going directly to London. I'm returning to my parents' home in Somerset."

He could see that I was on the point of refusing him, and he said in quite another voice, "Don't let me down, Bess Crawford. This is important to me, and there's no one else."

"Surely there's someone in Little Sefton who would agree to drive you."

"Undoubtedly. But the reasons why I'm so set on going would be common knowledge in the village, even before we'd cranked the motorcar. Let them believe I've taken a fancy to you—that my broken heart has finally begun to mend."

"Do you have a broken heart?" I asked, curious.

"There was a girl before the war. One I liked very much. She preferred someone else. It was generally assumed I was devastated. But the truth was, I liked her. I wasn't passionately in love with her."

Was he talking about Marjorie? Michael was glib, in my opinion. It could be the truth or it could be what he thought I wanted to hear.

But then it dawned on me that if he were not so handsome, people might well see him differently and accept everything he said at face value.

"If you go with me to Somerset, you'll have to put up with the scrutiny of my family. I don't as a rule bring young men home with me."

In fact, I never had. He sensed this, and said, "You knew Meriwether. Surely you must be curious about what happened to Marjorie. I don't mind if you are there when I talk to the staff or her friends."

"Lieutenant Hart—"

"Michael."

"Michael. I have only so much leave."

"One day. That's all I ask."

"Let me think about it," I said, to be rid of him. I could hear Alicia coming down the stairs.

He must have heard her too. He smiled at me, and was gone.

The next day I went to the early service with Alicia. It was a gray morning and the small church was only half full. As we took our places, Alicia said, "Not many people here today, I'm afraid. But then most of them met you yesterday. Their curiosity is satisfied."

I smiled and said softly, "Never mind. I've enjoyed my visit."

Alicia nodded. "Yes. So have I."

The organ wheezed into life in the dampness, and I noted that neither Michael nor Victoria was present.

As we walked home, I waited until we were out of earshot of everyone else, and said to Alicia, "I've been meaning to ask you. Did you know a Lieutenant Fordham? Did he come to Little Sefton, do you know?"

"Lieutenant Fordham? I don't believe I've ever met him. And if he came to Little Sefton, I was never aware of it."

"I wondered if perhaps he was a friend of Marjorie's?"

"I have no idea," she answered, but it was clear I'd inadvertently sparked her interest. "Is there any reason I should have heard of him?"

I was prepared for that question and smiled. "He died not long after Marjorie. And the same inspector was looking into his death as well as hers. Coincidence? Or connection? Did someone from Scotland Yard come to Little Sefton?"

"I never saw him, but there was someone who came down. He broke the news to Victoria, and asked about Marjorie's solicitor, and the like. He spoke to Constable Tilmer and the rector as well, then left. But Marjorie hadn't lived here for years, so I expect he spent most of his time in London."

"Did he question Michael Hart?"

"He was in France at the time."

"Michael told me Victoria believes there's something he knows about the murder—she keeps demanding that he tell her."

"I've seen her corner him in the street and even in the churchyard. That explains why he's taken to avoiding her. What does she think? That perhaps Marjorie wrote something to Michael? She didn't know what was about to happen to her. That doesn't make sense."

I hadn't considered letters. When I didn't answer straightaway, she turned to look at me.

"It *was* robbery, wasn't it? Marjorie's murder."

"I don't think her purse has ever been found."

We had reached Alicia's house, and as she lifted the latch, she said, "Michael has asked me at least twice to drive him to London. He feels that he could learn something that the police missed or overlooked. It seems so unlikely, and I'm not comfortable driving Gareth's motorcar. I told him so. He's bound to ask you. I think he feels helpless, and needs to be doing something. Even if it's a wild goose chase."

I didn't tell her he already had asked me. Twice. "I'm not going to London," I said. "I'm returning to Somerset." But I was still thinking about letters.

"He can be very persuasive," she said doubtfully. "You don't know how close I came to giving in, even against my better judgment."

"And I'm used to the blandishments of wounded men," I answered. "He won't sway me."

When I walked through the door in Somerset with Michael Hart in tow, it was worth any price to see my mother's eyes widen as I introduced him. She was in the sitting room writing letters to her circle of correspondents, and rose to meet us as I said, "Mother, may I present Lieutenant Michael Hart. He's on his way to London tomorrow, and I offered to give him a lift since he can't drive himself."

"This is a pleasant surprise," my mother said, recovering her manners in an instant. "Will you be staying with us, Lieutenant Hart?"

"I've already taken a room at The Four Doves," he told her, smiling.

"Indeed," said the Colonel Sahib, coming into the room behind us, to be introduced in his turn.

"Do sit down," my mother said hastily, and rang for tea.

Chapter Nine

Michael was of course invited to dine with us, and my father swept him off to the stables to see a new foal.

I went up to my room, changing my clothes quickly, and found my mother waiting for me as I came down again.

"Simon is coming to dine as well," she informed me.

"How cozy," I replied.

My father and Michael came in at that moment. He said, "I met Michael's father once in Delhi. He was there as part of a commission on its way to Burma."

The earlier frost in the air had warmed almost to cordiality. We had drinks in the drawing room and talked about the progress of the war and the garden party at

Little Sefton. We were just moving on to changes that the war had brought to London when Simon Brandon came in, greeted me, and shook hands with Michael. As he took his chair on the other side of my mother, Simon passed me an envelope.

"This came for you earlier today."

I thanked him and shoved it into a pocket until I could read it.

But as we were going in to dinner, Simon, falling back to walk beside me, said, in a low voice, "That came by special messenger from Scotland Yard. I met him in the drive earlier as I was coming to borrow your mother for half an hour."

I let him go ahead of me, turned to one side, and tore open the envelope.

There was just a brief message inside. And another photograph.

Did you by chance see this man at the railway station on the day in question? He's wanted for the killing of three women in Oxford. They were apparently accosted on the street, then followed home. The previous victims were shopgirls. He escaped the police and may have traveled to London. It's possible he saw Mrs. Evanson, just as you did. Inspector Herbert.

Dismayed, I read the message again. Was it possible they'd found Marjorie Evanson's murderer?

I turned quickly to look into the face of a man I was sure I'd never seen before. It was an older photograph, and I recognized the background: the gates of one of the colleges in Oxford.

He appeared to be of medium height, neither fat nor lean, with a long face that was too ordinary to draw attention. He had what looked to be light brown hair and dark eyes, and a mouth that was too small. He could have been a shop clerk or a lorry driver or the man sitting across the way in an omnibus.

I stared at the photograph for a moment, searching my memory. And then I went to the telephone and put in a call to London and Scotland Yard.

Inspector Herbert was not available, but I left a message for him, telling him that I hadn't seen the man in the photograph.

But as I went in to dinner, I thought how easily he could come up behind someone on a rainy street, and not even turn a head.

Everyone was waiting for me in the dining room, and I apologized for the delay without explaining why it was necessary.

As Michael and my parents carried the burden of conversation, I was silent, thinking about the dead shopgirls and whether Marjorie Evanson, blindly walking out of the station into the rain, might have attracted the notice of someone like the man in the photograph. It could have happened that way. He could have followed her.

But there were a good four or five hours between the time Marjorie Evanson was at the railway station and the time she'd died. Inspector Herbert had said as much himself. Was he clutching at straws?

I'd have liked to ask Michael what he thought, but it would be difficult to explain a communication from Scotland Yard without confessing how I'd been drawn into the case.

I happened to look up as the chutney was passed to me, and I met Simon Brandon's dark eyes, watching me speculatively.

And it was Simon who volunteered to drive Michael back to The Four Doves.

When they had gone, my mother said to me, "My dear, do you know what you're doing?"

"I'm only taking Michael to London to speak to the staff at Marjorie Evanson's house. He wants to hear about that morning before she left the house. Or if something was worrying her."

"But surely the police—?"

I shook my head. "Of course they must have done. But consider. If the police came here, would Lois or

Timmy or anyone else who worked for us tell them things they believed we might not want the police to know? For whatever reason?"

"I'd expect them to tell the truth."

"And they probably would, if you were innocent and the truth would help. But if you were guilty of some indiscretion, and they knew that if they told the police it would ruin your reputation, what then?"

She was fair. She was always fair. "And so Michael Hart hopes they will confide in him. Charming he may be, but their first loyalty will still be to their mistress, don't you think?"

"He's healing. He needs to focus all his energy on that. And instead I think Marjorie Evanson's death is weighing heavily on his mind. If he learns nothing of importance, he'll still be satisfied that he did all he could for her. And if he does discover something, then he can take it to the police."

"That would be the wisest move. Was he in love with her, do you think? That would explain his resolve."

"He was in France when she was killed and wasn't eligible for compassionate leave—she wasn't his wife or mother."

"Yes, I see what you mean. This is the least he can do for her."

My mother usually did see. I kissed her good night then and went into the passage toward the stairs.

Simon Brandon was waiting for me in the shadows by the door. He took my arm, opened the door, and led me out into the warm summer night. The sun had not yet set, and the distant horizon was a lovely illusive opal that turned the tops of the trees to a soft gold. A jackdaw, sitting in the top of the nearest tree, was singing to it, his breast a shimmering black like wet paint.

I walked a little way down the drive, knowing what was coming, listening to the crunch of stones under my shoes.

Finally he said, "How well do you know this man?"

"I don't. But he's trying to find out what happened to his childhood friend. And to do that, he wants to go to London. You can see for yourself he can't drive. I promised—since I was going to London anyway—that I'd take him." When he said nothing, I added, "I didn't suggest that he stay here. Nor did he."

"Were you going to London anyway?"

"I—in the long run. Simon, I saw the man with Marjorie Evanson the night she was killed. He got on the train and left her there. Now the Yard thinks she might have been the victim of a man who fled Oxford after three women were killed there. They were interested in Lieutenant Fordham before him. The Yard doesn't seem to be making any progress at all, and the only person who might answer their questions about where she intended to go after leaving the station is either dead or refusing to come forward. If Michael Hart can learn anything useful, it's all to the good. If he doesn't, he's done no harm."

"I understand why you feel you have a responsibility to this woman—" he began.

"I saw how desperate she was that night. Where did she turn? Perhaps she trusted the wrong person." I reached into my pocket and pulled out the message from Scotland Yard. "You see, Inspector Herbert has been using what I know to help him sort through suspects. I'm not involved, not officially. But he can send me a photograph and ask me a question."

He was staring up at the jackdaw. "This isn't the first time the Yard has asked you for information. How many photographs have you looked at for them?"

"Only these two."

"Stay out of it, Bess. You know what nearly happened the last time you got yourself involved in the troubles of another family. Leave this one alone."

"It's Michael Hart who is involved at the moment."

He turned to look at me. "There's something you ought to know. The Colonel has already spoken to me.

And I have my own suspicions. Michael Hart may not be what he seems."

"What do you mean? Did you know him before this?"

"I've never seen him before. But I wouldn't be surprised if he's become addicted to the medicines his doctors have been giving him to control his pain. When I took him back to the inn just now, his hands were shaking and his mouth was dry. You're a nurse. Be more observant. And think what it is you may be getting yourself into."

"I'm not getting myself into anything," I told him, furious at the lecture. "I don't intend to marry Michael Hart. I'm only driving him to London. Besides, fatigue and pain could cause the same symptoms."

Simon grinned. "Indeed. Good night, Bess."

And he walked away down the drive, leaving me there to look after him, torn between calling him back to tell him what I thought of his interference in my life and letting him go.

As I turned toward the house, I remembered what Mrs. Hart had said about Michael Hart, that he had refused sedation and was fighting his own way through the pain.

But *had* my father been suspicious, or had Simon simply brought him into the conversation to back up his own views?

I walked in the door, shut it, and continued down the passage to the study, where my father was sitting with a book open in his lap.

"Good night," I said. "I hope to get an early start tomorrow."

"Be safe, Bess," he said, but he didn't smile as he usually did when wishing me a safe journey.

I said, "Thank you for being kind to Michael Hart. I remember when I broke my arm last year, how frustrating it was for me, being dependent and helpless."

"He's strikingly handsome," my father said, finally smiling. "But I wouldn't introduce him to any of your flatmates. He's being ridden by his own devils."

"Drugs?" I asked baldly.

"I don't know what his devils are. He's very amusing, he answers questions openly and apparently truthfully, and he doesn't trade on his charm. But there's something behind the bonhomie that gives him no peace. It isn't your place to put that right."

"As I told Simon," I said, "I'm just driving him to London, not marrying him."

"See that you remember that," he said, and turned his attention to his book. "Good night, Bess."

I took my dismissal with the best grace I could muster, and went up to pack.

Snapping my valise closed, I found myself wondering if I had completely trusted Michael Hart. Even before Simon had made his remarks.

On the whole, I thought I did. I couldn't have said why. Except that he hadn't turned the full force of his charm on my mother.

The next morning I retrieved Michael Hart from The Four Doves and drove both of us to London.

He asked me where The Four Doves Hotel had got its name. For the sign showed only four gray doves.

"The house that once stood there was the pilgrimage guesthouse of a convent that had already fallen into ruin by the time of Henry VIII. The last of the nuns—four of them—were very old and had come to live in the guesthouse because there was nowhere else for them to go. But they still kept it open for travelers, in the care of a man they trusted. When Henry's men stopped there on their way to burn out the abbot of Glastonbury, they remembered that the house had once belonged to a convent, and they asked the manservant if there were any nuns still there. He told the soldiers that the only females he knew of were four doves in the ancient dovecote in the garden. Henry's men decided they would have the doves for their dinner. The servant was in great distress, because the dovecote had been empty for years, and that was where he'd hidden the nuns. He went out there, sick with fright, and told the nuns what he'd done. They said, "But didn't you know? There are four doves here, roosting for the night." And when the manservant lifted his lantern, he saw that they were right. He served Henry's men their dinner, and sent them on their way. And ever after, there were always four doves in the cote and the elderly nuns lived out their lives in peace."

Michael was silent for a moment. Then he said, "It's too bad life doesn't have such happy endings."

I replied, "Here is what I know about Marjorie Evanson. She had a sister, but often there was no love lost between the two of them. Her parents are dead, but Victoria was her father's favorite, and he appeared to spoil her. Marjorie went away to school and never really came back to Little Sefton. She married Meriwether Evanson, and her father seemed to make no objection to the match. While Lieutenant Evanson was in France, Marjorie must have taken a lover, because she was pregnant when she died—" I could have bitten my tongue.

"I didn't know that," he said, his voice strained. "Is it true?"

"Yes. It was discovered in the postmortem. It wasn't made public."

"That would explain why Meriwether killed himself, wouldn't it? He'd known he wasn't the father." He thought about that for a moment. "And does anyone know who this man might be?" He still hadn't got full control of his voice.

"He's a mystery. The police asked anyone who had seen Marjorie the day of her death to come forward. And he never has."

"Now I understand why Serena Melton asked that the funeral for her brother be private. And why he and Marjorie weren't buried together. Neither Victoria nor I were invited to the service, but she went anyway. And the Meltons didn't attend the service for Marjorie. That caused talk, I can tell you. But most people accepted the fact that they were still in mourning." He cleared his throat, angry with himself.

"I didn't know." It seemed vengeful to me.

"You couldn't have known. I'd thought it was because Marjorie was murdered. As if that had been her fault."

"Murder doesn't happen in nice families," I quoted.

He said something under his breath, the words whipped away by the wind as we drove east toward London. I had a suspicion he was swearing.

"Serena Melton. Do you know her very well?"

"Not well at all. We met at the wedding, and at a party or two in London after that. I didn't like her very much. Mainly because she didn't seem to care for Marjorie. Merry was all right. And Jack, Serena's husband."

"Who could have been Marjorie's lover? Someone she knew? A stranger she happened to meet on a train or in a restaurant or at a party?"

"I don't know. I told you, she changed. Her letters changed. Yes, all right, I was in France, and it's difficult writing very personal things that the censors will read before the person at the other end does. But I hadn't thought—I don't know what I thought," he ended. "It's hard knowing your husband could be shot down any day he flies. I thought that might have put strains on Marjorie's marriage. That she was afraid to love him too much."

We drove in silence for a time.

Then Michael said, easing his injured shoulder, "She was in love with Meriwether. A blind man could have seen that. I don't know what could have gone wrong."

"He crashed twice. He was badly burned the second time. It must have been frightful to realize that the man you knew and married was so disfigured that you might not even recognize him. She could have turned to someone for sympathy and his kindness made her vulnerable. She had only to sleep with him once. She needn't have loved him. Or he her."

"In some way that's worse." Michael Hart turned to look at me. "You seem to know what she was feeling. How such things happen."

"It's not surprising," I told him. "I've dealt with soldiers of every rank. I've written their letters home, and I've read them their letters from home. Marjorie wasn't alone in her fall from grace." Three years of war had had other costs besides the long lists of dead and wounded. "I think it's time you told me the truth. Were you in love with Marjorie Garrison?"

He wiped his good hand over his face, as if to conceal the agony there. "God help me. I was."

We said nothing more for the rest of the journey.

We were coming into London when Michael roused himself and said, "I haven't been very good company, have I?"

"I was thinking. Marjorie's house was also her husband's home. You've been assuming that the staff would speak freely to you. But what if they won't? Out of loyalty to him as well as to her?"

"I've considered that too. But it was Marjorie in trouble—Marjorie who was murdered. I don't think Victoria came here to question the staff. I don't know that she cared enough; she would have left that to the police. As for Serena, she sent her husband to box up Meriwether's belongings. She never even told them Merry died. She left that to the family solicitor."

"How did you know this?"

"I telephoned the house as soon as I came to stay with my aunt and uncle. I wanted to know about Marjorie's things. What was to happen to them."

I suddenly remembered Alicia's remark about letters.

"Why is the house still open, if both Marjorie and her husband are dead?"

"I can't answer that. But I rather think Victoria and Serena are squabbling over it. And until that is settled, it's being run as if Evanson and his wife are expected to return."

"Fully staffed?" I was surprised.

"As fully as any house can be staffed today. They're paid to the end of the quarter, anyway."

"But if Marjorie died first, and then Lieutenant Evanson died, I don't understand the problem. If she willed everything to him, then all their property was his to dispose of, and so Serena must now be the owner of the house."

"It's not that simple. Marjorie inherited the house, you see. It was in her mother's family, and her mother's sister—her aunt—lived there until her death. Marjorie could have wished it to stay in the family."

Weaving through traffic, I said, "It takes time to settle affairs. But I understand now why you were so intent on coming here."

London was crowded, men in uniform looking for places to stay, families coming to see loved ones off to France or hoping to meet them on leave, everyone demanding a room and no rooms to be had. But Michael found one. He walked into the Marlborough, not far from Claridge's, and came out again in a quarter of an hour, saying, "A room for four nights. I doubt I'll be here that long, but a bird in hand is wisest."

I wondered how he managed it. But I had no intention of asking.

Hesitating, unsure how to put my question, I said, "Can you cope with one arm strapped to your body?"

"Well enough. It's awkward as hell, but I can do up buttons on my own, comb my hair, shave, and even brush my teeth. What I can't do are laces. But they'll send someone up. I'm not the worst case they've come across."

I nodded, told him to be ready the next morning at nine, and left him and his suitcase to the tender mercies of the ancient doorman.

Chapter Ten

When I reached the flat, Diana and Mary were there, eager for news. Then Diana was off to make her train in time, and Mary said, "You're braver than I am, Bess, to do what you're doing for a woman you don't know. It will be ages before you have another leave like this. Don't waste it chasing shadows."

But I did know Marjorie, in a sense. That was the problem. I'd watched her photograph give her husband hope. And then I'd seen her in person, unaware of why she was crying or who the man was, but a witness to such wretchedness that she couldn't hold back her tears even in this very public place. And whatever she had done, she hadn't deserved to be stabbed and thrown into the river to drown, unconscious and unable to help herself. I could still see her rush away into that sea of umbrellas, and if I'd had any idea what lay ahead, I'd have found her somehow and brought her back to the flat with me. I don't know how I could have solved the problems she was facing, but I'd have tried.

That was hindsight. And I couldn't dwell on it. Yet in a way I was.

I met Michael Hart at nine o'clock the next morning, as promised. He was waiting for me on the steps of the hotel when I drove up, and he directed me to the Evanson house in Madison Street.

It was tall, three stories with two steps up to a pair of Ionic columns supporting the portico roof. Curved railings to either side graced the steps, and above the porch was a balcony with a white balustrade.

I lifted the knocker, wrapped with black crepe, and let it fall, smiling at Michael Hart to cover the trepidation we both suddenly felt.

No one answered the summons. And then, out of the corner of my eye, I saw the flick of a drapery as someone peeked out. It was quickly pulled to again. After a moment a middle-aged woman in the black dress of a housekeeper opened the door, apologizing profusely to Michael.

"Mr. Michael. I'm so sorry, sir! Truly I am. But we've been besieged by newspaper people and curiosity seekers. There was a woman here a fortnight past swearing she could find the murderer for us if she could come into the house and touch something belonging to the dead. That was the last straw. I shut the door in her face, and we decided that we wouldn't open it again to anyone."

She was ushering us into the small square hall, and then into a drawing room decorated in pale green and cream, urging us to be seated.

"How are you, sir? We heard about that shoulder. You must have been in great pain. I don't see how you can bear it, even now."

I saw Michael's mouth twist in the beginning of a grimace, and then he smiled and said, "I try not to think about it, Mrs. White. This is Sister Crawford, my nurse. She agreed to accompany me to London. I'm not yet well enough to travel on my own."

Mrs. White made polite noises in my direction, clearly relieved that I represented nothing more than Michael's nurse.

"I understand, Mr. Michael, truly I do. My grandson just came home with half his foot shot off. He can't bear to put it to the floor yet."

Changing the subject he said, "I don't know what's happening, Mrs. White. I know Marjorie is dead, that she was murdered. Victoria hardly speaks to me, and she won't tell me what progress the police are making. This is the first time I've been able to come up to London. I want to find out anything I can that will help."

"There was an inquest, sir. I was there, and horrible hearing it was. Mrs. Evanson's death was put down to person or persons unknown and left open for the police to pursue their inquiries. But I don't think they have any. They came here after her poor body was found and searched the house for evidence, but I don't know what they was hoping to find. And then the solicitor, Mr. Blake, came to look for her will, and he left empty-handed as well. I told him she'd been speaking of changing it, but I doubted anything had come of it. He knew nothing about that. The police came again, asking us more questions about her state of mind, who might have called at the house, who she might have gone out to meet. I gave him the best answers I could, but I really didn't know much. She wasn't herself these past months."

"How so?"

"She had one of her meetings here. Of the ladies with husbands who fly those aircraft—February, I believe it was. And it upset her. They talked about such terrible things, Mr. Michael. I heard them discussing how burned flesh feels when you touch it, and what it's like to lose fingers or toes to fire, and the like. One of the women arrived in tears, and I think her husband had just been reported dead. Burned alive in his Sopwith."

I felt a shudder, remembering the pilot of the Albatross going down in flames. As angry and frightened as I'd been at the time, he too had a family somewhere grieving for him.

Before Michael could ask another question, Mrs. White was saying earnestly, "Mrs. Evanson cried herself to sleep that night. I could see how red her eyes were the next morning. She went out in late afternoon, and although she'd told me she'd be at home for dinner and there would be no guests, she didn't come in until close on to ten o'clock and that wasn't like her to stay out with no word. But I smelled cigarette smoke on her coat as I put it away and helped her get herself into bed. And she didn't tell me anything. Usually it was, 'Oh, I ran into such and such a one, and we decided to have dinner together.' And tell me what she'd had to eat, and how dreary the menu was or how bad the service, or how kind the waiter had been when she couldn't even cut her meat with a knife, it was so tough—she was lonely, she missed the lieutenant something fierce, and I was there to listen if I could. But it all stopped that night. I thought she must have been angry with me."

A woman beginning an affair? Or one caught up in an emotional tangle, and turning to the first sympathetic ear. And then having to be secretive, unable to speak freely, and so falling back on silence.

That gave me an interesting time frame. February. Her husband was in France, just joining a new squadron, his first and last crashes in the future. I'd been told that Lieutenant Evanson was a very good pilot, with quick reflexes, an understanding of the machines he flew, and the good sense to know when to fight and when to run. Most of the young, green pilots joining a squadron had to be restrained from trying to be heroes before they had even learned the rules of engagement with the very well-trained German fliers. And often they died in their first encounters with the enemy, too easily tricked into doing something rash that exposed them to a sure shot. The Germans liked to hunt in packs, lurking where they couldn't be seen, but ready to come in for the kill when the opportunity arose.

Michael was asking if any of the other staff had found Mrs. Evanson more willing to talk about her days and evenings.

"Nan—you remember her, sir, she's from Little Sefton, Mrs. Evanson brought her to London with her—she remarked to me that Mrs. Evanson was quieter, and later she told me she thought she was worried. That she cried in the night. We put that down to the lieutenant's first crash. But he walked away from that one. Still, it must have frightened her to know how close he came to dying then."

"Did she bring any strangers to the house? That's to say, women or men you didn't recognize? Someone she hadn't known before Merry went to France?"

"She didn't. No. Except of course for the ladies whose husbands flew. That changed from week to week, it seemed. But one of her friends, Mrs. Daly, stopped by, and as I showed her into the drawing room here, I heard her exclaiming, 'Marjorie! At last. I haven't seen you for ages. Come and dine with us tomorrow night.' But I don't think Mrs. Evanson went. I didn't help her dress for such a dinner."

"No letters from strangers? No messages? No—flowers or the like?"

"You mean, was there a man hanging about? I was beginning to wonder myself, when she paid particular attention to how she looked. And then she was at home nearly all the time, morning, noon, and night, refusing all invitations, and sometimes not leaving her room until late in the afternoon. What's more, she wasn't eating properly. Skipping a meal, saying she wasn't hungry and would take only a cup of soup."

"The day she—died," I asked. "What happened that day?"

She turned to me as if she hadn't expected me to have a voice. "Miss?" She shot a quick glance at Michael, and he must have nodded, because she answered, still looking at him, as if he'd asked the question.

"The police wanted to know as well. She was unsettled in the night. Mrs. Hall, the cook, came down to start the morning fires, and she found Mrs. Evanson in the kitchen, her eyes red, and she said she'd been horribly sick before dawn, could Mrs. Hall make her a cup of tea as soon as the fires were going. Mrs. Hall got her the tea and a pinch of salt to put on the back of her tongue to stop the nausea, and she went back to bed. But later she got up, dressed, and went out. She said she had a train to meet. She didn't come home, and we thought perhaps she'd met the train and stayed with the friend she was expecting. I thought she looked very upset to be meeting a friend, but we supposed it was someone from her women's group who had had bad news."

"And no messages came for her, no one stopped here looking for her?"

"There was the note, before she left. Brought round by messenger."

"Did she read it?" I asked, for the first time feeling that we were making progress.

"I don't know if she did or not, Miss. She put it in her purse because she was in something of a hurry."

And her purse had never been found.

I asked, remembering Serena Melton's lie, "Was she wearing any special jewelry when she left that day? A brooch, or a bracelet, a fine ring? Something that might tempt a desperate man to rob her?"

"Of late she hadn't worn much in the way of nice pieces of jewelry," Mrs. White answered. "I'd have noticed if she had."

We stayed another half hour, speaking to Mrs. White for a little longer, and then to Nan and another maid, and finally to Mrs. Hall, the cook, and the scullery maid who helped her. Mrs. Hall told us that if she hadn't known better, she'd have guessed Mrs. Evanson was in the family way, she'd been so ill in the night.

"But of course the cuts of meat the butcher's boy brings us these days, you never know whether they've turned or not."

"Was anyone else ill that night?" Michael asked her.

"No, sir. Just Mrs. Evanson."

No one could tell us who had been on that train. I'd have given much for a name, to hand over to the Yard.

Michael thanked them all for their care of their mistress and promised to see they were given good references when a decision was made about the house. I could see that they were grateful and relieved.

Outside, we found the day had turned from early sunshine to clouds that seemed to hang over the city and hold in the heat like a wet blanket; I was grateful for my motorcar rather than trying to find a cab.

"Take me back to the hotel," Michael said abruptly, in as dark a mood as the day.

I nodded, cranking the motorcar and driving us to the Marlborough. As the man at the door helped him to descend, Michael said, "Find a place to leave this thing, will you, and come in. I'll be in the lobby."

With some misgivings I did as he'd asked, and when I got there, he'd found a table in one corner of the lounge, quiet and private, and had already organized tea for us.

As I sat down, Michael said, his voice low and angry, "If she had to turn to someone, why not *me*?"

"You were in France," I pointed out.

"Yes. Damn the French and their war. We wouldn't have been drawn into it save for them."

I couldn't point out that it was the Belgians we had come into the fighting to save. He wasn't interested in logic, he was looking for somewhere to lay the blame.

"I don't think she really loved him—" I began, but he gave me such an angry look that I broke off.

"Do you think it makes me feel any better to know that she picked someone she didn't love to give her comfort?"

"I didn't mean it that way, Michael, and you know it. I think she was used—that she was vulnerable and unhappy, and whoever it was saw that and took advantage of it."

"Don't make excuses for her."

I stopped trying to talk to him and lifted the lid of the teapot. It had brewed long enough and I filled our cups.

I didn't really want tea, but it gave me something to do with my hands while he mourned for a love he'd never really had, except in his own heart.

After a time, I asked, "What would you have done, if she'd come to you, Michael? No, don't bite my head off. I'm trying to think this through."

He glared at me all the same, but after taking a deep breath, he said, "I'd have tried to comfort her. I'd have offered her a friendly shoulder to cry on and fought down whatever feelings I had, so that she wouldn't know. I'd have taken her somewhere quiet for dinner and talked to her, tried to make her see that she couldn't do anything about her problem except cry it out, then face it. And I'd have stood behind her, whatever it was, until she was all right again. She wouldn't have wound up in my bed. I wouldn't have done that to her or to Meriwether."

"But someone must have done. Perhaps not that first night. But on another. It's what must have happened. And she might not have foreseen where it was leading."

Or she might have seen it, and needed that reassurance that she was loved and wanted. Swept away on a tide of feeling that as soon as it passed would leave her hurt and ashamed and possibly pregnant.

I knew of three nursing sisters who after a very difficult time in France came home with nightmares and an emotional void that led them in the end to turn to someone to reaffirm that life went on. A love affair, a foolish liaison, and sometimes slashed wrists had been the outcome, and all three had returned to France chastened and quiet. There was often no real outlet for shattered nerves except the courage to see them through alone.

Michael was saying, "I still find it hard to believe. Not Marjorie."

"You've seen her differently, that's all. And part of it is what you wanted to find in her. Only Marjorie Evanson could really know Marjorie."

"I need a drink," he retorted. "Not this damned tea."

"No, you don't. Are you going to fail Marjorie as well? Did she disappoint your expectations, and so you're going to walk away angry and hurt because she wasn't as strong as you'd have liked her to be?"

"Damn you, you see things too clearly," he said, almost turning on me. But then he settled back in his chair. "You have a point. I'm no better than anyone else, am I? It's not Marjorie that I'm crying over right now, it's my own hurt."

"A very real hurt. But it won't help us to find out who killed her."

"No. But when we do find out, I'm not going to the police. They can have him when I've finished with him!"

I left Michael sitting there and walked out of the hotel. Coming down the steps, I looked up in time to see two men in quiet conversation on the pavement not ten feet from me. They shook hands, and the older man, the one facing me, touched his hat politely as he was about to enter the Marlborough. The other moved on. I had seen only his back, but I had a feeling I knew him.

I had already taken a half dozen steps in the opposite direction when I realized that the other man must be Jack Melton.

I turned and went after him, calling to him. A very forward thing to do—my mother would have been appalled—but I wanted very badly to speak to him.

He swung around, frowned at me, and then said, "Miss Crawford," in a very cool tone of voice as he removed his hat and stood waiting impatiently for me to explain myself.

"I'm so sorry," I said, lying through my teeth—I was no such thing. "Do you have a moment?"

"I'm late for a meeting—but yes, I have a moment."

It would have been better to return to the hotel, but Michael Hart might well still be in the lounge just off Reception.

I said rather too quickly, "I made no mention of it when I was a guest in your home. I thought it out of place to bring it up so publicly. But I think you should know that I saw your sister-in-law, Marjorie Evanson, the evening she was killed. Perhaps this will help you narrow the search before your wife—" I broke off.

His face lost all expression, smoothing into flat planes of light and shadow without any emotion. "Indeed. The police never said anything to me about this. You were with her . . . ?" He left it there, waiting.

"No, I saw her. I'd just come in on the train from Hampshire. She was standing directly in my path." I hesitated. "She was crying. Terribly upset. I couldn't help but notice. And there was a man with her. He boarded the train, and she walked away alone. I lost her in the rain and the crowds. I never saw her again."

"How could you possibly have recognized Mrs. Evanson?" His voice was cold, now, and very hard. "What is it you want, young woman? Is this an attempt at blackmail?"

I was so angry I stared at him, speechless. Then I found my voice. "Commander Melton," I said in the tones of a ward sister dealing with an unruly patient,

"I didn't wish to distress Mrs. Melton while I was at Melton Hall, but I nursed Lieutenant Evanson in France and had just accompanied him and other patients to Laurel House the day Mrs. Evanson was killed. Your sister-in-law's photograph was with him day and night. I'd also seen it not half an hour before taking the train to London. I couldn't possibly have mistaken his wife's face, even in such distress."

He had the grace to look ashamed. "I'm—sorry. This has been a terrible business, and my wife is still grieving for her brother. We have both been under considerable strain—" He broke off, aware he was running on. Then he asked, tightly, "Did you also recognize the man with her? Please tell me who he was."

"I'm afraid not. He was an officer in the Wiltshire Fusiliers, and I have a good memory for faces. I believe I'd know him if I saw him again."

He digested that. "And have you spoken to the police?"

"Of course. And I told them what I'd believed at the time, that she was distraught enough to have done herself a harm. Instead she was murdered. I can't help but wonder why she was in such great distress."

"Surely that was obvious. She was saying good-bye to her lover. Who else could it have been?" There was contempt in his voice.

"I don't know," I told him. "We've all assumed . . ." I realized then that there could be another reason for the officer's coldness. "Perhaps he was sent to offer her promises, or, more likely, considering her distress, to tell her she couldn't rely on the other man. Rather cowardly of him, if that's true, to send an emissary. And what sort of man would be willing to take on such an onerous duty, even for a friend?"

"I liked Marjorie," he admitted after a moment. "If she had turned to me, I'd have quietly found a way to help her, even though I disapproved of what she'd done. But she didn't. I've had to watch my wife suffer through the shock of her death and then Meriwether's death. Just now I find it hard to feel any sympathy for Marjorie's despair."

"Whatever happened on that railway platform, that person bears some responsibility for Marjorie's death. If it hadn't been for him, she'd have been at home, out of danger." My voice trailed off as I looked up at the entrance to the Marlborough at that moment. Michael Hart was standing there glaring at me. He couldn't have overheard what I'd been saying. Not at the distance between us. Could he?

Jack Melton followed my gaze in time to see Michael Hart turning away, walking stiffly back into the hotel.

Serena's husband looked from his departing back to my face, then he said sharply, "If you want to know who Marjorie could have turned to, there's your man." And he started to walk away.

"He was in France," I said, stopping Mr. Melton with an outstretched hand. "Out of reach. Who else—?"

"Was he? Out of reach?" Melton asked. "I would have sworn he was in England."

And he was gone, leaving me there in the middle of the pavement, in the path of those passing by.

By the time I'd collected myself and gone back up the hotel steps and into the lounge, there was no sign of Michael Hart. I asked Reception to page him for me, and then to send someone to his room.

But he was nowhere to be found.

At the flat, Mary was washing up the last of the dishes. I went to my room, murmuring something about letters to finish, and instead sat by the window thinking about what Jack Melton had just said about Lieutenant Hart.

Truth? Or lies?

But why should he lie?

I'd seen the fleeting expression in his eyes when he recognized Michael Hart at the top of the hotel's steps. Antipathy, certainly. Anger as well. But was the anger directed at Michael or what Jack and I'd been discussing?

Impossible to know the answer. Still, I'd made a mistake talking to him about Marjorie. But I'd heard his attempts to rein in Serena's vehement emotions, and I'd believed we might discuss Marjorie Evanson's last hours and look for something, anything, that could lead us to the truth.

I remember my mother telling me as a child, "Bess, my dear, you can't always expect others to see things as clearly as you do." I didn't always remember that lesson.

I'd failed to take into account that the man was also a husband.

But I'd learned something in the encounter with Jack Melton. Marjorie must have met that train with high hopes that she could share the burden she was carrying. And she walked out of the railway station knowing that there was no help in that direction, whether the officer she'd met was her lover or someone she thought she could trust.

What's more, her husband had just returned to England, and she must have felt the pressure of time catching up with her. She might not have known the exact date, but she would have known from Meriwether's letters that it would be soon.

And if she was three months' pregnant, it would be increasingly difficult to hide the fact. Something had to be done. Was she considering ridding herself of the child? Finding a place for it with another family? But that would mean leaving her husband for six months while she hid herself away somewhere. And it would very likely destroy her marriage. Did she expect the father of her child to marry her if she were divorced by her own husband? Did she love him at all?

Impossible to know. But that rejection as the train pulled out most certainly sharpened her need to find help somewhere.

But if she had known that Michael was in London . . .

I caught up my hat and purse and with barely a word of explanation to Mary, went down to my motorcar.

Marjorie's housekeeper wasn't happy to see me again. It struck me that she thought I was meddling, behind Michael's back. "We've told Lieutenant Hart all we could," she began.

"Yes, of course you did," I answered quickly, before she could shut the door in my face. "He forgot to ask if you could give him the names of one or two of her closest friends? I've come alone because he needed to rest."

"Is he in terrible pain?" she asked sympathetically. "There were new lines in his face. I don't remember them being there before. He was never one to take life seriously, always a smile." She stood aside and I stepped into the entrance.

"He tries not to be dependent on drugs." It was what his aunt had told me.

"That's good to hear. There was a footman once when I was a girl. He was addicted to opium. Mr. Benson—he was the owner of the house where I was maid—locked the poor man in his room for a week, to cure him. I never heard such screams and cries, begging to die one minute and cursing us all in the next breath. We thought surely he'd die."

"It must have been terrifying."

She took a deep breath, as if shoving the footman back into the past where he belonged. I wondered if she'd had a fondness for him once.

"Names, you said. At a guess, her two closest friends were Mrs. Calder and Mrs. Brighton. Mrs. Brighton lives one street over, at Number 7. I've returned a book Mrs. Evanson borrowed, that's how I know. Perhaps she can tell you how to find Mrs. Calder."

Calder. I knew that name. A distant cousin. Was this the same woman?

"And the ladies who attended the group meetings for wives and widows? Were they close to Mrs. Evanson?"

"They came and went, you see, there was no time to make real friendships."

I could understand that. "Thank you," I told her. "This is a beginning."

I left my motorcar where it was and walked the distance.

But there was black crepe on the door of Number 7, encircling the knocker. The folds were still crisp and new.

I hesitated and then lifted the knocker anyway, and a red-eyed maid came to the door. She said immediately, "Mrs. Brighton isn't receiving. If you care to leave your card?"

"I'm so very sorry to intrude," I said, and prepared to turn away. Then I asked, "I've just come to London from Somerset. I was to meet Mrs. Calder here—I didn't know—" I gestured to the black crepe. "She must have tried to reach me and I missed her message. Do you know how I could find her? I'm afraid I left my diary in the hotel."

A shot in the dark. But it found its mark.

"She called only this morning," the maid said, and gave me what I wanted before she quietly shut the door again.

I drove to Hamilton Place, and found the house I was looking for at the corner of its tiny square.

As I got out, I stood to one side as a nurse wheeled a wounded man along the pavement. He was in a chair, his eyes bandaged, one arm in a sling, a leg missing. I smiled at the sister, and then went up to knock at the door.

Mrs. Calder was in. I was shown into a small sitting room, and she rose to meet me, a query in her glance.

She was a tall woman, rail thin, with fair hair and blue eyes. I introduced myself as a friend of the Evanson family, and she frowned.

"Indeed? I don't recall meeting you at Marjorie's," she said, suspicion in her tone.

"I'm not surprised," I said easily. "I've been out of the country." Her eyes dropped to my uniform. "I was one of Lieutenant Evanson's nurses."

"You know he's dead."

"Sadly, yes. Matron told me on my last visit to Laurel House."

"What brings you to see me?"

"I was in Little Sefton only a few days ago. I understood from Alicia Dalton that you're related to Marjorie Evanson."

She was still wary. I searched for a way to convince her I meant no harm.

"It seems to me that very little progress has been made in finding out who killed Mrs. Evanson. And it matters to me, because her husband died when he shouldn't have. Not medically. He'd passed the crisis. He was counting on seeing his wife as soon as possible. Someone took that away from him. I don't want her murderer to escape justice."

"But why come to me? You should be speaking to Victoria Garrison, Marjorie's sister."

If it was a test, I was ready for it.

"With respect, I don't believe I should. We had words in Little Sefton. She thought Serena Melton had sent me there to spy."

"And were you?"

"No."

Helen Calder sighed. "There's no love lost between them. A pity, but there you are. Even tragedy failed to bring them together."

"There's more. I have reason to believe that Marjorie had met someone, perhaps six months ago. It's possible I've seen this man. I don't know his name, but she met him at Waterloo Station the night she died. I happened to be coming up from Laurel House, and it was sheer coincidence that our paths crossed."

"Marjorie had a good many friends. It could have been any one of them."

"She was so distressed. Crying, in fact. I don't think that was like her. Do you?"

After a moment she said, "No, she wouldn't have made a scene. Not Marjorie. But I'm afraid I can't help you. It would be—prying. And she's dead."

"This polite conspiracy of silence is all very well and good," I pointed out, a little angry with her. "But I think Marjorie would approve of a little 'prying' if it meant her killer was found out."

Helen Calder studied my face for a moment, and then nodded. "You're absolutely right, you know. We've all taken such pride in closing ranks to protect her memory. I never considered the fact that we were protecting her murderer as well. But you see, people do ask about her death, and I've gotten quite good at fending off gossipmongers. Heaven knows there have been enough of them. But even if I answer your questions, what possible good will it do?"

"I myself stepped forward when there was a notice in the newspapers asking for any information about Mrs. Evanson on that last day of her life. I met with an Inspector Herbert at Scotland Yard. It was not as difficult as I'd expected." I smiled. "Sadly, I don't think what I told him about seeing her at the railway station was very useful. But it did fill in a part of their picture about her movements after leaving her home earlier in the day."

She said, "Yes, all right. There was a man. I don't how she came to meet him. She told me he was in

London just for the day, and they talked for a bit. And then he asked her to join him for dinner. I know this because Marjorie mentioned it casually in another context, that it brought home to her just how much she missed Meriwether and the things they often did together. It pointed up her loneliness, she said, and she was left to face that. 'I shan't do that again,' she told me. 'It's too painful.' "

"Did she tell you the man's name?"

"No, and I really didn't care to ask. I didn't want to make more of the event than she already had done. I was hoping it would come to nothing."

"But she saw him again?"

"She must have done. I met her coming out of a milliner's shop with a hatbox in her hand. She greeted me sheepishly, as if she hadn't wanted to run into anyone she knew. I was about to tease her when it occurred to me that perhaps she was dining with that man again. There was almost a schoolgirl's furtiveness about her."

"Can you be sure it was the same man?"

"I must believe it was. Marjorie wasn't the sort to take up with strangers, and it was no more than a month after the first dinner."

"What happened next?"

"It was almost a month later—two months after that first dinner—and she was standing waiting for a cab, and I saw she'd been crying. My first thought was that she'd had bad news about Meriwether, and she answered that she'd had a letter from him only the day before and he was all right." She shook her head. "Looking back, I wonder if she'd broken off with this man. It was the last time I saw her—she began to refuse invitations, keeping to herself after that. There was this group of women she worked with. I told myself at the time that listening to their experiences was doing her more harm than good. I should have made an effort to see her, but I had my own worries, and I kept putting it off. To tell you the truth, I thought she might feel compelled to confess, and I didn't want to know."

"Do you perhaps know of a Lieutenant Fordham?" I asked.

Mrs. Calder frowned. "Ought I to know him? Do you think he was the man Marjorie was seeing?"

"I have no real reason to believe it. His name came up in a different connection. But I'd like to ask, if Marjorie were in trouble—of any kind—would she have turned to you for help? And if not to you, where would she go?"

"She didn't come here. My housekeeper would have told me if she had called. I wish she had." She shook her head. "There's really no one else she was close to. Except for Michael Hart. But of course he was in France."

"If you could ask among her friends? It could lead somewhere."

"Yes, by all means. I'm ashamed now that I didn't do something. You're very brave to take on this search. It should have been me."

But she hadn't wanted to know.

I told her how she could contact me, and thanked her.

Sadly, we were still no closer to finding Marjorie's killer.

I was outside on the pavement, preparing to crank the motorcar, when I realized that she hadn't asked me if Marjorie was pregnant.

Did she know already? Or was this something else she didn't want to hear?

Chapter Eleven

As I was about to pull over at the Marlborough Hotel, I saw a face in a cab window that caught my attention. Serena Melton. She appeared to be very upset.

I swerved back into heavy traffic, ignoring a horn blown in disgust, and fell in behind her cab, wondering where she might be going, although it was more likely that she was coming from somewhere instead.

But I was right. She was going. I trailed her back to the house where her brother and his wife had lived. She asked the cabbie to wait and went up the steps to knock at the door.

There was no answer. She waited for a moment and tried again. And again no one came to answer the summons.

She was coming back down the steps, when I turned in behind the cab and called to her.

"Serena? Imagine running into you in London. Could I take you somewhere?"

She looked at me, and after a moment paid off the cabbie and came to join me in my motorcar.

"What brings you to London?" she asked. "I thought you were in France again."

"How are you?" I asked her instead of answering. Then, "Is anything wrong?"

"I've just had a most unpleasant conversation with someone who knew my brother's wife. It was very upsetting."

"In that house? The one you were just coming out of?"

"No, no. That's my brother's house. I was hoping to have some tea and a lie down, before taking the train home."

"Are you any closer to finding out who killed your brother's wife?" It was baldly put but there was no other way to ask.

"How did you—oh. The weekend at Melton Hall." She sighed, pulling off her gloves and then after a moment putting them on again. "It's been the most hopeless task. But the police are still sitting on their hands, doing nothing. I spoke to the inspector in charge this morning. He tried to assure me that everything possible was being done. But it isn't. I know it isn't."

"It's likely—" I began, but she interrupted me, turning toward me with anger in her eyes.

"His latest theory has to do with someone from Oxford. I don't know that Marjorie even knew anyone there. He's grasping at straws."

I couldn't explain what I'd been told about the reason the police were searching for that person. It wasn't my place to pass on such information if the police had not. And so I said, "Do you have any idea what your sister-in-law did that day?"

"The police have told me that she went out in the early afternoon and never came back. She knew Merry would be arriving that day, and I'd assumed she would go at once to see him. I was intending to visit him the following day, when he was a little more rested from his journey. But of course the police were at our door before I could go. And it was left to me to tell him what had happened. I couldn't understand how she'd come to die in London. I thought there must be some mistake. They'd had some difficulty in identifying her—her purse was taken—and if her housekeeper hadn't spoken to the constable on their street, the police wouldn't have known who she was as soon as they did."

It was, for the most part, what Michael had learned from Marjorie's housekeeper.

We were nearing Kensington Palace. I said, "You remarked earlier that you'd just had an unpleasant conversation—" I left it there.

"I wish you hadn't reminded me. This woman had the audacity to say that people were talking about Marjorie long before she was killed, and that she was asking for trouble, walking down by the river at night on her own. She made her sound like a common tart, looking for custom. It was there, in the tone of voice she used."

"What sort of talk was there?"

"That she was avoiding her friends, insinuating that she must be in some sort of trouble. Well, someone in London knows where she was that evening. Why won't he or she tell us the truth?" Her voice was rising again, and she fidgeted with her gloves as if they had offended her, not the woman. "I blame Helen Calder. She ought to have noticed something. Marjorie would have listened to Helen if she'd spoken up. In the beginning, before it had got too far. But she shut her eyes, didn't she? The sort of woman who wasn't willing to put herself out for anyone, safe in her own rectitude."

It was a harsh indictment, not really warranted, but I'd seen Helen Calder's willing detachment even when she suspected that Marjorie was growing too fond of the man she'd been seeing. I didn't believe that she could have changed the situation, but I could understand Serena Melton's feeling that she might have made a difference.

"There must be a reason why she—" I began.

But she interrupted me for a second time. "We're speaking of behavior that led to murder. I would have said something, if I'd had any inkling that Marjorie was being talked about. I'd have confronted her and told her what I thought of such selfish conduct."

"Are you saying that her—that an affair had something to do with her death?"

She cast a withering glance in my direction. "When you flout the rules of society, you leave yourself open to the consequences of your actions. If she'd been at home, if she'd been with respectable friends, she would still be alive and Merry would still be alive."

All pretense that Marjorie had been killed in the course of a robbery had been dropped. I don't think Serena was aware of it, the volatile mixture of distress and anger, grief and frustration blinding her to everything else.

We drove in silence for a time, and then she said, "I might as well go home. I don't feel like facing any more blank faces and lies. The people who could really help me are Marjorie's closest friends, but they're fiercely loyal. Or else Victoria has told them not to talk to me. I wouldn't put it past her." She flicked a glance in my direction. "Marjorie's sister. I can't abide her, and neither could Marjorie."

The pent-up feeling of helplessness driving her must be exhausting, I thought, for there were new lines around her mouth, and circles beneath her eyes.

I said, "Would your brother want you to go through this anguish, trying to get at the truth?"

"I don't know whether he would or not. But if the shoe were on the other foot, he'd have moved heaven and earth to find out who had killed me. I can do no less. Just because I'm a woman, I'm not going to walk away from this."

I couldn't have said whether Lieutenant Evanson would have felt that way. But then he hadn't lost his sister while I was caring for him. I couldn't have guessed how angry he would have been, or if he'd have left matters to the police.

"Would you mind dropping me at the station? I'm sorry to ask you to turn around. But it would be a kindness."

I did as she asked, and when she had left the motorcar, she turned back to me and said, "If you hear anything about Marjorie, anything at all, you would let me know, wouldn't you?"

Now there was a conundrum. I hadn't told her what I knew. And I couldn't in good conscience promise to keep her informed. And I wasn't sure I trusted her to act wisely if she did learn the truth.

"Serena—" I began.

But she said bitterly, "You're just like the rest, aren't you?"

"No," I said sharply. "I will go to the police if I hear anything that's helpful in finding her murderer. That's what everyone should do."

"Liar," she answered, turning her back.

And she was gone, marching toward the station as if she were marching to war.

In a way she probably thought she was.

I took Michael, still protesting, back to Little Sefton.

"I've made a promise to your doctors," I told him over his protests when I finally ran him to earth at the Marlborough. "After I keep it, you're free to do as you like."

He was not in a good mood. As we threaded our way through London's traffic—mostly bicycles, military convoys or vehicles, omnibuses, and the occasional lorry trying to make deliveries to the next shop—I let him sulk.

He did it beautifully. But I was immune to his blandishments.

When we were in the clear and running through the countryside beyond London, I said, "I came looking for you earlier. Where were you?"

At first I was sure he wasn't going to tell me. Finally, he said, "I went to Scotland Yard."

Surprised, I asked, "And did they have news for you?"

"They would tell me nothing." There was suppressed anger in his confession. "Apparently I'm a suspect in Marjorie's death."

"But—you said you were in France."

Yet Jack Melton had told me he was not.

He turned to look at the passing scene, as if he hadn't heard me. Then, grudgingly, he went on. "I haven't said anything about it. I was given forty-eight hours' leave. A foreign object in my eye. I was sent to a specialist in London. My men were in rotation, I could be spared. He removed the particle, gave me drops and a patch, and I went straight back to the line. I didn't actually lie. Everyone thought I was in France. I let them go on thinking it. But the Yard stumbled on the truth."

"I don't understand."

"I hadn't heard from Marjorie for three months. Just—silence. I wrote to Victoria, but she wouldn't answer. That worried me more. I tried to get word to Meriwether, to ask him if everything was all right. But it didn't get through. When my eye was inflamed, they thought I might lose it, and I was given the choice of seeing someone in Paris or in London. Luckily, I knew a chap in school whose father was an eye surgeon in Harley Street, and the doctors at the Front approved."

"And did you see Marjorie?"

"No. I sent her a telegram the day before, telling her where I would be, begging her to come and sit with me for a bit. Either she didn't get the message or she had something else on her mind. She never came."

He was staring at a field where cows grazed, and so I couldn't read his face.

"And you didn't go to the house? Why not?"

"I was told not to leave the surgery. Not to move for twenty-four hours. I waited all that day and the next for her, and she didn't come."

"You went back to France, not knowing she'd been killed?"

He didn't answer.

"Michael—?"

He turned to me, his face twisted with grief and anger. "Do you know how many times I've wondered if she was on her way to Dr. McKinley's surgery when she was killed? How many times I've wondered if she might have lived if she'd been with me instead of out on the street somewhere and vulnerable?"

And Marjorie's housekeeper had said she went out earlier in the day and never returned. From the train station, could she have been on her way to see Michael? Was the timing right?

Catching sight of the next turning, I asked as I slowed for it, "You couldn't leave the surgery?"

"Dr. McKinley told me not to jar the eye in any way. He left me in a darkened room and his wife brought me my dinner and my breakfast the next morning."

"So you weren't supervised?"

"I was there whenever they looked in on me," he said, which wasn't necessarily the same thing.

I let a little time pass.

"Was it your child she was carrying?"

"No," he said quietly. "It was not."

And this time I believed him.

We arrived in Little Sefton late in the afternoon. I took Michael directly to the house of his aunt and uncle.

As I helped him get out of the motorcar, stiff from the drive down, he said, "Thank you, Bess Crawford. For taking me to London."

"I'm sorry it wasn't more helpful."

"It made me feel less useless. As if I'd at least tried to find the truth." He nodded to me, picked up his valise in his good hand, and walked up to the door. There he turned, and with that smile that seemed to light up the world, he said, "Give my regards to Sergeant-Major Brandon."

I laughed in spite of myself.

I went on up the street to Alicia's house and knocked at the door. She was surprised to see me but greeted me with friendly warmth. "I didn't expect to find you on my doorstep. But do come in. I'll put on the kettle and make sandwiches."

I thanked her and joined her in the kitchen as she worked. It was her cook's day off, and she was rummaging in the pantry for cold chicken and a pudding as she said, "This is my dinner, but I dine alone far too often. It will be nice to have someone to share my meal."

We ate it in the kitchen, and talked about everything but the war.

"I'm tired of knitting and growing vegetables to save room in the holds of ships for war materiel," she said as we ate our pudding. "I'm restless, I want to do something useful, really useful. But Gareth won't hear of turning the house into a hospital or my going to London and finding work. I type, you know."

"Do you? You'll be in demand."

"I think what he really wants is to know that nothing has changed at home. Not the village, not the house, not me. That it's all there to come back to."

"A good many soldiers feel that way. It's what sees them through."

"He sent me photographs in the last letter but one. Would you like to see them? His father gave him a camera for his birthday and he's been using it to capture memories, he said."

"I'd love to see them." I had a long drive ahead of me, but she had been good enough to invite me to dine, and I owed her a few minutes of my time.

She went off to find the letter, and I finished my pudding, looking out at the kitchen garden and the outbuildings and the quiet peace of late afternoon.

Alicia came back with the envelope, and took out a sheaf of photographs. "He found someone who could develop these for him. They cover a year or more. I was so pleased to have them, because now I know what his world is like."

But the photographs were not his world as it truly was. It was a tidy look at war that made me want to cry. Had Gareth chosen to spare his wife, or was he afraid that the censors would object to the truth and confiscate these photographs?

There were tents pitched in neat rows, well behind the lines, like an encampment for troops on parade. Artillery that was silent, the gunners standing grinning in front of a jumble of empty casings. A group of French children, smiling for the camera, their faces unmarked by fear and despair. I turned it over to see the name of the village where this was taken, and it was well south of the lines too. There were several photographs of his fellow officers posing absurdly, as if they hadn't a care in the world. But I could see the tension around their eyes, belying their antics. There was even one photograph of Meriwether Evanson's aircraft, with Meriwether standing proudly with a hand on the prop, his face only partly shadowed by his cap. Alicia pointed him out to me.

"I should have sent that to Marjorie, but I couldn't part with any of these for a while . . ." She let the words trail off as she handed me a few more photographs from another envelope.

Here were another group of officers standing together at a crossroads, a line of soldiers and caissons and well-laden lorries passing behind them.

I recognized the uniforms—the Wiltshire Fusiliers. And third from the left was a face I knew.

Staring at it, I said, "Do you have a glass? I'd like to see this one a little more clearly."

"I think there's one in Gareth's desk."

She went away and I tried to contain my excitement while I waited.

Alicia came back with a small magnifying glass that she said was a part of Gareth's stamp collection, and I took it from her, holding it above the photograph.

I'd been right. The third officer from the left was the man I'd seen with Marjorie Evanson at the railway station.

I turned the photograph over. The caption just read: *Friends meeting by chance.*

"Do you know who these friends are?" I asked her.

"Just the two on Gareth's right. I don't know that one."

"Could I possibly borrow this, if I promise to return it safely?" I asked. "Just for a few days."

She was reluctant to part with it, but in the end allowed me to take it with me.

I thanked her for my meal and set out for Somerset.

The light was with me most of the way, the long light of an English summer evening, a warm breeze blowing through the motorcar, the world looking as if it had never been at war. And then I caught up with a field ambulance carrying wounded to a nearby house that had been turned into a clinic, taking the rutted drive in first gear.

My first thought on leaving Alicia's house had been to find Michael and ask him if he recognized the man standing at the crossroads with Gareth. But I wasn't sure that was wise.

And so I went to the one person I knew would find the answer for me without asking questions.

Simon.

It was beginning to rain hard as I drove up the drive and put my motorcar in the shed where it lived while I was in France.

I pulled the shed doors closed and made a dash for the side door of the house.

My mother, startled by the apparition meeting her in the passage, said, "Oh. I didn't hear you coming."

"I'm not surprised. It's pouring down out there. Mother, did Simon come to dine tonight? Is he still here?"

"I expect he is. Where's your handsome young artillery officer?"

"Back where he came from."

"You decided not to keep him?"

I laughed. "His heart belongs to someone else," I said lightly and went up to change out of my wet clothes.

At the sound of voices, Simon came out of my father's study. He greeted me with raised eyebrows. "Have you abandoned young Hart to the tender mercies of The Four Doves again?"

"Alas, I was afraid he might be taken up for murder," I responded.

Simon laughed, but it was wry amusement.

In fact, I was telling the simple truth.

"But that reminds me," I went on, taking the photograph from my pocket. "I'd like very much to know the identity of the man third from the left. It's important."

Simon still had contacts with men he'd known while serving, both in my father's regiment and in others that had crossed his path. It was very likely someone would recognize that face.

He looked at the photograph, read what was written on the reverse, noted the uniform, then regarded me with interest. "Where on earth did you find this?"

"It was quite by accident," I told him. "A matter of pure luck."

"Let me see what I can do." He pocketed the photograph and turned to speak to my mother as she came into the room.

I'd always thought she was the only person on earth Simon Brandon would obey without question—next, of course, to the Colonel Sahib. He would have walked through fire for her sake. There were those who whispered that he was in love with the Colonel's lady, but his devotion had very different roots.

My father eyed me with interest as I came into his study. "What, no lost sheep? No crusades to lead? You've abandoned all hope of saving some poor soul?"

I laughed. "Sorry. I'm between causes at the moment."

"That's rare," he said, his suspicions aroused, but he said nothing more, changing the subject with the ease of long practice.

We were just going up to bed when our village constable bicycled to the house and asked to speak to me.

I went to the sitting room, where he'd been shown, and my father accompanied me.

Constable Boynton greeted me and said, "There's been word from Inspector Herbert at Scotland Yard, Miss Crawford. Someone took a shot at Lieutenant Michael Hart in Little Sefton an hour and a half ago."

"Michael?" I exclaimed, bracing myself for bad news. "Is he all right?"

"He's unharmed. In fact, he reported the incident himself. He was walking in the garden. No one heard the shot, no one saw the shooting. Inspector Herbert wishes to know if you could put a name to his assailant."

My first thought was Serena Melton. I wouldn't have put it past her to shoot—and miss—with the weapon that wasn't in the gun cabinet where it belonged. But I'd seen her onto the train. No, I'd dropped her at the station, I corrected myself. I had no idea which train she'd taken.

On the other hand I could see that Michael Hart could easily have invented the entire incident to take himself off the Yard's suspect list. And mine.

"Please tell Inspector Herbert I can't help him in this matter. I wasn't there, and I don't know who could have tried to shoot the lieutenant. I'm sorry. But if I learn anything more, I'll be in touch."

"Thank you, Miss. And my apologies to Mrs. Crawford for disturbing you so late," Constable Boynton said, and took his leave.

As the door closed behind him, my father said, "You're making a habit of being consulted by an inspector at Scotland Yard these days?"

"Not really consulted," I said, trying to make light of what had just happened. "I was there, in Little Sefton, only a few hours ago." But how had Inspector Herbert known that?

The constable in Little Sefton must have remembered my motorcar and reported that I'd just brought Lieutenant Hart home from London. The fact that Inspector Herbert knew such details indicated all too clearly his interest in Michael.

Which told me that the murderer from Oxford hadn't proved to be the Yard's man. In spite of what the Yard had told Serena Melton.

"Indeed," my father was saying thoughtfully. "I don't believe you were telling the whole truth when you refused to help Constable Boynton."

The Colonel Sahib knew me too well. "I didn't refuse. I just didn't want to make false accusations,"

I answered him. "Not when I had no real proof to support them."

"Very commendable. And is there any remote possibility that we shall be in danger in our own garden?"

"If in fact someone actually shot at Lieutenant Hart, it would have been a very personal matter. And not one that I'm likely to be involved with."

"I'm delighted to hear it. Perhaps I should have a word with this Inspector Herbert. I don't care to see you dragged into inquiries."

"I wasn't dragged into anything. I happened to be a witness to two people having a conversation in a railway station. I knew one of them but not the other. And the one I knew was later murdered. But hours later, long after I was sound asleep in my flat. The trouble is, the other person, the one I didn't recognize, could probably give the police a great deal more information— that is, if he could be found. He's been conspicuous by his absence."

There. It was out in the open. The whole story. Mostly.

"And Michael Hart is involved? How?"

"He'd known the dead woman for many years."

"But he's not a suspect."

I hesitated a heartbeat too long in answering that.

My father gave me a straight look but said no more. He held the sitting room door open for me. Simon had gone, and my mother was waiting to speak to my father after I went up the stairs. I knew very well she'd have the story of Constable Boynton's intrusion before they followed me up to bed.

I couldn't sleep. I dressed, then went quietly down the stairs and out the door, looking up at the wet night, the trees softly dripping rain, the sounds of night creatures loud in the stillness.

Simon, wearing rain gear, came up behind me as I started to walk along the stepping-stones that led around the house. I wasn't going farther than the little gazebo my father had put up in the garden there for my mother, but of course he had no way of guessing that.

He said, "If you're thinking of going to Little Sefton tonight, I'll drive you."

I shook my head. "There's no point in it. I'd come no closer to the truth than the police have done. Did my father tell you what Constable Boynton wanted to speak to me about?"

"Of course," he said, grinning. "Your mother had it out of him as soon as you were out of the room. He walked down to see me afterward."

"What did she have to say about the shooting?"

"As I recall, her exact words were, 'I wouldn't worry, if I were you, Richard. I think young Mr. Hart is looking for sympathy.'"

Trust my mother to see into the heart of the matter.

I said, "If he came to speak to you, what are you doing here? It's late."

"I had a feeling you might decide to go to Hampshire."

"This time you were wrong."

I could see a flash of something in his eyes before he turned away. "It occurred to me that Lieutenant Hart's death—if he'd been killed tonight—would bear a striking resemblance to Lieutenant Fordham's."

I hadn't linked the two. Yet. But Simon was right, in time I would have.

I woke up the next morning with a headache. Rare for me, because I seldom had them. But I hadn't been able to sleep until close on four o'clock because my mind was trying to sort out the tangle of events.

A nurse is trained to observe. It's her duty to see what is happening to the patient in her charge—she's the eyes of the doctor on the case. Any changes must be noted, and she's expected to know what they represent: a sign of healing, of a worsening of the patient's condition, the onset of new symptoms, or a simple matter of indigestion. We're expected to know when to summon Matron or the doctor, and when to cope on our own.

Use that training, I told myself. Don't jump to conclusions.

There had to be some evidence somewhere.

Marjorie had spent five hours that were unaccounted for. She could very well have walked to the nearest hotel and used a telephone to reach someone. But that person hadn't come forward. She could have taken a cab to the house of a friend. But according to Helen Calder, she had been cut off from her friends—she had told Helen herself very little, for that matter, and then only in the early stages of the affair. She could have confided in a complete stranger in a tea shop, someone who would listen but not judge. That person hadn't come forward either. She couldn't have traveled very far between the time I saw her and when she was killed. Perhaps an hour in any direction, if she were meeting the person she'd telephoned. But no restaurant or other public place had contacted the police to say she had been seen.

Very likely she never left London.

And Michael was in Dr. McKinley's surgery. Marjorie knew that.

Had she walked the streets for a time, working up her courage to talk to an old friend? And then made her way to the surgery after hours, when the doctor was least likely to look in on his patient? She wouldn't have wished to arrive with her face blotched by tears.

I could see the police point of view there.

I wondered who had told them that Michael was in love with Marjorie? Otherwise, they would have interviewed him and moved on, since he had no apparent motive. Was it Victoria?

Of course police suspicions would have been aroused by the fact that he had said nothing about seeing her that night. Unless he swore she had never come there. Michael could hardly have stabbed her in the surgery. And if he disobeyed orders and left, he risked the doctor finding him gone.

Where could one go to commit a quiet little murder?

If someone had intended to throw Marjorie's body in the river, surely it was easier to do the deed nearby, rather than having to transport a body any distance. It was dark there, with London wary of Zeppelin raids. A well-lit river was a navigator's delight. That might explain why Marjorie was still alive when she was put into the water—it would be impossible to make sure she was dead.

Michael had said that he was haunted by the possibility that Marjorie had been killed on her way to meet him.

If that were true, had Marjorie told someone where she intended to go, and that person had prevented her from reaching the surgery?

Walk with me for a little while. We can talk by the water, it's quiet there. Then you can go on to the doctor's surgery . . .

That was a far more realistic possibility than encountering a stranger.

Back, then, to someone she knew.

Had she told the man at the railway station where she was going? I hadn't seen him descend from the moving train, although Inspector Herbert had asked me specifically about that point. But there was the next station.

First Lieutenant Fordham. Then Michael Hart. The only person I could think of who would have a reason to shoot both men was Serena Melton. She was obsessed, searching for the baby's father. And I wondered if Jack suspected that, if it had been the reason he'd been afraid of blackmail.

I'd fallen asleep on that thought.

Ignoring the headache as best I could, I dressed and went down to breakfast. My parents had already eaten theirs and gone. The sun was out again, the rain only a memory.

I could imagine my father driving to London to have a word with Inspector Herbert. But he had a good head start, I'd never be able to catch him up.

I drank a cup of tea, ate some dry toast, and went out to the shed where I'd left my motorcar. It was low on petrol, and I was about to take it to the smithy-cum-garage to see to that.

Simon was coming around the corner of the house. He had a tennis racket in his hand, and I realized that he and my mother must have been playing. "Who won?" I asked.

"I did. By the skin of my teeth. Where are you going?"

I told him.

"I'll see to the petrol. Then I'm off to Sandhurst."

"Business or pleasure?" I hoped it was my photograph that was taking him there.

"I've to see someone there on War Office business," he said. "After that I intend to bring up the photograph."

I thanked him, and then asked if he knew where my father had gone.

"Something came up. He's on his way to Portsmouth to meet someone. That's how I was dragooned into a game of tennis, in his place."

I wasn't sure whether to believe him or not. Portsmouth—and London afterward?

And then I did, when Simon said, "You'll stay close to home while we're away? I don't like the idea of shots flying about in gardens. Besides, your mother wouldn't mention it, but I think she'd like a little time with you."

I'd have liked to go to Little Sefton and ask Michael Hart about the shots fired at him. But I could hardly knock at the Harts' door and boldly ask about an event that had occurred hours after I left. I persuaded myself that if Simon was successful in identifying the man, I could return the photograph to Alicia as promised. And she was sure to tell me what had happened, and it would seem very natural to speak to Michael then.

Besides, Simon was right about my mother.

"I promise," I told him, and with a nod he was gone.

Chapter Twelve

I was just coming up the avenue of lime trees later that day when I heard Simon's motorcar pulling in behind me.

"Were you able to put a name to that face?" I asked, hope rising.

"Unfortunately, no."

My spirits plummeted. "Oh" was all I could manage to say.

Simon smiled. "I can't work miracles, Bess. He's in a territorial regiment. They come and go, those charged with their training barely getting to know them before they're shipped to the Front. Besides, it's not a very clear likeness. And at the moment, I must go up to London."

To my eyes it was. Or had I wanted it to be the right man? With his cap on, shading his face—but that's how I'd seen him at Waterloo Station.

"Let me go with you." I put on my most innocent face.

He was instantly suspicious. "Why?"

"I have some shopping I'd like to do."

He nodded. "All right. After breakfast, then."

I was ready the next morning when he came knocking at the door a little after seven. My mother had given me a long list of things she needed and couldn't find locally.

We drove in silence for a time, and then he said, "Look, Bess. This is all well and good. But you need to spend more time with your family."

"I feel guilty enough," I told him. "But I also feel responsible. Day after day, I watched Lieutenant Evanson cling to that photograph of his wife, and on the long journey home, I helped him count the hours until he saw her again. He was stoic, never complaining. Only, I was the one who saw her—he never did. He wasn't even well enough to attend her funeral. Then he killed himself, slowly, patiently, until he'd succeeded. He was one of mine, Simon. He should have *lived*."

He reached over and took my hand. His was warm and safe and comforting. "You can't save all of them, Bess," he said gently. "That's the trouble with war. Men die. Your father and I close our eyes and see a thousand ghosts. We know they're there, but we can't stare too long at their faces. We have to move on. Put the living first. There are already enough monuments to the dead." His voice was bitter as he finished.

I said nothing, too close to tears, and I knew how he disliked tears.

After a while he released my hand, and then he changed the subject.

Simon hadn't particularly cared to see me go into nursing, but when the war came, it was what I wanted to do. If I couldn't fight with my father's regiment, as a son would have done, I could at least keep men alive to fight again another day.

Simon had decided that the rigors of learning my trade would discourage me. But mopping floors, changing dressings and bedpans, sitting with the dying, and standing by without flinching when horribly wounded men came through the tent flap had toughened me in ways I hadn't expected. If my father's son could face death on a battlefield, my father's daughter could certainly face the bloody ruins of brave men.

India and the other places where my father had been sent in the course of his career had also helped me cope with the ugliness of what I had chosen to do. Death and disease, poverty and despair were just outside the compound gates in Agra and other places. I had only to ride a mile in my mother's carriage to see maimed lepers and begging children, ash-covered holy men lying on a bed of hot coals or a starving family covered with sores. I knew early on that life for some was very hard and for others much more comfortable.

"A penny," my companion said as we drove through the next small village.

"I was thinking about India."

"I dream of it sometimes. Do you?"

"Yes—oh, Simon, stop, please!" I reached out, my hand on his arm.

He did as I'd asked, pulling in behind a baker's cart. I was out of the motorcar almost as soon as it came to a halt.

"Captain Truscott!" I called to the Army officer just walking into a bookshop. He turned and recognized me at once.

"Miss Crawford! How good to see you. What brings you to Maplethorpe?"

"I was passing through, on my way to London."

"I'm leaving for London myself in half an hour. Have dinner with me tonight."

"The Marlborough?"

"Yes, indeed. Shall I come for you?"

I told him where to find me and that Mrs. Hennessey was the guardian at the gate. "Let her see that you are the most responsible officer in the entire Army, and she'll come upstairs for me."

He laughed. "Seven, then?"

"Seven."

And I was back in the motorcar before the baker had finished his delivery at the tea shop next to the bookstore.

"You've thrown over the dashing young lieutenant for a captain, I see."

"He was at the Meltons' house party. He knew Marjorie Evanson and her husband."

"Which explains why you leapt out of a moving motorcar to chase that man into a bookstore and beg him to take you to dinner tonight."

"I did no such thing," I answered indignantly.

Simon laughed. "That's how your mother would see it."

That was true. I don't know why I had rushed after Captain Truscott, but it had been a spur-of-the-moment decision. It was a bit of luck to find him again at all.

We reached London and Simon set me down at the flat, where I went up to look for anyone who might be there. But I had it to myself, and I decided that my first order of business was to speak to Inspector Herbert.

He was not at the Yard, having been called away to deal with a problem in Bermondsey. The elderly constable who escorted me to his office and back down the stairs again took pity on me when he saw my disappointment. "He's got a meeting tomorrow at eight o'clock with the Chief Superintendent. If you are here at nine o'clock, he'll make time for you."

I thanked him and left. I'd expected I'd be staying over in London, anyway. The problem would be persuading Simon to stay too.

By the time I reached the flat again, having stopped along the way to find items from my mother's list, I discovered Simon waiting for me, leaning against the wing of his motorcar, arms crossed.

I gave him my packages and he stowed them in the motorcar. Three more he carried inside for me, where Mrs. Hennessey gave him permission to take them up the stairs to the flat, while she watched with an eagle eye. "He's a very attractive man. Friend of the family or not," she murmured to me. "And there are standards to maintain. The families of my young ladies expect it."

I suppressed a smile. If Mrs. Hennessey didn't trust Simon, the most trustworthy of men, I wondered what she would make of Lieutenant Hart. Temptation incarnate.

But dear soul that she was, she did her best to safeguard those of us who lived in the flats above, and we all loved her.

When Simon came down again, we went to his motorcar and he took me to lunch. I'd wanted to ask him what he'd learned, but he was in a dark mood and I knew better than to push. We talked about other things—where I'd gone shopping, what I'd heard from my flatmates, news of mutual friends, everything under the sun but what was uppermost in my mind.

And then, at the end of our meal, as the waiter set our trifle in front of us and walked away, he finally said, "I've found the name of the man in that photograph. Are you sure you want to hear what I've learned? Or shall I send it along to this Inspector Herbert of yours, and let it be finished?"

"Is it someone you know—or my parents know?" I asked, suddenly worried.

"No."

"Then tell me, please."

"He's Jack Melton's brother."

I sat there, stunned.

I hadn't expected the man to be someone I knew. But then I'd never actually met him, I reminded myself. Only his brother. Serena's husband. Still, it was too close to home for comfort.

"What is his name?" I couldn't remember ever hearing it.

"Raymond Melton. He's a captain in the Wiltshire Fusiliers. And in France at the moment."

I took a deep breath.

"It can't be. No, I don't think he would dare—Serena's brother's *wife?*"

"You know nothing about the man. What sort he may be." Simon's voice was harsh. "Go to Scotland Yard, tell Herbert what you've learned, and leave it to him."

"But it doesn't make sense," I said, dabbing at the trifle with my spoon, not wanting to meet Simon's eyes.

"That's because you don't want to believe it."

"It will break Serena Melton's heart. She'll never forgive him. And she will blame Jack as well."

"Why?"

"Because her brother died of grief. She didn't care all that much for Marjorie, even when they married. But she loved her brother with all her heart."

I had wanted to find this man, to keep the inquiry on track. And as is common with most meddling, what I'd learned would have repercussions. Once Raymond Melton was questioned, Serena would give Jack no peace until he told her all he knew.

Still, so much fit together. Marjorie would have met Raymond Melton. And if she had run into him in

London one day, she would have had no qualms about dining with him. Even Mrs. Hennessey, a stickler for propriety, wouldn't have batted an eye.

"Why was he in England five or six months ago? It couldn't have been an ordinary leave. He must have been here longer than most."

"He was seconded to General Haig's staff, and he was coordinating supply shipments. They were being held up, finding transport was a problem with the German submarines taking such a toll. London was his base. From there he could visit Manchester or Birmingham or Liverpool with relative ease. He also had a staff motorcar at his disposal."

"I can't imagine what she could possibly have seen in him," I said crossly. "He seemed so—distant. Michael Hart is so much better looking, if it was a fling she was after. And he loved her, he wouldn't have walked away from her and left her there all alone."

"Raymond Melton didn't kill her. He couldn't have. I asked. He caught the train and reached France precisely when he should have."

But trains were slow. He could have borrowed a motorcar, using the excuse that he'd missed his connection.

Simon was saying something that I didn't catch. "Sorry?"

"He's married, Bess. Raymond Melton is married. They have two children."

I recalled the boy and girl I'd seen at Melton Hall the day Mary and I arrived. Raymond Melton's children? Very likely, though she'd referred to them as cousins.

"Oh, dear God. What am I to do, Simon? It will ruin *their* lives."

"This is why I didn't want to tell you." He signaled the waiter. "I'll take you back to the flat and then speak to Inspector Herbert myself. He'll know how much will have to come out during the inquiry, and how much he can keep from the newspapers for the time being. Leave it to him. Then I'll drive you back to Somerset."

He didn't say, bless him, that I should have handed Gareth Dalton's photograph to Scotland Yard. Then I'd have been ignorant of the connections. Like the ostrich with her head in the sand.

"I have a dinner engagement with Captain Truscott," I answered distractedly. "It would be unkind to break it. Besides, Inspector Herbert is away."

"Then I'll wait and drive you home tomorrow."

Rousing myself, I said, "No, that's not the right way to handle this, Simon. I made a promise to Inspector Herbert. I told him I'd let him know what I discovered. I'll speak to him myself."

We argued that point for a good five minutes, and then Simon capitulated.

"It may be the best way after all," he said. He settled the bill and then led me out of the restaurant. "What matters is to put this behind you as soon as you can."

We had reached the pavement when I remembered something. Hearing a quick indrawn breath, Simon turned to me. "What is it?"

"I ran into Jack Melton outside the Marlborough Hotel when I was in London with Lieutenant Hart. I felt an obligation, I don't know why, to tell him that on the night she died I'd seen Marjorie with a man I didn't recognize, and I think I said something about the Yard searching for this man, to help them with their inquiries. And he told me that I ought to be looking instead at Michael Hart. Little did he know." I paused. "Or did he? No, somehow I have a feeling that Raymond Melton keeps himself to himself."

Simon swore under his breath in Urdu, thinking I wouldn't recognize the words, but I did. Bazaar life is very colorful. A child's ear soon picks up bits and pieces of Hindi and Urdu. I quickly learned which words I could and could not repeat in front of my elders.

"How close is he to his brother, do you know?"

"I can't answer that," I told him.

"Then the sooner you get to the Yard, the safer you will be." He shook his head. "There's something wrong with this whole affair, Bess. Don't you feel it as well? Something rather—sinister. You've learned too much, for one thing, and for another, the murder of Marjorie Evanson was particularly vicious. Don't tempt her killer, whoever he may be, to try again."

"But Raymond Melton is in France." I wasn't as convinced as Simon was.

"For the moment."

"Do you think he knows where she was going after the train left?"

"Would she tell him? Perhaps she would, to make him jealous."

What had been set in motion that rainy evening in the railway station? Was that only the tip of the problem, the more visible half? What about Michael Hart?

I realized all at once that we were standing in everyone's way as they came and went from the restaurant, forcing them to part like the Red Sea around us.

"We can't discuss it here." Simon took my arm and led me to the motorcar, holding my door for me. He turned the crank with more than his usual vigor, then got behind the wheel. "We can't talk in your flat either. Where would you like to go?" When I didn't answer, he said, "Scotland Yard? Even if Inspector Herbert isn't there, we'll tell someone else what you know. It will be finished, Bess."

"Yes," I said. Reluctantly. But I knew he was right.

As it happened, Inspector Herbert had just returned from Bermondsey, and we had to wait half an hour for him to make his report to his superiors. Finally I heard his footsteps, loud on the bare floorboards, as he came down the passage, and then he opened his office door and was shaking hands. I explained Simon's presence, and after that we all sat down.

I had a distinct impression of cold feet—they wanted to carry me back out of the room again as fast as possible. But it was too late.

"Well," Inspector Herbert was saying. "What brings you here, Miss Crawford?"

Simon opened his mouth but I forestalled him.

Inspector Herbert listened carefully as I told him what I knew about the man at the station. And he asked to see the photograph that I'd given Simon.

"It belongs to someone. I promised to bring it back to her as soon as possible."

He was busy scanning the face of Raymond Melton. After a moment, he reached into his drawer and drew out a looking glass. "You're quite sure this is Captain Melton?" he asked after a moment, still bent over the picture. He reached up to turn on the lamp at his elbow and brought it closer. I thought to myself that by the time he gave that photograph back to me, Inspector Herbert would have memorized Melton's face.

Straightening up, he turned off the lamp, set the glass back inside his drawer, and leaned back into his chair. "What did Marjorie Evanson say to this man, on that rainy evening in London?" he mused. "What did it set in motion, that meeting?"

"She may have kept her own counsel," Simon pointed out. "Given his conduct."

"Yes, that's possible. I expect she was too upset to dine anywhere, and she wouldn't wish to be seen by anyone she knew. We've looked into tea shops between the railway station and the river. Churches are more difficult—they're often empty at that time of day. She could sit quietly in one until she'd recovered, with no one the wiser. It seems unlikely that she'd turn to a friend—no one has come forward, at any rate. I'll try to bring Melton back to England for questioning. Although since he's made no effort to contact me, I don't have much hope in that direction. At least we have a witness who puts him there with Mrs. Evanson. We've tried to find others, but the stationmaster tells us it was very busy, and a weeping woman seeing a soldier off is too common. People try to pass by without looking, give them a modicum of privacy."

"If he's Jack Melton's brother," Simon commented, "he can't claim he didn't know she'd been killed."

I confessed, "I've told his brother about seeing a man with Marjorie the night she died. But I didn't know then who he was. I was trying to help Jack Melton get to the truth before his wife did. She's frantically searching for someone to blame. Serena Melton is likely to do something rash. And it won't bring her brother back."

Inspector Herbert was staring at me, weighing up what I was saying.

"Yes. Well. I don't think any harm has been done." He leaned forward, his elbows on his cluttered desk. "Since you didn't know his brother, and you aren't likely to meet him, Commander Melton won't be unduly worried. The likelihood is that his brother hasn't confessed his adultery, anyway. Especially if he learned Mrs. Evanson was murdered that evening. Is Captain Melton married, do you know?"

"Yes." It was Simon who answered. "So I've been informed. There are two children."

"All the more reason to keep his—relationship—from everyone. Doesn't speak well of his character, does it?" Inspector Herbert turned to me. "It's amazing that you found this photograph. Well done."

I said, giving credit where it was due, "It was Sergeant-Major Brandon who put a name to the face."

Inspector Herbert smiled. "You can safely leave this matter to us now. Which reminds me, about Michael Hart—"

I had done enough damage, talking out of turn. "I see no reason for him to lie. If he says he was shot at, then he was. The local people will probably discover it was boys who came across their father's service revolver and were tempted to try it." I cast about quickly for a way to change the course of the conversation. "You haven't told me—has that man from Oxford been found?"

"He was apprehended in Derby. I don't think we need to concern ourselves with him any longer."

"And Lieutenant Fordham?"

"Ah. That's another matter."

I waited, and after a moment he said finally, "Lieutenant Fordham knew Marjorie Evanson in London, before she was married. His mother was a friend of her late aunt's. As he had never married, we wondered if the friendship had been renewed while he was convalescing. Mrs. Evanson escorted him to medical appointments on a number of occasions. He was one of several wounded she volunteered to work with. She would meet a train, see that the patient got to his destination and then back to the train."

That explained why no one in Little Sefton knew of him, and why Marjorie's staff didn't know the name.

They had been hired after her marriage to Meriwether Evanson. Michael had helped select them.

But why had she let her aunt's staff go?

It seemed that everything I learned generated more questions.

I thanked Inspector Herbert, and he nodded.

"Finding this photograph was a piece of luck. We've been on the point of setting this inquiry aside for lack of new information." He smiled ruefully at Simon. "You'd think, in a time of war, when England is fighting for her life, people would put their petty differences aside and work together. But crime never goes away. We're shorthanded here at the Yard, but the number of cases seems to climb by the day."

It was a way of reminding us that he was busy. But I had one more question for him. "Captain Fordham," I said. "How did he die? You never told me the outcome of your investigation."

At first I thought he would tell me it was police business and not mine. But he said, "That's a very odd affair. There is a small lake on the Fordham property. At one end a bridge crosses to an island just large enough for a stone table and benches. Summer picnics and that sort of thing. As far as we can determine, he walked out onto that bridge one evening and shot himself. He went over the low parapet into the water, but he was already dead. The weapon went with him, and we haven't found it yet. The water is rather deep just there and quite murky."

"Was it really a suicide?" I asked.

"We believe now that it must have been. But we can't be sure. No note, you see, and his family can't think of a reason for him to take his own life. He didn't use his service revolver. That was still in the armoire with his uniform. He was wearing trousers and a white shirt when he died. His family is adamant that he wasn't grieving over Mrs. Evanson. They refuse even to consider suicide."

"Which leaves murder? Or was his wound severe enough to drive him to do something drastic?"

"A stomach wound," he said. "Very unpleasant, I'm told." He reached for a folder, pulling it in front of him but not opening it. A sign that our visit had ended.

We exchanged polite farewells.

Dismissal as well, telling me that the Yard no longer required my efforts.

He rose as I did, reached across the desk to shake hands with Simon Brandon, and came around to accompany us to the door, where a constable was waiting to see us out of the Yard.

Simon had nothing to say until we had reached his motorcar, and then he turned to me before he opened my door.

"It was really very clever of you to discover who the officer with Marjorie Evanson was."

"It was more a matter of seeing what was before me. And of course making Alicia's acquaintance in the first place. She wouldn't have thought to show those photographs to an inspector from the Yard. I don't think her husband knows Raymond Melton, by the way. Alicia did recognize the other two men. He probably just happened to be with one of the other men at that crossroads." I smiled, remembering. "I like Alicia. She's been busy matchmaking, you know. She suspects there's a growing attachment between Michael Hart and me. There was, of course—a murder."

Simon laughed in spite of himself. "You're impossible," he said, opening my door.

And then he was suddenly quite serious, one hand on my arm to make certain I was paying attention. "But mark me, Miss Elizabeth Alexandra Victoria Crawford, you will heed the advice of Inspector Herbert and leave the death of Mrs. Evanson to the proper authorities to solve. You're in enough danger in France; I don't wish to spend every leave pulling you out of trouble before it comes to your mother's ears!"

He invariably brooked no nonsense when he used my full name.

I wisely said nothing.

When he got behind the wheel, he added for good measure, "And that includes the suicide of the unfortunate Captain Fordham."

I was actually thinking about his death and wondering if the weapon would ever turn up, deep end of that lake or not.

As if he'd read my mind, which I was sometimes convinced he could do, Simon turned to me and said, "Bess."

Chapter Thirteen

I spent the afternoon in Mrs. Hennessey's apartments ironing the uniforms I'd soon be packing to take back to France. It was cooler there, and getting the collars and cuffs stiff enough was always hard work. I had had to do one set over again.

Mrs. Hennessey was having tea with one of her friends. I was grateful for the use of her iron, and having to concentrate on what I was doing kept my mind from dwelling on Marjorie Evanson and Captain Fordham.

Simon had gone to his club, refusing to leave London without me.

"If I do, you'll just get up to mischief of some sort," he'd told me.

"You aren't showing up in the Marlborough Hotel, to sit across the room and scowl at poor Captain

Truscott, are you?" I'd demanded before shutting the door behind me. "The poor man's hands shake badly enough as it is."

"Captain Truscott appears to be a decent enough sort. No, I'll wait here on the street to make certain he brings you home at a reasonable hour. Mrs. Hennessey may even ask me in for tea."

I slammed the door in his face, and heard him laughing all the way back to the motorcar.

Ironing cuffs and aprons isn't a soothing activity. By the time I was dressed and waiting for Captain Truscott to call, I was not in the mood for dinner and was beginning to wonder why on earth I'd been so eager to see him again.

He arrived on the dot, and Mrs. Hennessey, bless her, climbed the stairs to our flat and told me he was waiting.

He smiled as I came down, saying, "It was good to see you again. I'm looking forward to dinner."

Frederick Truscott turned out to be a very nice dinner partner. It made up for the Marlborough's very indifferent menu. We had a number of friends in common, and that kept conversation rolling comfortably all the way to the hotel. "I've borrowed Terrence Hornsby's motor," he told me. "And so, like Cinderella, I must have you at home before the stroke of twelve. He's driving to Wales tonight to visit his family."

"I haven't seen him in ages! How is he?"

"Bullet clipped his ear. Still looks rather raw there, but he's glad it wasn't his head. He says he needed it, although some of his friends are in serious debate over that."

Which sounded just like Terrence. I laughed.

While we were on the subject of absent friends, I said quite casually, "I only discovered today that Jack Melton's brother is a serving officer. A captain in the Wiltshire Fusiliers. I don't think Jack mentioned him when we were at Melton Hall."

"Someone told me they were estranged, though not why. I've never met him."

"He's married, I think?"

"I couldn't say."

We swapped other names, and then, against my better judgment I asked, "Did you know Captain Fordham?"

His face lost its humor. "Sadly I did. A loss there. He was a good officer."

"Was he by any chance acquainted with Marjorie Evanson?"

"Strange you should mention that. The police asked his family about a connection when they came to inquire into his death. Apparently he did know her."

"How well?"

"I've no idea, really. Marjorie was good company. I was fond of her myself." Changing the subject, he asked, "When do you go back to France?"

"In another five days."

"Bad luck. I leave the day after tomorrow. Said my good-byes at home and came up to London to put that parting behind me. Easier that way. Where is your family?"

"Somerset. I haven't spent as much time with them as I'd promised."

"Was that your elder brother in the motorcar with you?"

"Good heavens, no. That's Simon Brandon. He was my father's sergeant-major at the end of his career."

A light dawned behind his eyes. "You're not Colonel Richard Crawford's daughter, are you?" When I nodded, guessing what was coming, Captain Truscott said, "My God. He was a fine officer. We've a man in the Fusiliers who served under him. He knows more about planning battles than half the general staff."

I could agree with that. There had been complaints that the generals were fighting the wars of the past. My father and Simon often refought the battle of the Somme over cigars, and it always put them in a rotten mood.

We discussed my father for a bit, and then suddenly, we'd finished our pudding, drunk our tea in the comfortable lounge, and it was time to go.

I said, as we walked through Reception and out of the hotel, "Can you think of any good reason for Captain Fordham to kill himself?"

"I don't know that we need a reason," Freddy Truscott answered somberly. "What keeps you going is your men. You don't let them down. Fordham lost most of his men in a charge ordered against a section of line that reconnaissance had indicated was poorly defended and certain to fold. But the Germans had put in a concealed machine-gun nest during the night, and they held their fire until Fordham and his men were within easy range. They were wiped out—he was one of only a handful of wounded who somehow made it back to their own lines. The rest were dead before they knew what they were up against. He blamed himself for trusting HQ. He felt he'd betrayed the dead, and refused all treatment when they got him back to the nearest aid station. One of the nursing sisters put a needle into his arm and that was that. He was more sensible when he came out of surgery."

I recalled the incident—although I hadn't known it was Captain Fordham who'd fought the nursing staff. Diana had been there, had witnessed the struggle to treat the wounded man, and she had told us about it. Even she hadn't learned why the officer had gone mad, only that in spite of his severe injuries he'd fought like a tiger.

But this went far to explain Fordham's suicide. Still, if he'd been intent on taking his own life, why wait until he was nearly mended?

Trying for a lighter note on which to end the evening, I asked Freddy if I could write to him in France.

He said, "I was trying to get up the courage to ask just that."

And then it was time to say good-bye. As we stood outside the door of Mrs. Hennessey's house, I wished him safe in France and he held my hand longer than was needful. "Thank you, Bess, for a happy evening. I've enjoyed it more than I can say."

With that he was gone, walking to the borrowed motorcar with swift strides, not looking back even as he drove away. I watched him go, watched his taillights vanish around the far corner of our street, and with a sigh, said a silent prayer that he would come home whole. Then I turned and went inside. Where had Simon got to?

I hadn't learned a great deal about Raymond Melton, and only a little about Lieutenant Fordham.

But as I climbed the stairs to my flat, calling good night to Mrs. Hennessey who had come out to ask me if I'd enjoyed my evening, I wondered why Jack Melton and his brother were estranged. Because he knew what sort of person Raymond Melton was?

What had been the fascination there for Marjorie? Attention when she needed comforting, her fears for Meriwether smoothed away? Sometimes very cold men could be utterly charming when it served their purpose. I preferred someone like Michael Hart, who made no bones about flirting, enjoying it and expecting no harm to come of it.

Like the woman at the garden party, I remembered as I drifted into sleep. Henry's wife, who had been amused by Michael's flattery, gave it back in full measure, and made both of them laugh.

Someone was knocking at the flat door. I heard it in my dreams before I realized that the sound was real. Surfacing from sleep, I tried to think what time it was, and if I'd overslept. I fumbled for my slippers and my dressing gown and made my way through the dark flat. But the windows told me it wasn't the middle of the night, as I'd first thought, or late morning. Dawn had broken and the first rays of the sun were touching the rooftops opposite.

I opened the door to Mrs. Hennessey, her gray hair in a long plait that fell down over the collar of her dressing gown.

"What is it? What's the matter?" I asked, thinking she must be ill.

"My dear, it's Sergeant-Major Brandon. He says it's most urgent that he speak to you. I do hope it isn't your parents—"

My mind was racing ahead of me as I brushed past her and went headlong down the stairs, nearly flinging myself into Simon's arms as I tripped on the last three steps.

"What is it?" I said again, tensed for the blow to come.

"I told Mrs. Hennessey not to frighten you," he said, angry. "It's a police matter, but important enough to make sure you were safely here."

Mrs. Hennessey had seen me come in. She could have told Simon—and then I realized that he had been frowning with worry until he saw me on the stairs.

"Do you know a Mrs. Calder?" he continued, and I tried to concentrate on what he was saying.

"Calder? Yes—she's a friend of Marjorie's. Marjorie Evanson."

"She was attacked last night and nearly killed."

"She—" I began and had to stop to catch my breath. "*Nearly* killed?"

Mrs. Hennessey had made her way down the stairs and said to Simon, "If you wish to use my sitting room—"

He thanked her and we went into her flat, where a lamp was burning in the small room where she sat in the evening. She asked if we'd like a cup of tea, but Simon shook his head. With that she left us alone, but knowing Mrs. Hennessey, she wouldn't be far, even though she knew that Simon was a family friend. Her staunch Victorian upbringing wouldn't allow her to eavesdrop, but she would be able to hear if I screamed or had to fight for my virtue, since I was not properly dressed to receive a gentleman.

Simon must have read my mind because he smiled grimly and said, "You had better sit over there. God forbid that we should not observe the proprieties."

I sat down on one side of the hearth and he took the chair on the other.

"Mrs. Calder?" I reminded him.

"She had gone to dine with friends. Mr. and Mrs. Murray put her into a cab at the end, and she went directly to her house. That's been established. But she didn't go in. The maid waiting up for her was drowsing in her chair, but she would have heard any disturbance on the doorstep."

"Then it was someone Mrs. Calder knew," I said. "She wouldn't have gone anywhere with a stranger, not after what happened to Marjorie Evanson." I tried to think. "Have the police found the cabbie?"

"They have, and he doesn't recall anyone walking along the street or standing in the shadows of a tree. But he's an old man, he might not have noticed. At any rate, she got down at Hamilton Place, paid the cabbie, and the last he saw of her, she was walking toward her door. An hour later, a constable walking through Hamilton Place heard something in the square, and alert man that he is, went to investigate. He discovered Mrs. Calder lying in a stand of shrubbery, stabbed and bleeding heavily. She's in hospital now and undergoing surgery. No one has been able to question her. But she wasn't robbed or interfered with in any way. Because of the unsolved attack on Mrs. Evanson, someone, probably the Metropolitan police, thought to bring in Inspector Herbert."

"Oh, dear." I put my hands up to my face, pressing them against the flesh, trying to absorb everything Simon was telling me. And then I realized that it *was* Simon telling me. Letting my hands fall I said, "How is it that you know all this?"

"Inspector Herbert put in a call to Somerset—he must have thought you were going directly home, but he was taking no chances. You father called me at my club. I came directly here." He paused. "Bess. How much did this Mrs. Calder know about Marjorie Evanson's love affair? Did she know the name of the man?"

"She told me she didn't—" But Serena Melton believed Mrs. Calder knew more than she wished to tell even the police. That she found her cousin Marjorie's behavior distasteful and was trying to distance herself from it. "Serena Melton believes she does. And if that's true, someone else could as well." Michael Hart had not suggested we talk to Helen Calder. The thought rose like a black shadow in my mind. Had he believed that if Helen knew the name of the man Marjorie had been seeing, it was possible that she also knew Marjorie intended to meet him that evening?

I pushed the thought away. There could be a little jealousy there, because Helen really was a cousin, and Michael was not. But the thought lingered.

Simon was saying, "The police can't be certain that her attack is related to Mrs. Evanson's death, but they're treating it as likely."

"She must know who it was. She isn't the kind of woman who would take risks. Is she—will she survive?" With critical stabbing wounds, infection was often the deciding factor in living or dying.

Simon shook his head. "It's touch and go, I should think. My first responsibility was to look in on you. To see if you'd also been lured out into the night. Mrs. Hennessey couldn't stop a determined killer."

He was right. If someone knew just what to say—that my mother had suddenly taken ill or something had happened to Simon or my father—I'd go with them. Especially if I thought Mrs. Hennessey had allowed them in this emergency to come directly to my door. It would never occur to me that she was already dead. What, then, had someone said to Mrs. Calder that made her turn away from her door and follow him—or her?

"I'm wide awake," I said. "It's no use going back to bed. Do you think, if we went to the hospital, Matron might tell me about the surgery and what the prognosis is for Helen Calder?"

"It's worth trying."

I left him there in the sitting room and went up to dress. I decided to wear my uniform, though I sighed when I put on the nicely starched cuffs and apron that I'd ironed only hours ago.

Simon drove me to St. Martin's Hospital, where we made our way to the surgical wards. But Mrs. Calder was still in surgery, I was told, and not expected to be brought into the ward until she was stable.

I asked where she had been stabbed, but the sister I spoke with shook her head. "I haven't seen her file. Only that I'm to expect a female patient with repairs of severe knife wounds."

Frustrated, I went to where Simon was sitting in the room in which families awaited news, and said, "She isn't out of surgery yet. It could be some time."

"It was worth a try," he said. "I'll take you home and we'll come again in a few hours."

I was agreeable to that, but we met Inspector Herbert as we walked down the passage. He'd been in the small staff canteen helping himself to a cup of tea. He looked tired.

Surprised to see us there, he said to me, "You're in uniform."

"Indeed."

"I hope you weren't thinking of interviewing Mrs. Calder before the police spoke to her." He smiled, but it was also a warning.

"I was worried. I met her for the first time only a few days ago."

"Did you indeed?" He gave me his undivided attention. "And what did she have to say to you?"

"She couldn't give me the name of the man Mrs. Evanson had been seeing, but she'd been concerned for some time about what she believed to be a developing affair. And she was under the impression that Mrs. Evanson had broken it off several months before her death. Well before she could have known she was pregnant. But I didn't say that to Mrs. Calder."

I went on to tell him what little I knew.

Inspector Herbert nodded. "This time her purse wasn't taken, and so we had her identity at once. Then when the police went to inform her family, her mother said, 'Dear God, first Marjorie and now Helen.' That was when we made a connection between the two women, and I put in a call to Somerset." He looked down at the hat he was turning in his hands. "I must say, I never expected a second murder." He looked up again, and after a brief hesitation, he added, "The constable who found her said that she was barely conscious when he bent over her, but she spoke someone's name. Her voice lifted at the end, as if she were posing a question. 'Michael?' she said."

"Michael—" I repeated before I could stop myself. "Er—what is her husband's name?"

"Alan."

"Oh."

"Oh, indeed."

I said, "If you're thinking that Michael Hart did this, you're mistaken. He couldn't, given his injuries. Ask his doctor." I tried to remember. "A Dr. Higgins."

He'd given Michael permission to accompany me to London; he must know the case well enough to make such a judgment.

"I'll be speaking to his physician," he assured me. "But for all we know, he could be malingering."

I thought about the pain I'd read in Michael's eyes, the struggle with the sedatives. The whispers that he was addicted to them. But I didn't bring these matters up. My testimony would be considered biased.

"It will be hours before Mrs. Calder is awake," I told him. "If she's still in surgery now. We might as well all go back to bed."

But he shook his head. "That isn't what the Yard pays me to do. I'll be there the instant she opens her eyes."

Just then Matron came down the passage, calling to Inspector Herbert. "Mrs. Calder is being taken to a private room. She isn't awake and won't be for some time," she said, echoing what I'd just been telling him myself. "But you may go in and see her, if you wish."

He turned to accompany her. I gave Simon a swift glance and followed in Inspector Herbert's wake.

Matron was saying, "The damage is considerable, but we'll know more tomorrow. Whoever her attacker was, he stabbed her twice. She was wearing a corset, and luckily the staves deflected his knife. There is a laceration along her ribs, the bone scraped, cartilage torn, but the blade didn't reach her lung. Then he stabbed her in the stomach, and nearly succeeded in killing her."

We went into the small private ward, and looked down at the patient's wan face. I didn't think she'd be speaking to anybody for some time. She had lost quite a bit of blood, and the surgery had been stressful as well.

I studied her face. She was no longer the vigorous woman I'd seen only a day or so ago. Even with the bandages, she seemed to have shrunk into herself, thinner and somehow vulnerable. I felt a surge of pity. If she had been thrown into the river, as Marjorie Evanson had been, she wouldn't have survived at all.

Matron was saying, "You'll observe that she was also struck on the head from behind. We saw that injury as we were pulling her hair back." She gently turned Mrs. Calder's head and parted her heavy hair to show us the wound. "I would say that she was knocked unconscious and then cold-bloodedly stabbed while she was unable to defend herself."

"Then there's a chance she didn't see her attacker." Inspector Herbert bent down for a closer look.

"True." Matron eased the patient's head back onto the pillow and arranged her hair.

Inspector Herbert then turned to me. "Any thoughts?"

"You were at her house? The servants' entrance is just below her door—down the stairs behind the railing and into a kitchen passage, I should think." It was a common enough arrangement. "If someone waited there, the cabbie wouldn't have seen him. But he'd have had to be quiet."

"As the cabbie left, it might have covered the sound of his footsteps coming up," Inspector Herbert agreed. "I'll speak to one of my men; we'll see if another cab dropped off a passenger earlier. The question is, how did he know she was out? Or when she would return?"

"He may have been there earlier, and seen her leaving. And waited."

He nodded. "Whoever it was took a great risk. One cry and someone might have come to a window. Unless he persuaded her to walk into the square, then struck her from behind. That may be why she said the name Michael the way she did. As he came up the tradesmen's stairs, she must have been surprised and called out to him."

Matron gestured to us, and we walked out of the ward together, closing the door behind us. Inspector Herbert asked that an extra chair be brought to him, and he sat down before the closed door. He pointedly bade me good night.

I left, having pushed my luck as far as I thought it ought to go.

I accompanied Matron back to the hall where Simon was waiting, my mind busy with the problem of why a dying woman had spoken Michael's name. I went over what she'd said to me when I called on her. I hadn't brought up Michael's name—and neither had she.

Simon took me to the Marlborough Hotel and commandeered a breakfast for the two of us. I sat there toying with my food, thinking about Mrs. Calder.

"It makes no sense," I finally said aloud.

"It isn't supposed to. You aren't Inspector Herbert."

I smiled. "I don't think he's exactly happy with this turn of events either."

"Eat your breakfast."

I did as I was told. I wanted something from Simon and the easiest way to persuade him was to cooperate. At least the breakfast was better than the dinner the night before and I was hungry.

"How was your evening?" Simon asked, echoing my own thought.

"Captain Truscott is a very nice man. You needn't use that tone of voice."

"What tone of voice?"

"The one that sounds disapproving and nosy."

Simon laughed. "Actually, I think you're probably right about Truscott."

"He told me something about Captain Fordham that made a lot of sense."

He groaned. "I thought you'd been warned off that topic."

"I was. I can't help it if Freddy knew the man."

"I see. You'd better tell me."

I did. Simon nodded as I was finishing the account.

"He's right," Simon told me. "There's delayed shock, you know. As long as Captain Fordham was recovering from his wounds, he could put France out of his mind. But as soon as he knew he was nearly ready to return to the Front, the truth had to be faced."

"Then why didn't he use his service revolver?"

"I expect he didn't wish to. I expect he didn't feel he had a right to use it."

That was a very interesting observation.

I sighed. "Poor man."

"He wouldn't be the first. And he won't be the last. Don't you remember Color Sergeant Blaine? It was much the same story."

I did remember. It was in Lahore, and Color Sergeant Blaine was in hospital recovering from wounds. He slashed his wrists one night, without a word to anyone. And my father said Sergeant Blaine blamed himself for losing his men in an ambush on the Frontier. He felt, experienced man that he was, that he should have foreseen it. No one could have, my father told my mother. But Sergeant Blaine had never lost a troop before.

"You're very wise, Simon. But what became of the handgun that Captain Fordham used? Solve that mystery too."

"It's buried deep in the mud under the bridge where he was standing. It fell from his height and through the height of the bridge. Enough force to bury it in the soft soil at the bottom of the lake."

But the police had searched, and still hadn't found it.

I finished my tea, and sat back in my chair. "Will you drive me to Little Sefton? I'd like to speak to Lieutenant Hart before Inspector Herbert sees him."

"Do you think that's wise?" Simon asked.

"I don't know what's wise anymore. But Inspector Herbert has a second victim now. He's probably already under a good deal of pressure to take someone into custody. Michael Hart would solve all his problems. As soon as the inspector speaks to

Helen Calder, he'll order Michael's arrest. See if he doesn't!"

"That could be later this afternoon or evening. Are you convinced that Michael's shoulder wound is as serious as he claimed?"

"You know as well as I do that severely wounded men can go on to do heroic things before they collapse. He's a soldier, he could stab her if he had to—wanted to. What would be impossible for him to do is carry or drag her into the square afterward." I bit my lip, then added, because I knew Inspector Herbert was already considering it, "It could explain why she was found in the square and not taken to the river, as Marjorie was."

"Yes, I'd considered that myself." He signaled to the waiter. "I'll take you to Little Sefton, only because I feel safer with you under my eye. And then you'll go back to Somerset and stay there."

"I promise."

But I crossed my fingers behind my back, just in case.

Simon took me to Little Sefton, then did as I asked, driving away after leaving me on Alicia's doorstep. He was to return in precisely two hours. He wasn't happy with that arrangement, but I promised to stay with Alicia.

I had the excuse of returning the borrowed photograph, but I needn't have worried about my welcome.

She was delighted to see me. From the twinkle in her eye, I knew what she was thinking, that I couldn't stay away long because my heart was given to Michael Hart.

She said nothing about that as she led me into her sitting room, and asked if the photograph had helped.

"Indeed it has," I told her. "The only problem is, that officer is in France just now."

Looking at the photograph I'd given her, she said, "He looks like a nice sort. And if he's someone Gareth photographed, he must be all right."

I changed the subject, asking if the village had been reasonably quiet since my last visit.

"That's right, you haven't heard, have you?"

I knew what must be coming. "What's happened?"

"Michael Hart was walking in his aunt's garden. Pacing it, more likely. Mrs. King was passing by, and she said he had the face of a bear, so she didn't stop to speak. And not a quarter of an hour later, he went raging in to see Constable Tilmer, claiming someone shot at him. But Constable Tilmer couldn't find anyone who'd heard one shot, much less two. And with all the windows open because of the warm evening, you'd have thought someone must have heard it."

"What happened then?"

"Constable Tilmer searched the gardens and the back lanes, and told the Harts that all was well, the excitement was over. But Michael wouldn't hear of it. He demanded that the constable ring up Scotland Yard and report the incident directly. And then we all went home to bed and that was the end of it."

"Who could possibly want to shoot Lieutenant Hart?"

"That's what everyone is asking. Jason Markham claims it was a jealous husband." She laughed at that. "If so, he had very poor aim."

The village was taking the incident very lightly, finding amusement in it.

"But why should Michael make up such a story?"

"Too many drugs, everyone says. Hearing things." She shrugged.

"Is that true?"

"I don't know how the rumors got started. But they did. I imagine it was when Michael first came here to rest after they had worked on his shoulder. He wasn't himself at all—barely able to speak, and even when he did he didn't always make sense. Slept much of the day and paced his room at night—I could see for myself once or twice that his lights were on until the small hours. And his shadow passing between the lamp and the window, back and forth, back and forth. Even when he finally came outside where people could see him, he was pale and often sweating and his eyes looked right through you."

"Such wounds can be terribly painful. And the shoulder is awkward—difficult to sit down, difficult to lie down, difficult to stand. So you don't rest. Even when you're so sleepy you can hardly stay awake."

"I hadn't thought of it that way," Alicia admitted. "It sounds pretty grim, doesn't it?"

"It is grim," I said. "And something to help with the pain is necessary."

"He told the rector when he first came here that the next surgery would be drastic. And he didn't want to survive it."

I could understand. Michael was used to being noticed. He was handsome and charming and amusing. People enjoyed his company. But a man with only one arm was usually pitied, not admired. And amputation at the shoulder would be ugly.

Alicia suggested a walk, and I agreed, thinking that if Michael saw me with her, he might come out and speak to us, saving me from having to find a proper excuse for calling on him.

"It helps the day go by faster," she admitted as we leisurely strolled by the Hart house. "Walking, knitting, taking care of the gardens—anything is better than worrying about Gareth."

And I was right, not five minutes later, as Alicia and I were retracing our steps, Michael Hart came out his door and moved purposefully in our direction. We were just by the churchyard when he caught us up.

Alicia hastily recalled that she must have a word with the rector about flowers for the coming Sunday services, and left me alone.

"You came back," Michael said as soon as he was near enough.

I could see that he had taken his pain medication last night, for his eyes looked dull, and his hands shook a little.

"Alicia was just telling me about your narrow escape."

"Hardly that," he said, an edge to his voice. "Since I imagined the entire incident. I'm surprised Scotland Yard didn't call to inform you of my delusions."

It was too close to the truth for comfort.

"Yes, they do seek my advice regularly. They dare not make a move without me."

He had the grace to apologize. "I'm sorry. I wrenched my shoulder ducking the first shot. Afterward I had a long couple of nights."

Men who had been at the Front often ducked when a motorcar backfired or there was some other loud noise. It was a reflex action, learned to save their lives and not as easily unlearned in a peaceful setting like one's uncle's garden.

"And you never saw anyone. Or heard anything except for the shots?"

"You sound just like Constable Tilmer," he told me sourly. "If I'd seen who it was, I could have named him to the police. Or lacking that, described him."

"What makes you so certain it was a man?" I asked.

That gave him pause.

"I just assumed it was," he said after a moment.

"And why would someone shoot at you?"

"I don't know. Unless someone believes I learned something in London that made me a threat."

"Such as?"

He surprised me with his answer. "If someone learned that I went to Scotland Yard. He—she—could believe I went there to pass on information."

"Then why kill you now? If the Yard already knows what you've learned."

"I haven't worked that out yet."

"Are you sure you heard shots? I mean, as opposed to something that sounded very much like shots."

"I've spent two years in France. Do you think I'd confuse a farmer scaring crows with a shotgun for a pistol shot?"

"No."

I walked a little way toward the church, then turned again and walked back to where he was standing. "How did *two* shots miss you? *Both* of them?"

"Think what you like," he snapped and strode away.

I shook my head at his attitude, then hurried after him.

"Michael. Be sensible! Listen to me."

He stopped and turned a stony face toward me, already rejecting what I had to say.

"If whoever it was missed you both times, then it tells me the person aiming at you wasn't used to firearms and was either out of range or couldn't hold the weapon steady."

"I wouldn't put it past Victoria," he answered bitterly.

But I thought it was more likely to be Serena. She'd talked to Inspector Herbert. And so had Michael. For all I knew, she had seen him leaving the Yard.

If it was Serena, this could be the second time she'd fired at a human being. And the first time she had hit her mark, which would have frightened her if she hadn't intended murder.

"I remember the first time I fired a revolver. I missed the target and nearly hit a troop of monkeys in a tree. It was six weeks before they ventured that near again."

He was smiling at the story about the monkeys, but his mind wasn't on what I was saying.

"Did the police at least search for the spent bullets?"

"A cursory search. I went back later to look on my own. But it's a garden, for God's sake, and finding anything would be a miracle."

"Let's have a look together."

He was about to refuse me, but I stood there waiting, and finally he said disagreeably, "All right, then."

I wanted very much to tell him that handsome is as handsome does. But that would be sinking to the same childish level.

Still, I was tempted.

And what would Alicia think when she came back to find I'd gone off with Michael Hart? That her stratagem had worked?

We walked in silence to the house where he was staying with his aunt and uncle. The grassy path branched about three-quarters of the way to the door, and stepping-stones led to a gate in a well-trimmed hedge. Through that I found myself in a very pretty formal garden. Small boxwoods lined the paths in a geometric pattern, dividing the beds. Along the far side of the garden, matching the hedge at the front gate, was a bank of lilacs, which must have been beautiful in the spring, their fragrance wafting to the chairs set out on a narrow stone terrace, rising above two shallow steps.

"What's behind the lilacs?"

"The carriage drive to the stables. Beyond that a small orchard."

"So someone could have come as far as the lilacs without being seen."

"Yes. That was what the police suggested as well."

"And where were you standing?"

"I was in the center, by the little sundial, my back to the lilacs. The house had felt stuffy, and I'd come out here. But I couldn't sit still, so I walked as far as the sundial, stood there for several minutes, and was just turning back to the terrace when I heard the shots."

He was right. Finding the spent bullet amongst the beds of roses, peonies, larkspur, and other flowers in full bloom, much less the loamy earth they were set in, would be a miracle.

But I looked anyway. If only to satisfy my own ambivalence about whether or not there were any shots at all. I asked him to stand where he had been at the time, and then I cast about, looking under leaves, in the earth, even in the blossoms themselves. After ten minutes, he said impatiently, "I can't stand here much longer. You aren't going to find anything anyway. Let's sit on the terrace before I fall down." He did look rather gray in the face.

I am stubborn. Just ask the Colonel Sahib.

"Go ahead and sit. I'll look a little longer."

And five minutes later, my fingers, scything gently through the soil around a rosebush in the next bed over, came up with something hard. I picked it up, brushed it off, and looked at it.

It was a readily identifiable .45 bullet.

Triumphant, I carried it to Michael and dropped it into the palm of his hand.

"Persistence," I said simply.

He grinned at me. "And your fingers are filthy."

I regarded them wryly. "So they are."

"Now perhaps someone will believe me!"

But there still remained a shadow of a doubt. Michael Hart possessed his service revolver, and he could just as easily have fired that shot into the rose-bushes himself, in the hope that the police would believe his story.

I sighed. "I must go back to Somerset. I'm here on sufferance anyway. My family is convinced that you're a blackguard and I'm in danger of being shot in your company."

The grin deepened. "It's a lie. Your mother adored me. Stay, and I'll take you to dinner somewhere."

I shook my head. "Thank you, but I must go." I rose to leave, and then said, "Michael. What if we never discover who killed Marjorie? If the police can't do it, it's not likely that anyone else will succeed where they failed. And they keep jumping about, first this and then that likelihood. They won't keep searching forever."

"I'll keep looking if it takes me the rest of my life," he told me grimly. "I won't desert her as everyone else has."

I said good-bye and left. Alicia was watching for me, and smiled. "I saw you walking with Michael Hart to his aunt's garden. Beautiful, isn't it?"

I agreed and then told her I must return to Somerset.

She said, "You two didn't quarrel, did you?"

Several times, I answered silently, then told her, "He's not at his best today."

"Don't let that discourage you. I think he rather likes you."

I smiled and said, with heavy irony, "Thank you, Alicia. You send me away happier than when I arrived."

"Did he tell you," she went on, "that Victoria, Marjorie Evanson's sister, had a very public quarrel with him, just this morning. I don't know what precipitated it. He was walking toward the church when she stopped him and suddenly there were loud voices and everyone turned to see what was happening."

"What were they saying?"

"Marjorie was buried here in the churchyard. Did you know that? Not with her husband but with her family. When her body was released, Meriwether's sister refused to let her be laid to rest in their family plot. I don't know if Meriwether was told what her decision was. I think he'd have been very angry. But she told Victoria in no uncertain terms that Marjorie was no longer considered a part of their family."

I hadn't known that or I would have visited her grave when I was here for the garden party. But I should have guessed that Serena would carry her anger that far. She hadn't come to the service.

Alicia was saying, "At any rate, Victoria accused Michael Hart of spending too much time there. I know he's been there a few times, not what I would call an inordinate number, but she seemed to feel that having caused her sister so much grief in her life, it was keeping the scandal alive for him to be seen there so often."

"She believes that Michael Hart was the other man?"

"I think she's always been very jealous of the attachment between Marjorie and Michael. And so she thinks it was an unhealthy one."

"What does the rest of the village have to say?"

"They're of two minds, at a guess. Those who liked Marjorie believed the best of her. If she fell from grace, they say, it was out of loneliness. Those who are closer to Victoria and her father seem to think that Marjorie betrayed her family as well as her husband."

"Never mind what the truth might be?"

"Never mind," she agreed, nodding. With a sigh, she said, "I know how easy it is to fall from grace. I miss Gareth so terribly sometimes that I cry myself to sleep. I'm always afraid to answer the door, for fear Mr. Mason is on *my* doorstep this time, to deliver bad news. Sometimes after his leave is over and he's been gone for months, I can't quite remember the sound of my husband's voice, or see his face as sharply as I did before. And one day someone comes along who is kind, thoughtful, his touch is real, and he's *there*, and one is so hungry for companionship, for someone who admires one's hair or makes one laugh, or just brushes one's hand as he helps one into a motorcar, that one is susceptible. Suddenly one is alive again, and you tell yourself that you might well be a widow already and not even know it—"

She broke off, flushing with embarrassment. A little silence fell. Then she said, "I've never succumbed. I've been faithful in thought and deed. But I'd be lying if I said that I could throw the first stone at Marjorie." Wryly she added, "That's why I so enjoy your feelings for Michael. It lets me feel something vicariously."

Misreading my expression of annoyance, she said, "I've made you self-conscious, haven't I? I'm sorry. Let's change the subject."

"All right, then. Why would Victoria make such a public display of her feelings? Why not speak to Michael quietly, privately, and ask him to be more discreet?"

"I rather think she wants the world to see him as an adulterer. She wants him to be an object of contempt."

"Or she's jealous." I leaned back in my chair and regarded the ceiling. "Do you think Victoria might decide to shoot at him?"

"At Michael? But why should she?"

"I don't know," I told her truthfully. "Perhaps to frighten him. To make him leave Little Sefton and return to that clinic. To make him a laughingstock. Or to return to the idea of jealousy, to rid herself of him so that she wouldn't be reminded day in and day out that he still cares for Marjorie, but cares nothing for her?"

"I hadn't thought of it in that light," Alicia said, considering my words. "But she's always had an uncertain temper. Spoiled children often do. She might very well decide to shoot at him—knowing that she would miss him, I mean—just to be vindictive."

"Would you walk with me to the churchyard, and show me Marjorie's grave?"

"Yes, of course. Let me get my shawl." She was back in only a moment. I took one last look at the photograph I'd returned and then together we walked down the street to the churchyard.

There were any number of new graves, the earth still brown, and others where the grass was just a tender green. I tried not to think that for every man who died of wounds here in England, hundreds of others were buried in makeshift cemeteries in France.

The Garrisons were buried in a cluster of graves on the right side of the church. Besides Marjorie's mother and father, there was a brother who had died at the age of six, and her grandparents, two uncles and their wives and a number of older-generation Garrison relatives. Marjorie's grave was on the far side of her brother's, as if Victoria had elected to keep for herself the space that was next to her father. After all, Marjorie, the first to die, was in no position to argue.

There were colorful fresh flowers on the raw earth. I recognized some of them as varieties I'd seen in the garden belonging to Michael Hart's aunt and uncle. I could in a way understand Victoria's complaint, for these tokens were there for all to see and speculate about. They also pointed up the fact that Victoria hadn't planted any flowers by the headstone herself. There were pansies and forget-me-nots and other low-growing blossoms rampant on the other graves. Michael was making it plain that Marjorie didn't deserve to be ostracized by her family as well as her neighbors.

We were standing there together when the rector came around the corner of the church and spoke to us. He remembered me from the fete, and told me he was happy to see me again.

"Alicia has been rambling about in that empty house long enough," he went on. "It's nice that friends can come and stay. We hope we'll see more of you."

I smiled and thanked him.

Looking down at the grave, he said, "Did you know Mrs. Evanson?"

I told him the truth, that I had nursed her husband and brought him home to England to recover from his burns, and I left it at that.

"He was a very fine man," the rector told me. "The sort you're happy to see marrying one of the young women in your parish. A tragedy that he should die of his wounds after coming so far."

"Yes." I gestured toward the grave at my feet. "Tell me about his wife."

"A thoroughly nice young woman. I shouldn't wish to speak ill of the dead, but she was not really happy here. She didn't see eye to eye with her sister or her father. I never understood what lay behind that. I was glad when she made a life for herself in London."

"Did Victoria visit her there?"

"She went to London a few times," he said, frowning, "but I don't know that she visited Marjorie. I remember asking for news, once, when Victoria had been up to see a play. She told me she'd been too busy to call on her sister." He smiled sadly. "A shame, really, they had only each other."

He left us then, and Alicia said, "You know, you really ought to speak to Mrs. Eubanks. She's the rector's cook now, but she was the Garrisons' cook until she had words with Victoria's father and walked out. That was ages ago, before the war. I'd all but forgotten."

I glanced at the watch pinned to my apron. A cook would be starting preparations for dinner very shortly, but it wouldn't take long to ask my questions. "I'm so glad you remembered. And there's just time." I started for the rectory.

"I'll go with you!" Alicia said eagerly.

"No, that's probably not a good idea. If she's kept any secrets all these years, she might well not wish to make them public now. And you live in the village."

"But that's not fair—it was I who told you about her—"

"Alicia, think about it for a moment—"

She was angry. "I've helped you thus far. It's really unkind of you to shut me out now. And I was the one who introduced you to Michael."

"Alicia—"

"No. You've just used me, that's all. I should have guessed. Victoria said you would, you know. The day of the fair. I told her she was trying to make trouble, but I see now she was right." She turned and walked away, hurt and disappointed.

I felt my own anger rising. I liked Alicia, I wouldn't have upset her for the world. But thanks to Victoria's meddling, she had taken what I'd said in the worst possible light.

I called to her, told her I was sorry, but the damage had been done. She kept walking, and disappeared through her door without looking back. I started after her, and after a few steps, stopped. It was useless. Even if I could persuade her that I'd been wrong about Mrs. Eubanks, Alicia would think I was apologizing because

I still needed her help, not because I meant it. Otherwise she would have come back when I called to her. I couldn't help but wonder what else Victoria could have said, then recalled Alicia's parting words about Michael Hart. She had enjoyed matchmaking, but Victoria had poisoned that as well.

With a heavy heart I crossed the churchyard to the rectory gardens, and made my way to the kitchen yard and up the path to the outer door. It led into a passage littered with boots and coats and umbrellas that had seen better days, and thence into the kitchen.

I opened the door, and the woman up to her elbows in flour and dough looked up, ready to say something, then stopped short.

"Oh—you aren't Rector. If you're looking for him, he should be in the vestry just now. At the church."

"Are you Mrs. Eubanks?" I asked. But of course she must be. Short and compact, she was graying, although her face was unlined. I put her age at perhaps fifty-five.

"I am. And who might you be, Miss?"

"My name is Elizabeth Crawford. I'm a nursing sister, and one of my patients was Lieutenant Meriwether Evanson," I began. "I was with the convoy that brought him to England for treatment of his burns."

I explained that I was visiting with Mrs. Dalton, and she nodded. "I think I saw you with her at the garden fete."

"Yes, I was here then as well."

"The poor man. We heard that he barely survived a fortnight after his wife's death. I met him a time or two, you know. He came here to speak to Rector in regard to marrying Miss Marjorie."

"I've been learning a little about her as well. Alicia Dalton said that you could tell me more about her than anyone else in Little Sefton. Would you mind?"

We talked for a while about the Evansons, and it was clear that Mrs. Eubanks would have been glad to go to London with them as their cook, but she had already, as she said, "gotten used to Rector's little ways, and he to mine."

"I understand there was no love lost between Marjorie and her sister."

Mrs. Eubanks's lips thinned into a hard line. After a moment she said, "I know Rector preaches that it's wrong to hate anyone, but I come as close to that as never mind when it comes to Miss Victoria. She's a piece of work." She had been making dough as I came in, and now she turned it out onto a floured board, and began to knead it vigorously. I hoped it wouldn't be tough as nails as a result.

"Was she always so rude?"

Mrs. Eubanks turned her head to listen, decided that no one could overhear us, and said, "Rudeness isn't the half of it. My sister Nancy, God rest her soul, worked with Dr. Hale, and when Miss Marjorie's dear mother went into labor prematurely, he took Nancy with him to help. She was very good with women in labor and newborns. She had that way about her."

"Did she? That's a gift."

"To be sure it is. Well, Mr. and Mrs. Garrison had only been married the seven months when Miss Marjorie was born, and she had that breathing trouble that so often carries off those little ones born before their time. But my sister and Dr. Hale kept her alive, and though she was sickly for months, she survived and began to thrive. It was a miracle, and Mr. Garrison paid my sister handsomely for her services, so grateful he sang her praises to everyone who would listen."

I couldn't quite see where this was going, but I looked encouraging and hoped she would continue. But she set aside the dough and put the kettle on, as if the subject were finished.

"I could do with some tea," she said, getting out cups and the milk pitcher, and a bowl of precious honey to sweeten it. Then she went to a cupboard and brought out a plate of biscuits.

That done, she and I sat down at the table, and she picked up the thread of her story. "All was well, then. The next child, a little boy, was born in winter with a weak chest as well, and he didn't live very long. After that came Victoria, and she was a lusty, healthy little one, kicking and crying with such strength, you wouldn't believe it possible. There was only four years difference in their ages, and Miss Marjorie adored her sister. But when Victoria was about twelve, their mother died."

The kettle was on the boil, and Mrs. Eubanks stopped to make the tea. When she had poured our cups, she sat down again.

"Miss Marjorie and her mother were always close, I expect because she nearly died. And Miss Victoria was closer to her father, they were always out and about together. She followed him everywhere, as soon as she could walk. Slowly, with malice, that girl set out to turn her father against her sister. Little things at first, the spilled milk, the broken vase, any small mishap, and it was blamed on Miss Marjorie. Even when the old dog died. Victoria swore Miss Marjorie had poisoned it. When she was old enough to understand such things, she told her father she didn't believe that Miss Marjorie was his true daughter, that her mother must have been pregnant when she married. And she would point out little things—the fact that Miss Marjorie looked more like her mother, and not at all like her father—I don't know what all. The housekeeper was a friend of mine, and she'd tell me tales that made me want to cry. But in the end, Victoria Garrison got her way, and Mr. Garrison came to hate his own daughter, hated the sight of her, and nothing her mother could say changed his mind. Miss Victoria had her father's love, but now she wanted all of her mother's, and when she saw she wasn't going to get it, she made the poor woman's life a misery. And her father stood by, letting her do it. It was as if he didn't have the courage to come right out and attack his wife himself. But he enjoyed seeing her unhappy."

In spite of the tea, I felt cold. "How vicious!" I said. "Are you sure—"

"Oh, I'm sure. Once I found Miss Marjorie sitting in a corner of the rectory porch, crying her eyes out and wet to the skin. Her sister had flung a pan of hot water at Miss Marjorie, then told her father that Miss Marjorie had spilled it on purpose to get Miss Victoria into trouble. I took her home and dried her off in my kitchen and fed her her dinner there too, before sending her up the back stairs of her own house to her bed. The next morning her father wouldn't let her eat her breakfast until she'd apologized for lying."

"But did you tell the rector—anyone—what was going on?"

"I thought about it, but I could do more for the child than Rector could, because I was there. And if I'd told, I'd have been sacked. Mr. Garrison had been a wonderful man, stern but fair, but he'd changed, he was cruel and cold. Then after his wife died, he turned bitter. You might say a child couldn't do such things, but she did."

"Then what happened?"

"When the will was read, Mrs. Garrison's, I mean, she'd left money to Miss Marjorie, and as soon as she was of age she walked out the door of that house, went to London, and never set foot in it again. Even when her father died and she came for his service, she stayed here in the rectory."

"You've given me food for thought," I told Mrs. Eubanks. "And I'll keep what you've told me in strictest confidence."

"Oh, you can tell whoever you like. I don't mind. Mr. Garrison is dead himself now. And there's nothing Miss Victoria can do to me. Rector wouldn't let me go for a dozen Miss Victorias. He'd not know where to find anything and would starve to death if he had to cook for himself or do the wash." She was secure in her own worth. But I wondered if she'd have spoken quite so freely in Alicia Dalton's presence. It was one thing to assert that the rector would keep her on, but the parish priest served at the discretion of his vestry.

"Tell me about your sister."

"Nancy died young. Her and Dr. Hale were killed one icy morning coming back from a difficult lying in. Mare slipped first, then overturned the carriage, and horse, carriage, and my sister went into the river. Dr. Hale was thrown out and his back was broken. He lived a few hours, long enough to tell everyone what had happened. Otherwise I'd not have been surprised to find Miss Victoria had had something to do with the accident—young as she was."

The venom in her voice was palpable. I think she had talked to me not because I'd known Marjorie's husband but because this had been bottled up inside for so long it was like a boil in need of lancing, the pressure was so great and so painful.

"How old was she at that time?" I couldn't help it, I had to know. The story had left me shocked as it was.

"Fourteen."

We finished our tea. I saw Mrs. Eubanks eyeing the chicken, ready to garnish and put into the oven, and I knew that now she'd told her story, she was ready to get back to work on the rector's dinner.

I thanked her and rose to leave. She said, "I don't lie, Miss Crawford. I never did. What I told you is the truth. Not that it matters now with Miss Marjorie gone, and all. But it's been on my mind of late, hearing of how she died."

I left her to her cooking and walked around the rectory toward the road. I had hardly got to the end of the rectory's drive when I saw policemen just coming out of the Harts' house, and between two constables walked Michael Hart, his face black as a thundercloud. In front of them strode Inspector Herbert, mouth grim, eyes looking neither right nor left.

Chapter Fourteen

I stood there rooted to the spot, not sure what to say
or do for all of several seconds.

And then I was striding across the street and brush-
ing past Victoria Garrison, who was standing in the
middle of it, a gloating expression on her face.

She said, as I passed her, in a voice pitched for my
ears only, "He's going to the hangman, and there's
nothing you can do to prevent it."

I ignored her. She wasn't the only person watching
as Lieutenant Hart was being taken into custody. Alicia
was there, looking stricken, and others I recognized
from the church fete.

I caught up with Inspector Herbert as he came
through the Harts' gate. He started with surprise when
he saw me, then glowered.

"What are you doing in Little Sefton, Miss Crawford?"

"Visiting friends," I snapped, "and it's just as well I'm here to tell you you're making a mistake."

"Mrs. Calder isn't completely out of danger and they are keeping her sedated. But the doctors and the nursing sisters have told me that as she rouses a little, she repeats the name Michael over and over again. When she does, she's restless, and they believe she's afraid in whatever limbo she's in. A deeply rooted residual fear from her attack that she can't face."

It made sense, of course, but I wasn't ready to give up so easily.

"Nonsense," I said briskly. "That's merely one interpretation. I've sat beside men who were hardly more than boys, as they recover from surgery. They call for their mothers—or if they're married, sometimes for their wives. Am I to believe that these soldiers feel their mothers are responsible for their wounds?"

"It's not the same," he began.

"How can you be so certain? I've never once heard them cry out the name of a German soldier or the Kaiser."

"You're being ridiculous." But I could see he was weakening.

By this time Michael and his escort had caught up with us. He said sharply, "Elizabeth. Stay out of this."

"Oh, do hush," I retorted, barely glancing at him. Turning again to Inspector Herbert, I asked, "What other evidence do you have that Lieutenant Hart is guilty of murder?"

"He was in London the night that Marjorie Evanson died. And again last night."

I turned to Michael, surprise in my face. "But that's impossible!"

He had the grace to look ashamed. "I'm sorry—"

"We found the marks. He dragged her. He's strong enough to do that one-handed. He gripped the collars of her clothing and dragged her into those shrubs. We found the bits of grass and earth on the heels of her shoes."

I swallowed hard. "And no one saw him? It was a summer's evening, and no one was looking out a window on Hamilton Place, to see a man loitering or to see him with Mrs. Calder, or in the square?"

"No one. I had men canvassing the street at eight o'clock this morning."

"How did he get to London? He required permission from his doctors before I could take him there."

"If you'll step out of the way, Miss Crawford, we'll finish our business here and take Lieutenant Hart to London."

Behind them I could see Michael's aunt in the door, her face white, her hand to her mouth. Next to her stood her husband, his face pale with shock.

I turned to Michael. "Who took you to London? Whose motorcar did you use?"

"My own," he said harshly. "Victoria agreed to drive me."

I stepped back, then. "Where was she when you were supposed to be killing Mrs. Calder?"

"Ask her. I left her at the theater. She wanted to see *The Man Who Vanished.*"

I whirled on Inspector Herbert. "Have you verified that?"

"I spoke to Miss Garrison earlier. She paid for her ticket, handed it in, and took her seat. That much is certain. She was waiting outside the theater when Lieutenant Hart was to return for her. I have three witnesses to that."

A voice behind me said, "Let it go, Bess."

It was Simon. I didn't know he had already come back for me. I said, "But—"

And he repeated, "Let it go."

I took a deep breath and moved out of Inspector Herbert's path. He went directly to the motorcar he had waiting, and Michael passed me without a glance, taking his place in the vehicle as ordered. One of the constables was driving, and he slowly moved through the spectators cluttering the street; I felt like bursting into tears.

Not from frustration but from anger. Helpless, furious anger. At Inspector Herbert, at Victoria Garrison, and at Michael Hart as well.

I let Simon guide me to where he'd left his motorcar and got in without a word.

"I'm sorry, Bess," he said as he stepped in beside me. "Truly."

"He's not guilty. Inspector Herbert will come to his senses and realize that for himself."

"Very likely." Looking over my shoulder, I could see Alicia. Her expression was pity vying with doubt.

"You don't mean that. You're just trying to make me feel better," I added, as the village disappeared behind us.

"I'm not, my dear girl. I'm agreeing with you."

I glanced at him, and saw that he was telling me the truth.

"I thought you didn't care for the handsome lieutenant," he said after a time. "You certainly put up a brave defense on his behalf."

"I respect the fact that a Scotland Yard inspector has a great deal more experience in these matters than I have, but he's been floundering from the start, Simon.

There could be any number of reasons why Mrs. Calder is saying Michael's name over and over again. Inspector Herbert should have waited until she could speak before taking any action. What's more, it could be that Victoria is lying."

But I knew she wasn't. The police had already looked into that too.

Then where had Michael gone, when he left her at the theater?

Simon glanced at me. "If he's innocent, Bess, Inspector Herbert will have to let him go. You needn't worry."

I closed my eyes, trying to read Michael's face as the policemen had brought him out. I could see it still, and what I read there was anger, not innocence. He hadn't protested, I had. And I could feel my cheeks burn with the memory.

Not because I was ashamed of my defense of him. But because I knew that Inspector Herbert would see it very differently. Like everyone else who had been a witness to that scene, to him it would point to my feelings for Michael, rather than any objectivity on my part.

And then I knew what I had to do. There might not be another chance. "Please—Simon—I must go back. It's important," I told him urgently.

He slowed, but said, "It's not wise, Bess."

It took several minutes to convince him, but in the end he reluctantly turned back toward Little Sefton. I touched his arm in silent gratitude.

The crowd had dispersed, although a few people stood about in knots, whispering. I ignored their stares as we passed.

I left Simon in the motorcar and went up the walk to the Harts' door. Someone had already begun to draw the drapes, as if trying to shut out the stares of neighbors.

Feeling every eye in Little Sefton pinned to my back, I knocked at the door, and after a time, an elderly maid opened it and told me that the family was not receiving today.

"I understand," I began.

And then Mr. Hart was in the passage behind her, saying, "It's all right, Sarah. Let her come in."

He led me into the drawing room, the walls painted a pleasing yellow with white trim and a soft green in the drapes. They had been pulled, making the room seem dark and rather claustrophobic. As if he sensed my reaction, Mr. Hart went to a table and lit the lamp sitting there.

He appeared to have aged, his face still pale, lines etched more deeply than I remembered.

I said, "Forgive me. I'm so sorry to intrude."

"You defended him out there."

"I don't believe he's guilty. Could you tell me what the police said, and what happened when they told Michael what they wanted to do?"

"I feel it's my fault," he said, taking the chair across from mine. "He'd asked me again if I would take him up to London. But I wasn't very keen on driving that far, and besides, this is our busiest time at the farm. I asked him why it was so important to go just then. He told me he needed to speak to Helen Calder. I don't know if you're aware of it, but she's related to Marjorie on her mother's side. He didn't say why, only that he wanted to see her in person, rather than telephone her. It was an arduous trip for him—the last time, after he'd gone there with you, he was exhausted for two days."

In my mind's eye, I could still see Helen Calder lying there on her cot, pale and unresponsive after her surgery.

"I don't understand; if it was so important, why didn't he call on her when I drove him to London?"

Mr. Hart shook his head. "Michael has always been impetuous. It might not have mattered then, you know. And with this wound, he seems to be unable to settle to anything. I know he's in great discomfort at times. I hear him pacing at night. The doctors think he's developing a tolerance to the sedatives he's been given, and it requires higher and higher doses to help now."

I wondered what relief he'd be given in a prison infirmary or cell.

"Did he tell Inspector Herbert about wanting to see Mrs. Calder?"

"I'm afraid—in my ignorance, you see—that I told him. Michael was sleeping when they came, and his aunt went to rouse him. Sometimes that's difficult. Meanwhile, the police asked if he'd just returned from London, and I told the inspector that he had. I was asked why he'd gone to London, and I told them. I saw no reason not to, and I had no way of knowing why they were here."

And that had been damning.

"Were you present when they questioned your nephew?"

"Oh, yes, I insisted on being present. We've always had him in our care, you see, and I could tell from Michael's face that something must be wrong."

"Did he tell them he'd spoken to Mrs. Calder?"

"He told them he'd gone to her house, and apparently they already knew that. But she wasn't at home. He told the maid at the door that he would wait for a time. But after a while his shoulder was hurting badly, and he left." Mr. Hart took a deep breath. "Inspector

Herbert told me Mrs. Calder is very seriously injured and hasn't regained consciousness after her surgery."

"It's true. We can only hope that when she does, she'll remember who attacked her and why."

But even as I said the words, I knew it was very unlikely that Mrs. Calder would remember anything after leaving her friend's house. Not after such loss of blood and the ensuing surgery. The mind has a way of blotting out what it doesn't wish to think about.

"I must apologize for asking this," I said, "but it's important. Had Michael been violent as a child? Angry, moody, sometimes acting rashly? Or has he acted this way only on his leaves from France?" If there was anything like that in his Army records, it would be used against him.

"No, no," Mr. Hart said, alarmed. "There's been nothing of the sort. He came to us while his parents were abroad. And as a boy, he was very much the way you see him now. Nor has the war changed him, although I've seen a darker side of him of late. This wound has tried his patience. He was never one to sit idle."

Whatever Mr. Hart preferred to believe, war did change men. I'd seen it in India and in the wards of the wounded. It was just that some were better at hiding it than others. And the darker side he spoke of might be a sign that Michael could explode into violence in the right conditions.

If only Helen Calder had come to her senses before Inspector Herbert came down to Little Sefton.

I thanked Mr. Hart, and told him I'd let him know as soon as I heard anything about Helen Calder.

"Poor woman. I didn't know her well," he said as he walked with me to the door. "She and her mother didn't come to Little Sefton very often. And she was a little older than Marjorie." With his hand on the latch, he turned to face me, and I could see the effort he was making to hold himself together. "I can't quite come to grips with any of this. My wife is making herself ill with worry. If Michael isn't released soon, I hesitate to think what will become of us."

I wished I could offer some comfort. I smiled and said, "Early days, Mr. Hart. We'll face that bridge when we must cross it."

He nodded, but the heart had gone out of him.

As I stepped out the door, I cast a glance toward the street, but the curious onlookers had gone about their business. There was only Simon, waiting for me in his motorcar. Mr. Hart quietly closed the door behind me, hoping not to disturb his wife.

Simon opened my door and as I settled myself in my seat, he reached out, and without speaking, held my hand until we had left Little Sefton far behind us.

When we arrived in Somerset, my mother was full of plans for a dinner party she was giving the next night, a chance for me to see and greet old friends. Her enthusiasm was jarring, in the mood I was in, and the Colonel Sahib gave me a quizzical look, one that said he sympathized but that I owed my mother the courtesy of entering into the event in the spirit she'd have wanted.

Simon, the coward, had vanished the instant the words *dinner party* were spoken, and there was no one left to spare me Mother's good intentions.

And so I was swept off to see what the kitchen could manage that was halfway edible, and there was no time to sit down and think through events. That, clearly, was everyone's intention.

I barely had time to wonder how Michael, for his sins, was faring, languishing in gaol. I hoped he was absolutely wretched.

My mother did ask, in passing, if I would wish to invite that handsome young lieutenant as well. I realized that she hadn't heard the latest turn of events. I didn't have the energy to explain them to her, and so I told her that I didn't think he would be available.

The Colonel Sahib, having spoken privately to Simon, wondered, as I walked into his study, if he should anticipate a passionate plea for his intervention if matters looked grim for my lieutenant.

"He's not my lieutenant. If he was anybody's lieutenant, he was Marjorie Evanson's. Besides, I'm sure Simon also told you it wasn't likely that Michael would be in custody for very long."

"He did seem to think that Lieutenant Hart had acted rather foolishly, going in to London."

"The worst part of it is," I said, wandering from the window to take a chair across from his, "the woman he was desperate enough to ask to drive him to London is no friend of Marjorie Evanson's. I think she was pleased to see Michael taken up."

"Are you certain about that?"

I told him what Mrs. Eubanks, the cook, had had to say.

"Of course servant gossip can't always be relied on for truthfulness," he pointed out. "But when there's heavy smoke, there's often fire."

"I think she told the truth as she sees it," I agreed. "She didn't like Victoria, and so she was ready to lay all the blame at her door. But everyone—Alicia, the rector, Michael himself—had also told me that there was no love lost between the sisters. Marjorie left home as soon as she could after her mother died, and her father did nothing to stop her from going. The wonder is, he didn't think of disinheriting her, once Mrs. Garrison was dead."

"And that may well be Victoria Garrison's problem. In spite of all she'd done to make him believe the first daughter wasn't his, in the end he had doubts."

I looked at him. "You *are* clever," I said. "It would explain so much."

After a moment, I went on. "Granted, I haven't known these people for very long. But I was drawn into their lives because I was a witness to what happened. If the police had found Mrs. Evanson's killer straightaway, that would have been the end of it."

"Not every murder inquiry leads to someone being taken into custody, much less tried and convicted. God forbid that Mrs. Calder should die, but if she does, and there is no explanation of why she had called the lieutenant's name in extremis, a shadow will hang over him for the rest of his life. It might be better to have a trial and clear him of any culpability."

"What if he's convicted?"

"There's that risk as well." My father paused. "Who would you suggest as the murderer the police are looking for?"

I shook my head, feeling tired suddenly. "I don't know."

"Then you can understand Inspector Herbert's dilemma."

I smiled against my will. "I would very much like it to be Victoria."

My father laughed. "From what Simon tells me, this Inspector Herbert is no fool."

"He tells you that because Inspector Herbert advised me to stay out of the Yard's affairs."

"Good advice."

For what was left of the afternoon, I helped my mother plan her dinner, shaking out the best table linens, stored away in lavender, and helping with the polishing of the silver and then I washed glasses and dried them carefully. She and I worked side by side in contented silence or chatted about whatever I needed for my return France.

And all the while my mind was busy with what the Colonel Sahib had asked me: Who had killed Marjorie Evanson?

I was no closer to an answer by the end of the day.

The menu, given all the shortages of food, presented a problem. Sighing, my mother said, "Do you suppose we could ask our guests to bring their own chickens?"

I laughed.

Then, changing the subject as she so easily could when one least expected it, she added, "You may as well tell me what is going on. It will save me from having to cajole your father."

I was saved—quite literally—by Nell appearing in the doorway.

"Miss Elizabeth," she said, "there's a message for you. The boot boy, Sammy, from The Four Doves, just brought it round."

I took the folded sheet she held out to me, and opened it.

A hasty scrawl read:

I've just been told. Is it true? Please, will you come and talk to me? It was signed *Serena Melton.*

I refolded it and turned to my mother. "We might not need those chickens after all."

As I left the room she answered, "I hadn't had my heart set on them, you know."

I drove to The Four Doves, wondering all the way there if Serena Melton had somehow discovered Scotland Yard's interest in her brother-in-law, Raymond. I didn't see how she could have found that out—or my role in identifying him. Her husband, Jack, was important in the cryptology section, but that gave him no influence with the police or even the Home Office. But then news sometimes had a way of leaking out. Someone else could have heard and then called him. I'd already confessed to him that I'd seen the man.

The doors to the inn were standing wide, allowing late sunlight to pour through into the small reception area, gilding the polished wood of the floors. The woman behind the desk greeted me warmly as I came in. Gray-haired and gray-eyed, she could pose for one of the original doves. But she had taken her son's place running the little inn when he went off to war, and had managed to keep it up despite the lack of nearly everything from paint to food.

"Good afternoon, Mrs. Cox," I said. "I've just received a message from a visitor. Is she still here?"

"Yes, I put her in the small parlor. She was reluctant to come to the house. Heaven knows why."

I knew why. The last time we'd met, Serena had called me a liar.

I thanked Mrs. Cox and started for the parlor. "Shall I bring you tea? We don't have any biscuits today, I'm afraid."

I knew she needed the business, and agreed that that would be nice. But I doubted Serena Melton would stay long enough to drink it.

She was standing when I walked into the little parlor, as if she had been pacing the floor while waiting to see if I would come to her or not.

"Miss Crawford," she said as soon as she saw me. "Bess."

"Hello, Serena." We hesitated, decided not to shake hands, and I sat down.

It took her a moment to rally herself, and then she said, "I hope you've forgiven me for the things I said when we parted at the railway station. I was under considerable strain, and it seemed then that everyone was set against me. I felt an obligation to find out who the man was in Marjorie's life—I owe that to my brother—but it has been a very difficult task I've set myself, and I have no experience to guide me."

It was a long preamble. I was beginning to feel a little ill at ease.

"I can appreciate your determination, Serena. But I think the police are better at getting to the truth."

"But they haven't. In all this time. Until now. I'm told you were there. And I need to know if I can believe—if it's true, is it the same man who seduced her?"

"I—really don't know, Serena. I'm as much in the dark as you."

"But you were *there*," she pressed. "You must know something. I don't fault you for not telling me, not after the way I behaved earlier. Still, for Meriwether's sake, if not mine, perhaps you'll tell me what you know."

Thinking she might be more willing to reveal her sources now, when she wanted something from me, than after I'd answered her questions, I said, "First, I'd like to ask you how you knew that I was present."

The door opened and Mrs. Cox came in with the tea tray. Smiling, she set it down on the table next to me, and then quietly withdrew.

Busying myself with the pot and the cups, I asked Serena how she preferred her tea, all the while wondering how much I could safely tell her about that night in the rain when I'd seen Marjorie Evanson.

I nearly dropped the cup I was about to hand her when she said, "Victoria Garrison telephoned me. She felt I ought to know. I can't think why—she and I had words over where her sister was to be interred. To be honest, under the circumstances, I didn't want Marjorie lying next to Meriwether and Victoria didn't want Marjorie to be returned to Little Sefton. Even when Merry was alive, I didn't see Victoria very often, and I could tell she and Marjorie never got on. I wasn't sure whether she was gloating or intended to be kind when she telephoned me."

Oh dear, I thought, rapidly reassessing what it was she must be wanting me to tell her. I'd come all too close to revealing more than I should, because it was on my mind and not hers.

"Do you mean when Michael was taken into custody?"

"Yes, yes. The police had come to arrest him for the attack on Mrs. Calder, as well as Marjorie's murder. Is it true? Did he do those things? I'd suspected he and Marjorie were close, even before she married my brother. But if he killed her, was he also her lover? I must know. Michael always struck me as someone who used his charm for his own advantage. I never could tell when he was serious or not. But he's been in France, or so I'd thought, and it never occurred to me to look in his direction until now."

"I think the police have probably made a mistake," I said. "I don't know Michael all that well, you see. I was there, yes, but I couldn't quite understand why the police feel he killed Marjorie. He admits he was in London at the time—"

"So I have heard," she interrupted eagerly. "He was there, he had the opportunity. I'd persuaded Jack to find out who was in England around that time, but I never even thought about Michael."

"But he was here to have his eye treated—and he's recovering from other wounds now. It's hard to believe he could have managed either attack. Physically, I mean."

"You don't know what men are capable of when they put their minds to it," she informed me darkly. "You aren't married, you don't know how determined they can be."

"No, you don't understand, he ran a terrible risk, medically. If his eye had hemorrhaged, he could have lost his sight. And now he was likely to do serious damage to his shoulder. After all the surgeries and the pain he's had to endure, I don't see him taking that chance. It could mean losing his arm. And he realizes that. It would be foolish."

"It might seem foolish to you," she told me, "but we can't know what was in his mind."

"If he was her lover—and I'm not convinced of that—why should he then wish to kill her?" And I asked myself, why was she weeping copiously on Raymond Melton's shoulder, if it was Michael who had got her pregnant? Unless Michael, not knowing he would be in London, had asked a friend to act for him.

"She might have told him it was over, that Meriwether was coming home and she wanted to go back to *him*. Jealousy is a powerful emotion. Sometimes people who are as handsome as Michael can't accept rejection. They're used to being adored."

She had worked it all out in her mind. Just as Inspector Herbert had done.

"Yes, of course that's possible," I argued. "But then why should he want to harm Mrs. Calder?"

"Perhaps she just found out he was in London then, and Marjorie had already told her about a man she was seeing. Helen Calder realized what that must mean, and she could have told Michael what she intended to do, giving him the opportunity to do the right thing and turn himself in. I don't know Helen Calder well, but she is very conventional, isn't she? Or maybe she herself really didn't want to get involved with the police."

Mrs. Calder *was* rather conventional. It would explain why Michael urgently wanted to go up to London. Could Serena be right? But why had he told his uncle he was intending to see Mrs. Calder? Why not claim he needed to visit a doctor? Why did he take a knife with him?

When I hesitated, Serena said, "He couldn't be sure, could he? That she wouldn't go to the police herself? It's possible he only wanted to persuade her she was wrong."

"Serena, you've made a very strong case. But it's mostly conjecture. There's no way of knowing how true it really is."

Her face hardened. "Victoria told me you'd argued with the police inspector. And you're standing up for Michael now." She set her teacup aside. "She told me too that you were in love with Michael Hart. All I wanted to know is, was Victoria right? Can I believe her, that the police actually took him into custody, that he's not just helping them with their inquiries? Marjorie didn't trust her sister. Can I?"

I let out my breath in a sign of frustration. "In the first place, I'm not in love with Lieutenant Hart. I've told you, I hardly know him. In the second, it's true he was taken into custody, and that I was present. And yes, I did argue with the inspector. I thought his case a very poor one. Medically I didn't see how Michael Hart could have attacked those two women. But Inspector Herbert is convinced that it was possible. And finally, Victoria Garrison is a troublemaker. The only reason I can think of for her to telephone you and tell you about Michael is to stir up your grief all over again. She settled her score with you. Don't you see?"

Standing, she said, "I shouldn't have come. I just want to see the end of this business, so that my brother can finally rest in peace."

I felt like telling her that her brother might have found that peace if she herself hadn't told him the whole truth about his wife. It had been unnecessarily hurtful. The only reason I could think of for her not to shield him was her own jealousy. That she was both shocked and gloating that Marjorie had fallen so far from grace. And now it was Serena who needed to find some peace.

I said, "Serena. I can understand that you want to see Marjorie's murderer caught—"

"He got around you just as he got around Marjorie, didn't he? You can't see beyond that, but I can. I can see him clearly."

She marched to the door, self-righteous indignation in every stride.

I waited until she had reached it, then asked, "Serena. Someone shot at Lieutenant Hart earlier this week. Whoever it was missed him both times. Was it you?" That stopped her cold.

I added, "There was a weapon missing from your husband's gun cabinet. A revolver, at a guess."

"You are grasping at straws, aren't you? Jack carries a weapon when he's in London. For self-protection, because of the work he does. I'd hardly call that 'missing.'"

And she was gone.

I could hear the outer door of The Four Doves shutting with what might be called some force.

Setting the cups back on the tea tray, I went to thank Mrs. Cox and settle the account for our tea.

She said, "Your visitor was crying when she left. Is everything all right?"

Surprised, I answered, "She hoped for good news."

Mrs. Cox nodded. "We could all use a little of that."

I just wished Helen Calder would regain consciousness and tell us what she remembered. Good news—or bad—but better than this limbo.

The dinner party went exceedingly well, our cook outdoing herself with the chickens and even with a lovely French tart for the sweet. I couldn't help but wonder where she had found the sugar for the glaze.

Most of all I enjoyed the guests, many of them friends of my parents, a few of them friends of mine. Diana was in London and arrived in high spirits, flirting with Simon, although Mary had told me it was likely she would be engaged by the autumn. Another of my flatmates, Elayne, was a surprise. I hadn't seen her in weeks and we had much to catch up on. She too was expecting a proposal, she said, and I was happy for her.

Even Melinda Crawford had traveled all the way from Kent. She and my father were distantly related, and both her husband and her father had served in India in their time. As she leaned on Simon's arm as we went in to dinner, she said, "When this wicked war is finished, I want to go back to India. I've unfinished business there. Will you take me?" Overhearing that, I made a promise to myself that I would go with them.

Throughout that dinner, I enjoyed watching my mother's face. She loved entertaining, did it well, and was a clever hostess. I smiled at her down the table, and won a smile in return.

My leave was nearly up. I felt a twinge of regret, knowing how much this time meant to my parents.

Chapter Fifteen

I had wanted to see Alicia Dalton before I left for France, to apologize again for hurting her feelings. But there was much to do the morning after the party, and I couldn't leave all of that to my mother and Nell. And I was waiting for news of Helen Calder. Diana had promised to find out what she could.

Simon had driven Melinda Crawford to the train and my mother had taken the last of the chicken, made up as a fricassee, to two elderly women in the village. My father had been summoned to Sandhurst for a ceremony of some sort, and I was rather at loose ends.

Remembering that Victoria had telephoned Serena, I decided I would return the favor.

As the call was being put through, I realized too late that I should have left well enough alone. This was borne in upon me by the coldness in Victoria Garrison's voice when I told her who I was.

"I should have thought I would be the last person you wished to speak with," she said. "After what happened the other day."

Refusing to be drawn, I asked, "Miss Garrison, did Lieutenant Hart tell you why he wanted to go to London?"

"Why don't you ask Inspector Herbert? I've told him what I know."

"It was you who took Michael there. And so I'm asking you."

"Someone had told him I had tickets for that play. I didn't twist his arm, he came to me. He said he would very much like to see it. I was surprised, but I was glad of the company, driving back after the performance. And then later, when we reached London, he hurt his shoulder getting out of the motorcar, and he was in pain. He couldn't sit still, and even before the curtain went up, he walked out, saying that he needed air. I offered to go with him, but he told me to stay there, he wouldn't be gone very long. When he hadn't returned by intermission, I went to look for him. I missed a part of the play searching. The doorman told me he thought he'd seen the lieutenant leave the theater. I couldn't think where he might have gone. I went back to my seat, and toward the end of the last act, he was there, looking as white as I'd ever seen him, his hands shaking. I drove him home, and he had very little to say for himself. I was very angry with him; I thought him selfish, to ask to come and then to ruin my evening."

"Did he tell you where he'd been?"

"He said he'd walked until he was too exhausted to walk any longer. He found a cab and was driven back to the theater."

"Did you believe him?"

"I didn't know whether to believe him or not. I wondered if he'd had no interest in the play after all, and had only used me to bring him to town."

"Could the people who had the seats nearest you swear that you were alone until the end of the play?"

She was angry then. "Are you suggesting that I wasn't there either?"

I hadn't been, I'd just wondered if she'd been lying, but she was furious and said, "You won't get him off, you know. However much you try. I tell you, I was lucky that he didn't decide to kill me on the way home. I didn't know then that he was a murderer."

"But I don't understand why you should think he would harm Marjorie. Or had any reason at all to attack Helen Calder. If he couldn't bear to sit still, he might well have tried to walk instead."

There was silence for a moment, and then she said, "There was a dark smear on his sleeve. I pointed it out to him, and he said he'd stopped for a glass of wine and spilled some of it, then tried to wash it out with cold water. The sleeve was still damp; it must have been true."

I couldn't decide if she was telling the truth about that. Her voice seemed a little different, somehow. Or had I imagined it? "That still doesn't explain—"

"The next day, a friend telephoned to tell me about Helen Calder. She knew that Helen was a connection on my mother's side. She lives across the square, she'd watched the police come and go from the garden, and she'd sent her husband to find out what had happened. He told her that Helen Calder had been the victim of a knifing, and he thought she must be dead. But his wife had seen an ambulance come and then leave. I expect she hoped that I might know more about the attack. She said Helen Calder's assailant hadn't been found."

"I still don't see the connection with Michael Hart," I pressed.

"My friend—Mrs. Daly—told me she herself had seen a young officer with his arm in a sling come to Helen Calder's door, earlier in the evening. He spoke to the maid, then left to sit in the garden for a time before walking away."

My heart sank. Whether that maid knew Michael by name didn't matter, her description of the caller would be enough. That, coupled with Victoria's statement about the stained sleeve, would be telling evidence.

"Do you really believe he killed Marjorie?" I asked, as soon as I could collect my thoughts.

"Oh, yes. Once the police asked me if I was aware that he was in London on that same day, I knew it must be so. Someone got her pregnant, did you know that? The police told me she was pregnant when she died. If Michael had found that out, I think he would have killed her out of sheer jealousy. I was convinced from the start that she must have written to him in France and confided in him that she'd had an affair. She always had confided in him, why shouldn't she turn to him now? I kept after him to tell me if he knew the name of the man she'd been seeing, and he swore he didn't. I was starting to believe him. Did you know he hadn't even told his aunt and uncle that he was in London that night? But he must have told Marjorie. He'd found a way to get leave and confront her."

Her voice changed again, and I wished I could see her face. "He never got over her marriage, did you know that? He always thought she'd marry *him*. I remember him at the wedding, looking as if he'd like to snatch the bride up and ride off with her across his saddle bow."

That made a dreadful sense. After the man at the station, Raymond Melton, walked away from her, Marjorie would very likely have turned to Michael.

"But why should he kill Helen Calder?"

"How should I know? Perhaps he's still trying to find out Marjorie's lover's name. For all I know, Michael intended to kill him next."

But Helen hadn't known who the man was. At least she told me she didn't.

"Someone shot at Michael. Perhaps it was the same person who killed Marjorie and tried to kill Mrs. Calder."

"You are pathetic," she said. "Don't you know what that was about? I knew, the minute I heard about it. Michael was trying to kill himself. And he failed. He couldn't quite bring himself to do it. So he invented someone shooting from the bushes, to spare his aunt and uncle the truth. Someone was bound to have heard the shots."

I felt ill, unable to think of anything to say. I hadn't considered suicide.

Victoria interpreted the silence and laughed. "It's rather shocking, isn't it, to realize he's in love with a dead woman. He hasn't let her go. But you're like all the rest, that's why you came to his defense when the police wanted to take him away. Even dead, Marjorie still has him in thrall."

There was a sudden break in her voice, and I realized that she was talking about her own sense of loss, not mine.

And then before I could answer, she added harshly, her voice hardly recognizable, "They won't hang him, you know, until that shoulder is fully healed. But hang him they will. Mark my words. And it will be my testimony that will put the noose around his neck."

There was a click at the other end of the line. Victoria had hung up before she gave herself away.

I stood there for a moment, the receiver still in my hand, then put it up.

Victoria was angry, vindictive. But Michael had sealed his own fate when he lifted the knocker on Helen Calder's door. If the maid knew him by sight or could identify him, the police had all the evidence they wanted.

For a fleeting moment I wondered if Victoria had tricked Michael, and while he was walking off the pain in his shoulder, she had taken advantage of his absence to kill Mrs. Calder herself. From the start I'd been surprised to hear that Michael and Victoria had gone anywhere together, much less London. Why had he asked? Why had she agreed?

Could Victoria stab two women?

I could have asked Michael—but he was beyond reach.

Feeling closed in, I went out into the gardens, thinking to refresh the vases we'd arranged for the dinner party.

Now that he had Michael in custody, would Inspector Herbert still summon Raymond Melton to England to make a statement? Or would that be left to the KC who was preparing the prosecution? I wanted to hear just what had been said at that meeting in the railway station. If Captain Melton had made promises, he had given them grudgingly, and they had provided no comfort. Marjorie deserved better.

I was ready to go back to France, but I wanted very badly to be here when Helen Calder regained her senses. And time was running out.

My father met me as I came through the garden doors into the passage.

"Hallo." He took one look at me. "I've seen Pathan warriors with happier faces. Care to talk about it?"

I smiled. "I just had a conversation with Victoria Garrison. She could probably hold the Khyber Pass single-handedly with a fork." As he laughed, I went on, "I've been trying to decide if Lieutenant Hart is the sort of man to want to kill himself."

"Do you mean before his trial?"

"No, earlier. According to Victoria, no one fired at him as he walked in the garden. The only reason I can think of for a suicide attempt is guilt. And why two shots?"

"It's hard to miss with a revolver if you're serious about using it." He led me to his sanctuary, the study full of trophies from his years in the Army, and offered me the chair across from his. "Especially twice. Unless one intends to miss. In which case, it's a cry for help."

"If it was a cry for help, he covered it up very well indeed." I stared into the golden glass eyes of a Bengal man hunter, a tiger that had killed fourteen villagers before my father brought it down. "More important, I'd like to know if he lied to me. And if he did, what else had he lied about? Conversely, if it was Victoria's lie, it could have other implications. There's a big difference between being shot at and shooting one's self." I turned to look at my father. "I also have to wonder why Victoria agreed to drive him into London—and I'd give much to know what they talked about on the way. I do know he didn't tell her who he expected to see while there."

"It would be wiser, don't you think, to leave the entire matter in the capable hands of Inspector Herbert?"

"I have done. It doesn't stop me from wondering, or from weighing up what I know or suspect."

"And you'd be content to see Victoria Garrison as a murderess."

"It's entirely possible that she could have killed her sister, and tried to make it appear that it was a random act of violence on the part of someone nameless and faceless in London."

"That's a damning comment."

"Yes, but Victoria is so filled with something—hate, envy, jealousy—a wanting—that she might have seen her chance and taken it before she'd even considered what she was doing."

"Women don't usually carry a large knife in their purses."

Which was an excellent point. I smiled. "You've just shot down my best argument for Victoria as a murderess."

"I'm not saying it couldn't be done, only that she would have had to plan carefully." He considered me. "I'll be just as happy to see you back in France, if you want to know the truth. Out of reach. You ask too many questions—if the police are wrong about Michael, then you will need to be cautious."

"Being shot at by Germans is preferable to being stabbed by Englishmen?"

"Absolutely. Just don't tell your mother I said that."
He paused. "If you must go back to London before you
leave, do take Simon with you."

I promised, and felt the eyes of the Bengal tiger
follow me from the room.

My distant grandmother, who had followed her officer
husband to Brussels in June 1815, and helped nurse the
wounded brought in from Waterloo, was not certain
until well into the next evening whether her husband
was among the living or the dead. Reports had come
in placing him in the heat of the battle, and various
accounts had listed him as dead, severely wounded,
or missing. But she had held to her faith in his ability
to survive, and her words to him as he finally walked
into the house they had taken in Brussels had been,
"My dear, I'm so sorry, there seems to be nothing for
your dinner."

My mother, dealing with the ravages of this war's
shortages, still managed to put a decent meal on the
table, and I was reminded of Mary's remark that a
country house fared better in trying times.

It was Simon's night to join us, and we were finishing our soup when he said, "You'll never guess
who I ran into as I was coming out of my meeting
today."

I thought he was talking to my father, then looked up to realize that he was speaking to me.

I named several retired officers we'd known in other campaigns, and he shook his head each time.

"I give up. Tell me."

"Jack Melton."

I stared at him. "You didn't mention his brother, did you?" I wouldn't have put it past Simon to have engineered the meeting for the sole purpose of finding out what I would like to know about Raymond Melton.

"I did ask how his brother was. It was the decent thing to do," he said, smug as a cat with a mouthful of canary feathers.

"Well, then?"

"He's presently near Ypres. You might keep that in mind when you go back to France next week."

"Little good that will do me. I've no idea where I'll be sent next. What else did you learn?" I asked.

"That Melton wasn't particularly at ease talking about his brother. His answers were short, as if it wasn't a subject he was comfortable with." Simon Brandon had dealt with men all his adult life—soldiers, prisoners, angry villagers. Men in trouble, afraid, lying, angry, vindictive. He could read them without effort because it had become second nature. I knew he could read me as well, and oddly enough, it was one of the things that made me trust him.

I set aside my soup spoon. "When I learned that the man was his brother, I found myself wondering if what I'd said to Jack Melton outside the Marlborough Hotel in London might not have put him on to Raymond as the man I'd mentioned. I didn't describe him of course. But Jack was rather short with me as well. Almost rude, in fact. Still, he must not have said anything to his wife—she'd have brought it up when she came to Somerset to see me."

"Very likely not," my father put in. "On the other hand, by the very nature of his work in cryptology, Melton isn't likely to be talkative. He can't afford to be, given what he reads every day in dispatches and intercepts. After a while, secretiveness must become a way of life."

"It's more likely that he prefers to steer Serena away from suspecting his brother was the man with Marjorie. She's angry enough to cause trouble. And that wouldn't go down well with his superiors either." I'd had a taste of how angry she could be, and how hurtful. "But it's rather two-faced of him, isn't it? Protecting the man who seduced his brother-in-law's wife."

"I expect," my mother said, surprising us all, "Mr. Melton feels that since Marjorie Evanson is dead, and her child with her, there's no point in ruining his brother's marriage, career, or life. It's finished. And so he can simply put it behind him."

It was a very perceptive remark.

"And now," she went on, "perhaps we can dispense with murder as a subject for dinner conversation."

Not five minutes later, I was summoned to the telephone. I almost failed to recognize the voice at the other end.

"This is Matron speaking—"

I thought she meant Matron at Laurel House, and was about to greet her warmly when the voice continued, "—at St. Martin's Hospital in London."

"Yes, Matron. This is Sister Crawford."

"I thought perhaps you'd want to know that Mrs. Calder is out of danger and has been removed from the surgical ward to the women's ward. We have kept her heavily sedated, to keep her quiet. But that's been reduced, and I expect her to regain consciousness in a few hours."

"I should like very much to be there," I said. "Will I be permitted to see her?"

"I see no reason why not. Unless Scotland Yard objects."

"I'll be there," I promised. "And if she awakens before I arrive, will you tell her that I'm on my way?"

"I'll be happy to," she said, and rang off.

I hurried back to the dining room. "I must go to London tonight—as soon as may be."

Simon was already pushing his chair back. "I'll drive."

My mother said to me, "I suggest you finish your meal first, my dear. Ten minutes shouldn't matter, not with Simon at the wheel."

And so we finished our dinner in almost indecent haste, and then I was rushing upstairs to change and fetch my coat.

I was tense on the drive to London. The hours crept by, and Simon said little, his concentration on the road intense.

It was late when we walked through the doors of the hospital and asked for Matron.

She greeted me, and with a warning not to tire her patient, she turned me over to a young nursing sister. Simon was asked to remain outside. He touched my arm and said quietly, "I'll wait in the motorcar."

I nodded, grateful, and then I was shown to a bed near the middle of the ward. A small lamp burned above the bed, leaving the rest of the room in darkness. I could hear the quiet breathing of other patients, and one moaned softly.

Helen Calder's eyes were closed, and she appeared to be sleeping as well as I took the chair by her bedside. She must have heard the slight rustle of my skirts, for she stirred a little and bit her lip as if in pain.

I said in a low voice that I hoped would carry only to her ears, "Helen? Do you remember me? It's Bess Crawford."

She opened her eyes, focusing them with some difficulty at first. And then she said faintly, "Oh yes. Of course. How kind of you to come and see me. My family has just left—"

"Then you'll be tired. I just wished to be sure that you were recovering. Is there anything I can do to make you more comfortable? Is there anything you need?"

The young woman in the bed behind me coughed a little, and then slept again.

"The sisters have been so good," she said. "But I hurt—"

"I'll ask them to look in on you," I promised. "I was so shocked by the news," I went on. "Do you have any memory of what happened?"

"I remember dressing and leaving the house, looking forward to dining with friends. And then I woke up here and didn't know where I was." She frowned. "I'm told I was attacked—knifed. As I came home alone. Is it true?"

"I'm afraid so."

"But who would do such a thing?" A tear ran from the corner of her eye down her pale cheek. "I've never harmed anyone. Not ever . . ." Her voice trailed off.

"You're safe, now." I touched her hand. "Let the police deal with it." Her fingers closed tightly over mine.

"Bess—it's frightening that I can't remember. They tell me it happens. The shock, they said." She moved restlessly. "I'm told it will all come back. Only I'm not sure I want it to."

"If it starts to return, ask a nurse to send for the police," I said, trying to soothe her. "They'll want to know. It will help them apprehend whoever did this."

"Yes, that's what Inspector Hemmings—no, that's not right—" She closed her eyes. "I didn't imagine him—" She was still drifting in and out of consciousness.

"Inspector Herbert," I said. "From Scotland Yard."

"Was he here? Did you see him?"

"I've spoken to him before, about Marjorie Evanson."

"That's right. You were anxious to find out who killed her."

"Did he—did Inspector Herbert ask you about Lieutenant Michael Hart?"

"I can't think why he wished to know if I'd seen him last night—no, it wasn't last night, was it? I'm so confused."

"It doesn't matter," I answered her, though I felt myself go cold.

"He told me I'd been calling Michael's name when I was found and brought to hospital. But that makes no sense. I'd have asked for my husband, wouldn't I? Not for Michael."

"Perhaps you were thinking about him."

"Not at dinner—afterward—"

I told myself that I must stop now, before I heard more than I wanted to hear. If she brought back some fleeting memory that would damn Michael, it would all be my doing. But truth is something I'd been taught to value. I couldn't walk away from it, whatever the consequences.

"Afterward?" I asked, before my courage ran out.

But she had drifted into sleep, and I recalled my promise to speak to one of the sisters and tell them she was in pain.

Still, I sat there for another several minutes, in case she awoke again. Then, after a brief conversation with the ward sister, I left, feeling very depressed for Helen Calder's sake and my own.

I was just walking down the steps of the hospital, taking a deep breath of the cooling evening air after the familiar smells of the wards, and nearly passed Inspector Herbert without noticing him, so distracted that I just registered a man coming toward me.

"Miss Crawford," he said, stopping me. He frowned. "Not questioning my witness, I hope?"

"I'm a nurse," I replied shortly, "and the patient is someone I know."

He nodded. "How is she? She wasn't making much sense earlier."

"The ward sister tells me she's doing as well as can be expected. The fear, as always, is infection. From the knife, from bits of cloth driven into her wounds, from the surgery itself. She's healthy and that's in her favor. They're still sedating her for her pain." It was a cowardly comment, but I told myself that it was also true.

"I was just on my way home and decided to stop and ask if she was awake again."

"She's asleep at the moment. Or she was when I left the ward."

"Did you speak to her?"

"Briefly. She told me you had called earlier, and that she couldn't remember what had happened. She added that she was afraid to remember. I tried to assure her that she was safe now and it would be all right. Which of course isn't really the truth—if she does remember, she'll relive that night for years. If not while she's awake, then in her dreams. Is there any possibility that you could send for her husband? It would be a comfort to her."

"I hadn't thought of that. I'll see what I can do."

"Will you let me see Lieutenant Hart?" I asked. "I'm going back to France in a few days. I'd like to hear what he has to say about his arrest."

"I don't think that's useful," Inspector Herbert told me. "He's allowed no visitors. Only his lawyers."

"May I write to him and expect an answer?"

"I wouldn't advise writing him."

I took a deep breath. "What if all this evidence is just circumstantial? Will you hang the lieutenant and let the real murderer go free?"

"Hardly circumstantial, I should think," he answered, a little annoyed with me. "You've been a great help with this inquiry, Miss Crawford. But as I've said to you before, you must now leave the rest to us."

He started to walk through the hospital doors, but I stopped him.

"Have you found Captain Melton?"

"There's no hurry there. He's at the Front, and we've time before the trial to interview him. I think even you will agree that he's not our murderer."

"He can speak to Marjorie Evanson's state of mind—" I wanted to add that men died at the Front. Waiting was a calculated risk.

"And you have already done that. Quite admirably." He touched his hat, and went through the main doors, holding them open for a pair of sisters just coming off duty.

There was nothing I could do.

Simon was waiting for me, but I said, "I need a little time . . ."

He nodded, and I began to walk to clear my head, but I'd not gone twenty paces when I heard Inspector Herbert call to me.

I stopped and he caught me up.

"I wanted to ask—it's not my business to ask, but are you in love with Lieutenant Hart?"

I must have looked as exasperated as I felt. "If anyone else asks me that question, I will gladly box his ears. Or barring that, kick him in the shins."

He smiled. "I'm sorry. As a policeman I must know how to judge your evidence. It has been impartial to a certain point. It's necessary to understand if that has in any way changed."

"If I'm asked to testify in court, you may be sure I shall tell the truth, as I will have sworn to do," I answered stiffly.

"It won't come to that. Your statement will be sufficient. Good night, Miss Crawford. I wish you a safe journey back to France. And hope that you will return to England safely when your tour of duty is finished."

He touched his hat again and went back the way he'd come. I stood there looking after him as he passed through the hospital doors without looking back, thinking to myself that he was a fair man, but like many fair men, once he'd made up his mind, he wasn't likely to find any reason to change it.

Chapter Sixteen

I must have walked another hundred yards or more. And then someone spoke just behind me, and I nearly jumped out of my skin.

It was Simon Brandon. He'd been following me at a distance.

"It's late, Bess, and that direction isn't wise."

I realized that I'd left the hospital well behind me, and ahead was a short, cluttered street with rather run-down shops and a pub or two, their doors shuttered. The street itself was dark, empty, dustbins casting long shadows. At the far end, two men stood in the shelter of a doorway, the lighted tips of their cigarettes glowing red. They seemed to be intent on their conversation—I could just hear the murmur of voices—but I turned and together Simon and I started back toward the motorcar.

"How is she?" he asked. "I saw Inspector Herbert come out again to speak to you."

The clanging of an ambulance speeding toward the hospital drowned out my voice. After it passed, I told Simon what Helen Calder had said.

"It's very likely she'll never remember, Bess. And that leaves Lieutenant Hart in a limbo of sorts. She could have cleared his name—or she could have condemned him. It might work in his favor that she doesn't recall the attack. On the other hand, there may be assumptions that aren't true entered into evidence."

We had reached his motorcar, and he held my door before continuing. "There are witnesses who heard her call out to Michael Hart. And the police will act on that evidence instead." He turned the crank and then got in next to me. "Why did she call his name, do you think? She was in great pain, bleeding heavily. Why not call for her husband. Or a sister. Someone connected with her family."

"I don't know," I told him truthfully. "And when I asked her, she told me Michael wasn't at the dinner party. Then she added, 'Afterward.' Did she mean that she'd seen him after the dinner party? Or was she going to tell me something else?"

"There's no way to know. You must prepare yourself, Bess. This case is going to trial, and there's nothing to be done about it."

I turned to him. "Simon, attend the trial for me, if I'm in France. I want to know everything, what witnesses are called on either side, what they testify. What the rebuttal is. And the verdict—you must be there to tell me what the verdict is. I don't think they'll give me leave. Inspector Herbert told me that my statement was sufficient. Please? I need to know all of it."

"Shall I sketch their faces as well?"

"That's not amusing, Simon."

He nodded, threading his way through light traffic. "Sorry. I was trying to lighten your mood."

I hadn't realized that I had been so intense. "Please?"

He turned to me, his face in shadows cast by the canvas roof. "I promise, Bess. If it will give you any comfort. But there's nothing more you can do. Don't let it haunt you. Your patients will suffer if you do."

"He wouldn't let me see Michael. Or write to him. Inspector Herbert, I mean. He doesn't want me to contact him in any way. Will you try to see him? I want to know how he's planning to fight these charges."

"I'll do my best."

I settled back into my seat as we left the busy city streets behind us and found the road leading to Somerset. "Thank you, Simon. And, Simon—don't tell Mother or the Colonel Sahib that you're doing this for me. It will only worry them."

I saw Simon's mouth tighten into a straight line. "And I'm not to worry?"

I didn't know how to answer. And so I said nothing.

My mother closed my valise, sighed, and said, "When your father went off on a dangerous mission, I was so grateful to have a daughter. She would never walk in harm's way, I told myself. I won't lose a night's sleep over *her* out in hostile territory. My only worry will be whether or not she chooses wisely when it comes to marriage. And look at what this war has brought me."

It was the closest she'd ever come to admitting to worrying. And I thought perhaps it had been the sinking of *Britannic* last year while I was aboard that had brought her fears out into the open. With a broken arm, I couldn't have fended for myself in the water, if we hadn't had time to launch the boats, and I could well have drowned.

I smiled, glad I hadn't told her about the German aircraft strafing us at La Fleurette. "I shan't be in any danger. It's my patients you must say a prayer for, every day."

My father came just then, to carry the valise down to the motorcar. After he'd gone, my mother said, "He would prefer that I didn't tell you, Bess, but I think you ought to know this. Your father has been in touch with Lieutenant Hart's aunt and uncle, suggesting a good barrister if they haven't already found one to their liking. They were in such a state of shock and were grateful for his advice."

I felt a mixture of shame that I hadn't thought of calling on them again and a surge of hope that my father believed Michael was innocent.

I said, "Then the Colonel Sahib agrees with me."

But she dashed my hopes almost at once. "I think it's more a case of the Army looking after its own, whatever one's regiment. The lieutenant's own commanding officer hadn't called on them yet. He's still in France."

"Thank you for telling me."

"I'd like to know why you're so sure he's innocent?"

"I drove him to Somerset and then to London, and back to Little Sefton. I'd have known if he were a murderer. And I didn't feel it."

"Hardly evidence that would sway a jury," she said.

I embraced my mother, and she returned it fiercely. "Be safe," she whispered into my ear, then let me go.

As I walked out the door to where my father and Simon were waiting with the motorcar, I found myself remembering a lesson in ancient Greek history: how the women of Sparta sent their loved ones into battle with the brave words, *Come back with your shield—or on it.*

How many women over the millennia had fought back tears to smile and wish their men safe?

The door shut behind me, and I didn't look back. My father held my door for me while Simon turned the crank. And then we were on our way.

My father walked me to the gangway of my ship, took me in his arms for a brief moment, then stepped back, smiling.

As Simon bent to kiss my cheek, I murmured, "Don't forget!"

And then I was at the rail, waving, and we were pulling out, our escort already under way.

I wondered afterward what premonitions my family had felt before my departure. I'd had the strongest impression of an undercurrent of concern. It hadn't been like Simon to kiss me, nor my father to put his arms around me. Whatever foreboding there was, I began this next posting far from the front lines and well out of range of danger. I'd been there several weeks when I heard from Simon.

He had gone over Inspector Herbert's head and found a way to speak to Michael. It must not have been a very successful visit, for Simon reported that the shoulder was healing well although it appeared that Lieutenant Hart wasn't recovering the use of that arm. VAD therapy wasn't available in prison, and so there was no hope for a successful convalescence. With gallows humor, Michael Hart had told Simon that it wouldn't matter, he wouldn't live long enough to worry about it. But Simon rather thought he was worried.

My father reported that Michael's family had retained the barrister recommended to them, and they felt he might well save their nephew.

It occurred to me that my father had written those lines to encourage me, as much as to report on the legal issues.

We were sent shortly after that to a new hospital, one with severely wounded patients from all over the Front. This was well behind the lines too, and I was beginning to think my father had had a word with someone about his only daughter.

I was becoming a favorite surgical nurse among the staff, and this kept me too busy to think or worry about anyone, myself included.

And then I was sent to another forward hospital, a receiving station for wounded brought in by stretcher bearers rather than ambulances. We could hear the guns, see their flashes all night long, and sometimes their screams as they raced overhead deafened us.

We had just cleared out a contingent of our own wounded when the Front moved forward three hundred yards in that salient, and suddenly the men I was working with wore the field gray of German uniforms.

I'd heard several nurses state flatly that they wouldn't touch German wounded, Edith Cavill fresh in their minds. She had been shot by firing squad for staying with her duties to her own wounded when the Germans had overrun that part of Belgium. They had called her a spy, and rid themselves of her.

But as I looked at these men, some of them so young and frightened, others stoic in their pain, I could hardly turn them away.

I spent endless hours working over them, sorting the more serious cases from those we couldn't move until they were stabilized, listening to the ragged breath of the dying, holding the hands of those facing surgery, trying to discover the names of those who couldn't speak.

I soon forgot that this was the enemy. But for their uniforms and their language, they could have been any soldier from our own armies. I gave them all the care at my command, and cried when one of them died in my arms.

Their officer, his foot badly lacerated by shell fragments, hobbled around the tent speaking to each one of his men, comforting and reassuring them, taking down their names in a little leather book along with a description of their wounds, so that there would be a record of where they were and why.

Twice I asked Hauptmann Ritter to sit down and let me examine his foot, but he shook his head, continuing his rounds. Finally I stood in front of him, forcing him to stop and face me.

"You are risking infection that will cost you your foot and possibly your leg as well. It might even kill you. Is that what you want? If so, it's a poor example for these men who are letting us care for them."

I wasn't certain he understood me until I saw a flash of anger in his blue eyes, and he said in passable English, "I am responsible."

The Colonel Sahib would have liked him in other circumstances. They saw eye to eye on the duties of command.

"Yes, well, you can be just as responsible once I've cleaned and disinfected that wound, then bandaged it."

He gave me a look that was withering, and then as he turned he saw that the men on cots around him were listening with open interest to hear what he would say.

It must have taken enormous effort to quell his pride and let me lead him to one side where his foot could be examined properly. He refused to let his men out of his sight, but I found a bench where he could sit and rest his foot on a wooden crate.

And it was a nasty wound. I summoned one of the doctors and he came to have a look as well.

"You could lose this, you know," he told Herr Hauptmann. "And with it your career in the Army." He fetched what he needed and began to clean the foot and remove any fragments still buried there.

I watched as the muscles in our patient's jaw tightened, and I knew what sort of pain he was enduring, refusing to show weakness.

I realized that not only the German soldiers but Dr. Newcomb himself was watching Captain Ritter with interest.

Dr. Newcomb did what he could with the wound, then said, "This will require surgery. We must get him and those five men over there back to where they can be taken care of."

Ritter wanted no part of being separated from his men, the walking wounded already being lined up to be taken under guard to a processing center for prisoners, the others to remain here until they were fit to move.

It took some argument and persuasion before Captain Ritter accepted the fact that he had no choice in the matter. He finished the entries in his small notebook, then reluctantly allowed us to put him in the ambulance waiting outside.

I was the transport nurse, and after making certain the other critical cases were as stable and comfortable as possible, I climbed into the seat next to the driver. Captain Ritter called from the back, "Claus is bleeding again."

I got out and stepped into the rear of the ambulance. And Claus had indeed pulled at his bandaging, blood already welling in the wound in his chest. I worked to stop the bleeding, and finally succeeded.

Captain Ritter said bitterly, "The war is over for him. I don't know whether to mourn for him or congratulate him."

I stayed with Claus, sending Captain Ritter to take my place next to the driver, who gave me a long look. I knew what he was asking—if this German officer was to be trusted next to the driver, where he could try a mischief.

I said, "Captain Ritter understands I am exchanging places in order to keep this soldier alive. He will give me his word to respect this decision."

Captain Ritter smiled at me, and I knew he'd been weighing his chances. But he nodded, and closed the ambulance door on me before hobbling painfully to the front of the vehicle.

We set off along the rutted road, lurching and swaying like some mad creature in the throes of despair. It was always a wonder to me when a severely wounded man survived this ride. I felt bruised and battered as we pulled in at the hospital and I could turn my patients over to the staff waiting there.

Captain Ritter thanked me for my care of his men, and then said, "I have learned one thing in life at least. When I have given up all hope, there is still something to live for. I swore I would never be taken prisoner. And here I am, a prisoner. But I shall write to my wife now and tell her that very likely I shall survive the war after all. She will have a little peace, knowing that. It will be my good deed."

"There's no shame in being taken prisoner," I told him. "You are no use to your country dead."

He smiled. "I shall remember that. Good-bye, Fräulein." And he was gone, supported by two orderlies, followed by an armed guard.

I was to think about Captain Ritter when my mail at last caught up with me.

When I have given up all hope, there is still something to live for.

Michael Hart was speaking almost those same words to Simon Brandon that same afternoon. Only I wouldn't hear about it for another two weeks.

Chapter Seventeen

When Simon's letter arrived, the envelope was worn and splattered with mud. At least I hoped it was mud. I opened it gingerly, and drew out the sheets inside.

Unfolding them, I looked at the heavy, angular strokes of his pen, and I had a premonition of bad news.

Bess, it began,

I am writing in haste, as there is a chance I shall be able to send this letter tonight. As you asked, I attended the trial. It was brought forward because Mrs. Calder regained some memory of events the night she was stabbed. Only a partial memory as it turned out, but she was able to tell the police that she'd received a message from Lieutenant Hart asking her to meet him. This was verified by her maid, who had brought the letter to her from the post. She replied that she had a dinner engagement that night—would it be possible for him to come another evening. He answered that he would meet her at nine thirty, if her dinner party ended in good time. She agreed, and was surprised that he wasn't waiting in her house. Instead he came toward her from the shadows at the corner of her house, and she called to him to join her. That was the last thing she remembered. Because the doctors had ordered a long and careful period of convalescence, it was decided to move the trial date to accommodate the medical needs of the chief witness. I spoke to the barrister who had taken Hart's case, and he felt that judgment could go either way—conviction or acquittal depending on the view of the jury when the evidence was presented. He believed your evidence regarding events at the railway station would be crucial, as it indicated that Hart was not Mrs. Evanson's lover, and therefore had no reason to kill her to protect himself from charges that he was the child's father. As she was already married, Hart could hardly be considered a jilted lover or cuckolded husband.

This removed one motive for murder, and such circumstantial evidence as there was required a suitable motive. And Mrs. Calder could be shown to be recovering still, and perhaps not perfectly certain about what she thinks she remembers.

He had told Hart how he expected to conduct the trial, and had every expectation that his principal agreed with the plan.

The trial began on a Monday, and the general feeling was that it would last five to seven days. Your father had told me he had also arranged to attend, and we met outside the courtroom, taking our seats just as Hart was brought in.

His shoulder had healed sufficiently for the more conspicuous bandaging to be reduced to a padded sling. His counsel objected to the prison doctor's decision, believing it gave the jury a false impression of his ability to use that arm. Still, it was rather obvious that the shoulder was held awkwardly as he came up the stairs into the dock. I thought he appeared to be under considerable strain, but otherwise he seemed to be in control and aware of his plight.

When he was asked how he would plead, his counsel rose to speak, but Hart was there before him, and to the absolute horror of most of the

*spectators, he said quite clearly and without
emotion, I plead guilty to both charges.*

*Pandemonium reigned for all of a minute, his
counsel begging for time to confer with his client
and nearly drowned out. When the bailiffs had
restored order, the judge turned to Hart and said,
Do you understand the consequences of your plea?
And Hart replied quite steadily that he did and
was ready to accept them.*

I put the letter down, staring at nothing as the
words brought me so close to that courtroom that
I could imagine the scene quite clearly, Lieutenant
Hart in the dock, his counsel and the KC staring
alternately at him and at the judge, unable to fathom
what was happening. After all, everyone had been
prepared for a trial, not for the rug to be pulled pre-
cipitously from under their feet. And in the center
of this maelstrom, his face pale but determined, was
Michael Hart.

The effect on the jury must have been momentous.
The trial couldn't continue.

But what in heaven's name had possessed him? Why
had he thrown his chances to the winds, and ignored
the advice of the barrister retained to save him from
the gallows?

I sat there, my head reeling, my heart plummeting to the soles of my shoes.

It was the very height of foolishness, and it made no sense.

After a time, I picked up Simon's letter again and turned to the second page.

Justice Bromley asked if Hart had any more to add to his plea, and he was answered by a single shake of the head, then a very firm No.

I needn't tell you what happened next. The court had no choice but to accept the plea before them, and I thought of you when the judge reached for his black cap. He declared that the circumstances of the two attacks, both on women alone and vulnerable, and the brutal stabbing before one had gone into the river and the other abandoned to bleed to death on the pavement, left no room for compassion or understanding. And he condemned Michael Hart to be hanged.

The words seemed to roll around my head, echoing through the room where I sat in the early twilight, unable to reach out and turn on the lamp beside me. Light would make it true. Sitting here in the shadows, I could almost pretend that this letter had never come.

Or that Michael Hart had offered something, some crumb of comfort or explanation to his bald statement. Why? Even if he had done these things—which I still doubted—why had he admitted to them? Was it conscience?

How had I been so wrong about him?

I picked up the letter again, hoping that Simon had an answer to that question.

But he didn't. He and my father had left the courtroom with the rest of the spectators, all of whom were talking about this shocking turn of events.

Simon ended the letter with a final paragraph.

I tried to speak to his barrister, but the man refused to hear me. I had the feeling he was too angry to trust himself to talk to anyone. The Colonel and I decided the best move now would be to see Hart. If we can gain access to him. If he will see us. I have considered tearing up this letter. Or not sending it until we've heard what he has to say. But in all fairness to you, my dear girl, it had to be sent. I wish I could be there when you read it. I wish I had better news.

And it was signed with his name, nothing more.

I reread the letter, still trying to absorb it.

Why would Michael Hart condemn himself? What did he know that had made him confess to murder, whether he had done that murder or not?

And the answer was there in front of me.

I went back to the letter and looked for the words again. And there they were.

Simon's discussion with Michael's barrister:

He believed that your evidence regarding events at the railway station would be crucial, as it indicated that Hart was not Mrs. Evanson's lover, and therefore had no reason to kill her to protect himself from charges that he was the child's father. As she was already married, Hart could hardly be considered a jilted lover or cuckolded husband.

Michael had confessed because he didn't want the world to hear about Marjorie's lover, Marjorie's infidelity, Marjorie's shame. It would have had to come out. It would be in all the newspapers, the gossip of London, a nine-day's wonder, and at the end of it, Marjorie would have been seen as the woman who betrayed her severely burned husband, the husband who had killed himself rather than live with the truth.

Whether Michael was guilty or not, he had given her one last gift of love—his silence.

Still, the Colonel Sahib would have something to say on that subject. "Gallantry," he often told his men, "is an act of great courage under fire, of bravery beyond the call of duty. But if it kills your comrades as well or puts the battle in jeopardy, then it is arrant pride and foolishness. Learn to know the difference."

But then Michael was only putting himself in jeopardy.

I set the letter down and went to my small trunk. Lifting the lid, I searched through my belongings for the photograph of Marjorie Evanson that I still carried with me because no one else seemed to want it.

I found the frame, turned it over, and looked at the face of the dead woman, trying to think what it was about her that had made two men love her so fiercely.

She was quite pretty, with fair hair and what must have been blue eyes, but that wasn't the person, only an outward reflection.

There must have been some quality that the camera couldn't capture, something in her smile or a vulnerability that appealed to men.

There were prettier women—Diana, my flatmate, was certainly far more beautiful.

Possibly Raymond Melton had seen her as a challenge. Some men liked that.

It occurred to me that I should send this photograph to Michael Hart. If he hadn't killed her, he would take comfort in it.

Perhaps he would whether he had killed her or not.

But it seemed a betrayal of her husband, who had clung to this photograph through the darkest hours of his life.

And how Victoria Garrison and Serena Melton must be celebrating now. They had got what they wanted, both of them.

I took a deep breath and put the frame back in my trunk and closed the lid.

The practical question now was what to do about Michael?

Did I take him at his word? Or should I go on searching for a murderer?

I turned, pulled on my boots, and went to see Matron.

If I could have leave, I could go to England and try once more to get to the bottom of Marjorie Evanson's death.

But Matron, swamped with wounded, refused to consider my request for leave, although I told her that it could be a matter of life or death.

"We're shorthanded, Sister Crawford. And your love affair will just have to wait."

"It isn't a love—"

She cut me short. "You aren't the first nursing sister to come to me with such a request. Nor will you be the last. I was young, like you. I can appreciate the fact that your world feels as if it's coming to an end. But men are dying *here,* and I will thank you to concentrate on their needs, not your own. Selfishness has no place on the battlefield."

With that she dismissed me, and I had no option but to walk out of her office and return to my quarters.

Consoling myself as best I could, I wrote a letter to Simon, and set it out for the post. If only he'd told me when the date of execution was. But perhaps he didn't know. I had a feeling that Michael would ask that it not be delayed. And he would go to the gallows before Christmas.

A thought came to mind. Inspector Herbert had been in no hurry to send for Captain Raymond Melton, because he believed that my encounter with Marjorie in the railway station had sufficiently explained his role in her life: lover, rejecting her, unwilling to believe the child she was carrying was his—but in no way connecting him to her murder. His alibi was about as sound as one could be.

But what if I could break it?

I had two hours before I was scheduled to return to duty.

I set about searching for Raymond Melton.

My father had commanded a regiment. There were soldiers from that regiment scattered across France, combined with other units, making up the armies in the field.

I only had to find one or two of its present officers, and the rest would be easy.

It was three days before someone from my father's regiment was brought in to our station, and he was walking wounded, his arm laid open by machine-gun fire. I asked the sister who was already cutting away his sleeve if I could attend to the young lieutenant.

He smiled as I came over to him, and I think he believed I must be flirting with him when I asked his name.

"Timothy Alston," he said. "And yours, Sister?"

I told him, and added, "I expect you might know of my father. Colonel Crawford."

"My God, yes," he answered, giving me a very different sort of look. And then he winced as I began to clean his wound. "How is he?"

"Fighting this war from London, much to his chagrin."

"They still tell stories about his time in India, you know," he went on. "I never had the pleasure of serving under him. I joined after he retired, but I'd have been proud to be one of his men."

"He would be very pleased to hear that," I told Lieutenant Alston truthfully. "He misses his command."

"There was the tiger hunt that nearly killed a maharajah. Has he ever told you about that? The beast leapt right into the blind, directly in the face of the maharajah, and no one could move. The maharajah was certain to be clawed to death. And then your father swung a rifle and gave the tiger an almighty whack on the side of his head—there was no room to shoot, too dangerous, but the tiger turned, looked at your father, and everyone in the blind thought he was going to attack. Then the tiger wheeled about and leapt out of the blind, disappearing into the high grass before anyone could bring a gun to bear. They say he came back to that blind, you know, the day your father marched away, and stood there, head down, mourning the loss of a brave man."

I'd heard the story from others, and those who told me, his bearers among them, swore it was true. But I said only, "I expect the tiger was still looking for the maharajah."

Lieutenant Alston laughed. As I was binding the wound, I asked casually, "By the bye, have you run into a Captain Melton in the Wiltshire Fusiliers? I've been trying to find him. I was at his brother's birthday party."

"Melton? Name doesn't ring a bell. But I'll put the word out, if you like. One of us is bound to come across him."

I thanked him, turned him over to the doctor for suturing, told him to keep the bandaging clean for at least three days, and then he was gone, back to the fighting.

I wondered if he'd remember my request. But ten days later, I received a message from Lieutenant Alston. He told me that Captain Melton had been seen not three miles away, where he was in rotation from the Front.

This time, with Matron's blessing and the excuse of needing medical supplies, I commandeered an ambulance and went to find the Fusiliers.

They were well behind the lines, men stretched out on cots, even on the ground, or smoking and pacing, writing letters, shaving, reading—anything to put the war behind them for a few precious hours. The rows of tents gleamed in the morning sun, and I felt at home as I walked down between them. The guns were loud here, our own and the Germans', and the sharp chatter of a Vickers could be heard faintly in the distance. But tired men ignored everything but the pursuit of peace for as long as possible.

I smiled and asked for Captain Melton. The young officer who had risen to greet me looked around him and then said, "I expect he's still in hospital, Sister."

Alarmed, I asked, "Is it serious?"

"Um, I'd rather not say."

Which usually meant dysentery. I thanked him, returned to the ambulance, and found my way to the rear hospital where more serious casualties were taken.

The first sister I met as I walked through the door was young and flushed with excitement.

"Rumor says the Prince of Wales is coming here to speak to the wounded," she exclaimed. "Everything is at sixes and sevens."

I gave her a list of the supplies I needed, then asked if there was a Captain Melton in the officers' ward.

She pointed the way, then rushed off to finish my errand before the Prince arrived.

She was right that the hospital was at sixes and sevens. Another sister told me that the Prince was coming to pin a medal on someone. Victoria Cross, she thought. Someone else said that the Prince was coming to see one of his former equerries who was just out of surgery for life-threatening wounds.

Threading my way to the busy ward, I went down the row of cots and looked at each patient, hoping to find Captain Melton without drawing more attention than necessary to my visit. A few patients were heavily bandaged, and I asked quietly, "Captain Melton?" only to receive a shake of the head in return.

I nearly missed him. He was at the far end, a weak and exhausted man who had lost several stone of his original weight. His skin was gray, and his eyes sunken. But a second glance confirmed that this was indeed the man I recalled from the railway station.

I went to sit beside him, and after a moment I spoke his name softly, to see if he slept or was awake.

He turned his face toward me, and his eyes when he opened them were those of a dead man, no life at all in their depths, as if he had given up all hope.

Severe dysentery could kill. But I thought, he's weak, not dying.

When I said nothing, he spoke in a thread of a voice. "Whatever you gave me seems to be working. Thank you, Sister."

He was so far from the cold, heartless man who wouldn't comfort the distressed woman clinging to his arm that I felt a wave of compassion and was torn about bringing up the past. But this might be my only chance.

When—if—he recovered, he might be sent anywhere, and the next big push might be his last.

Steeling myself against softer feelings, I said, "My name doesn't matter, Captain Melton. But I happened to be at Waterloo Station when you were saying good-bye to Marjorie Evanson, just before you sailed for France." I gave him the date and the time, told him that it was raining hard, a summer rain that made it impossible for me to find Marjorie again as she was leaving.

He listened, his face changing to a coldness that made him seem more familiar to me than the wasted man lying on the cot as I'd approached.

"What of it?" he demanded.

"The police asked me questions about her and about you. I didn't know your name then, I found it much later when I saw some photographs taken by the hus-band of a friend." I hoped I could still consider Alicia a friend. "I had met your brother Jack only a few weeks before I saw that photograph. And so I know who you are."

"You've got the wrong man," he said, turning away from me. "Please leave."

"It isn't a mistake. I knew Marjorie by sight and I have a good memory for faces. I also recognized your cap badge. You don't look like your brother, I would never have guessed who you were. But cameras don't lie. You were with Marjorie that night."

He said nothing, keeping his face resolutely turned toward the far wall.

"She was three months' pregnant. Did she tell you that?"

No response, though I saw a muscle twitch in his jaw. It struck me that he was angry, not ashamed.

"She was murdered that same evening. Were you lovers? If you were, perhaps you can tell me who Marjorie Evanson would turn to in her distress, after you got on that train and left her to cope alone." I was guessing at some of what I was saying. "Please, if you know anyone she might have seen after your train left, it would help the police enormously and might even lead to finding her killer."

"He's been found." The three words were clipped, and I was right about the anger.

I was on the point of asking him who had told him, and then of course I remembered that he was Jack Melton's brother. Jack would have passed on the news. But had he realized when he did so that the man he was telling was Marjorie's lover? I wondered too who had initiated that telling of events. Had Raymond Melton asked? Or had Jack Melton volunteered? Perhaps a little of both. It was, after all, expected to be a sensational trial and indirectly the Meltons were involved through Serena and her own brother.

"The question is, have the police got the right man? I'm not very sure of that." I kept my voice steady, interested but impersonal. "I have to be impartial, and while I don't believe you could have killed her—after all, I saw you board that train—I can't help but think your evidence would be helpful. As mine was, for it told the police that she was alive at five forty-five that day."

He showed no interest in what I was saying. And so I pressed a little harder.

"Haven't the police asked you to provide proof that you didn't leave the train at the next stop, and then find someone to drive you to Portsmouth so that you reached your transport just before it sailed?"

His head turned, and his eyes met mine. There was fire in their depths, shocking in so weak a man.

"Get out of here."

"I should like your word that you never left the train. And then I will walk away, even though you've done nothing to help the woman you seduced and then left to deal with the aftermath on her own. I would have believed in her suicide that night. It's amazing that you never gave that possibility even a thought."

"I never left the train. My word."

We'd kept our voices low, in order not to disturb other patients or draw the attention of the ward sisters.

I sat there, looking into his eyes, trying to plumb their depths for truth.

"My word," he repeated, and I had to believe him.

As I rose to walk away, I watched his face. Something stirred there, and I wondered what it was. Satisfaction?

Satisfaction that he'd managed to drive me away with only a portion of the truth?

I wondered how hard Michael Hart's counsel had tried to find this man and establish his alibi, even if the Crown had not. But then, I reminded myself, they might have done, and when it was shown he hadn't left his train, they had not felt it worthwhile to bring him back to England. There was no getting around the fact that Raymond Melton had been in France when Mrs. Calder was stabbed.

I thanked him and turned away as I'd promised, feeling deflated and uncertain. But then I went back to his bedside and said, "Has anyone told you that Helen Calder was also attacked in the same fashion as Marjorie Evanson, and presumably by the same man? Or woman? The two stabbings so close together are most likely linked, because Mrs. Calder was a Garrison before her marriage, and a cousin of Marjorie Evanson's."

He stared at me. "I know Helen Calder," he said, eyes wide now with disbelief. "I was at Mons with her husband. Is she dead as well?"

"She ought to be. But she was found in time, in spite of loss of blood and emergency surgery to repair the damage done. There will be weeks of recovery ahead of her, but she's alive."

He went on staring at me, trying to absorb what I'd said. Then he asked, "Surely she was able to identify her attacker?"

"She has no memory of what happened. What little she recalls of the hours before she was stabbed point to the man the police took into custody. He's been tried, and will be hanged."

I fought to keep my voice steady as I said the words.

Captain Melton closed his eyes and lay there, spent. Then he said, "Poor devil, he must be out of his mind with worry."

I understood that to mean Mrs. Calder's husband. I couldn't help but think that this man had shown more pity for a fellow officer than he had for the woman he'd used, if not loved.

I left then, walking swiftly down the center of the ward, and in the distance I could hear shouting, loud huzzahs, and assumed that the Prince had finally arrived. A piper began to play, the pipes wheezing and then settling into the melody. I'd always liked the pipes, and listened for a moment to what the man was playing. It was, I realized, "God Save the King," in honor of the Prince's father.

I slipped out a side door, in low spirits and not in the mood for a spectacle. For that's what it would be, and rightly so. Men needed to know that the royal family remembered their sacrifice. Reaching the ambulance, I discovered that the sister I'd given my list to had set several boxes in the rear, where the stretchers usually went. Grateful to her, I drove back to my own unit, and turned the boxes over to the nurse in charge of stores.

And then I went to my own quarters and sat there as darkness fell and the rains came again, turning mud to a treacherous slickness and breeding a miasma of odors that seemed to cling to the walls and my sheets and the very air I was breathing.

I could understand now why Inspector Herbert, far more experienced in such matters than I could possibly hope to be, had discounted finding Captain Melton. He had indeed taken the train to Portsmouth and boarded his ship as scheduled and landed in France at the required time. While it had been important to identify the man with Marjorie Evanson and the likely father of her child, the instant he'd stepped into his compartment on the train, his alibi was secure.

Then where was there any small, overlooked fact that would save Michael Hart?

Or was the right man going to hang at the time set for him to climb the stairs to the gallows?

Why was it that I couldn't be satisfied with what was looking more and more like the truth?

Chapter Eighteen

The next two and a half weeks were busy. I was coming to realize that this war was producing nothing but dead and wounded men. No glorious victories, no great advances into German-held territory.

There was talk that the Americans would be coming to France, but even so, it would be months before they could take the field and make a difference. By that time, it appeared that England and France would be bled dry.

I was too tired to do the arithmetic, but it seemed to me that for every yard of ground won or lost, the toll was enormous. If I, a nurse in the field, could see this happening, why did the men in staff positions, the men who made both the daily and the long-term decisions about fighting the enemy, not look at the casualty lists and find another way to win?

I was reminded of my great-grandmother at Waterloo. There the English squares held despite charge after charge by Napoleon's best troops. And at the end of the day, in spite of the slaughter, the squares still held, and Napoleon was forced to retreat. Not a very decisive victory, attrition at its worst. And without the backing of Blücher's men, arriving in the nick of time, the tide might have turned the other way. But at least the battle lasted only that one day. And by the next evening, my great-grandmother knew whether or not her husband still lived.

I was coming off duty when I encountered Dr. Hall just coming on. We smiled wearily at each other, and he asked, "Do you sleep?"

"Not very well," I answered truthfully.

He nodded. "Nor I. Well. We do our best."

"Yes, sir."

"I've had word we're to be relieved in the next fortnight."

This was news I hadn't heard. It revived me a little and I said, "Another convoy home?"

"Very likely. Would you like to be listed as the transport nurse?"

"I would indeed."

He nodded a second time. "I'd heard that you had approached Matron about leave some time ago. Was it important? Or perhaps I should ask, is it still important?"

I told him the truth. "An officer I know has been convicted of murder. I'd have liked to have been at his trial. Since then, I've not received any news of the date he's to die. Either that or no one wishes to tell me when it will be. I keep hoping for some fresh evidence to prove that he's not guilty. I'd like to see him a last time and hear what he has to say."

Dr. Hall regarded me with interest. "He's more than a friend?"

"No, sir. Just—a friend. But I feel rather responsible for his situation. I was a witness in the case, though not called on to give evidence in court. I was in the right place at the wrong time. And what I saw proved to be important. An attempt on my part to help the police uncover the identity of one man in the case led them to another man, but it seems to me that there were problems with evidence. And circumstance conspired to put the worst possible interpretation on that evidence. Given my friend's wounds in two instances, I can't see how he could have committed the crimes he was charged with. But the police surgeon must have seen the matter differently. And so my friend will hang."

"Interesting," Dr. Hall said. "What sort of wounds?"

I told him about the particle in Lieutenant Hart's eye, and then about the damaged shoulder.

Dr. Hall looked at his watch. "I don't have time to pursue this now. But if you'll meet me when I come off duty, I'd like to hear more."

I thanked him, thinking he was trying to be polite and would have lost interest by morning.

But I was wrong. I was sitting in the canteen finishing my tea when Dr. Hall came looking for me.

He took the chair across from me, and said, "I'm so tired I could sleep on my feet. But talk to me, and if I can stay awake, I'll give you my opinion. It won't make any difference to the Crown, or to the case in hand. Still, I might be able to set your mind at ease on the medical issues."

I tried to marshal my thoughts, and then told him as concisely as I knew how the way the murders had occurred and what Michael's physical condition was at this time, after his shoulder had healed. At least to the best of my knowledge, which was superficial at the very least.

Dr. Hall stirred his coffee—he had picked up the French habit of drinking coffee, as so many others had done during this war—and considered the medical implications.

"He could have done these things, in spite of his injuries—that is to say, if he didn't care about the physical damage and was prepared to take the risk."

I wondered if his barrister had ordered a physician to examine Michael's eye. He hadn't complained—but then he wouldn't have, would he? If he'd disobeyed the doctor's instructions?

He must have read my face.

"My dear, you must understand that people who kill are not marked by the brand of Cain. They appear no different from you or me. It's hard to believe sometimes that someone we know well—or think we know well—could do horrible things. But they can."

He was right, of course he was.

I smiled, trying to make it appear bright and accepting.

"Thank you. I needed impartiality."

He cocked his head to one side. "The position as transport nurse is still yours. Sometimes it's better to learn the truth firsthand."

He was a small man, graying early, lines forming around his eyes that would not go away even when he slept for a week. But his hands were gentle in the operating theater, and they worked miracles with torn flesh and sinew and bone.

I sighed. "You're very kind."

"No," he said, finishing his coffee and getting to his feet. "I'm just very tired."

We brought the wounded to England and I discovered I'd been given ten days' leave.

I went home and surprised my parents. As I stood in the doorway, they stared at me as if I were a ghost, then they rushed to greet me, talking at the same time, laughing with excitement, sweeping me into the family circle with such warmth it was as if I'd never been away.

I said nothing about Michael Hart. Not then, nor at dinner. But after my parents had gone to bed, I pulled on a sweater against the night's chill and walked the mile to the cottage where Simon Brandon lived.

He hadn't come to dinner. He hadn't come to welcome me home. My parents hadn't mentioned that he was away. So where was he?

I could hear a night bird calling as I went up the lane and came to the path to the cottage door.

The house was in darkness except for a single lamp in the front room.

I stood for a moment on the step, then lifted my hand to the knocker. It was shaped like an elephant's head. Simon had had it made in Agra at a little shop where a man sat cross-legged and spent his days carving useful objects. A rectangular length of brass had been fitted to the back of the head, and the plate was also brass. It had a musical ring as I let it fall.

I didn't think he was going to come to the door. But after what seemed like a very long time, the door opened, and Simon stood there in shirt and dark trousers.

"I was waiting," he said, and stepped aside to allow me to enter.

I had always liked the cottage. It was strictly a man's home, of course, filled with a lifetime's treasures and memories, but as tidy as a sergeant-major's quarters in camp.

I moved into the parlor as Simon closed the door behind me and I took the chair that had always been mine, by the window overlooking the garden.

"The news isn't good," he said, coming in to join me, but not sitting down. "He's stubborn, your Michael Hart. He asked that his sentence be expedited. Mrs. Calder isn't doing well. Preparing herself for the trial has taxed her strength. And of course there was no trial. As such."

"He's not my Michael Hart."

Simon nodded, then said, "The execution is set for a fortnight tomorrow."

I couldn't stop myself from reacting. I had thought, before Christmas. *Months* away.

More than enough time, surely. But there was almost none.

"You didn't write," I accused him.

"No. He refuses to see you. He asked me to wait to tell you until it was—over."

"He did it for her, you know. To prevent what she'd done being opened up for the public to gawk at and whisper about."

"I think he did it for himself as well. That arm will probably be useless for the rest of his life. He can't live with that. So why not die for a good reason?"

"It's stupid! There was a chance—you said so as well—that the trial could have ended in an acquittal."

"At what price to Mrs. Evanson's reputation?"

"Well, he hasn't considered one thing. And I intend to bring it to his attention. Can you or the Colonel arrange for me to see him?"

"I told you. He refuses to see you."

"He may refuse. But you might tell him that I am bringing a photograph of Marjorie to take with him to the gallows."

Simon's face had been in shadow, but suddenly I saw the gleam of his teeth as he smiled. "My dear girl. I bow to your brilliance. But where will you find a photograph of Mrs. Evanson in ten days' time?"

"I've had it since I went to Hampshire and learned that Meriwether Evanson had killed himself. Serena refused to put it in his coffin. Matron couldn't bear to throw it away, and so I took it. I had thought—if I'd considered the matter at all—that I might somehow put it by Lieutenant Evanson's grave."

"You had told me the photograph went with Evanson from France to the clinic. But not that it was now in your possession."

"It was—personal. Whatever she did, whatever reason she might have had for doing it, he loved her more than living."

Simon went to the sideboard in the dining room. I could hear him collecting two glasses and a decanter. It was whiskey he brought back with him, and a small carafe of water as well.

He poured a small measure of the whiskey in a glass, added water to it, and passed the glass to me, then poured himself a larger measure without the water. Holding his glass out to me, he said, "Welcome home, Bess."

I drank the whiskey. They say Queen Victoria drank a small tot each night before retiring. If she approved of it for herself, it would do me no harm. But I wasn't sure I really cared for the taste of it, a smokiness that caught at the back of my throat and belied the smoothness of the first swallow.

Simon smiled and took my glass from me before I'd finished it, setting it on the table. "It's late. I'll see you home."

"I can find my own way."

"I'm sure you can. But I shouldn't care to face the Colonel tomorrow if I allowed you to walk that mile alone." He drained his own glass and set it down.

"Who killed her, Simon, if Michael didn't?"

"I don't know. Who had the most to lose?"

I stepped through the door he was holding for me and out into the night. "Raymond Melton? He had a career in the Army, a wife. He could have lost both if the affair had come to light. As it surely must have done."

"But he was on that transport ship."

We walked down the path side by side and turned into the lane.

"Victoria? She was jealous of her sister from childhood."

"Why then? Why wait until that moment?"

"Because with the child of her affair, she would have had to come home to Little Sefton and back into Victoria's life?"

"Possible, of course. On the other hand, Victoria might well have relished her sister's fall from grace."

"There's that. Serena, then, for what Marjorie was about to do to Meriwether."

"That's far more likely. Except that Serena told her brother the truth about Marjorie, after she was dead."

"I think that was her own pain speaking. She hated Marjorie and wanted her brother to hate his wife too." I sighed. "A tangle, isn't it?"

"Which brings us full circle, back to Michael."

We walked on in silence, shoulder to shoulder. As Simon lifted the latch on the door to my parents' house, he said, "I'll go to London tomorrow."

"And I'm going to Little Sefton. I want to speak to Michael's aunt and uncle. After that, I must go to London and look in on Helen Calder. She must be feeling rather awful after her testimony sent Michael to trial."

Simon said good night, and waited outside as I shut and locked the house door. I stood in the darkness at the bottom of the stairs and watched him out of sight. Then I turned toward the stairs, intending to go straight to my room.

My heart leapt into my throat. There was someone on the stairs, standing there in silence, watching me.

All at once I recognized the shape of my father.

He must have known somehow that I had gone to see Simon.

He said only, "Is everything all right?"

"Yes. Simon is going to London tomorrow. I'm going to Little Sefton myself. And then to London. There isn't much time . . ."

"For what it's worth, my dear, I don't believe he killed Marjorie Evanson."

My father knew men. He'd fought with them, led them, listened to them, disciplined them. Little escaped his notice, and he was a good judge of character.

I went up the stairs to him and hugged him.

"Thank you for telling me that," I said.

"You smell of whiskey. Brush your teeth before your mother comes to kiss you good night."

I promised, and we went up the remaining stairs to bed.

Between my own fatigue and the whiskey, I slept soundly.

I wondered if that was what Simon had intended.

The next morning I said good-bye to my parents and set out for Little Sefton.

It was well into September now. I'd first taken this road in early June, with high hopes that I could in some fashion bring to light a name that would lead the police to Marjorie's killer. Now I drove with a sense of desperation goading me.

A fortnight today. That's all the time I had. And even if I found new evidence, the courts would have to be persuaded to hear it and act upon it.

The urgent order of business, however, was mending my fences with Alicia.

The first person I saw was the rector, who greeted me warmly and asked if I'd been in France again.

I told him I had, and then said, "Still, I heard about the trial. It must have been terribly trying for Michael's aunt and uncle."

He shook his head. "I've offered them what comfort I could. And I've written to Michael, to ask if I could serve him in the days to come."

"How has he answered?"

"Sadly, with silence." He looked up at the weathervane on the church tower as if it could point him in the right direction. "I've never counseled a man facing the gallows. I've prayed to find the right words, when the time comes."

"I'm sure you will do," I replied. "Do you think I could speak to Mr. and Mrs. Hart? I know Michael pleaded guilty, but I also believe I know why he did. If I'm right, then it may be that he's innocent of murder."

The rector stared at me. "You mustn't raise false hope," he warned. "It would be very unkind. They have been in seclusion, I don't believe it would be wise."

"Which is worse for them, thinking Michael is a murderer or watching him die knowing he's innocent? I've wrestled with that question for hours. I think I'd find comfort in knowing the truth. In knowing that my own flesh and blood is dying for what he believes in, not because he has done something appalling."

But he remained steadfast in his belief that I would do more harm than good.

I left the subject there, and asked instead, "How has Victoria Garrison taken this news?"

The rector said, "Walk with me to the rectory, won't you?" I nodded, and as we crossed the churchyard, he went on. "Victoria Garrison troubles me. She was eager to give her evidence. And when proceedings were halted almost before they had properly begun, she was beside herself with anger. I was there that first day myself, I felt it was my duty, you know. If young Hart looked out at the crowded courtroom, I thought it might be steadying to find a familiar face. Victoria was waiting with the other witnesses, and when the trial ended abruptly, a bailiff must have gone to tell them that they were free to leave. And so we ran into each other on the stairs, and I was shocked. I had expected distress, disbelief, even. But her face was flushed with fury. I asked if she was all right, but she turned on me and said, 'I've been cheated!' in such a savage tone that I stepped back, and she hastened out the door and into the street. I've been at a loss ever since to understand."

I thought I did understand. Victoria had wanted her pound of flesh, to hear in open court a discussion of the sins of her sister. I couldn't imagine that Michael's fate moved her—she had been eager to see him taken into custody.

I had wondered before if a woman could have stabbed both victims. It was possible. But was it likely?

Given Victoria's hatred of Marjorie, it could have happened. But how did Victoria know about the love affair before her sister's death? Or about the child? Surely Marjorie hadn't confided in her. And so Victoria couldn't have killed her.

There was the problem. If Marjorie had been living her life quietly in London, Victoria had no reason to be aware of her situation.

The rector, suspecting my inner struggles, invited me to have lunch with him. "My excellent cook always makes more than enough sandwiches for one person," he ended. "It will be no imposition."

And so I did. There was a plate full of sandwiches, with a dish of summer apples stewed in honey. "We've been keeping bees," the rector told me. "Have you tried honey in your tea?" There were also small potatoes baked in milk and grated cheese.

We talked about the village, and I confessed that I'd come to mend fences with Alicia.

He smiled. "She was saying on Sunday last that she wished it had never happened. I think if you go to her door, she will be glad to see you."

I wasn't as certain. But I promised I would try.

After our meal, against his advice, I went to knock at the door of the Hart house.

A maid opened it and told me that Mr. and Mrs. Hart were receiving no visitors.

"Will you tell them that Elizabeth Crawford has called and would like to speak with them?"

She went away and after several minutes came back to say that the Harts would see me.

Surprised and grateful, I thanked her and was taken to the small sitting room with its comfortable furnishings and a lovely Turkey carpet.

I could see at once that Mrs. Hart's eyes were puffy and red from crying. Mr. Hart appeared to have aged in only a matter of weeks.

He said, as I was shown into the room and the maid had closed the door behind me, "Miss Crawford," and indicated a chair to one side of his own.

I answered at once. "I can't express what I feel. I wasn't allowed leave to come home for the trial. I doubt if I could have made a difference if I had. But I wanted to try."

Mrs. Hart said, "Michael expressly forbade us to attend the trial. He told us that it would be distressing and hurtful, and he didn't want us to see that. He didn't want to sit there in the dock and watch our faces. Now I think he knew, even then, what he was intending to do, and that's why he asked us to stay away. And it was the most horrible shock when the rector came to tell us what had happened. I refused to believe it then, and I still do. But most of Little Sefton feels that we stayed away out of shame for what he's done. And to make it all even worse, he won't let us come to see him one last time. I'm unable to sleep, I can't—we had him from a little boy, and there's no meanness in Michael. I want him to know that we love him still and would do anything—anything!—to keep him with us."

"My dear, you mustn't—" her husband began.

"Don't tell me not to cry! He was like my own child. How shall I go on, knowing what they've done to him?" She turned to me. "You stood up for him, there in the street, when they came for him. I never said a word in his defense—I was so shocked, my tongue seemed as paralyzed as the rest of me. But you kept your wits about you and defended him. I will always be grateful for that, Miss Crawford. You will always be dear to me because you did what I couldn't."

I took her hand. "Let me tell you what I think. It may not ease your suffering, but it could explain what happened in that courtroom. Michael was informed while he was in prison that although his shoulder has healed, he won't regain the use of that arm. I don't know if that's true or not. There are trained people who are doing wonders with such wounds. I do know that he isn't the only solder to feel his life is over because he's lost the use of a limb or an eye. It isn't an easy truth to live with. I'd like to believe that he decided then to protect Marjorie's name and reputation by stopping the trial before it had begun. He's always loved Marjorie. It would be like him to see this as a noble gesture, a very good reason for dying and ending his own wretchedness."

Mr. Hart stared at me. "I— If I hadn't been so blinded by my own grief, I would have seen that for myself. It's possible. Very possible." He smiled for the first time, although there were tears in his eyes. "That foolish boy. But dear God, what are we to do?"

"I don't know," I answered truthfully. "But perhaps if we talk about the people who knew Marjorie best, we might find something that could help."

"Victoria." Mrs. Hart's voice was cold and angry. "She tried to ruin Marjorie's life, and now she's ruined Michael's. Did you know, Miss Crawford, that she went to Meriwether Evanson shortly before the marriage, to tell him that Marjorie was very likely illegitimate? He showed her the door, and said that if she ever said as much to any other living soul, he and Marjorie would take her to court for defamation of character. I think she was a little afraid of him after that. He came to Michael afterward to ask what sort of person Victoria was. And Michael told him how she'd alienated Mr. Garrison and Marjorie, to the point that Marjorie went to live in London. Meriwether swore Michael to secrecy, and he never broke his word until a week before he was taken into custody. He wanted us to know what Meriwether had said—that Victoria was evil. To beware of her."

"Then why did he let her drive him to London?"

"Because he was desperate to go there," Mr. Hart replied, "and I'm really not comfortable driving such distances now." He put his hand to his heart as if in explanation. "I asked him to wait a few days, that I'd find someone to take him. But he was impatient, he said there was something he had thought about, that he must ask Helen Calder, although he wasn't about to tell Victoria his real reason for speaking to her. Michael had been rereading Marjorie's letters to him, but he didn't have all of them. He believed Mrs. Calder might remember what he was searching for."

I leaned forward. "What was it he was hoping to ask her? I expect to see Mrs. Calder tomorrow. Perhaps I can ask her instead."

"I wish I knew," he replied. "I didn't understand the urgency, you see, or I'd have risked the journey myself. I've regretted that bitterly. I would have been with him instead." Michael's alibi, which Victoria couldn't—or wouldn't—give him.

"Could Victoria have been suspicious enough to follow him?" I asked. "If she was jealous of Marjorie, she could have been jealous of Helen Calder as well. She might have jumped to the conclusion that he had used her to see Mrs. Calder." But even as I said the words, I thought about Mrs. Calder's long, thin face. And she was a few years older. What was there to be jealous of?

But jealousy didn't always heed reason.

Small wonder Victoria was eager to testify at the trial. She would have enjoyed twisting the truth if it put Michael Hart in the worst possible light.

"Just how much did Victoria know about Marjorie's life in London?" I asked after a moment. "Did she go up to London often, after her father's death?"

"If you want to know what I think," Mrs. Hart said, "she went to spy on her sister."

"My dear," her husband cautioned, "we couldn't be sure where she was going when she left here."

"Well, you saw her often enough at the station in Great Sefton. Where else could she have been going at that hour but to London? It isn't as if trains pass through Great Sefton as often as they do in Waterloo Station or Charing Cross! There are only two a day, the morning train to London and the evening train to Portsmouth."

"She was fond of the theater and the symphony," her husband reminded her. "And Mrs. Toller mentioned that Victoria volunteered there, arranging programs for the wounded. I've told you before."

"Yes, that's all well and good. It doesn't convince me she wasn't spying on Marjorie."

I said, "Perhaps there was a man, someone she cared about."

But they would have none of that. Not Victoria, they said. They weren't even certain she'd cared for Michael, except for the fact that he belonged to Marjorie.

"She wanted him because she couldn't have him," Mrs. Hart declared. "And what she can't have, she despises."

I tried to pin Mr. and Mrs. Hart down to precise dates when they'd seen Victoria in Great Sefton, but too much time had passed.

When I left the Harts, I wondered if Michael had weighed the grief his decision had inflicted on them. Protecting the dead was admirable, but the living counted too.

From there, I went to call on Alicia.

Her face was cool when she answered the door.

I said quickly, before she could shut it again, "Please. I'm so sorry that I made you angry on my last visit. It was wrong of me to exclude you when I spoke to the rector's cook. I thought I was being wise, and I was only being selfish." I stopped, seeing no softening in her expression. "I've only just come back from France. I couldn't get leave for Michael's trial. And he's to be hanged next week." I wanted her to know that I hadn't been in England since the day of our quarrel.

"I was shocked by your behavior when he was taken into custody. To argue with the constable and that man from Scotland Yard on a public street was unseemly. It embarrassed me. After all, I'd introduced you to every-one here."

I didn't think that had bothered her as much as my interviewing the rector's cook on my own. But I said, "It was the only chance I had to speak up. I had to stand up for what I believed to be true at the time."

"And he confessed, didn't he? To murdering one woman and attempting to murder another. I couldn't believe it, but I expect he did it to save his aunt and uncle the ordeal of a trial. At least in that he showed some courage."

I didn't argue. What good would it have done?

After a moment she said, "What brings you back to Little Sefton?"

"I came to offer my support to Mr. and Mrs. Hart. They are guilty of nothing, except perhaps for loving Michael and still believing in him."

"He wasn't their child. As Victoria has been busy pointing out."

"I don't think they consider whose child he was, only that they are losing him before very long." I hesitated, and then said, "Speaking of Victoria, I hear she was often in London. Did you ever go with her to a play?"

Grudgingly she answered me. "I did once, yes. I didn't enjoy it very much. I didn't know anyone there, and I felt guilty enjoying myself while Gareth was in France."

"I understand that."

"No, you can't. You aren't married. The man you love isn't likely to be killed in the next push, or at risk of dying in an aid station before you even hear that he's been wounded."

I realized then that she hadn't heard from him for a while. And looking more closely, I could see that she had passed sleepless nights as well.

"I'm sometimes the last caring face they see," I told her gently. "I often write letters for the dying. I know that their last thoughts are for those they love."

She burst into tears then, unable to hold them back, burying her face in her hands. "You don't know. No one can know."

I took her arm and led her into the house, then sat with her as she cried. After a while I went to the kitchen and found the kettle, put it on, and made a pot of tea. She was quieter when I came back to the sitting room, and drank her tea obediently, sniffling at first, and finally dully sitting there, worn and worried.

"I'm so sorry," she said in a muffled voice. "I've been out of sorts, worrying. There's been no news for weeks and weeks."

"If there is bad news, you will know. It won't take weeks and weeks."

Taking a deep breath, she set her teacup aside. "Thank you, Bess," she said simply. "And I'm so sorry about Michael. I feel responsible, I introduced you to him. I didn't dream—"

"No, that's all right." I rose to take my leave. "Will you be all right now?"

"Yes, sometimes it just overwhelms me, the worry about Gareth."

Following me to the door, she added, "I *am* sorry about Michael. I know you were beginning to care for him. But you'll forget in time. There will be someone else."

I didn't contradict her. I thanked her for the tea and asked her to write to me if she felt like it.

I had reached the walk, heading for my motorcar, when she stopped me.

"Bess?"

I turned.

"I think Victoria was seeing someone in London in the winter. But it must not have come to anything. It was over by the spring."

"Did you know who it was?"

She shook her head. "I only heard the gossip. Someone told me he was an officer. And Mrs. Leighton swore that he was married. She saw them coming out of a mean little restaurant near Hampstead Heath. Those were her words, 'a mean little restaurant,' and she interpreted this as proof he was married, because he hadn't taken Victoria somewhere nice in London."

I thanked her, glad we were parting as friends, and walked back to the church, where I'd left my motorcar.

I'd just turned the crank and stepped back when someone came up behind me.

I turned, expecting it to be Alicia again, but it was
Victoria Garrison.

"I thought that was your vehicle, hidden in the
shrubbery where no one would notice it."

"Hardly the shrubbery. If I'm not mistaken, those
are a stand of lilac. What is it you want, Miss Garrison?
To gloat?"

"Well, you won't be marrying Michael Hart. I've
seen to that."

I stood there stock-still, feeling my jaw drop. I
snapped it shut and tried to think of something to say
that wouldn't tell her how angry I was.

"Do you mean you were so willing to drive Michael
to London because you thought he might be falling in
love with me?"

"He wanted to go. I accommodated him. I didn't
stab poor Helen, and he did."

"You don't believe that."

Something flickered in her eyes. "How do you know
what I feel?" she demanded in a different tone of voice.
"How dare you even suggest you know me?"

"You just suggested that you knew me well enough
to believe I was in love with Michael Hart and he with
me. Well, let me disabuse you of that notion. What

drew the two of us together was your sister's murder. Nothing more, nothing less. I liked Michael, I still like him. But if he were freed tomorrow, I wouldn't marry him. I'm not in love with him and never will be."

"Alicia said—" She stopped.

Ah, the power of gossip! And the damage it can do.

"Alicia has been matchmaking. She's a happily married woman, and she wants everyone to be just as happy, because it's all she can cling to with Gareth at the Front. I'm sorry if I've disappointed you."

I got behind the wheel, and she came to stand by my door, pinning me there. "I don't believe you."

"Perhaps that's because you were in love yourself not long ago. And like Alicia, expect that everyone else is looking for someone to care about."

For an instant I thought she was going to step closer and slap me. I could see her hands clenching at her side. A mixture of emotions passed across her face, anger and something else that was barely controlled. I'd wondered if she could kill. And now I knew she could. I drew back a little, but she leaned toward me. After looking around to be sure no one was near, she said through clenched teeth, "Have you ever seen someone die on a gallows? That handsome face will be black and swollen, hardly recognizable, and I hope that's what you see in your dreams for the rest of your life!"

I caught my breath.

Meriwether Evanson had called Victoria evil. And now I knew he was right.

What she had done to her mother and father, to her sister, what she had hoped to do to Michael, and what she had just said to me, spoke of a deep-seated streak of cruelty.

Driving away before she could change her mind and do something rash, I was glad to see the last of Little Sefton.

I was halfway to London before I was calm enough to go over again what I'd said to Victoria Garrison. I'd been angry, and yes, a little frightened by her, so the words were lost at first. In the end, they came back to me. What I'd said hadn't angered her—it was the fact that I knew something she wanted to hide.

If Victoria had had a romantic fling in the winter, it hadn't survived. I couldn't help but wonder if he, whoever he was, had thrown her over for someone else. Married or not.

I turned the bonnet of my motorcar toward London, and when I got there, I went directly to the flat. It seemed a haven, just now. It was late afternoon, and Mrs. Hennessey was out.

I climbed the stairs with a heavy heart, and reached for the latch of our door, but it opened under my hand. Someone was here.

I walked into the flat, and Mary glanced up from the letter she was writing. After one look at me she frowned.

"Have you lost your last friend, or your last penny?" she demanded, and capped her pen before setting it aside and moving into what we euphemistically called our kitchen, to make a pot of tea.

"I'm in low spirits," I admitted. "I've just been very rude to someone who was rude to me first. And I'm trying to save a good friend from hanging, and I am in the early stages of panic, because he goes to the gallows next week."

She looked up from measuring the tea and said, "Who's going to the gallows next week? Anyone I know?"

"Michael Hart. He was convicted of the murder of Serena Melton's brother's wife. Marjorie Evanson. And of attacking a distant cousin of Marjorie's, with the intent to kill."

"You do have an unusual range of friends, Bess," she retorted. "I hope you're saying he's innocent?"

"God knows. The evidence against him was strong, but the feeling was, he could very well be acquitted. He had a very good barrister—Mr. Forbes for the defense—who was certainly sanguine about his chances. And then to everyone's amazement and shock, he changed his plea to guilty in the first minutes of the trial."

"Ah. I remember now. He's extraordinarily handsome. I saw his photograph in some broadsheet or other."

"No doubt. They thought it was going to be a notorious, scandalous trial, and instead he disappointed everyone."

Mary brought the tea to the table, and set out the cups. "Drink this, and then tell me everything from the beginning."

"You know a part of it—"

"Doesn't matter. Start at the start. I won't be able to see any solution if I don't know it all."

I didn't like telling Mary all about the Garrisons and the Harts and the Meltons. She knew Serena, after all. But Mary is the soul of discretion, and what I said to her would be treated like the confidence it was.

The afternoon had faded into early dusk by the time I'd finished, and the teapot was empty, the biscuits she'd found in the cupboard, hard and stale as they were, had been finished as well. There's something about eating a sweet that raises the spirits.

I sat back, tired by the tale and tired from the emotions of the day and the long drive. "Well. There you have it."

She picked up the cups and the teapot to do the washing up, and it was while she was working that she said, "I hesitate to tell you this, Bess, but you're right. The evidence is very strong against your Lieutenant Hart."

"He isn't mine," I said testily, "although everyone is busy insisting that he is."

"All the same."

"Yes, I know. But there's just enough doubt . . ." My voice trailed away. Then I said, "But why do I have this sense of failure? I'm a fairly good judge of character, Mary. How could I be so wrong about the man?"

"I expect the reason is that you don't believe strongly in his motive. That he killed Marjorie Evanson because she was seeing someone else. But he knew her husband, and it seems to me that a decent man wouldn't kill a married woman because she'd been dithering with someone else instead of *him*. He was more likely to lecture her on her behavior and make certain that the man was out of her life altogether. Simon would have done that, wouldn't he? If you stood in Marjorie's shoes? Well, you aren't married of course, but you know what I mean."

It was typically convoluted—Mary was good at convoluting—but she was also very sensible and practical. It was what made her an excellent nurse.

"I do see." I was already feeling better. "And even if he went to Helen Calder's house, I can't understand why he would have a reason to kill her. But that's the problem, she can remember that he was coming, but not why, or if he was the one who stabbed her."

"Who knew he was going to her house?"

"His aunt and uncle. Unless of course Victoria was suspicious and followed him."

"Who would Victoria tell?" Mary asked. "If she saw him at the Calder house and was angry enough to do a mischief?"

"I—I'm not sure," I said slowly. "Why would she tell anyone?"

"You said there was speculation that she'd been seeing someone in London. A man. What if he was the same man who killed Marjorie?"

"That makes no sense."

"It would do, if she has made a practice of spoiling Marjorie's chances."

"But he wasn't the one who got Marjorie pregnant."

"You can't be sure of that."

"But I can. I told you, I spoke to Raymond Melton while I was in France. He was the man I saw with her at the railway station that evening. She was dead only a few hours later. And he was on his way to Portsmouth.

He couldn't possibly have killed *her*. We're back where we began."

"Didn't you say he denied leaving that train?"

"Yes."

"What if he's telling the truth? What if *he* wasn't her lover?"

"I saw the way Marjorie was clinging to him. In distress—despair." I gave it some thought. "You're saying that he was there at the station with her, and she'd told him the truth about her circumstances—but he wasn't her lover."

I'd dismissed that idea earlier.

I went on slowly, "But if she did indeed confide in him, and he wasn't the man responsible for getting her pregnant, then he must have known who that man was. That's why he was there." I remembered the small flicker of satisfaction in Raymond Melton's eyes when I confronted him in the ward. He had told me the literal truth—but not the whole truth. "And she contacted him because the other man refused to speak to her after the affair was over."

"That happens," Mary said. "All too often, in fact. Remember Nan Wilson, who was in love with that Frenchman who was here with the diplomatic corps? He was some sort of military attaché. And when he went back to France, and she found herself in trouble, he sent her letters back unopened, marked address unknown."

I did remember.

It would explain so much. I'd wondered why Marjorie Evanson had let herself be seduced by Raymond Melton. After all, her own father had been the same sort of cold and uncaring man. I understood why he'd offered no comfort, kissed her cheek so perfunctorily. I remembered how he'd walked away without looking back—even if the love affair was over—to make certain she was all right. He had done his duty, he had listened to her pleas for help, told her he could do nothing about her situation, and calmly boarded his train.

It was such a calculated and callous act that I was stunned.

Who would Raymond Melton do such a service for?

The answer was simple.

His brother Jack.

Chapter Nineteen

"**J**ack Melton." I whispered the name aloud, as if by hearing it spoken, I confirmed it. And then I thought, Poor Serena.

How frantic she had been to put a name to the man who was responsible for Marjorie's plight, and I'd heard her husband pretend to advise her as if it were his dearest wish as well that those weekend parties be successful. And all the time, the man she was after was within arm's reach. He'd let her anger and her determination make her life a misery, and he'd even expressed his concern about her to me. Had she also secretly prayed that the man she was looking for wasn't her own husband? It would explain so much about her, her shrillness, her rudeness, her frustration.

What had made her suspect him of having an affair?

Did she suspect him of murder as well as adultery? Surely not.

I remembered the day I'd encountered Jack Melton outside the Marlborough Hotel.

He had known that Michael Hart was in England the night that Marjorie Evanson was killed. But how could he have known? Unless she had told him herself.

How easy it would have been for Raymond Melton to find a telephone in Portsmouth on his way to the docks, and put in a call to his brother to say that the meeting with Marjorie hadn't gone as well as expected. Or that she'd made threats. As a last resort, she could even have brought up Michael's name.

He's in London tonight. I'll speak to him, and we'll see how Jack feels then about not talking to me himself . . .

It wasn't out of the realm of possibility. Still, conjecture wouldn't stop Michael from hanging.

I said to Mary, "I'm so sorry—these are your friends!"

She answered me with a sigh, then said, "Serena is my friend. And she will need me when the truth comes out. As it must, Bess. Don't you see, she's a victim too. She's already lost her brother. We can't leave her to the mercy of a man like that. What if *she* discovers he's a killer?"

I found a telephone and called my parents, first to tell them that I was in London now, and second to ask my father if there was any news from Simon.

My father said gently, "Bess. My dear. I don't think Michael will wish to see you. You mustn't let yourself hope."

"But how can we do anything for him if he won't answer questions? His aunt and uncle are grieving. He ought to think of the living as well as the dead."

"Will it do if Simon or I go to see him?"

My heart plummeted. I wanted to see Michael, I wanted to see for myself how he was bearing up, and whether pleading guilty had weighed heavily on his conscience—or freed it. I wanted to see whether he had any use of his shoulder and arm, or if the case there was as hopeless as he'd been told. But how to explain this to my father—or for that matter, to Simon—without arousing their protective instincts, thinking to spare me added grief? If Michael was guilty, I could accept it. If he wasn't, it was a terrible waste of a man's life and reputation to die in the misplaced belief that he was sparing Marjorie.

I couldn't stand in judgment of her—but her affair had touched other lives, led to her murder, the death of her husband, the attack on Helen Calder. I saw no good reason to add another death to that list. Especially since it could mean that the real murderer went free.

I wasn't sure we would ever know what drove Marjorie Evanson into a love affair. The truth may have died with her. That was how it should be.

My father's voice came down the line.

"Bess? Are you still there?"

"Please, if he can be persuaded to see me, I still want to go. If he absolutely refuses, then Simon should go in my place. Michael knows him. I'll make a list of what I need to learn. It's important. Otherwise I wouldn't insist."

"It would help if I knew—have you any information that could overturn the verdict? I'll speak to Inspector Herbert if you have."

"I'm not sure. I'm leaving now—I'm going back to Little Sefton. There's something I must do there."

"Not tonight, Bess. That's not wise. Wait until morning."

"There aren't enough mornings left." I tried not to let what I was feeling seep into my voice. Wailing would do no good. "Please, will you speak to Simon?"

"I promise."

That was enough for me.

"If you promise not to drive anywhere tonight."

I was caught on the horns of a dilemma.

Finally I said, "Yes, all right, I agree. I'll leave a list of the questions with Mrs. Hennessey tomorrow morning. Will that be all right?"

"As long as it isn't a letter. And if you have a personal message, let Simon give it orally. Prison officials are strict, Bess, and you don't want him to be turned away."

"Yes, thank you. Good advice!"

I hung up and left the hotel, deciding to walk back to the apartment, to clear my head.

The exercise was good, the air cool and fresh, the streets for some reason nearly empty. Then I recalled that it was the dinner hour, and most people were at home, where they belonged.

As Mrs. Hennessey's house with its wartime flats came into view down the street, I thought how helpful Mary had been in putting what I'd learned into perspective. Despite her friendship with Serena. I'd been fortunate with my flatmates. Diana and Mary and the others had been good friends and the sort of women who made sharing a flat bearable. Mrs. Hennessey was dependable, caring, and willing to look in on us if we were ill. I felt safe here.

Opening the outer door, I saw her peering out her own door, and then she came to greet me.

"You look tired. Have you just come home from the Front?"

"I've been in Somerset," I told her. But that wasn't altogether true.

She came closer, as if to see me better. "You aren't grieving for that young man they just took up for murder?"

"No, not grieving. Just sad. I'm not sure he's guilty."

"If a judge feels he is, then he is," she said, nodding. "They're nobody's fools, are judges."

"No." I didn't feel like arguing with her. But talking about Michael suddenly reminded me of Inspector Herbert. I turned around and started back through the door I'd just come in. "If Mary comes down to ask for me, tell her I'll return shortly."

I thought about driving, then decided to find a cab. But that wasted precious minutes, and I was almost on the edge of my seat as I reached Trafalgar Square. Scotland Yard was within walking distance now.

The constable guarding the door told me that he thought Inspector Herbert had already left for the day.

"It's very important. Could you ask to be sure?"

He must have heard those words—it's very important—a thousand times over, but he nodded and went away to find out where Inspector Herbert might be.

I felt I had waited an hour or more, but then the constable came back, and with him another man, a Sergeant Miller, who led me up the stairs and down the passage to Inspector Herbert's office. I thanked the sergeant, took a deep breath, and knocked lightly on the door.

Inspector Herbert's voice bade me enter. But as I walked through the door, his face changed. "They said a young woman—no one gave me your name."

"They weren't sure you were here. May I speak to you?"

"If it's about Michael Hart's execution, there's nothing I can do to prevent it."

"I haven't come about that. But I'd like to know— were you in the courtroom when he pleaded guilty?"

He hesitated. "Yes. I was," he said finally.

"What did you think? What did you feel?"

"Surprise, like everyone else. I'd been told our case was sound, but that it wasn't a certainty. For one thing, Hart is a handsome man. He had some public sympathy. A male jury wouldn't be swayed by that, of course, but even jurors have wives and daughters. I was prepared for anything, to tell you the truth. But not for a guilty plea. I expected Hart to take his chances."

"Do you know why he did it?"

"I have my suspicions. The prison surgeon's report, that Hart's arm is likely to be useless, was a factor, I'm sure. In fact, I was told he was put on a suicide watch after the doctor completed his examination."

"Have you visited Michael in prison?"

Inspector Herbert, who had been speaking directly to me as I stood there before his desk, looked toward a filing cabinet against the left-hand wall. "No. I saw no point in going there. I don't think he'd have cared for my sympathy."

"The other reason for his plea was to spare Marjorie's memory and reputation. He wouldn't have wanted her name to be dragged through the court."

"There's that," he conceded.

"Can you arrange for me to see Lieutenant Hart?"

"I don't feel that's wise. Besides, he's asked to have visitors turned away. There was a list." He fished around on his cluttered desk, and came up with a sheet of paper. Reading from it, he said, "Victoria Garrison is at the top of the list. She's the sister of his first victim."

I made no answer. Looking up, he said irritably, "Do sit down, Miss Crawford. I don't bite."

I sat down and waited.

"The next names on the list are his aunt and uncle. After theirs comes yours."

I took a deep breath. I'd expected that, but it still hurt.

He set the list aside. "For what it's worth, I believe he cared for you, Miss Crawford."

"That's nowhere near the truth, Inspector, and you know it. He loved Marjorie Evanson. No one else. I believe he liked me, as I liked him. That was as far as it went."

Caught in trying to be kind, Inspector Herbert was flustered. He set the list aside and turned to look out at the reflection of London's lights against the low clouds that had been rolling in for the past hour or so. When he turned back, he was himself again.

"Miss Crawford, just what is it you want?"

"I want to tell you a story. You owe it to me to listen—I gave you considerable help in closing this inquiry."

"I don't have time—"

"I shan't be long." I wasn't overawed by Scotland Yard. As a nurse I'd learned to deal with patients, their families, Matron—who could be far more intimidating than Inspector Herbert—impatient doctors, and officers of every rank. Still, I would need to be brief, on the mark, or I'd lose this one chance.

"For one thing, I spoke to Captain Melton in France. He's in hospital there—or was, before I left.

He admitted to being in the railway station with Mrs. Evanson, but wouldn't admit that he was her lover. I'd thought he was. And for a time, so did you. In fact, you had decided not to pursue questioning him, as his statement was irrelevant to Mrs. Evanson's murder. His alibi was the train to Portsmouth."

He was wary now. "And that's it?"

"He was very smug during our conversation. He finally told me that he had not left the train before Portsmouth. I realized later he could have telephoned someone before boarding his ship. Remember, I couldn't understand why he left her there, without even seeing that she had a cup of tea in the canteen or someone to take her home. Why he was so distant."

"Very callous of him, I agree. But get to the point, if you please."

"That is my point. If he wasn't the child's father, why was he there that day? Because Melton knew the man who actually was her lover. And he had been sent there to deal with Marjorie, if he could. Somehow I wasn't surprised—Raymond Melton was hardly the sort of man to attract someone like Marjorie Evanson. What's more, I also realized he was too much like her father."

"You're concluding that we still don't know the name of her lover. Does it matter?"

"If you had seduced a married woman and suspected she was carrying your child, how many people would you tell? And if you needed a friend to help by meeting a weeping woman in a very public place, where would you turn?"

Inspector Herbert hesitated. Then against his will he said, "I doubt I'd have told anyone. I'd have dealt with it myself."

I smiled. "Because you're an honorable man. You wouldn't have enticed Marjorie Evanson into doing something that was going to ruin her life." Then I asked, "Do you have a brother, Inspector Herbert? If you dared not be seen in a compromising situation because you were often in London and your face was known because you were at the Admiralty, would you have asked your brother to meet this nuisance of a woman for you? After all, he was passing through on the train and in the short stopover here, he could give her a message for you. And the message was, since the affair had been over for months now, you couldn't be sure the child she was carrying was yours. And that you were sorry, but there it was."

"I don't have a brother." He paused, watching me. "But Melton does."

"Of course if your brother had agreed to do this for you, you'd want to know—before he sailed for

France—whether he'd been successful in putting this distraught woman off. You'd ask him to find a telephone before he took ship."

"Miss Crawford, you told me that you'd not come here to stop Hart's execution."

"I haven't," I said. "I thought perhaps you'd like to hear what went on after that conversation I witnessed at the railway station. I've tried to piece it together from actual facts. It isn't all my imagination."

"Yes, I understand. And it's just as well to have this matter closed." He cleared his throat.

"And there are telephones to be found in Portsmouth, are there not? It would be possible to put in a call. Perhaps only three words: *I got nowhere.* Then report to your transport in good time and arrive in France in good time."

"Yes, all right."

"Of course, allowing for the time to travel from London to Portsmouth—several hours—you'd probably await your brother's call in London. Not at home. At the Marlborough Hotel, for instance. Or a quieter place where you weren't readily recognized. There was always the possibility that it would take more than three words. That there was a problem that the brother couldn't handle in your place."

Inspector Herbert said nothing.

"You would have had to know where to find Marjorie, of course. And your brother would have been instructed—in the event something didn't go as planned—to ask her to meet you at a time and place where you could deal with the unpleasant situation." I paused. " 'I'll have to call Jack when I reach Portsmouth. Meet him at nine o'clock at this park or that small restaurant where neither of you is known, or by the river, where you'd have a little privacy.' And Marjorie would have walked for a while, to get her emotions under control, then hurried to make sure she wasn't late at the designated place, just in case it was a trick of some kind. You might say you hadn't seen her and left, or that you were early and couldn't wait. Which meant she would have to see Michael afterward, when she knew for certain what she wanted to tell him. She would have met you and walked a little way with you, along the river, talking about what was to be done. She wouldn't have been afraid. And so you could have stabbed her at any time. It was raining, there weren't many people strolling by the river on such a night, and you'd take your chance when it was offered, whatever you had to promise in the meantime. It was too dark to see if she was dead, so for good measure you shoved her into the river. To drown."

"A very neat reconstruction, Miss Crawford. I doubt that it's more than that."

"Yes, well, Jack Melton had a better reason for murdering Marjorie than Michael Hart had. What's more, he gave himself away when I spoke to him outside the Marlborough Hotel weeks ago. I told you about that encounter, because I'd lost my temper and confessed to him I'd seen the man with Marjorie at the railway station. He lost his temper as well, accused me of blackmail and then told me that Michael Hart had been in London the night she was killed. If Jack Melton was spending a quiet evening at home, how would he know that? No one did. Except for the physician who treated Michael, and possibly Marjorie Evanson, if she knew about his eye. She might well have told Jack Melton what she was planning to do, a threat to hold over him, to make him keep his promise. She'd had time to think about it. Four hours at the very least."

I'd finished. Before he could reply, I stood up and added, "My reconstruction is as valid as yours, I think. Who knows which is actually right? Probably only Jack Melton and Michael Hart. Although I think Jack's wife is beginning to wonder. What will happen to her if she works it out as well? Thank you for your time, Inspector. I am sorry that I ever led you to Michael Hart, but that's water over the dam, I'm afraid."

As I reached the door, he said to me, "We would have found him in time."

"Or would you have interviewed Raymond Melton, as I did, and seen that brief flicker of satisfaction when he told me he never left the train before Portsmouth? Of course he never left it. He needn't have. Good-bye."

And I closed the door before he could say anything else.

A constable was waiting to escort me to the street, and I stepped out into the night air, feeling it cool and fresh on my face, and found myself thinking that Michael would see the light of day for the last time when he went to the gallows.

One more day gone.

But not quite.

I went to see Helen Calder. To my surprise, she was at home. But I was informed that she wasn't receiving visitors.

"Tell her that it's Bess Crawford. Ask her if she'll see me for just a few minutes."

And she did.

I was taken back to the sitting room, which had been transformed with a bed and chair and the other accoutrements of a sickroom.

Mrs. Calder was already in bed, her hair brushed and hanging to her shoulders, wearing a very becoming nightgown in a pale lavender covered by a darker lavender shawl.

"Miss Crawford," she said, and I could hear the wariness in her voice.

"I haven't come to worry you," I told her straightaway. "I'm here to ask how you are. I haven't been back in England for very long or I'd have come sooner. Are you recovering on schedule?" For she seemed pale, her hands restless on the coverlet.

"The doctor says I'm quite recovered, but I don't feel that I am. I seem so tired, and I don't have the energy to go anywhere or do anything. This bed should have been taken down days ago, but I still find it difficult to climb the stairs." There was the underlying complaining note of the invalid beneath the words.

"You look so well," I said, asking silent forgiveness for the lie. "I was hoping for good news."

"I haven't slept well in some time. Not since—not for some time."

I understood. Not since her words had sent Michael Hart to trial. I said, "Never mind, that will come in time. You've been very ill, you know. It isn't surprising that you still feel a little uncomfortable."

"It isn't pain. I mean to say, I don't hurt. I'm just dreadfully tired."

And that was depression. Her feeling of guilt a burden she didn't recognize.

"Do you want to talk about Michael?" I asked gently. "Perhaps you'll feel better afterward."

She began to cry. "I can't help it. He was coming to see me—I expected him—and his was the name I spoke when that policeman found me in the garden."

"You told the truth, you know. As far as you remembered it. There's no guilt in that."

"But he's to hang, and how am I ever to forget that it was my words that sealed his fate? What if I haven't remembered it properly, what if it's confused because of my injuries, and I only remember next month or next year? When it's too late?"

"He condemned himself."

"He did it for Marjorie's sake, I've no doubt of that. He would do. When things appeared to be so hopeless anyway, he could at least spare her." She found a fresh handkerchief, but the tears hadn't stopped. "I find it so hard to believe that he could have killed her. Not when he loved her so. If he were that sort of person, he'd have killed her before she could marry Meriwether. I lay awake trying to see the face of the person who attacked me. I try and try, and nothing comes. What am I to do when—after—Michael is dead, and I see that face clearly? And know beyond a shadow of any doubt that it wasn't him?"

I felt pity for her. Her life would never be the same, through no fault of her own. And she was right, she would be forever haunted, whether the face came clearly to her or not. There would always be that uncertainty, and that burden of guilt.

I said, to change the subject, "Were they able to bring your husband home from France?"

"Oh, yes, he came. I was so grateful, I felt so safe when he was with me. But he had to go back, once I was out of danger. Compassionate leave, they called it. He was so angry, you know. He said if he could find the person who did this, he'd kill the man with his bare hands. And I think he would have done. I never told him about saying Michael's name over and over again. Then he was gone and it was too late."

"It was the only thing you could do." I hesitated. "Tell me, did you ever see Marjorie with someone named Jack Melton? Or hear her mention him?"

"I know him, of course I do. He's Serena's husband. He was at the wedding."

"But afterward. More recently, perhaps. Did Marjorie tell you that she'd run into him by chance?"

"I don't think so." She frowned, trying to remember. "But she probably wouldn't have. He's in London from time to time. He's taken me to lunch once or twice, and I'm sure he's taken Marjorie as well. You know how it is, London is so full of strangers these days. One walks down the street and feels as if one is in a foreign city. When one encounters a familiar face, it's almost a relief."

I tried to think of another way to bring up Jack Melton, without giving her more reasons for feeling terrible about Michael's fate. But then I remembered Victoria, and switched the subject again. "Did Victoria come often to London to see Marjorie?"

"Oh, never. She was at the engagement party of course, and the wedding. That's about the only time I remember seeing her at Marjorie's house. And she never came here. She knew how I felt about her, the way she'd treated her mother."

"I'm told she did come to London often, for several months in a row. And then she stopped coming. The Harts wondered if she was spying on Marjorie."

"Spying on her? I can't imagine why. Well, Marjorie did say that she had run into her while looking for a wedding present for a friend. That was in May, I think. But that was it, Marjorie was in a hurry and got out of the encounter as quickly as possible. She said Victoria wanted to know how Meriwether was, and seemed inclined to talk. But Marjorie wasn't in the mood."

And had Victoria's curiosity been tweaked, and had she followed her sister to see where she was in such a hurry to go?

I wouldn't put it past her.

"What is it that makes Victoria carry such a grudge? Was it just Michael? She seemed to have everything else she wanted—the house, Marjorie settled, out of sight and mind in London. What else was there to take away?"

"It's the will. Not many people know. The Garrison house was left to Victoria, of course, but the estate was divided fairly evenly. Much to Victoria's chagrin, let me tell you! There was a scene in the solicitor's office. I'd gone with Marjorie as moral support, and I was very glad I had, although it was a dreadful time, I must say! And on top of that was the way the trust was constructed. I don't understand all of it, but from what I gathered—what Marjorie gathered from the actual reading and told me—was distinctly odd. Neither daughter inherits anything outright."

"He forgave Marjorie—or at the end, felt some doubt about what he'd been told by Victoria?"

"I'm not so sure. You see, while both girls could draw on the income from their share of the trust, the capital wouldn't be distributed until both of them reached fifty. Past child-bearing age. At that time, the trust would be dissolved. However, if either daughter bore a child before that, and it was given its grandfather's name, the house and the entire trust would go to it at age twenty-one. There would be nothing left for Marjorie and Victoria."

I caught my breath. It was a cruel provision—it pitted sister against sister. And I had the fleeting thought that perhaps Victoria had inherited her father's mean spirit. After all, he'd turned against his wife and his daughter, and in the end, he'd punished both daughters for that. As Victoria had tried to punish Marjorie.

But Marjorie was expecting a child. Unless Meriwether was willing to acknowledge it and give it his name, the child would be a Garrison—Marjorie's maiden name.

What a revenge against her sister for all the grief that Marjorie had suffered!

It was almost shocking to contemplate what Victoria might do, given that knowledge. After all her scheming, she would have lost everything.

"Did anyone else know the contents of the will?" I asked.

"The servants were there for the reading; of course there was a small bequest to each of them. Then we were asked to leave. The final provision was read only to Victoria and Marjorie. As I mentioned, there was a terrific row, and none of us knew where to look. You could hear it, but not the words of course. Victoria screaming, and once, Marjorie laughing. If Mr. Blake hadn't been there, they'd have been at each other's throats. I expect Marjorie told her sister that as a married woman—the wedding was to be that October, you see—she might soon see Victoria evicted."

"How long ago was this? When did Mr. Garrison die?"

"In the winter of 1914. Six months before the war began. Meriwether had already told Marjorie that he wanted to fly, that he wanted above all things to be a pilot. Marjorie told me later that Victoria had said, 'If there's a war, I hope he's shot down and killed. It will serve you right.'"

Three years ago. The wounds would still be raw. And when Victoria had asked after Meriwether when the sisters met in May, it had not been a friendly overture—it had been a reminder that Marjorie hadn't had her child, and that Meriwether was still at risk.

"But if that's how the trust stood, why didn't Victoria marry as soon as possible, and have a child of her own?"

"And lose her house and her substantial income to it? Besides, I think she wanted to marry Michael and throw that in Marjorie's face. She might have taken the risk for him."

"I could almost believe that it was Victoria who killed Marjorie. That perhaps Marjorie had gloated about the child she was carrying. It would make sense."

"Oh, I'm sure Victoria isn't a murderer."

But it might explain as well why Helen Calder herself had been stabbed. If Marjorie had told her about the peculiar provision, and now she was about to tell Michael. Was that the question he was burning to ask Helen? It gave Victoria the perfect motive for murder.

Had I been wrong about Jack Melton? I hadn't known about the will when I spoke to Inspector Herbert. And I couldn't go back to Scotland Yard.

Helen Calder must have read the uncertainty in my face.

"You surely don't believe that Victoria attacked Marjorie? Or me? No, she may be vicious and uncaring, but she's no murderer. She's my *cousin*."

As if that prevented murder from happening in a family.

Helen Calder leaned back against her pillow. "You have successfully diverted me from thinking about Michael. That was very kind of you, Bess."

I said, "Did you know that Victoria tried to persuade Meriwether not to marry Marjorie? He was furious with her. I thought she was just being a spoiler. But perhaps she had the will in mind."

"I wouldn't be surprised. It was just the sort of thing she might do."

The Harts had called Victoria evil, but I wondered if seeing all her schemes come to nothing, she must have been beside herself with fury. And perhaps helping to destroy Michael had been the last act of vengeance open to her, in addition to seeing her sister's name dragged through the scandal sheets.

"I'm tired now. But I'm so glad you came to see me, Bess."

"I'm glad too," I told her, meaning it. "But remember, I'm a nurse, I know wounds. If you languish here, you'll never recover. Get up and dress and go out for lunch somewhere. It will do you the greatest good. You'll see."

But she shook her head. "I couldn't enjoy myself, knowing that Michael is counting the days down to his last. Perhaps—perhaps when it's over, I'll feel more like going out."

There was nothing I could say that would change her mind. I held her hand for a moment, and then left.

My own mind was in turmoil. None of the questions I'd left for Simon had anything to do with Victoria, only with Jack Melton.

If Helen Calder believed she carried a burden of guilt, she had no idea of the depth and breadth of mine at this moment.

I found a cab and gave him the direction of Mrs. Hennessey's house, then sat back in the anonymous darkness and told myself over and over again that I wouldn't fail, that I wouldn't be too late.

Chapter Twenty

To my surprise, when I reached Mrs. Hennessey's house and the cabbie had been paid, it was Simon Brandon who held the door for me to step out.

"Have you been to see Michael?" Those were the first words out of my mouth.

"I'm doing my best to arrange it. Have you had any dinner? You look distressed."

Standing there on the street looking up at him, I burst into tears.

He held me for a while, letting me cry into his lapels. Then he said briskly, "If you aren't starving, I am." He led me to his motorcar and put me inside. Coming around to the driver's door, he went on, "Where would you like to go?"

"Nowhere. I've been crying."

"So you have."

He drove through London, through the City, and came out on the far side of the Tower, down toward the river.

It was hardly what anyone would call a restaurant, just a few tables and a counter where during the day workingmen might sit and eat their lunch. Except for one man who looked half asleep at a table by the window, the place was empty. We walked in and Simon nodded to the aproned man who stuck his head out of what must have been the kitchen. Seeing who had come in, he nodded, then disappeared.

We took the table in the far back corner, and I expected to find it dotted with crumbs and spots of grease from the diners before us. But it was spotlessly clean, though worn, and the man reappeared from the kitchen with a cloth for it and our silverware. He brought Simon an ale, and asked what I'd have.

Simon answered for me. "Tea," he said.

The man disappeared again.

Intrigued, I said, "He knows you?"

"I've come here from time to time. He was a cook in the regiment. This was what he dreamed about, a small place of his own where there were never more than twenty people to serve at any one time."

I smiled in spite of myself. "I can appreciate that."

"He won't remember you. We'll leave it that way, shall we?"

Nodding, I said, "What do they serve?"

"Fish. It comes in fresh. He never says from where, but I would guess Essex. There are enough tiny coves and waterways there for a fleet of fishing vessels to hide if they even smell a German ship or U-boat. People have to eat. There's precious little food as it is."

"I thought all the channels were mined."

"Those who saw to it were absentminded."

We waited in silence until our plates were brought steaming on chargers and smelling heavenly of well-cooked fish, today's bread, and a surprising array of vegetables.

We began to eat, and I realized just how hungry I was.

Halfway through the meal, I said, "Do you want to know—"

"Not here. Just eat your dinner and put it all out of your mind."

I did as I was told, grateful actually for the respite.

When we'd finished and I'd drunk my tea, Simon got up to settle his account with the owner, and then we went out to the motorcar, driving back the way we'd come.

He found a place in a street above Trafalgar Square, and we left the motorcar there, walking down to the square and settling ourselves near the ugly lions. There was no one about, and even the traffic heading down The Mall was light.

"All right. I'm listening," he said.

I began to talk, slowly at first, then with gathering assurance as he listened without interrupting. When I'd finished, he leaned back against the wall behind him, and considered me.

"You've hardly been in England three days, and already you've managed to confuse yourself and me."

I laughed, as he'd intended. Then I said, "What am I to do, Simon? Will any of this help Michael?"

"We need to take what we know to his barrister. Name of Forbes. Find out if the man will listen to us at all. He was in an almighty fury when Hart did what he did."

"I should think he might have been. He must have felt betrayed. And people like that don't care to be ignored. It's losing face in a sense."

"I'll try to get in to see Michael. If he'll see me. But I think he might. You should keep your fingers crossed."

"Shall I try to see Mr. Forbes?"

He considered me. "A pretty face might have better luck. But I think the evidence in both Victoria Garrison's case and in Jack Melton's as well has merit. On the surface they cast doubts, because they are as good as the evidence Herbert gave the Crown. Whether they would hold up if investigated is another matter."

"Simon, there isn't time for a lengthy and thorough investigation!" My voice had risen, and a passing constable turned, then walked our way.

"Everything all right, then, Miss?" he asked.

I smiled as best I could. "Sad news, that's all. Thank you, Constable."

He nodded and walked off. Simon watched him go then turned back to me.

"I don't know what to tell you, Bess. You've done wonders, no one could have done more. If only we'd known before the trial—but there was no way to know."

"What you're saying," I retorted, "is that the chances are slim to none. And Michael will hang. Well, I won't be satisfied with exonerating him after his death."

"You have to face it. Your mother is worried about that. She wonders if you are—too fond of him."

"I won't die of a broken heart," I told him. "But I will have a hard time forgetting."

"You still must remember one thing, Bess. He may be guilty. There's always that chance."

"No," I said resolutely. "He wouldn't have killed Marjorie for the reason given. He loved her enough to let her live her life as she chose, even if it included marrying Meriwether Evanson and having an affair with a married man."

He was silent for a time, his mind a long way away from me. And then he came back and said, "Well. It's late. I've bespoken a bed at my club. Time to return you to the dragon."

"Mrs. Hennessey isn't a dragon, and you know it."

He laughed and gave me a hand to rise. It was warm and comforting. Then we walked in companionable silence to where we'd left the motorcar.

I slept that night, mainly because I was very tired, emotionally drained, and had taught myself to snatch sleep where I could and when I could. That training stood me in good stead once more.

Mary was up making tea before I dragged myself out of bed and walked into the kitchen, drawing the sash of my robe around me.

"Anything new?" she asked casually. And when I didn't say anything right away, she added, "I did glimpse Simon waiting for you last night."

Nodding, I told her about seeing Inspector Herbert and then speaking to Helen Calder.

"It's such a pity that she can't remember anything really useful about her attack. It would make a difference."

"We can't count on it."

"No. On the other hand, if you want my vote, I'll plump for Victoria. She's a nasty piece of work, anyway you look at her."

"If Jack was Marjorie's lover, he's no better. He knew she was married, he knew whom she'd married. It was a malicious thing to do to his wife, never mind Marjorie."

"I know Jack Melton," Mary said. "I don't know Victoria."

"Be glad. I must go and speak to a Mr. Forbes today. He was Michael's counsel."

"Forbes?" She frowned. "I think I went out with his son a time or two. I don't envy you. He has a reputation for eating prosecution witnesses alive."

I laughed. "Know where I can find him?"

"Not a clue. I never met him."

"I'll try the Inns first."

"Wear your uniform. It might get you in to see him."

"Clever thinking."

I went off to dress, wondering if Mr. Forbes might be in court today. I prayed he wasn't.

As it happened, when I reached his chambers, not far from the Inns of Court, he was preparing to leave to interview a witness. I was taken down a narrow passage to a room nearly overflowing with briefs and law books, a ladder leaning against the tall shelves, an empty hearth surrounded by a Victorian mantelpiece that would have done justice to a French château, it was so massive, and a desk with nothing more on it than an inkwell, a tray of pens, a blotter, and a small statue of blind justice sitting on a Purbeck marble base.

Mr. Forbes regarded me with impatience, which was rather more daunting than lack of interest. He was a spare man with graying hair that would have suited an Oxford don, overly long and quite thick. The spectacles he wore hid sharp blue eyes that were unpleasantly piercing.

A feeling of unspecified guilt materialized from out of nowhere and swept over me.

When I told him my reason for coming, he said shortly, "Lieutenant Hart made his decision. He took the case in the direction he chose, not the one I was prepared to follow. He refused any appeal. Young Mr. Hart is a fool. I washed my hands of him."

"Give me five minutes of your time, Mr. Forbes, and then tell me what advice you would give him now."

"Young woman, I don't know what reason you have to involve yourself in the affairs of a man condemned by his own words and sentenced to hang, but I suspect that if your parents knew you were here today, they would be appalled."

"Colonel Crawford is well aware of what I am doing." Well, not completely, but he knew how I felt about getting to the bottom of things. And I knew he'd back me up, then lecture me privately. "The question is a very simple one, Mr. Forbes. Do you believe that Lieutenant Hart is guilty, despite his chances of acquittal on all charges?" When he didn't answer, I added, "Do you believe that Michael Hart deliberately set out to damage your reputation by changing his plea at the last minute? Or did he act out of despair and a misguided attempt to protect Marjorie Evanson's good name?"

He stood up, looming over me, his mouth a long, thin line. And then he said, "I suggest you leave while I remember that you are young and in love."

"I am not in love," I told him, taking my courage in both hands and remembering that an attack is often the best line of defense. "I have certain facts to present to you. And you may well discover that they have some merit to them. But you won't know if you don't listen to them. It could be that Michael Hart hangs on the day allotted. I'll be back in France by that time. But I should like to see his name cleared in the end. That's probably all I can do for him. I believe he deserves that final redemption."

I wasn't sure where the words had come from. They were suddenly there on the tip of my tongue, and my emotions were already running high.

Mr. Forbes sat down again. "Very well." He took out his pocket watch and set it on the table before him. "You have your five minutes, Miss Crawford. Proceed."

I was certain he'd agreed because he thought that I would make a fool of myself, stumbling over emotional attempts to be clever. Then he could put me in my place and show me the door.

He had overlooked the fact that I was a nurse and accustomed to thinking clearly in a crisis.

I collected myself, as I had done in Inspector Herbert's small office, and outlined, as I had done there, the case against Jack Melton. And then with equal brevity, I outlined the case against Victoria Garrison.

Mr. Forbes sat there listening with his eyes on the watch before him, nothing in his face indicating whether he was actually heeding me or simply marking time.

I finished and rose to go. I could see his watch—I still had thirty seconds of my five minutes.

"You would do better," he said before I was out of my chair, "to have taken your facts to Scotland Yard."

"I did present my arguments regarding Commander Melton to Inspector Herbert. Sadly, I didn't know about Mr. Garrison's will, or I would have told him about Victoria Garrison as well. Did you know that Mrs. Evanson's solicitor couldn't find her will? The staff told us that she was considering changing it. She had a child to protect, and she must not have been certain her husband would accept it. Perhaps she wanted something from its father too—a promise to recognize it, as the price of his own sins. After all, the Meltons have no children."

Mr. Forbes said, "Miss Crawford. Casting doubt on the facts of the case will not help Lieutenant Hart. I remind you. He confessed. Of his own free will, in open court."

"Then what would stop this execution?"

"If Mrs. Calder remembers the night she was stabbed and can tell the police who attacked her. Assuming, naturally, that it wasn't Hart."

It was so unfair.

"I've spoken to her. She's been made ill by trying to remember. It's a medical problem, not a parlor game. Is there no other recourse?"

"Of course. Give the police the murderer himself. Or herself."

I thought he was playing with me now. That made me angry.

After a moment, he added, "I know Mr. Melton. I refuse to believe he'd kill someone, even in anger."

"Then you should never have taken Michael Hart's brief," I retorted.

I'd failed. But Mr. Forbes's remark most certainly reinforced the fact that Jack Melton, fearing damage to his own reputation, had sent his brother to meet Marjorie Evanson.

Mr. Forbes picked up his watch, restored it to his pocket, and made a fuss of settling the chain across his vest. I thought my words had stung, a little.

I rose and walked to the door. "Thank you for your time, Mr. Forbes."

My hand was on the knob when Mr. Forbes said, "You must also surmount the obstacle of Lieutenant Hart's refusal to be helped."

I turned to stare at him, accepting for the first time the fact that Michael would hang.

"Someone should have reminded him that while he's being gallant and selfish, Marjorie Evanson's murderer will live a long and happy life," he added.

I quietly closed the door behind me. As I walked down the passage past the clerks' rooms, I told myself that I'd done everything that was humanly possible. I could do no more.

Nevertheless, I refused to be reconciled to Michael's fate.

As I stepped out into blindingly bright sunlight after the dim, paneled walls I'd just left, Mr. Forbes's words echoed in my head.

Give the police the murderer himself. Or herself.

And that was going to be a challenge.

For a fleeting moment I wondered if Mr. Forbes had meant it to be.

Chapter Twenty-one

I walked nearly a mile before I looked for a cab to take me back to the flat.

I needed the exercise to counteract the depression settling over me. But it did little to help. I reminded myself that men could be incredibly stubborn and unconscionably blind at times, and that also failed to bring me any consolation.

Would Simon Brandon have any better luck talking to Michael in his prison cell?

Simon could be very persuasive when he wished to be.

But chances were, Michael had already reconciled himself to dying. I'd seen soldiers do that—make peace with the knowledge that they would very likely not survive, so that survival didn't enter into any decisions that they would have to make on the battle-field.

As the cab made its way around Buckingham Palace and the Royal Mews, turning toward Mrs. Hennessey's house and the flat, I looked out at the afternoon sunlight slanting across London's landmarks, and wondered what to do next. I felt at a loss, with no purpose.

How does one find a murderer in a matter of a few days?

In my careful reconstruction of the evidence against Jack Melton and Victoria Garrison, there had to be a flaw. But where?

I closed my eyes, reviewing everything I'd said.

And then I sat back in the cab, breathless for a moment.

Everything had fit to perfection. Except for one thing. How had Jack Melton known that Michael was intent on speaking to Mrs. Calder? Coincidence? Accident? If I knew the answer to that, I could eliminate him from my quest.

What had driven Jack Melton to murder a second time?

It wouldn't do to appear at Melton Hall and ask questions. Serena would show me the door, if her husband didn't.

I bit my lip, thinking. But my mind was a blank.

All right, then, save time and eliminate Victoria Garrison from the role as murderess.

We were just pulling up in front of Mrs. Hennessey's door. I hastily returned to the present and got out, paying the driver as I did. Above my head, the late-afternoon sun was turning the windows of our flat to gold.

It was the only time beauty entered the sensible little flat designed to be a home for a few of the hundreds of people who had descended on London at the start of the war to work in one capacity or another.

I went inside and climbed the stairs. If only Michael would listen to Simon and decide to help at last in his own defense. Wishful thinking indeed. How many people facing the gallows suddenly proclaimed their innocence? No one would even listen. But at least I could find out what he knew.

I had begun to make myself a cup of tea. Now I set the tin back in the cupboard, put the cup and saucer on the shelf, caught up my coat, and went flying down the stairs.

It made no sense to sit here in London. I needed to talk to Victoria.

I stopped at Mrs. Hennessey's door and knocked.

She didn't answer, but as I was about to turn away, the door finally opened. Her eyes still heavy with sleep, she said, "Oh, Bess, dear. I was just doing a little ironing—"

I smiled. She never liked to be caught napping in the afternoon.

"I have to travel to Little Sefton, Mrs. Hennessey. That's in Hampshire. The train leaves in half an hour. Sergeant-Major Brandon will be coming here looking for me. Will you tell him where I've gone? Tell him it's important or I would have waited."

"Of course, dear, I'll listen for his knock. Should you be going on your own like this? You'd make so much better time driving with him, given the way the trains are these days."

But I had no idea when I could expect him.

"I must hurry if I'm to find a cab. Please don't forget, Mrs. Hennessey."

"No, dear."

And I was out the door, hurrying down the street to the corner by the bakery where I hoped to find a cab. Nothing. I all but ran to the next block, heads turning as I passed more sedate pedestrians.

Finally a cab saw my wave and slowed down just in front of me. "Waterloo Station, if you please," I said, slamming the door even as I spoke.

It was the same train that Captain Melton had taken, and I nearly missed it. Crowded with soldiers, the corridor filled to capacity, and no seat to be had, I resigned myself to an uncomfortable journey. And then a young private noticed me. "Sister—" He shyly offered me his place in the first compartment.

Thanking him, I sat down, struggling to catch my breath. Scraps of conversation floated around me and over my head, but I paid no attention. I was hoping that Mrs. Hennessey wouldn't fall asleep again and miss Simon's knock at her door.

Settling myself at last, I watched the outer villages of London slip past and the sun begin to sink in the west, a great red ball of flame that cast long shadows over already misty landscapes. Lights were coming on in village houses facing east, and in the increasingly frequent farms. The weathervane on a church spire reflected the sun long after the churchyard below it lay in purple shadow.

Too beautiful an evening to be hunting a murderer.

The soldier on my left asked where I was going, and I smiled to myself. He was very young. I must have been two years his senior at the very least, but he was tall, broad shouldered, and about to do a man's job. So I listened to his stories about growing up in the Fen country and how different it was from the scenery turning dark before our eyes.

And then Great Sefton was the next stop, and I turned to wish him well, wondering if one day I'd see him in a surgical theater, or if he would even survive his first weeks in the trenches.

The lamps were lit in the station as I stepped down from the train, and I went inside to ask the stationmaster if he could find someone to take me to Little Sefton.

"I'll be glad to, Miss." He finished the list he had been making, looked at his pocket watch and then the waiting-room clock. "If you'll have a seat on that bench, I'll find Sam."

He came back a few minutes later with a girl of perhaps seventeen driving a dogcart. She smiled at me as I stepped out of the station.

"Here you are, Miss," he said. "Sam will see you safe to Little Sefton."

I thanked him and opened the gate of the cart, stepping in and taking my seat.

"Do you drive people to Little Sefton often?" I asked.

"Fairly often. My father kept a carriage for station use, but the horses were taken away. I've got only the pony left."

We trotted out of Great Sefton, leaving behind a comfortable little town that had a pretty High Street and a handsome church set on a green up the hill from it. As the air cooled with sunset, a mist rose, turning the dark countryside a ghostly gray. The lanterns on either side of the cart seemed to encircle us in a soft, dancing light as the flames flickered. But if the mist worried Sam or her pony, neither showed any sign of it.

"Do you know Victoria Garrison?" I asked, to pass the time.

"Miss Garrison? Yes, she used to travel to London frequently, but that stopped after several months. She said she was bored with the company."

"In London?"

"Oh, yes indeed. I couldn't imagine being bored with London. I'd give much to go there myself. But my mum says she can't do without me, and besides, London is a pitfall for the unwary." She laughed as she said it. "I'm the youngest, and she holds on tight."

"Yet she allows you to drive strangers in the dark."

"It's safe enough. Mr. Hale, the stationmaster, wouldn't call me out if he didn't think it was all right."

Which sounded like a good enough plan. I could see she managed the pony with ease on the dark road, and knew the way so well she could see it in her head, every dip and twist, every turn, and how long the straight sections were. The pony too was at home out here in the dark. I wasn't sure I would like driving back to Great Sefton alone—even though it couldn't be more than three miles. But Sam seemed to like the night and the silence.

We came into Little Sefton on the far side of the village from the part of it I knew best, passing closed shops and even a small pub, light from its windows spilling out into the dark street, turning the mist to a murky orange. The shops thinned and houses took their place, and I caught a glimpse of the church through a tear in the mist.

"Where were you thinking of being put down?" Sam asked, slowing the pony from a trot to a walk.

Suddenly I didn't feel comfortable walking up to Victoria Garrison's door. I realized I should have waited for Simon. But it was already late, and by the time he reached Little Sefton, everyone could be in bed.

"Um. Do you know the Hart house?"

"Yes, indeed. I see him doing his banking in Great Sefton. He always has a kind word. I heard his nephew is to be hanged next week. Sad, that. I don't ever remember having a murderer in this part of the county."

"Sad, indeed," I said.

She drew up in front of the house, but it appeared to be dark to me, as if the Harts were away or had retired early. "Wait here, will you, for a moment? I'm not sure anyone is at home."

"Dark as the grave," she agreed, and I stepped down.

I walked out of the cart's comforting pool of misty lantern light and up to the door. I could feel the clinging mist, and shivered, glad of my coat. I found the knocker, lifted it, and let it fall. It sounded overloud in the night, but that was mostly my imagination. I could feel my nerves taut with what lay ahead.

When no one answered my summons, I tried again. Would anyone answer my knock at this hour? The Harts had grown reclusive—they wouldn't care to be disturbed—and after all, they had no way of knowing who was at their door.

What to do now?

I lifted the knocker again and gave it a substantial blow against the brass footplate.

I was on the point of turning around and walking back to the cart when I saw a light quivering in the window on the other side of the door. Then the door was opened, the light from a lamp almost blinding me.

"Mr. Hart?" I asked, unable to see who was behind the light.

"Miss Crawford!" he exclaimed in astonishment. "What are you doing here at this hour? Is everything all right? Have you had news of Michael?"

"Could I come in and sit for a while? I want to go to Victoria Garrison's house, but not just yet. Would you mind?"

"No, certainly not. I forget my manners. Do come in." As I did, he saw Sam waiting in her cart. "Did you come by train?" he asked me, and when I nodded, he called out, "Thank you, Sam. I'll drive Miss Crawford back to Great Sefton. Good night."

She called a good night to him, and then lifted her reins. I heard her soft "Walk on" to the pony, and then I turned back to Mr. Hart.

"I'm so sorry to disturb you. Had you retired for the night?" I asked as he shut the door behind me.

"We've taken to sitting in the room at the back of the house. People see no light and don't come to call."

It was a pity that their lives were so changed by what had happened. I thought to myself that if Michael could see and understand this tragedy, he might take a different view of his own actions. But he couldn't think of anyone but Marjorie.

Mr. Hart led me back to the room where his wife was sitting. As the light preceded us down the passage, she called, "Who was it, dear?"

"Miss Crawford. She's come to sit with us awhile."

We had arrived at a sitting room where two other lamps were burning, and I saw Mrs. Hart get to her feet and stand there trembling. "It's not tonight, is it?" she asked me, as if I had come to share their watch when Michael died.

"I've been in London today, Mrs. Hart. I spoke to several people there. I wanted to come and talk to you."

She sank back into her chair, relief leaving her face pale, her eyes still haunted. "That's so kind of you, my dear. We were just having tea. Would you like a cup?"

"Oh, yes, please, I would."

Her husband disappeared and came back shortly with another cup and saucer. She poured a cup for me, and passed the dish of honey and the jug of milk.

The cup warmed my hands. I didn't know whether it was the night chill or my own anxiety that made them feel cold. I said, "I wonder if you knew the provisions of Mr. Garrison's will?"

"His will?" Mrs. Hart nodded. "I heard that the bulk of it was divided evenly between Marjorie and Victoria, although the house went to Victoria. Well, not too surprising, as Marjorie had a home of her own in London."

"Nothing else?" I asked.

"The usual bequests to the servants, and to the church," Mr. Hart answered this time.

"There was another provision." And I told them about it.

"I can't believe—" Mrs. Hart began, as shocked as I had been. "But then in the last year or so of his life, Mr. Garrison didn't seem to be himself. I put that down to his illness, but perhaps it wasn't. Spiteful, I call it. Small wonder Victoria never married, although I often wondered if she would have changed her mind if Michael had paid her the least attention."

Mr. Hart said, "Michael told us you'd said that Marjorie was expecting a child."

"It would have inherited—the will as I was told about it didn't specify a child in or out of wedlock, only that it bear Mr. Garrison's name. Which of course it would do, if Meriwether Evanson refused to acknowledge it."

"Serves her right," Mrs. Hart said shortly. "Victoria, I mean."

Mr. Hart said, "Are you suggesting that Victoria killed Marjorie?"

"I don't know," I admitted. "It's possible. If she had any reason to believe Marjorie was pregnant, she would have reacted strongly. She stood to lose everything— her house, her income. She would have viewed it not as an unintended pregnancy but as Marjorie's means of cheating her out of what she believed was rightfully hers. Just how far Victoria would have taken her fury is anyone's guess."

"I wouldn't put it past her to have a spy in Marjorie's house," Mrs. Hart said. "It was the sort of thing she would do, since she wasn't invited there unless there was no way to avoid it."

Michael had told me he'd helped choose Marjorie's servants, but that didn't mean that one of them hadn't been amenable to bribery for telling tales. I thought about that missing will Marjorie was on the point of changing. A spy would have been richly rewarded for passing on news that Marjorie was suffering from what appeared to be morning sickness and had begun to reconsider her own will.

"Do you really think that's possible?" I asked, turning to Mr. Hart.

"Servants are as greedy as the rest of us," he answered. "A few pounds added to their wages? It would have been tempting."

"And you've come to Little Sefton to ask Victoria about this matter?" Mrs. Hart wanted to know. "My dear, why don't you stay the night, and face this visit first thing in the morning? I'll be happy to lend you whatever you need. The guest room is always ready, it will be no trouble at all."

I believed her and was sorely tempted. But I would lose another day. And besides, Simon was coming to Little Sefton for me. "You're very kind, Mrs. Hart, but if I'm wrong about Victoria, I must look elsewhere. It's too late to call on the Meltons tonight, but I can be in Diddlestoke very early tomorrow."

Mr. Hart was staring at me. "The other person was Serena Melton."

I sat there, my cup halfway to my lips, and looked at him over the rim.

"What? The other person, you say?" I set my cup on the small table at my elbow. "I don't understand."

"I didn't think to mention it. She came to Little Sefton to see Victoria. It was the day Michael went to the play. But Victoria wasn't at home and apparently the maid and the cook had been given the afternoon off. She came here next to ask if Michael knew where Victoria had gone and how long it would be before she came back. She apologized. She didn't know anyone else in Little Sefton to ask."

"But—I didn't think those two got on well together. Victoria and Serena."

"They don't. You see, there's the matter of the house in London. The two of them haven't agreed on what's to become of it. Mrs. Melton feels that since Meriwether died after Marjorie, he inherits. Victoria's contention is that the house had belonged to Marjorie's aunt on her mother's side, and therefore reverted to the Garrison family. I expect Mrs. Melton came about that. She did say something about papers." He smiled. "We hear the gossip—and of course Michael knows a little about Marjorie's affairs."

I remembered something Michael had said about the house in London remaining fully staffed while the question of ownership was being resolved.

"I'd have thought they'd meet in London—neutral ground."

"Apparently she hadn't been able to reach Victoria, and as she was coming up from visiting a friend who lives south of us, she decided to stop by."

"And you told her that Michael had gone to London with Victoria." I couldn't help the undercurrent of surprise in my voice. It was so unexpected.

"I saw no reason not to," he said defensively.

Of course he wouldn't have. While the Harts disliked Victoria, they would have told Serena the truth if asked, unaware of what might happen as a result of a few words.

"I shouldn't worry about it if I were you," I replied, not wanting to add to their distress. "But I'm glad you told me."

"I hadn't given it another thought," he went on. "Until you mentioned the Meltons." And that was probably true as well. The point of Serena's visit had been to find Victoria, not to betray Michael.

"Did you tell Michael about Mrs. Melton stopping by?"

"I don't believe I did. We'd retired long before he arrived home."

"And Mrs. Calder—did you say anything about Michael going in search of her?"

"No, no. Mrs. Melton said she might catch them up before the curtain rose. She asked if they were having dinner before the play. I told her I thought not, as Michael wished to see a friend before dinner. At that point she said she thought she'd go directly home instead, that she was already rather tired."

"I think you did mention Mrs. Calder," Mrs. Hart said. "I'm sure of it."

"Absolutely not. I just said a friend. I'd have remembered."

"It doesn't matter." By the time Serena reached Melton Hall and told her husband, he couldn't have reached London in time to kill anyone. Unless—unless of course he was in London already, and she telephoned him to tell him she had arrived safely, but had missed Victoria after all.

She wasn't there. You won't believe this, but she and Michael Hart are attending a play together. Marjorie must be turning in her grave. No, I don't know what play—probably the one everyone is talking about . . .

Even so, even if such a conversation took place, it didn't link Helen Calder, Michael Hart, and Jack Melton.

Nothing had changed. I looked at the clock on the table by the window. I couldn't wait much longer. It would be too late to call on anyone.

I said, "I hadn't realized the time. I must go."

Mrs. Hart started to say something, then changed her mind.

Mr. Hart, rising, said, "I'll go with you. Let me fetch a coat. And a light." He paused to look out the window. "I don't think that mist has lifted."

"No, you mustn't—" I began, then thought better of it. Caution, my mother often told me, was the best protection. He was gone only a few minutes, returning with a lightweight coat over his arm and a torch in his hand.

"You'll be careful, won't you?" Mrs. Hart asked him, her eyes on me. "Not that I expect any trouble, but you never know, do you?"

We left her sitting there, and I wondered if she would go to a window and watch our progress, once the door was closed behind us.

I wrapped my arms around me against the damp, then realized that I was cold because of nervousness. Matching my pace to Mr. Hart's, using the torch as my guide, I tried to get my bearings. The mist gave everything a strange softness, changing shapes, obscuring distances. I thought in passing that the mist would delay Simon. He wouldn't care for that.

We walked in silence past other houses, shadowy forms with no details, their windows only a smudge of brightness. I heard laughter from one as a door opened and then closed, a brief rectangle that loomed and vanished. A dog barked, sudden and shrill, sending my heart into my throat. I thought we must be near the church on the other side of the road, but there was nothing to see. Three more houses, one with a cat sitting on a low stone wall, jumping down to twine around our legs as we came closer, before trotting back to wait for the summons to its dinner.

When we reached the walk to Victoria's door, through gardens that were black shapes until the torchlight touched them, Mr. Hart stopped.

"Here you are," he said, gesturing to a house I could barely perceive.

I said, "Will you wait here? She might speak more freely if I seem to be alone." He was about to protest, but I said, "Don't worry. I'll stay within calling distance. I promise."

He didn't like it, but he stopped, flicking off his torch, and I went on up the walk. Nearer the door, white flower blossoms glowed in the darkness on either side of the flagstones, guiding me to the door where two stone urns held topiary trees.

I lifted the knocker, still uncertain about what I would say to Victoria when she opened the door.

But she didn't.

I knocked again.

Nothing.

I called, "Victoria, I know you're at home. It's Elizabeth Crawford. Please let me in. It's important."

I thought she would ignore me, but she must have been near the door, because after a moment it swung open. She was standing there in the sudden glare of lamplight from the entrance hall, her face in shadow. I could feel her antipathy.

"I've told you. He'll hang, and there's nothing you can say to me that will move me to do anything about it." Her voice was quite calm, unyielding.

"I want to ask you about Jack Melton."

That caught her by surprise. She must have been expecting me to begin a passionate defense of Michael Hart instead.

"What about Jack Melton?" Her voice now was wary, but her face was still expressionless. I couldn't read anything there or in her eyes.

"He was Marjorie's lover. Did you know? We all thought it must have been his brother, Captain Melton. But it wasn't. What we don't know is how Jack Melton found out that Michael was on his way to London with you, the night Helen Calder was attacked. But Serena told him, didn't she?" I was probing, to see where it led.

"I don't know what you are talking about."

"She was here—Serena Melton—the day you drove up to London to see the play. She went to speak to Michael when you weren't at home. But his uncle told her Michael had gone with you, so she drove on to Melton Hall. And she must have told her husband why she'd missed you."

Victoria laughed. "You are desperate, aren't you?"

"I don't see how else it could have happened."

It was almost as if Victoria couldn't bear to let Serena take credit for something she hadn't done. "Jack was in the theater that night. He was with several American naval officers. When I realized that, I hoped he would see me there with Michael. But Michael hadn't come back. He was off somewhere nursing that shoulder of his."

"But you told him Michael had come to the play with you?"

"Just before the curtain went up, Jack noticed the empty seat beside me and came over to speak to me. He thought I'd come alone, and he made some snide remark about that. It irritated me. And so I lied. I told Jack that I was expecting Michael to join me at any moment, but he was close to discovering the name of Marjorie's lover from someone who knew her secret, and he must have lost track of the time. I said it to annoy Jack, and it did. He went back to his seat, and just as the lights went down, he made some excuse to the Americans and quietly left. He'd mentioned that they were sailing for New York the next day, so they weren't likely to gossip about his absence, were they?"

"You sat there in the theater and let it happen? You must have guessed—just because Michael let you down, you made Jack angry enough to go looking for him? But Jack took you at your word, didn't he? And instead of hunting for Michael, he must have gone directly to Helen Calder's. She was the only 'friend' who was likely to know Marjorie's secrets. And when she came home from her dinner party, he must surely have believed that she'd been out with Michael, telling him everything. Victoria, don't you see that your malicious remarks nearly got Mrs. Calder killed? When Jack came up behind her, she even thought it was Michael, because she was expecting him. Dear God. None of this needed to have happened. None of it." I felt sick.

"I went to see a play, and I saw it." She was unrepentant, and I caught a glimpse of that child who had tried to rearrange her family to her liking. "And you still can't prove which of them killed Marjorie, can you?" There was triumph in her voice.

She was right—she would most certainly lie in the witness box. But I said, "Surely—you deliberately taunted Jack about something you should have stayed out of. Victoria, if he killed Marjorie and attacked Helen Calder, what's to stop him from killing you after Michael is hanged, just to be sure his last link with your sister is broken? You've put yourself at risk, don't you see? You're wagering your life that Michael is the murderer."

"Jack told me Michael had killed her—that Michael was in London the night she died."

"She didn't 'die,' Victoria. She was stabbed, then thrown into the river to drown. That's murder."

"What if it was? She brought it on herself, didn't she? If you want to know what I think, she wanted a child, she wanted to see me thrown out of this house. They hadn't had any children, she and Meriwether, and it was very likely they wouldn't. I think she looked elsewhere. Even if that affair cost her her marriage. There was always Michael, faithful Michael, in the wings. Or so she must have convinced herself."

I wanted to tell her about Marjorie at the railway station. About the despair and the desolation. Instead, I asked, "How did you learn about Marjorie and Jack Melton? Did she tell you?" I couldn't believe Marjorie had, even out of spite.

"I saw them together. Quite by accident. They didn't see me, and I could tell by the way she stood there, hanging on his every word, that they were lovers. So I made it my business to take him away from her—"

She was peering past me, into the milky darkness. "Who's out there?" she demanded. "Who did you bring with you?"

"It's only Mr. Hart. Michael's uncle. He very kindly walked me this far because of the mist. He has his torch with him, to guide me back."

"I don't want him here."

"I promised—"

"I don't care what you promised. Send him away!"

I turned and called to Mr. Hart. "It's all right. Will you wait for me near the church? I won't be long."

"I'm not sure—" he began, unwilling to leave me here in the dark.

But I stopped him before he could say more. "Truly. It's all right. Please?"

The torch flicked on, and after a moment it moved away, toward the church on the opposite side of the street. I doubted he could see me very well from there, but at least he could hear if I shouted for him.

"You've got your way," I told Victoria. I should have turned and left then too, but there was more she could tell me, and for Michael's sake I stayed.

"You tried to trick me," she accused, angry now.

"No such thing. If I'd wanted a witness, I'd have brought him to the door with me. I doubt if he could have heard more than our voices."

"I tried to warn Meriwether that Marjorie was just like our mother—not to be trusted. And I was right, she had an affair, didn't she? I was proved *right*."

"And Jack Melton turned his back on her when she got pregnant," I retorted, defending Marjorie. "That was hardly something to be proud of."

She studied my face. "You don't understand, do you? I really didn't like my sister. I felt nothing when she died but relief. She was going to win—why should I weep over her? Or that child?"

"But murder—"

"I tell you, it was as if it had happened to a stranger. Someone you read about in a newspaper, cluck your tongue over her death, and then turn the page."

"Michael told me you believed he knew more about Marjorie's death than he was telling you."

"Jack said Marjorie had gone to see Michael that night before she was killed. I wanted to know if it was true." She looked away, and I knew then that she hadn't been sure whether to believe Jack Melton or not.

But in the end, she'd decided to sacrifice Michael Hart because it was her last chance to destroy everything that Marjorie had cared for. Jack Melton meant nothing to her, just a conquest. If Michael had shown any fondness for her, would she have protected him instead and thrown Jack to the wolves?

"Did you really sleep with Jack Melton? Just because Marjorie had?"

"I just let him think I would. He's a very attractive man, and he likes women. I thought, *Imagine that!* Serena's husband, a philanderer. And I knew it would make Marjorie wretched when he turned to someone else. Why not me? Besides, there's the house in London. Serena is being an idiot about it. She wants it to punish Marjorie. I want it because it *was* Marjorie's. I thought if it appeared I was going to lose it, I could convince Jack to put in a good word for me. With Michael up for murder, Jack owes me a favor."

It was amazing to see her vacillate. But at the moment, she needed Jack Melton for reasons of her own. For how long, if he didn't persuade his wife to let the house go to Serena?

"Were you ever in love with Michael Hart?" I asked her.

"I don't know," she said truthfully, "whether I wanted him to spite Marjorie or because I loved him.

Over the years the two feelings got so entangled I couldn't sort them out any longer. I was always afraid that when he looked at me, he remembered Marjorie. And in the end, I didn't want that." She moved slightly. "I'm tired of standing in the doorway, and I'm not about to invite you in. Why don't you leave?"

I thought perhaps I'd touched a nerve. That in spite of her denials, she had cared too much.

And then, as if she'd read my thoughts, Victoria said in a tight voice, "I couldn't marry him, even if Michael loved me a dozen times over. I can't marry anyone. My father saw to that in his will. So Michael might as well hang and be done with it. Marjorie would hate that just as much. The sad thing is, she isn't here to see it. But if there's an afterlife, she'll find out." She looked toward the church. "I don't see the torch. Mr. Hart hasn't come sneaking back up here, has he? I will deny everything, you know. If you try to use me to free Michael, I'll tell the world that you were so besotted with him, that you were willing to perjure yourself to save him. So don't bother to try."

"I could make a very good case for you as the murderer," I countered. "In fact, I already have, to Michael's barrister."

She stared at me, then said contemptuously, "I'm sure you could try. But who would believe you? Helen Calder can't remember who stabbed her. I called on her in hospital, to see." She held out her hands. "Do these look like they could drive a knife into someone's chest? Look at them." She drew her hands back, clenching them into fists.

We were standing full in the light pouring out of the open door. I thought I was safe as long as that was so. Mr. Hart could pick out two figures—even Mrs. Hart at her window must be able to tell there were two of us, although we were blurred a little by the mist. I turned, looking for Mr. Hart by the church. But then I saw a light bobbing toward the Harts' house, up the walk, to the door, then shutting off.

Victoria had seen it as well. I felt suddenly vulnerable.

She laughed. "He got tired of waiting for you, Mr. Hart. I don't blame him. I'm here alone in the house. I could kill you quite easily now, and there would be no one to see."

She was trying to frighten me. I laughed with her.

"You could try," I said. "You'd find I was your match."

I turned to go, but she pulled a revolver from her pocket. "Don't be so certain of that."

I stared at it.

"It's from Jack's collection. He gave it to me because I was traveling back from London on the train at all hours, and a girl had been raped and murdered two villages north of here by a soldier who got off at her station and followed her home." She held it in her hand like a gift, admiring it. "If you want the truth, I think Jack used it on someone and then wanted to be rid of it. He never said, but I expect I know who it was. An officer whose sister Jack had seduced. He'd told Jack that as soon as he recovered from his wounds, he was going to hunt him down and kill him." She looked up at me. "But that's Jack, you never know when he's telling the truth and when he's having you on."

"You've already shot at Michael, haven't you?" I asked, trying to distract her.

"I think Jack was hoping I'd kill Michael. But I'm no fool. I let the police deal with him instead." Still, I thought perhaps she had shot at him, and was reluctant to say so. Even here, with no one listening.

I turned and walked away. My skin crawled as I did, knowing that she had the revolver and not knowing what kind of shot she might be. I was halfway down the walk when she went inside and slammed the door.

I reached the street and turned toward the church, and beyond it, the Hart house, hoping that I didn't break an ankle on my way back. The mist was still heavy, and I felt enclosed in it, smothered. I couldn't understand why Mr. Hart had deserted me. It was so unlike him, and I felt very much alone.

And then someone put a hand on my shoulder, and I thought my heart would stop.

Chapter Twenty-two

I didn't scream, bottling it up in my throat. Instead I drew back my foot and came down hard on the instep of whoever was behind me.

Simon Brandon swore. "Damn it, Bess—"

I whirled, but he shushed me at once. "Just keep walking." He moved closer and took my arm. "Watch where you go." He went on when we were out of earshot of the house, "I was there, at the corner of the garden where she couldn't see me. Hart had warned me to stay out of sight. I heard most of it."

"You couldn't have. I didn't see your motorcar—"

"I left the motorcar at your friend's house. Alicia. I thought you were there. When she told me she hadn't seen you, I went to the Hart house. Mrs. Hart sent me here, and I found Hart just by the church. I thought it best to send him home."

"Did you see Michael?" I asked, remembering why he was here, why he was late. "Is he all right? Please tell me he'll let us help him!" I could deal with anything, once I knew Michael was willing to work with us.

"He wouldn't see me." Simon was curt, clearly still angry about what had happened at the prison. "Short of a full cavalry charge, there was no way to reach him."

"Did you leave a message for him? Anything that would make him see the light?"

"I told him he was a damned fool to hang for another man's murder. Whether the guards will carry that to him or not, I can't be sure. The only person who could get in to see him now would be his lawyer."

"I saw Mr. Forbes. I don't think he was impressed by what I had to say." I turned my ankle and nearly pitched forward, but Simon steadied me. "He told me to bring the police Mrs. Calder's attacker, and then they'd consider listening to me." I was still bitter about that.

We had reached the Hart house. "I must go and thank them. And tell them about Victoria."

"No. They live here. It's not wise."

"They know part of the story already," I protested.

"Listen to me, Bess. In less than a week, they could very well lose Michael. Don't make it any harder for them to face that."

"They sent me to Victoria. She knows Mr. Hart walked with me to her house."

He let me have my way. They were expecting us and opened the door almost at once. I thanked them for all they'd done to help. "As for Victoria—" I began, and saw hope shining in their eyes, even though anything I'd learned was not evidence. "As for Victoria," I went on, "she's so twisted by hate that she can't see herself clearly. Or anyone else, for that matter. But I don't believe she killed Marjorie."

"What about Melton, Serena's husband?" Mr. Hart asked. "Is there any hope there?"

"I think it would be best if Inspector Herbert spoke to him. I'm going to London now to try. I'll stay in touch."

Their faces had fallen into the sadness I'd seen when I arrived. They thanked me, Mrs. Hart gave me a kiss on the cheek, and they both wished me Godspeed. But I could see, all too well, that I had intruded on the careful shell they'd built around themselves this last week, and for a little time had made them feel anything was possible. And now they must build it up again, and mend the cracks I'd caused, to carry them through what was to come.

Simon and I wished them a good night, their door shut behind us with what sounded like finality, and we walked on through the heavy mist toward his motorcar.

"Didn't you think to bring a heavier coat?" he asked as I shivered.

"No. It was warm enough when I left London. This one will do."

Exasperated, he opened the boot and brought out a rug, handing it to me. I got in and hugged it to me, waiting for the shivers to subside. But they were the aftermath of my encounter with Victoria, not the night's chill.

He started the motorcar and said to me, "Where do you want to go, Bess?"

"Home," I said, "but I don't have that luxury. Scotland Yard."

Without answering, he pulled away from Alicia's house and turned the bonnet toward the northeast. I sat huddled in my seat, thinking about Jack Melton as the miles slipped by.

It was late when we reached London. Simon threaded his way through what was left of the evening's traffic, and found a space to leave the motorcar a few steps from the entrance to the Yard.

Coming around to open my door, he said, "Do you want me to stay here or come with you?"

"I spoke to him before. Let me try again."

The constable on duty told me that he thought Inspector Herbert had gone home.

"Could you send someone to see? Please. It's quite urgent."

But I was told that Inspector Herbert's door was closed and his light off.

"Is there anywhere I could sit to write a message? Something that can be given to him as soon as he comes back here in the morning?"

They showed me to an anteroom and brought me pen and paper. I sat in the time-scarred chair and tried to think what to say, how best to say it. Finally I wrote a few lines, signed my name, and folded the message.

It read simply,

I know now how Jack Melton discovered that Michael Hart was in London to visit Mrs. Calder. He was at the theater, with several American visitors, and he saw Victoria Garrison in the audience. They talked. Victoria was angry that Michael hadn't returned. She told lies concerning his whereabouts. Afterward Jack Melton made his excuses to his guests, and left the theater. Victoria continued to sit there, doing nothing to stop him. I believe he saw this as an opportunity to throw suspicion on Lieutenant Hart, just as he'd done before. That means he could have attacked Mrs. Calder. Mr. Forbes told me that if I could bring you evidence that showed someone else had stabbed her, you would consider reopening Michael Hart's case. Well, I've done that. It's up to the Yard to fill in the details. One more thing. I think you'll dis-cover that Jack Melton seduced Lieutenant Fordham's sister, and Fordham swore he'd kill Jack Melton when he'd recovered from his wounds. Victoria Garrison has in her possession a .45-caliber revolver. Jack Melton gave it to her. I'd see if Melton had used it to murder Lieutenant Fordham. I wouldn't be surprised if she shot at Michael as well. If you solve the Fordham case, you owe it to me to pursue Michael Hart's innocence. It would be a tragedy to discover after his hanging that you were wrong. I found a bullet in the Hart gardens. If you look, you'll find its mate there as well."

I handed my message to the constable, and asked him to see to it that Inspector Herbert received it as soon as he came in the next morning. I'd marked it *Urgent*, all that I could do.

Simon, waiting by the motorcar for me, said, "That was quick. Were you shown the door?"

"His office was dark. He's gone home. I left a message."

He held the door for me, then got behind the wheel.

"Bess, there are circles under your eyes. You've had no rest since you got home. You've done everything that's humanly possible. More, in fact, than anyone ever dreamed could be done. Michael doesn't want to be saved—for the wrong reasons, I must admit. Or perhaps he is guilty after all, and it's hard to accept. Who knows?"

I fidgeted with the fringe of the rug. "If I could talk to Jack Melton, I'd know whether or not he was guilty. I don't think Victoria is. She's just vicious, cruel, wanting to hurt because she's hurt. If she'd killed her sister, I think she'd have met me at the door with a knife in her pocket, not that revolver. It was probably to protect herself, not to shoot me. She knew who was at her door, she'd had time to plan what to do."

Simon chuckled in the darkness of the motorcar, a deep chuckle in his chest that reminded me of Michael.

"What's funny?" I demanded angrily.

"Nothing. You. Rationalizing why you weren't killed tonight."

"Well," I retorted, "if you'd thought I was in any danger, you wouldn't have let me walk down that path with my back to the woman!"

His mouth tightened into a hard line.

"You should go back to Somerset. Tonight," he said finally. "It's safer. I have a bad feeling about this business."

"I know. But I can't abandon Michael."

"In spite of all you've done, you can't be certain he's innocent. Your theories are no better and no worse than the one that put him in jail."

"I know. But by the same token, I can't be certain he's guilty. I don't want his death on my conscience. There must be something else I can do. I'll think of something, I'm sure I will. And I want to be here, in London, where I can act on it. It takes hours to drive in from Somerset. Besides, Inspector Herbert knows where to find me."

"He's not going to listen, Bess, he's already got his man. There are too many hurdles to leap now, he won't risk his career on what Michael Hart's friends have to say."

"Then tomorrow we go back to Michael's defense counsel. I have a witness now. He'll have to listen. And if he won't, we'll go to the newspapers."

"They won't risk lawsuits to print your accusations."

I was tired, my mind wasn't working as it should. But a night's sleep would make a difference.

I said stubbornly, "I won't go to Somerset tonight. If I have to, tomorrow I'll go to Serena and tell her what I know. Or to Jack Melton himself."

"I tell you, it isn't safe."

"Mrs. Hennessey is there. I'll be all right."

He stopped arguing with me then. "All right." He drove on, turning toward the flat, his face in the shadows. I knew he was very angry with me. I knew he'd seen me take a risk I shouldn't have, speaking to Victoria alone. But I couldn't go home.

"Simon?"

He said nothing, driving in silence, and I subsided into my seat.

The problem was, Michael had confessed. And because of that, all doors were closed. Simon was right. Battering at them was a useless exercise.

I collected myself, swallowed my frustration and the feeling of helplessness that made me so angry.

We were halfway to the flat now.

"Simon. Give me one more day. Please? And then I'll go to Somerset. I promise you. I was drawn into this business because I nursed Meriwether Evanson. I wish now he'd carried a photograph of Gladys Cooper, like thousands of other men in France."

"None of this is your fault, Bess. You must understand that. It would have happened even if you had never recognized Marjorie Evanson that night at Waterloo Station."

And that was true. Her fate had been decided months ago when she embarked on a love affair.

I took a deep breath. "One more day, please?"

"All right. Against my better judgment. One more day."

Ahead was the house. There were no lights showing. Mrs. Hennessey had gone to bed, and Mary wasn't in. I could pace the floor or sleep, it wouldn't matter.

"Thank you, Simon."

He walked me to the door and saw me inside, waiting until I had climbed the stairs and unlocked my door. I went to the window and drew back the curtains, then turned on my light.

He lifted his hat to me and got back into the motorcar.

For once I wished Mrs. Hennessey wasn't the dragon at the gate, that Simon could have come upstairs with me and had a cup of tea before leaving. I'd have known then that he was over his anger.

Sighing, I locked the outer door and made a cup of tea for myself. I sat there sipping it, my mind finally slowing down enough to sleep. And then, finally, I went to bed.

Chapter Twenty-three

I don't remember turning out the light, but I must have done, for I woke up some hours later to find my room dark, with only the star glow from the windows telling me it was still hours until dawn.

I drifted off again, dreaming that I was a witness to Michael's execution, standing there like stone as he climbed the steps to the gallows and his sentence was read to him by the warden. Then the executioner slipped a black bag over his head. I was thinking that the last thing he'd seen was a bare prison yard and my face. Overhead the sky was cloudy, not even the sun shining for him one last time, and I wanted to cry, but couldn't. There was a priest just behind Michael's shoulder, and as he turned to say something to the warden, I recognized Jack Melton's face. It was he who stepped forward to throw the lever, not the executioner, and I made myself wake up before the trap fell and Michael died.

I lay there breathing hard from the effort, trying to shake the last remnants of the dream.

And then I heard something that brought me wide awake in seconds.

Someone was trying to open the flat door.

Everyone here had a key, unless we were to be away for some time, in which case we often left it with Mrs. Hennessey. Elayne and Diana weren't due for leave for a while, and Mary was staying with friends. Pat had been in Egypt these past six months or more. The flat below us was empty as well, its occupants in Poona, India, just now.

I got up very quietly, and stood at the bedroom door, listening. It hadn't been my imagination. There it was a second time, the scratch of something hard against the plate. It was very dark at the top of the stairs, and finding the keyhole wasn't always easy.

My flatmates and I could locate it blindfolded, from long experience.

Someone was trying to get into the flat.

My throat was dry now. I ran through a swift inventory of possible weapons.

There was the knife we used to cut bread and make sandwiches, but I didn't think the blade was stout enough to drive into someone, and I had no intention of getting that close. Diana had a golf club in her room. She was trying to learn to play, and sometimes amused herself by putting into a glass wedged between the door and her trunk. I wasn't sure I could reach it before whoever it was got the door open. I didn't want to be caught empty-handed.

My tennis racket wouldn't do much damage.

Think!

For a fleeting moment I hoped it was Simon, come back to look in on me to be sure I was all right. But he wouldn't have come upstairs. Not without Mrs. Hennessey in tow. And he would have knocked.

The lock was old, and it didn't take long to force it open.

Whoever it was stood there on the threshold for a moment, letting his or her eyes adjust to the small amount of light there was in the flat. I couldn't tell if it was a man or a woman.

I stood still, not breathing, and heard the rustle of clothes and a first tentative step inside. There were five tiny bedrooms. Which way would he turn?

He made a move toward Diana's room—nearest the door—and I caught the flash of light from the window on something in his hand. A knife?

I was barefoot, and it occurred to me that I could reach the flat door quietly and lock the intruder inside, if I was fast enough, before he realized what was about to happen. My fingers searched for my key, which was lying on the bedside table—and they knocked it to the floor.

The clank was so loud it could have awakened the entire street. But I knew it had shocked him, as well. Taking advantage of that, I caught up my hairbrush and ran on silent feet, reaching with the other hand for one of the chairs in the sitting room, sending it spinning across the floor toward Diana's bedroom as I went. It too seemed to make a tremendous racket, and I heard someone swear as he tripped over it.

I had reached the open door. I was out of it in a flash, slamming it shut behind me and flinging the hairbrush over the banister to skitter its way down the stairs for all the world like flying feet. But before I could turn the key and then conceal myself in the shadowy alcove on the opposite side of our door, it was flung open. In the same instant, a hand came over my mouth and an arm encircled my waist, lifting me off my feet, shoving me into the alcove. Frantic, I began to kick. But just as suddenly I was released, and as I regained my balance, whirling to defend myself, I realized with astonishment that I was alone and someone was clattering down the stairs. No, *two* people—

My intruder was trying to escape. But who was at his heels? I rushed to the top of the stairs and leaned over the banister to peer into the dark well below.

And then in the faint light from the windows by the street door, I saw the second figure make a flying leap to close the distance between them and take the other figure in a headlong fall down to the entrance hall.

There were flailing fists and feet, grunts and a curse broken off in midsentence. I went down the stairs after them, and reached the bottom just as the two men crashed into Mrs. Hennessey's door, then rebounded into the far wall.

"He's got a knife—" I exclaimed, and then saw that it was in the hand pinned high against the wall, a long, wicked blade that wavered, then flew from open fingers as the intruder cried out. He was spun around as the knife slid across the floor, and the two struggling men went thudding into the outer door. I could just see the knife, and I dashed forward to pick it up, then moved out of the way. Just as I did, the sound of a fist hitting hard and landing squarely sent one of the combatants staggering back to collapse at the foot of the stairs, almost colliding with my bare feet.

The fight had been all the more deadly for being so silent, and not knowing who had won, I slid along the wall, groping for the entry light switch.

Simon Brandon turned swiftly toward me, blinking in the brightness of the light. I reached out to touch him, needing to be sure he was all right—there was blood on his cheekbone, just under his right eye. He said, "You should have stayed in your room. I wouldn't have let him reach you."

He put a hand on my shoulder—a comradely gesture I'd seen many times among soldiers—and then his fingers gripped hard before releasing me.

He gave his attention to the man who had fallen on his face by the stairs. After a moment, he turned him over with one foot, wary of a trick, and I knew as I saw his profile that it was Jack Melton. I looked at the vicious knife in my hand and shivered.

"He came to kill me."

Simon, his voice brusque, said, "He had to. You asked too many questions. You might have overturned—"

Mrs. Hennessey was opening her door, her hair in a long gray plait down her back and a cast-iron frying pan in one hand, shouting, "I'll have the police on the lot of you for breaking into my house—" And then her voice quavered to a stop.

She saw me standing there barefoot and in my nightgown, that wicked knife still gripped tightly in my hand, and then her gaze moved on to Simon, breathing hard by the door and examining bruised knuckles. I couldn't think when I'd seen him so angry. She stopped at the sight of Jack Melton, still slumped where he'd fallen, showing no signs of regaining his senses.

"It's all right, Mrs. Hennessey," I said quickly, trying to reassure her. "That man by the stairs broke into my flat. Simon stopped him before he could do any harm."

"Men aren't allowed upstairs," she said primly, and I felt a rising bubble of nervous laughter—the reaction to what had just happened—and I quickly suppressed it.

"I'm so sorry, Mrs. Hennessey," I began. "I didn't want him there, I assure you. He's killed at least one person, and injured another rather badly. If you'll hand me a coat or something, I'll see if I can find a constable."

"You'll do no such thing," she told me. "Go upstairs at once and dress, you can't be seen down here like that. I'll find the constable."

At a look from Simon, I did as I was told. It didn't bother me going up those dark stairs to dress, knowing that Simon was there by the outer door and Jack Melton was beyond harming anyone for the moment. But I wondered how I was going to feel later, when the dark at the top of the stairs, once friendly and safe, loomed ahead of me and I couldn't see what was in the shadows.

I dressed in record time, still buttoning my sleeves as I hurried down the steps again.

Simon had found some rope somewhere, probably from Mrs. Hennessey's flat, and had tied Jack Melton's wrists. He was busy now with the man's ankles, and none too gently.

I said to Simon after a glance at Jack Melton, "What were you doing upstairs? You know it's not permitted."

"I told you, I didn't like the idea of your staying in London. I left the motorcar round the corner and came back. Mrs. Hennessey was nowhere to be seen. So I waited in that dark corner you yourself were going to use. But we won't tell her that, if you please. I was down here in the entry."

Jack Melton was just beginning to stir, shaking his head to clear it, then coming to the conclusion that his hands were bound. He tried to stand up, saw his ankles were tied as well, and slumped back against the stairs. Raising his head, he glared at me. I was reminded then of his brother, any charm erased by cold anger.

"You were in my way at every turn," he said through clenched teeth. I thought his jaw must ache—I hoped it did. Simon had hit him very hard.

The outer door opened, and Mrs. Hennessey was back with Constable Vernon, a burly man with a square face and large hands. I'd seen him often on the street, and he'd nodded in passing. He came into the hall now and looked to Simon for an explanation.

Simon introduced himself, pointed to me, and said, "This man tried to kill the young woman you see there. The knife he was carrying is there on the table. Mrs. Hennessey can swear that Sister Crawford is one of her lodgers. And I'm here in place of her father, Colonel Crawford, who is presently in Somerset."

"That's true," Mrs. Hennessey said, nodding. "I know her family."

"If you'll go upstairs to my flat, you'll see how he broke in. I was lucky to escape." I shivered in spite of myself. "Inspector Herbert at Scotland Yard knows this man," I ended, pointing to Jack Melton. "He'll confirm everything we've said."

The constable nodded. "You can be sure we'll notify him."

No one had said anything about Michael Hart. But I was beginning to think we could at least hope. I felt almost giddy with relief.

After inspecting both locks, the constable took Jack Melton into custody, and the rest of us accompanied him to the nearest station where I told a sergeant my story, supported by Mrs. Hennessey and Simon. I realized that Mrs. Hennessey was the one they listened to most intently, their impartial witness. Little did they know.

Jack Melton said nothing, his head down, his shoulders stiff with suppressed anger, refusing to give his name.

Simon quietly supplied it, trying to keep me in the background. Then he added, "I suggest you send for Inspector Herbert at Scotland Yard. He may have an interest in this man."

"That will take some time," the sergeant on night duty said, looking from Jack Melton back to Simon. He was a middle-aged man, face lined and hair graying.

"It doesn't matter," Simon answered him. "Just see to Mr. Melton, and we'll be happy to wait."

The sergeant turned to me. "Were you harmed, Miss? You say he came into your flat. Did he hurt you?"

"The flat was dark. I didn't even know who was there—a man, a woman—but I saw the flash of what I thought was a knife. And so I ran, slamming the door while he was in one of the other bedrooms looking for me. He followed me but I was hidden, and I threw my hairbrush down the stairs so he'd think I'd gone that way."

"Why did you believe you'd seen a knife?'

"I was afraid, I was alone in the flat, Mrs. Hennessey was on the ground floor, asleep. And I happened to know Helen Calder, who had nearly died from stab wounds after she was attacked. I didn't want to be a victim too."

He considered me for a moment. Then he summoned a constable and gave him quiet instructions. The man left, and we sat there on the hard wooden benches, waiting. There was a large-faced clock high on the wall. I watched the hands creep through the minutes, and then an hour. Simon got up and paced, Mrs. Hennessey nodded where she was, her head sinking to her chest, her breathing heavy. I tried to keep myself from yawning, partly from reaction, and partly from sheer fatigue. Another hour passed, and I realized as I gazed across the room to where Jack Melton sat on one of the benches along the far wall that his anger had faded, and he was busy thinking, a harshness in his face that made me look away.

He must have followed Michael Hart's case. He must have known who Inspector Herbert was. He must have realized that he was in an almost untenable position. But he was a very intelligent man, and he was slowly coming to the conclusion that he would be able to talk his way out of this.

The question was, what would he say? And I thought I knew. He would claim that I had invited him to the flat—lured him there—in some foolish, desperate attempt to clear Michael's name. Everyone knew how hard I'd fought for Michael. And he could swear Simon was a part of the plot.

His head came up and his eyes met mine. I looked away, unable to hold his gaze. I saw the slight smile, as if he'd already won.

We were into the third hour now, and suddenly the outer doors opened and Inspector Herbert walked in, followed by two other men. He nodded to the desk sergeant, glanced at Jack Melton, then turned to me.

"Miss Crawford," he said.

I realized that he looked very tired. There were circles under his eyes, and lines about his mouth that hadn't been there before.

I got to my feet. "Inspector."

Turning to the sergeant, he said, "Is there a room where I could speak to Miss Crawford in private?"

"Just there, sir, second door. Inspector Knoles's office."

Inspector Herbert nodded, then waited for me to join him. Simon, who had been sitting next to Mrs. Hennessey, moved to follow us, but Inspector Herbert shook his head.

After the briefest hesitation, Simon sat down again. But I could tell he didn't like it.

I followed Inspector Herbert to the door of the office, and he held it for me, then shut it behind me.

"You've been busy," he said. "And stubborn."

"I had to be sure you were hanging the right man."

His smile was a grimace. "Why are you here with Jack Melton? It appears that he and Sergeant-Major Brandon have bruises on their faces and hands. Tell me why."

I explained what had happened. "I sent for you," I ended, "because you knew what it was I feared, and why. Otherwise what happened tonight seems inexplicable. But Jack Melton *was* in my flat, and he was armed, and I was there alone. I could have been badly hurt, like Helen Calder, or killed, like Marjorie Evanson. Tell me why this man was in my flat? I can't think of any reason except the fact that I knew too much about what he'd done. I didn't invite him there—Mrs. Hennessey can tell you I was in my nightgown when she came out of her flat to find Simon Brandon trying to stop Jack Melton from escaping."

He had listened patiently, his eyes on my face.

"I was out concluding a case when you came to Scotland Yard tonight. I returned to find your message. I went to Little Sefton, to have a look at that revolver while I could. When did you see Miss Garrison?"

I explained about my visit yesterday—was it yesterday?—and speaking to the Harts before going to see Victoria. I touched on her threat.

"And you tell me she was alive and well when you left her?"

"Yes, of course. Sergeant-Major Brandon can confirm that. And the Harts, indirectly." I felt the first surge of unease. "Why?"

"When I arrived in Little Sefton, I found the local constable, a man named Tilmer, in Miss Garrison's house. The sound of a shot had been reported to him, and he was investigating it when he discovered her lying on the floor of her sitting room. There was a revolver by her hand, and on the desk, a sheet of paper and an uncapped pen. It appeared she was preparing to write a note, then stopped."

"Victoria—Miss Garrison—is dead?" I hadn't liked her. She'd been destructive and cold and willing to inflict hurt. But her death shocked me. "But I don't understand—" I couldn't imagine her taking her own life. There was too much hate in her. People killed themselves for all sorts of reasons, but not for hate.

"A Mrs. Whiting reported that a motorcar stopped in front of her house. Her dog barked, and she looked out. The car stayed there for half an hour, then left. She didn't know the motorcar, she didn't know where the driver went. But the shot was heard before the motor-car drove away. Any thoughts on that?"

"I don't believe I've met Mrs. Whiting, but I must have heard her dog bark when I was walking by in the mist. There aren't that many motorcars in Little Sefton. She'd know most of them."

"Do you think that Miss Garrison was killed by Melton?"

"It's possible. I think he was afraid her anger would lead her to say things she shouldn't. He wants Michael to hang, you see. And the case closed."

"But there's nothing to indicate it wasn't suicide."

I shook my head. "She wouldn't. I just know—"

"Hardly evidence to present in a courtroom."

"I don't know how Jack Melton got to my flat. There must be a motorcar somewhere."

He looked at me and then excused himself, leaving me there in the cluttered little office. And then he was back, asking me again to go over what had happened in the flat. I told my story a second time.

Inspector Herbert thanked me, accompanied me to the reception area, and then asked for Mrs. Hennessey. For a moment she looked a little confused and frightened, then her back straightened and she marched ahead of him like a Christian on her way to meet the lions.

I didn't look at or speak to Simon. After ten minutes, Mrs. Hennessey came back, chatting comfortably with Inspector Herbert about "her girls," and he thanked her for her assistance.

Simon was the last to be taken away, and he was gone for a very long time. Jack Melton, restless and impatient, his hands no longer tied, took out his watch three times. And then Simon was back, his face inscrutable.

Finally it was Jack Melton's turn.

I watched dawn creeping in the station windows, the lamps paling before the sun's growing brightness. The dingy paint and the wooden benches seemed shabbier than before, the floorboards scuffed and worn. There was no money, no paint, no men to wield brushes, and all of us had realized slowly but surely that the cost of war was reflected in many small ways no one had ever imagined in the autumn of 1914 when it had all begun.

Inspector Herbert returned, nodded to Simon and Mrs. Hennessey, and then said to me, "Mr. Melton is for the moment helping us with our inquiries. I see no reason for you to stay any longer. You must be very tired."

"I'd like to know," I said, choosing my words carefully, "what's to come of this matter. Whether Mr. Melton will be released—whether I will be in danger again."

He said wearily, "It's been a long night, Miss Crawford. But I think it is safe to say that you have little to fear from Mr. Melton in the future."

"You'll compare that knife with the wounds Mrs. Evanson and Mrs. Calder suffered?"

"I think I know how to handle this inquiry."

"Do you—did he kill Victoria? I'm leaving for France—please, won't you tell me?"

"I can't discuss an ongoing investigation," he said. "My advice to you is to go home and go to bed, and leave this matter in our hands."

I stood there, trying to find the words to ask him if this would have any bearing on Michael Hart's case.

But he turned away, shook hands with Simon, thanked Mrs. Hennessey again, and walked back to the door of the small room where he'd interviewed us, shutting it firmly behind him. Was Jack still there, waiting? Or had they taken him away, out another door, where we couldn't see?

I looked at Simon, but he shook his head, and I followed Mrs. Hennessey out the door toward Simon's motorcar.

We drove in silence back to the house, and then Mrs. Hennessey said, "I don't know when I've been so tired. Bess, dear, do you think you could make a cup of tea for all of us? It would help me rest."

I wanted nothing more than my own bed, but we went into her small flat and I made tea while Simon found bread, sliced and buttered it, and added a small bottle of preserves to the tray. Mrs. Hennessey, her face lined with weariness, sat and watched us. I wondered if she was afraid, just now, to be alone, in spite of the daylight sifting through her lace curtains.

Pretending to eat, I managed to swallow a little of the bread with a bit of marmalade preserve perched on one corner, and I drank my tea. Surprisingly, it did make me feel much better.

Mrs. Hennessey wanted to know why that man, as she called Jack Melton, should wish to break into her house and attempt to murder one of her nursing sisters.

Simon said circumspectly, "It has to do with one of Bess's patients. I shouldn't worry about it. Melton is likely to find himself in far more trouble than he expected."

"But you were here, I didn't understand how you could have been here. I have quite strict rules, you see."

Simon's glance met mine. "I followed him into the house."

That made perfect sense to her. She nodded, and addressed her food with an appetite, finishing her tea, then turning to Simon once more, asking him if he should care to rest on her settee before going back to Somerset.

He promised her again that all would be well, and I washed up, tucked Mrs. Hennessey into her bed, and shut the door behind me when I had finished.

Simon was waiting on the stairs, sitting there as I'd seen him sit so many times in India, able to sleep without lying down or losing touch with his surroundings. I myself had learned to do much the same in the field, catching what little rest I could when I could.

He looked up as I shut the door of Mrs. Hennessey's flat.

"I asked him what this would mean for Michael Hart's situation. He said that at the moment he could see no connection."

I didn't need to ask who Simon meant. Inspector Herbert. "Did he tell you that Victoria had shot herself? I don't believe it for an instant! Oddly enough, I'd warned her about Jack. And surely there is some way to see if this was the same knife that killed Marjorie. It's out of the ordinary, he had a collection of American weapons. The postmortem—"

"Perhaps it would be wise to see that Mr. Forbes is told that Melton is in custody and why."

"He wasn't interested before," I said.

"Because it was only your word, without proof or the sanction of an arrest. Try again."

That made sense even to my tired mind.

"I'll write it now," I said, pushing away any thought of my pillow. "And I'll deliver it personally."

"No. Let me deliver it. His clerk won't turn me away."

"And then, Simon, I want to go home."

I heard the plaintive note in my voice, in spite of every effort to suppress it.

"Give me four hours. Then we'll see to the letter before leaving London," he promised.

I looked over my shoulder. "If he's released—if he can talk his way out of this night's work—will Mrs. Hennessey be safe? I have a feeling he's cleaning house."

"She's not important to him. You are. That's why it's best for you to leave London and let Inspector Herbert sort this out."

I went up the stairs, righted the chair that I'd left overturned, braced my door, and sat down at the table that served as a writing desk.

Two tries and a lot of thought later, I'd finished what I felt was a fair representation of the night's events.

By that time it was half past nine. I got myself together, went lightly down the stairs so as not to rouse Mrs. Hennessey, and went to find a cab. I was lucky on the third try, and I gave the driver Helen Calder's address.

The maid answered, and I apologized for calling so early but begged to see Mrs. Calder on urgent business.

After a wait of some minutes, I was taken to Helen Calder's bedroom. She was awake and lying on a chaise longue with a coverlet over her knees. She was dressed, this time, and not in her bed, but her face was still wan, without spirit.

She greeted me warmly, looked again at my face, and said with concern, "Bess, I don't think I've ever seen you so weary."

"It's been a long night, Helen. Is there any way you can be sure who was waiting for you when you were stabbed?"

"I've tried, my dear. Heaven knows I've spent hours trying to remember."

Which was sometimes the wrong way to go about it, but that was neither here nor there.

"Jack Melton tried to kill me last night. And it's possible he murdered Victoria, though the police at the moment aren't certain whether it was suicide or murder."

Her eyes were wide with alarm. "Are you all right?" She looked me over, as if expecting to find bandages bulging beneath my coat or my skirt.

"I was lucky. I got away. But it could have ended very differently. The police have Jack Melton in custody, and are talking to him." I hoped I was right, and he was still there at the police station. "I don't think you have anything to fear from him, but a word of warning. If he's given bail, turn Jack Melton and his wife from your door, if they come here. Just to be safe."

She said, "Are you suggesting that it was Mr. *Melton* who attacked me? Not Michael Hart?"

"I don't know how to answer that. Yes, I believe it's possible. Whether it's right or not, I don't know. I hope the police are looking at the possibility that the knife he had with him when he attacked me could have been used to kill Marjorie and wound you. But that may not match after all. I'm just suggesting prudence."

Frowning, she said, "Yes, prudence by all means. I'm so confused."

"You mustn't be." I rose to leave. It wouldn't do for Simon to find I was not there at the flat. "It's for the police to look into these things. And to make interpretations. We can only trust to them to find the truth."

Helen Calder said earnestly, "I have given so much thought to what happened to me—because I don't want to believe it was Michael. I don't wish the Meltons any harm. I have no reason to want them to go through what I've gone through over Marjorie's death. But the truth will be a blessing, Bess. Poor Victoria, I'm sad for her, and I wish her life could have turned out differently. I think in the end her father punished both his daughters for what they had done between them to ruin his marriage. I think as he aged, he drew into himself and wanted to believe he hadn't been wronged by his wife."

I said good-bye, and she replied, "Will Michael die?"

"God knows. And the Crown."

She nodded, and I saw that her eyes were heavy with tears as I shut the door.

I was back at the flat a mere fifteen minutes before Simon came to fetch me. I looked in on Mrs. Hennessey, made her a fresh pot of tea, and set the tray across her knees before saying good-bye.

"You're going back to France again. Do be safe, my dear child. I will pray for you."

"Mary will be here tomorrow or the next day. Tell her good-bye for me as well."

And then I was gone, out the door, into Simon's motorcar, and we were on our way to Mr. Forbes's chambers. Simon said nothing, and when we had found a place to leave the motorcar, he went in with the letter in his hand.

I had wanted to do it myself, I had wanted to see this finished. But he was right. He would hand the sealed envelope marked *Private and Confidential* to Mr. Forbes's clerk, and the clerk would hand it to Mr. Forbes. And it would be read.

We drove on to Somerset, and were silent for most of the journey. I slept a part of the way, finally giving in to the need for a little respite.

It wasn't until we were pulling into the drive that Simon said again, "You have done all you can. And Inspector Herbert will not wish to have an innocent man's death on his hands. We must leave this to Scotland Yard and Mr. Forbes. If, in spite of everything, Michael Hart goes to the gallows as scheduled, it is his choice, Bess. You must see that and respect it."

I touched my face with my hands, as if to relieve the pressure I felt behind my eyes.

"I will have to, won't I? But it seems such a waste."

"How many soldiers have you watched die because they lost the will to live?"

"Too many."

"That's what Michael Hart has done, whatever gallant name he attaches to his decision."

"Thank you, Simon. For everything."

"One final thing. Let the Colonel take you to the train in London. I think he wants to do that."

I nodded, understanding.

And then for the next several days, I played the daughter of the house on leave, and gave neither of my parents a moment's anxiety. But my thoughts were in that prison with Michael. And I couldn't pull them back.

My train left the day before Michael's hanging.

My father drove me to London and Waterloo Station, to see me off for Portsmouth this time.

I stood there thinking that it had all begun here, that I had stood here and watched Marjorie Evanson in tears talking to a man who was nearly as callous and coldhearted as his brother. I had been an impartial witness then. I had tried to keep that personal distance, but events had drawn me further and further into the vortex of a murder investigation. I had got too close to people and perhaps hadn't been as objective as I could or should have been.

But Simon was right. I had tried. And there had been no messages for me from Inspector Herbert, either in London or in Somerset. I wanted so badly to ask him if there was any hope. But I knew he wouldn't tell me.

I chatted brightly with my father and then watched as the train pulled into the station, steam roiling in the cool night air, knowing that in a matter of minutes, I would be on my way to war again.

We had said our good-byes in Somerset, but I held the Colonel close for a moment and kissed his cheek. "I'll be all right," I said.

"You'd better be," he told me lightly. "Or the Kaiser himself will answer for it."

I laughed, as he'd intended me to do. I had just turned to face the train when there was a flurry of movement to one side of us, and the crowd of people seeing off or waiting for loved ones parted a little. A woman came hurrying through the gap, and I didn't recognize her at first, her face was streaked with tears, a handkerchief in one hand.

And before I could catch my breath or even move, Serena Melton was upon me.

She lifted her fists and beat against my coat, blows that forced me back a step, and I felt the presence of my father just behind me, his hands reaching for my shoulders to move me behind him, out of danger.

"You selfish monster!" Serena was crying, her fists flying, and heads turned to stare at us. "You came to my house and betrayed us. Callously, without thought for anyone but Michael Hart. You used us and everyone you met, to save him. I know all about you, I know what sort of woman you are. My husband has never hurt anyone in his life, do you understand me?"

My father had come between us, and her blows fell on his outstretched arms.

"It's Serena Melton," I managed to say.

But she wasn't finished. Her voice was strident, thick with emotion, and she'd lost all sense of anything but punishing her tormentor. I wondered what lies Jack Melton had told her, and where he was.

"You *used* us, you cold, uncaring bitch. Sister of mercy indeed. You're a disgrace to that uniform you're wearing, and I hope the Germans do for you what I can't, shoot you down like the animal you are!"

And then she was gone in a whirl of skirts, shoving her way through the staring throng. A policeman had come up, drawn by the screaming.

"Anything wrong, sir?" he asked, not seeing Serena as the wall of watchers closed around her.

My father said, quite clearly, "A demented woman I've never seen before just attacked my daughter without any provocation. As witnesses will attest. Will you see us to the train, Constable? It's been a very trying moment, my daughter is very upset."

It was true, the Colonel had never met Serena. But the words were comforting, even though they were partly lies.

I didn't know how my father looked. I knew my own face was flushed with shame and horror, and one of Serena's fists had caught me on one cheek. It ached, and I was close to tears. Angry tears, helpless tears. But I held my head high, and walked with my father and the constable toward my compartment on the train. I saw the constable have a word with the conductor. I was settled in my seat by the window, my belongings stowed safely, loved and cosseted and given the moral support that made my courage possible.

Then my father said rapidly, "Sticks and stones, Bess. She's distraught. But it tells you something, doesn't it? It tells you that someone heard you, and that someone is doing whatever can be done."

"I feel such pity for her."

"She must have known, Bess. She must have been afraid from the start that it was her husband."

And so she'd become a detective to find a lie, not the truth.

"Murder is never kind. To the victim, to the survivors. Not even to the murderer him- or herself. Let it go, be safe, and concentrate on why you're in France."

He was right. I kissed him, smiled—albeit most likely a tremulous one—and settled back into my seat.

And then we were pulling out of the station. There was no sign of Serena, but I lowered my window and leaned out to watch my father's tall, broad-shouldered figure out of sight.

No one had come into my compartment, crowded as the train was. My father's parting gift to me. Forward I could hear male voices singing one of the interminable verses of "The Mademoiselle from Armentières," that bawdy drinking song that the troops seemed to love even when sober.

I leaned back and closed my eyes, seeing only emptiness and darkness ahead.

Chapter Twenty-four

At dawn the next morning, I could hear the guns in the distance as the ambulance that had been waiting for me and a half dozen other nurses rumbled and bounced toward our destination, a field hospital behind the line of trenches.

I watched the sun rise, and it was a fair day, and I could think of nothing but Michael walking out the door into the prison yard and looking up at that bright sky for the last time. I had pictured it before—but only as a dread possibility. This morning it was real. I turned away from the other nurses and fought back my tears.

If only Marjorie hadn't succumbed to the seductive advances that Jack Melton had made. If only she had listened to his brother there in the station, and not seemed so desolate that Raymond Melton had reported to his brother that there was no hope of keeping her from telling someone—Michael or her husband—what she had done.

If only I hadn't been in the station that rainy evening. I wouldn't have known any of these people, I would have watched this sunrise untouched by the pain of a man who would rather die than live.

But that was wrong. It wasn't Marjorie's fault. It wasn't mine. The blame must fall where it belonged. And I truly believed that it would. I had met a number of good people in the course of these last months, and some terribly cruel ones. Because I believed in doing my duty and telling the police what I had seen in that railway station, I had got involved. And that was nothing to be ashamed of.

We hit a deep rut just as the sun reached above the horizon, and I knew that if nothing had stopped his execution, Michael Hart was dead. Quickly, his neck broken, his body already limp and without that force that came with life.

I said a swift prayer for his soul. As the sun moved higher, touching all the blackened and ruined countryside with a golden light, as if trying to hide what war had done to it, I said another for Mr. and Mrs. Hart.

And then we were at our destination, and I had to put Michael and all the rest behind me. There were wounded already waiting for us, men in dire straits, and my duty was to them.

But my last thought as I was handed down from the ambulance by the middle-aged driver comforted me. I would have done nothing differently, even knowing what lay ahead.

We had worked for three days almost without stopping. I hardly had the time to eat or drink or find a bed to fall into. I was already tired, but it was forgotten when I took my turn as theater sister and then as the night nurse for the recovering wounded.

And I counted it a blessing, because there was no space in which to think or mourn or remember.

Finally the lines of wounded dwindled to twenty, and then to ten, and then to five, and then to an empty doorway.

I took off my cap to let the fresh breeze of another dawn cool my face for one brief moment, before putting it on again to walk down the rows of wounded and surgical cases, making certain, before going off duty, I had told the sisters coming on what to watch for. Bleeding here, shock there, nausea across the way, and in the far corner, septicemia. The dread of blood poisoning.

I signed out, walked some fifty yards to the quarters that had been pointed out as mine, and found my things piled in a corner, the bed as fresh as it was when it had been made up days ago.

Sorting out my belongings, I found a towel and toothbrush and a bar of precious soap and went to find where I could wash my face and hands before I slept.

An orderly showed me, and I was just starting in that direction, wondering if my feet could carry me that far and then back again, when a man came running toward me, calling my name. He wore the insignia of the signals corps.

I turned and waited, thinking it was a summons back to the theater, and I knew I was in no condition to go.

"I'm Sister Crawford," I told him, as he caught me up. "What is it?"

He reached into his pocket and pulled out an envelope, much creased and more than a little grubby from the touch of many hands.

"This came through in a diplomatic pouch, marked very urgent, Sister. Someone sent it up by a rider, but I didn't receive it until yesterday. And they told me you couldn't be disturbed."

He held it out to me, almost reluctantly. We had learned that urgent messages often brought bad news.

I tore it open, dreading to see what was written there.

Just a few words, and they swam before my eyes until I could focus on them.

Execution delayed indefinitely for new evidence. Weapon that killed Victoria also very likely the weapon used to kill Lieutenant Fordham. Further investigation into Evanson murder and Calder wounding. Forbes expects no less than full pardon, but it will take time. Thank God, there is now time available. Rejoice.

And below it was my father's name and rank and former regiment.

He signed himself that way only on momentous occasions, to mark the importance of them.

I looked up, and saw that the signals corporal was watching my face as I read. I had even forgotten he was there.

Crumpling the letter in my hand, I flung my arms around him and whirled him in a wide circle, laughing and crying at the same time.

"Here, Miss—!" he expostulated, face beet red, caught completely off balance.

"It's good news, good news," I said, letting him go and trying to remember the dignity of a nursing sister. "I'm sorry, but I had to share it with someone."

He touched his cap, smiling. "Yes, Miss. Glad to be of service. Anytime." And then he was trotting off toward wherever he belonged, and I reread the letter again.

They had gotten it to me in record time, my father, my mother, and Simon, pulling God knew how many strings to make certain it reached me as soon as possible, before I had mourned a man who still lived.

Shoving the letter into my pocket, I picked up the scattered soap and towel and toothbrush, and went on to wash my face.

I couldn't help but notice when I reached a mirror that it was smiling broadly, my face, and the fatigue that had been grinding me into the ground only ten minutes ago had vanished.

Sparing a moment of pity for Serena and the dark road I knew she was following now, I remembered the living and the dead as I scrubbed my face.

Meriwether Evanson, Marjorie Evanson, even Victoria Garrison.

My father was right. Murder was never kind. To the victims, depriving them of a natural span of life and happiness. And also to the survivors, who must live with reminders of what might have been.

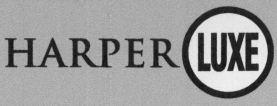